Vanilla et Motricium Oleum

ALINA COMSA

BOOK 2 OF THE LOST HOPE SERIES

Vanilla et Motricium Oleum, Book Two of the Lost Hope Series

First published in Great Britain in 2024 by: Malum Canticus Books

Edited by: Siiri Becker

Cover design by: Malum Canticus Books

Character Art by: @lrdeinfierno

E-book ISBN: 978-1-7385278-2-3

Print ISBN: 978-1-7385278-3-0

Contents

Blurb

My entire life I've been bound by loyalty—first to my family and then to my country—arrogantly confident in my decisions and instincts.

Finding my wife engaged to another man obliterates the foundation of everything I've ever held true.

It's only fitting that I end up back home, in Lost Hope—yet my wounds start to heal here. They scar with each day passing by. Nine years later, all that remains is a gruesome picture of the culmination of my worst decisions carved on my body.

My only reprieve is HER and her sweet vanilla scent.

The quintessential good girl—and painfully beautiful—she's the town's sweetheart and the balm to my shriveled soul.

I'm as hopeless as the town's name when my cruel past breaks us apart... until she returns, pregnant with my child and thinking the worst of me.

My loyalty demands that I keep her close, while my darkness whispers she cannot be trusted. She left me once when I needed her the most. She'll leave again when I least expect it.

We strike a feeble truce for the sake of our unborn baby, and my heart doesn't stand a chance against her.

The instinct to keep my distance fades into nothingness with every stolen kiss and healing touch.

But is she strong enough to stand at my side when the ghosts of our pasts threaten to obliterate our feeble foundation once more?

Welcome to Lost Hope

This book has wrecked me. In all the best and worst ways. Welcome back to Lost Hope, the small town hidden in the mountains, where wandering souls come to find a place to hide, and instead, find a place to heal.

I hope you enjoy the laughs, and tears. But mostly the laughs. Tatum's story has all the feels and all the turmoil that comes to life from navigating the choppy waters of emotional trauma.

For the best reading experience, it is recommended to start with *Lege et Lacrima* and continue with the order the books are released in. Each novel has the spotlight on a different couple, but the main story continues in subsequent books.

Latin words and their meaning in Vanilla et Motricium Oleum:

- **Vanilla et Motricium Oleum:** Vanilla and Motor Oil.

- **Lege et Lacrima:** Read It and Weep.

- **Laxo:** To loosen; To relax. **Used as:** Released from all commands.

Because my main characters have gone and made friends with a burly, surly Irishman, expect to find some very creative Irish swearing. It's the accent, I'm telling ya'. I can't help myself.

TRIGGER WARNINGS:

I take mental health issues with the utmost seriousness. I don't speak in the name of anyone but myself. The issues portrayed in *Vanilla et*

Motricium Oleum are issues portrayed not as textbook and not generalised, but based on my opinions, views, or reactions. Not two experiences are identical, and not two individuals survive through them in the same manner.

If you ever find yourself in any of the situations depicted, please find help. You are not alone.

The following sensitive subjects are touched in the book, either by mention or graphic depiction, and I've done my absolute best to treat them with the sensibility and care these subjects deserve.

Vanilla et Motricium Oleum has the following trigger warnings:

- Drug use (with and without consent)

- Sexual assault

- Death of a parent (mentions)

- Cheating

- Bullying

- Domestic Violence

Your mental health is a priority.

Vanilla et Motricium Oleum is the second book in the Lost Hope series of interconnected standalone novels. It's a surprise-pregnancy romance with a pinch of suspense, complete with HEA, and a cliff-hanger introducing book three of the series. This book is intended for readers 18+, with explicit scenes, mature language, touching on sensitive topics, and more.

Playlist

❀Eamon - F*ck it, I Don't Want You Back❀
❀Eminem ft. Rihanna - Love the Way You Lie❀
❀Korn - Freak on a Leash❀
❀Sunrise Avenue - Fairytale Gone Bad❀
❀Skillet - Comatose❀
❀Lady A - Need You Now❀
❀Michele Morrone - Feel It❀
❀Ben E. King - Stand by Me❀
❀Jessie J - I Got You (I Feel Good)❀
❀Marc Terenzi - Love to be Loved by You❀
❀The Police - Every Breath You Take❀
❀Korn - Slept so Long❀
❀Maroon 5 - Sugar❀
❀Savage Garden - Truly Madly Deeply❀

Dedication

For my dearest friend. Pisi, I don't have the power to change fate, as much as I wish I did. But I can give you a full happily ever after on paper. That's all I've ever wanted for you. My world is a better place with you in it.

This is for anyone who's ever had their choices taken away from them. Life is hard, and then it's downright difficult. You are strong, you are capable, you are a survivor. Your voice is worth hearing. Keep fighting.

I've never been reckless. Not a day in my life. From childhood and all through adulthood, discipline and careful planning have been instilled in me, flowing through my blood like red cells and oxygen.

Every word out of my mouth is carefully thought out. Every action and every decision are weighed against an extensive pros-and-cons list. From enlisting into the Marine Corps—following in my father's footsteps—to marrying my high school sweetheart, everything I've done in my twenty-six years of life has been risk-assessed and planned to a T.

So it makes no sense why I'm not sticking to the plan right now. It makes no sense why I fall back from my brothers-in-arms' tight, protective formation when we're under strict orders to stick together and get to the rescue point.

The scarf wrapped around my mouth doesn't help as thick, humid air coats my throat with heat and sand particles. Sweat drips in my eyes as I squint into the unrelenting sun bearing down on us.

There's nowhere to hide.

No trees, no buildings, just a few dilapidated wooden cabins scattered around, and sand dunes as far as the eye can see.

My gloved hand taps the bulletproof vest, underneath which the damned papers are hidden in the chest pocket of my camo shirt. The rage in me shifts and gurgles, demanding its pound of flesh. Demanding blood and retribution. Too bad the target for the restlessness reaching a boiling point inside my chest can't be found in this godforsaken, sand-filled hell.

No. The traitorous bitch is back in the States, fanning her surgically-enhanced face with our divorce papers—fucking the man she chose to cheat on me with.

"Carter!" Cole's thunderous voice crackles into my comms. "Where the fuck are you, man?"

My eyes scan the golden desert for my team—the team I let move away from me while I was questioning my sanity in marrying the witch of Lost Hope. *And all my decisions since.*

"Your nine o'clock. Hundred yards behind," I mumble back, shame coating my sun-burned face.

"Move your fucking ass into formation. NOW!" Cole orders, and my feet unfreeze. I trudge through the fine desert grains crunching underneath the soles of my combat boots, but don't make it more than ten steps in their direction when a bullet whizzes through the air. The burn of the shot so fucking close to my head stops me in my tracks.

A second bullet whizzes past my ear, and my muscles stiffen, my whole body locking down. Air remains trapped in my lungs, my heart-beat sluggish and dull. My eyes see nothing around me but sand and more sand. There's nowhere to hide, nowhere to go. I can't feel my limbs by the time realization hits.

I'm a goddamn sitting duck.

Reckless.

So fucking reckless to break away from my team just to ponder the full extent of Amanda's betrayal.

"OPEN FIRE! GET DOWN, GET THE FUCK DOWN NOW!" Cole's voice booms through the comms.

I faintly hear the strained words, but the order doesn't register. Nothing does through the adrenaline spiking my blood, poisoning me with images of home—of who I thought was my home just six months prior. A surprise visit for us turned into a surprise divorce for me.

And the bitter reminder is protected in the inner pocket right next to my shriveled heart.

THE DOOR OPENS with an ominous creak, and my steps falter in the entrance of our apartment when a masculine chuckle sounds from the living room. My duffel bag slides off my shoulder and hits the wooden floor with an echoing thump.

Hurried clicking steps bring my beautiful wife in front of me. My beautiful wife, dressed in a crimson mini dress, so tight on her slender body it looks painted on. My beautiful wife, with her platinum hair artfully braided in a crown atop her head, and her plump lips slicked with fire-engine red lipstick.

My stomach recoils, turning upside down. I swallow down the nausea and take a tentative step closer to her. Her amber eyes flash cold, and her lips turn in a grimace. A man's arm hooks around her waist and pulls her behind him.

"I get it, man. Mandy is not a woman you easily get over. But she doesn't want to reconcile. Sign the papers and return to where you came from."

"Goddammit, Carter. Drop to the fucking ground, you mother-fucker!" Jake's desperate voice crackles through my ear, yanking me out of my head and into the present.

It takes a single moment for me to retreat into my head, and that single moment is enough to completely lose sight of my team. A fine mist of coppery dust paints the air, and the shots are coming in heavy. He wants me to drop down. I'm already as down as it gets.

"If you're not on your ass in the next second, I'll put a bullet through your knee myself," Cole threatens, and the rage inside, combined with the last of my self-preservation instincts, forces my knees to bend and drop to the ground.

The fury making my blood boil pushes me face-first in the heated sand, my whole body flat to the earth, cheeks and nose buried in golden, scorching grains. My eyes, gritty with dust, look for an exit.

She may have ripped my heart out of my chest, but I'll be damned to the darkest pits of hell if I let her claim my life, too.

I'm at the top of a tall dune. If I manage to roll down the slope, I'll be better protected and could return fire—give my own team a fighting chance.

The jagged thunder of firing guns gets closer to me, and I barrel-roll faster, the speed of my movement in tune in my hammering heart. I'm so close to the edge, I can practically taste my last chance on my tongue.

Reckless.

Idiotic.

I had no business falling behind and jeopardizing the safety of my team. I had no business giving the traitorous bitch a second thought. But no, I chose today of all days to let my rage get the better of me; to let her betrayal live rent-free in my head.

If by any miracle I get out of here alive, I swear this is the last time she occupies any measure of space in my mind. This is the last time she's messing with my head. From this second until the last day I have left on Earth, Amanda is dead to me.

Blinking all thoughts of my failed marriage away, I stop my momentum with the heel of my boot. My palms push into the abrasive sand, and I lift my body into a plank, assessing the actual threat in front of me.

Shadows are dancing chaotically in the thick coppery mist. I can't make out friend or foe. Can't report my position either since I don't want to blow my already precarious hideaway.

I crawl on my elbows and knees, trying to gain an advantage, but I'm moving in blind.

"You better be goddamned alive, Carter," Jake hisses, and hope surges in my chest that at least one of them is still in one piece.

Air whooshes out of my lungs as my right thigh explodes in a mess of fire and sand. White-hot agony courses through me when my bone shatters and the flesh protecting it gives way to bullets and shrapnel before I faceplant back in the sand.

There's no way out of this now. Letting my arms fall listlessly at my sides, I feel the tacky wetness of my blood pooling underneath me, soaking the starved, sun-heated ground. I roll to my back, my eyes unfocused, the clear blue of the sky painted with crimson fog.

Sand, blood, despair, mistakes. My recklessness brought me here.

"Shit. What did you do that for, you cunt?" Jake's face comes into my field of view, his sweat dripping onto my skin. "You fucking moron," he curses, grabbing my arms in a steel grip and dragging me away through crushed rocks and pebbles.

The cuts and scratches on my back are nothing but afterthoughts when I know I left half of my blood at the bottom of that goddamned dune. If the bleeding doesn't kill me, the infection settling in surely will.

"Cover Hayes," I rasp, my throat refusing to sound any more words.

"Don't you worry your pretty little head about Cap. He's not a fucking idiot like you," Jake scoffs. His lips keep moving, but the blood rushing in my ears makes it difficult for me to focus on every word out of his mouth, so I stop trying, watching the blue expanse of the sky instead.

His grip around my forearm tightens, his voice penetrating through the spell I'm under. "We're covered. Help's on the way, so don't you dare die on me here. I plan to leave a goddamn hero. You owe me for the rest of your life."

My chest shakes as a garbled chuckle escapes its confines. Jackson Camden will be known as the hero to my dying damsel in distress. At least there's *some* silver lining.

I shudder when the pain in my thigh disappears abruptly, as if a switch is flipped. I know what it means when there's no more pain. I know my end is near.

Hot, thick air suffocates me while guilt chokes the remaining life out of me. I failed my team; I failed my family.

My stomach somersaults, and dry heaves wreck my weakened body. Single-handedly, I just broke the hearts of all my loved ones.

The pressure on my arms from Jackson's grip disappears too, while images of my father, mother, Selena, and Sawyer float in the air. My eyes roll into the back of my head, and I'm ready to give in to the numbness; ready to let the darkness lingering at the corners of my eyes swallow me whole.

A heavy weight falls on top of me like a boulder, forcing the air out of my lungs in a violent rush, yanking me out of my brush with death.

"C-Camden?" I call out to the man passed out on top of me. "Jackson! W-wake up, man. No, no, no, no... Jackson..."

Fear is poisoning my blood now. My unfocused eyes scan the sand, looking for threats. Rage returns with a vengeance, overpowering all other feelings and thoughts. It writhes in my veins, demanding justice for my brother. Demanding I get up, shattered leg be damned, and protect Jackson.

My heart pounds with renewed energy as I grip the revolver hidden in the pocket of my camo vest. A shimmering dark mirage at the corner of my eye lets me know the enemy who hit Jackson in the back like a coward has come to finish the job.

I have one shot before my energy drains in the sand with our combined blood. My arm lifts and my fingers tense on the handle as a jolt travels through the exhausted tendons of my forearm, like an electric bolt. The shadowy figure drops with a pained thump when my bullet flies true with the last of my strength.

My eyes lift to the sky. It seems unfair the sun is shining on the clear blue expanse when a tornado of guilt and disappointment wrecks me inside.

They say your whole life plays out in your mind in the seconds before you're gone for eternity. I don't know what I expected to see in these moments.

But a pretty as fuck face, framed by dark twin braids, and a pair of soulful, brown eyes weren't it.

I've never been reckless. Not a day in my life. Not until I paid for my recklessness with two lives and a bitter *What if.*

Chapter One

Maevis

Nine years later

I pull my woolen coat tight around my body as the freezing November air hits me with my first step out of Lalah's door. I spin on my heel and smile at my friend. My arms itch to hug her, but I'm well aware of her aversion to touch.

"Thanks for hosting all of us. I had a great time," I say. And I really did. The last two years, my Thanksgiving celebrations consisted of a rushed lunch at my father's side at the Forrest Falls Care Home and a lonely dinner on the couch in front of the TV.

"I should thank you and Annalise for the delicious food. I'm sorry I left it all up to you." Lalah grimaces, her red lips twisting at one corner.

Cole, her tall, dark, and delicious not-boyfriend—according to Lalah and the speech she held just last week during our planning session at Dine&Dash—throws a meaty arm around her shoulders and pulls her to his side. His pale-green eyes drink her in. I'm willing to bet half my bakery he's as in love with her as she is with him.

"You were in no shape to cook today, Supernova." When his mouth presses to the top of her head, a twinge of envy shoots through me.

This, right here. This is what I want. Someone to look at me the way Cole looks at Lalah, like she's his sole reason for living.

"Alright, Cupcake. Say your goodbyes. Your carriage is heated and awaiting." A swarm of butterflies takes flight inside my belly when Tatum's raspy voice heats the back of my neck.

That twinge of envy? Puff. Gone.

The someone I want to look at me the way Cole looks at Lalah?

That's Tatum Carter.

Mechanic extraordinaire, former Marine, my forever crush since childhood, and current partner in this back-and-forth tango we've been dancing ever since Lalah moved into town.

Lalah and her not-boyfriend are new transplants to Lost Hope. She came to us a shell of a woman, cagey and untrusting, six months ago. Between Tatum, Annalise, and me, we forced ourselves into her life, slowly chipping away at her shields, getting her to warm up to us, and we're all better for it.

But it took a snowstorm, bringing a knight in shining tattoos to her doorstep, for Lalah to soften and drop her walls. If anyone can manage to bulldoze through her fortress, that's Cole, and I have the feeling he'll put a ring on that finger as soon as he's sure she's not a flight risk.

I know the stoic ex-Marine, currently working with my twin as a firefighter for LHFD, will lay his life at her feet to make her happy. Cole's past hasn't been easy either.

He lost his mother and her husband back in July and has had to retire from the Marines when he's been named guardian for his step-sisters—ten-year-old Eliza and nearly three-year-old Clara.

Tatum steps into me, and I shiver under my coat. Not because of the rapidly dropping temperature, but from the heat emanating from him. All I want to do is lean back and have those tatted-up arms of his wrap around me. But I can't.

I'm a thirty-three-year-old divorced woman with the crush of a four-teen-year-old. No joke. That's when these pesky feelings I have for the man at my back started. These pesky, *unreciprocated* feelings.

His hot-and-cold games leave my head spinning, and I'm too much of a coward to actually go for what I want.

I don't have the best track record with my taste in men. I thought my ex-husband was a decent man, and he was. Until he wasn't. Until he buried me in debt while he was getting his cock sucked by a twen-ty-year-old on our sofa. Until he...

The sharp thud of palm-slapping-fabric takes me out of my head and back to Lalah's house, where the two muscled giants back-slap in that cool-bro-half-hug way only men can pull off.

Tate takes a step back and picks up the bags heaving-full of leftovers before his long, thick fingers entwine with mine, leading me toward his running truck.

He pulls the door open for me, grinning when I stare at the tall monstrosity. I'm merely five-foot-three in a tight-as-fuck dress. There's no way I could lift my knee high enough to reach the foothold without splitting it at the seams.

His husky chuckle has a direct line to my panties—panties that are getting uncomfortably wet and cold. His hands grab my hips and lift me onto the passenger seat, an embarrassing squeak escaping my lips at the sudden movement.

I slide hurriedly across the heated, buttery leather as he shuts the door behind me. A grateful sigh slips past my lips when my out-stretched palms are hit with hot air from the vents.

His masculine scent of pinewood and wilderness, with just the smallest hint of motor oil, fills the cabin of the truck as he hoists himself into the driver's seat. I can't help the full body shiver washing through me at his nearness.

His eyebrows crease together, his full lips twisting in a grimace. "You're still cold, Cupcake?"

I tentatively nod my head. It's not like I can actually tell him his mere presence and scent are enough to have me shivering as I repress the urge to climb him like a tree.

In one swift move, he lifts the center console and his arm pulls me to him, sliding me all the way onto the leather bench until my thighs are pressed firmly to his, and my upper body is nestled close to all the rock-hard muscles hidden by his jacket.

"There, that's better," he muses, fastening my seatbelt over my hips, and with a pat to my thigh, we're on our way to my apartment.

The heat of his body mixed with the rumbling of the engine—and the overload of carbs I stuffed myself with tonight—envelops me, and soon enough my eyelids flutter closed. I fall asleep pretending he is mine, I am his, and we're on our way to the home we've created together.

Gentle fingers brush over my forehead, followed by soft kisses on the top of my head.

"Maevis, babe, we're here. Wake up, sugar. Let's get you inside and into bed," Tate whispers while the arm around my shoulders tightens, holding me closer.

My eyelids flutter open, my head tipping back on the headrest. Cornflower-blue eyes drink me in, a small crinkle at their corners betraying the amusement in his gaze. Amusement, and something a touch darker, something that looks a heck of a lot like lust.

My mouth is so close to his, all I have to do is purse my lips for us to touch.

I clear my throat and push away from him, my cheeks blazing red in embarrassment and frustration. His sigh fills the truck before his door clicks open, and I take my cue from that to push open my own door and scramble to the ground, praying I don't break an ankle in the process.

"Stubborn woman," he mutters when he reaches me. "Couldn't have waited two seconds for me to open the door for you and help you out?"

"S-sorry. I-I didn't realize that was what you were doing," I croak, my eyes lowered to the ground. I can't look at him after I made a fool of myself twice in the span of one minute.

He reaches inside the truck and picks up one of the goodie-bags before his palm settles at the small of my back, urging me toward the stairs leading to my one-bedroom apartment over my bakery, Suga'High.

"What are you doing?"

"Seeing you to your door, obviously," he snaps, my heels and his boots thumping on the metal steps.

"You don't need to do that, you know? Open the car door for me or see me to my door." Why would he? I'm just a friend to him, despite all the flirting we've done in the past few months.

It's not like it's the first time he's led me on. I gained the courage to go out again at the beginning of this year, so Annalise made me join her and Drake at JC's Pour, a bar on the outskirts of Lost Hope, more than once.

And more than once, Tatum was there.

Buying me drinks.

Dancing with me.

Leaving without me at the end of the night.

There's only so much rejection a girl can take.

His palm flexes at my back, fisting the fabric of my coat as we reach the landing in front of my door. In one quick move, he pulls me behind him and barks, "Stay back. What the hell happened to your window? Don't you know it's dangerous having a window right above your lock?"

I peek from behind him at the bright-green painted door, and a gasp escapes my lips when I see the glass shattered. I try to push him away, desperate to check if the door is still locked, but he doesn't budge.

He twists the knob, and thankfully, the door remains shut.

"Maybe there were kids playing. Sometimes they do come back here for their snowball fights," I mumble, trying to find a reasonable excuse that won't make me fear sleeping in my own bed.

He pries the key from my hand and walks in first. Luckily, the entrance hallway is closed off, otherwise my whole apartment would have turned into a freezer with the jagged hole in my door.

He turns to me, his shoulders somehow wider in the narrow space we're both trapped in. His blue gaze scans my face, bright eyes boring into the depths of my soul.

"I'm sleeping on the couch tonight. I'll fix your window tomorrow. Better yet, replace your whole door with one that's not so... breakable," he declares.

"You'll do no such thing. Drake can take care of it in the morning." I don't know why I'm fighting his offer to stay. I would be more comfortable if he slept here, but I also don't want to be a damsel in distress who needs to be constantly rescued.

I'm sick of being pitied. Poor Maevis with no mother, a sick father, and an abusive, two-timing, shit-excuse of an ex-husband. Poor Maevis, who constantly has to be rescued by her father or her twin brother.

Tate's thick, callused fingers wrap around my jaw. My breath hitches, a tinge of unease curling in my stomach, but he just tilts my head back, forcing me on my tippy-toes so we're nose to nose.

"Don't fight me on this, Cupcake," he grits. "If I have to sleep in my truck with an eye on your front door, I will. But I know I'll be a hell of a lot more comfortable here."

His minty breath washes over my face as each of his patronizing words hit straight into the center of all my insecurities. My lips part, ready to give him a piece of my mind. Who does he think he is? Who died and made him my keeper?

Yeah, I want him to care for me because he wants me, not urged by some weird sense of responsibility he has because I'm Lalah's friend, and he adopted her as a sister.

His bright eyes turn black, with only a thin circle of blue surrounding his pupils, and his lips curve in a predatory smile. His knees bend until our noses touch and my legs weaken. I've never been this close to him before, and now twice in one evening is too much, too soon.

"Don't fight me, baby," he whispers a plea before his mouth descends on mine.

Plump, firm lips part mine and his tongue wastes no time plundering my mouth. Tatum kisses me into submission, in a duel of hot, wet strokes of his tongue against mine. A primal growl escapes his throat, and I swallow it in my chest for safekeeping.

My hands find purchase on his shoulders, short nails gripping his jacket, before sliding up his corded neck into his soft hair. Trembling fingers find the elastic holding his golden locks together and rip it away. A curtain of blond silk falls around our faces, enclosing us in a cocoon of privacy and need.

He sucks my bottom lip into his mouth, teeth nipping at the swollen flesh, his eager tongue caressing away the sting. "You taste as sweet as I imagined you would," he murmurs.

His large palm presses against the back of my head, pulling me closer to him, plastering me to his hard chest. His mouth is unrelenting, trailing open-mouthed, wet kisses along my jaw and down my neck. Jolts of electricity travel from where he sucks on my skin, straight between my legs.

"Tatum..." I moan his name when his teeth scrape my earlobe.

A hand shoves its way between our glued bodies, and my woolen coat slides down my shoulders and onto the floor with a soft thump. The same hand rips at the zipper of his leather jacket before my own hands help it off his straining body. All the while, his lips continue their torment, trailing down my collarbone, and into my small cleavage.

My lack of tits bothers him not one bit as he groans into my chest. His lips are fervently nipping and kissing my skin, his straight, Roman nose pushing the silk material of my dress aside, baring me to him.

"Fuck, sweetness. You're killing me. The taste of you drives me insane. Vanilla may be my new favorite fucking flavor."

My body stiffens, the molten desire put out by ice-cold dread as *that* word echoes in my head. My limbs grow heavy and numb under the weight of hellish memories I thought I'd long put behind me, but are now playing on repeat before my damp eyes.

My breath hitches in my chest as my insecurities rear their ugly heads. My heart pounds erratically, not in anticipation, not in celebration of my very first kiss with Tatum, but in shame.

"Vanilla Maevis, the blandest of flavors. That's who I married, the most boring flavor in the goddamned state."

My fingers shakily untangle from Tatum's and push at his shoulders, trying to get him away from me. He freezes with my lace-covered nipple in his mouth, releasing me with a wet pop and taking a step back.

"What did I do?" he asks, concern dripping from his tone in stark contrast with the childish pout tugging down his swollen bottom lip.

"N-nothing. I just... I'd like you to leave now."

Chapter Two

Tatum

With tousled dark locks, pink silk dress askew, plush lips swollen and puffy from my kisses, the prettiest of flushes creeping up her chest to her cheeks, Maevis Barlowe has never looked more beautiful.

And sad.

Why the fuck is Mae sad when I just had my teeth on her nipples and my cock busy drilling through the zipper of my jeans to reach her?

"If you don't want me to touch you, I won't." *How the fuck did I read the situation so wrong?* "But I'm not leaving." My hands move in front of me, palms up in a placating gesture, trying not to spook her further. "Do you want to tell me what happened?" I plead with my eyes.

Her big, round eyes still have the deer-in-the-headlights look, but now that I've stepped away from her, it frustrates me to no end that I can't clearly see her. My hands fumble blindly on the wall until I reach the switch, and warm light floods the small hallway. I look back at her and my stomach rolls at the tears threatening to spill from her long lashes.

I'm back in her space in less than a second, my palm cradling her jaw, thumb sweeping at the hot tears rolling down her cheeks. "Sweetness, you're scaring the fuck out of me. Talk to me, babe. What did I do?"

Her head nuzzles into my calloused palm, and the worry pouring in my bloodstream dims a fraction. She sniffles her pretty button nose, and I can't help but bend down and kiss the wet, freckled tip.

"You called me 'Vanilla'. Vanilla is the blandest of flavors," she whispers, her rich-brown eyes downcast, trained on the tattoos on my forearm.

I bite my cheek so hard I taste blood in my mouth trying not to laugh. Laughing right now would bring me nothing but a swift knee to my already suffering balls and a kick in the ass straight out the door.

"There's nothing boring about vanilla, Cupcake," I rasp in her ear.

"The sweetest of flavors, compliments every single dessert." My tongue trails down the side of her neck to her shoulder, licking the aroma embedded in her skin. Her breath hitches and her silky skin pebbles in my wake.

"The most indulgent scent. Regardless of where I am, if I smell vanilla in the air, it reminds me of home. It reminds me of you." My nose burrows in her hair, a deep inhale filling my lungs with her comforting scent. Sweet. Floral. Maevis.

My palm hits the wall above her head, and I lean on my forearm, towering over her. My other hand releases her jaw, fingers trailing down her collarbone, over her hardened peaks, trekking over the softness of her belly, following the pink patterns of her dress to the hem hitting mid-thigh.

My fingertip rubs the smooth, creamy skin of her thigh, sliding higher and higher until it reaches the wet lace barrier separating me from heaven.

I bend my neck, capturing her heated gaze with mine, my lips a breath away from hers, and whisper, "Vanilla sex. The best kind. Crisp white sheets, your silky hair fanned out around us, your tits bared to me to kiss and suck and lick and bite, your creamy thighs spread out, pink, swollen pussy glistening with our combined arousal as you take me again, and again, and again."

The mewling sound escaping her throat has me grinning, and it takes everything in me not to hook my fingers into the dainty lace I'm busy petting with lazy strokes, and rip her panties off her, burying my fingers to the knuckles in her tight channel.

"Yeah, Cupcake. Vanilla sex. Where I take you in long, lazy thrusts. Where I get to savor your pussy one hard inch at the time." My mouth touches hers as I whisper my next words, "Vanilla's the most intense of flavors. My absolute fucking favorite."

"Tatum..." she moans, her greedy fingers reaching under my T-shirt, burning the imprint of her palm on my abdomen.

"Tell me you want me, Maevis," I command. I'm one kiss away from snapping. My blood boils inside of me with the urge to take her. To make her mine right here, in the freezing hallway, on the goddamn wall.

"I want you," she whispers, gripping my steel cock through my jeans. I grunt in her mouth at the absolute bliss spreading through my veins as she strokes me with one hand, struggling to unbuckle my belt with the other.

And so I do what I wanted to do just seconds ago. With a flick of my thumb, I rip the lace off her body and bury my fingers in her hot, greedy pussy. Her channel grips and flutters around me, wetness pooling around my fingers as I move them in and out of her, working her up, stretching her out.

My tongue follows the same rhythm as my fingers, fucking her mouth in lazy strokes, my hips jerking, impatient to get their turn between her legs. I drink in all the keening noises she makes in the back of her throat, and step closer, trapping her between me and the wall.

I want to rut into her like a dog in heat. My heart pounds in my chest, and I feel like Icarus flying too close to the Sun. Nearly nine years of longing are coming to a head tonight.

Nine years where I watched her from afar, wanting her, missing her, too much of a goddamn coward to do anything about it.

I barely survived Amanda. If Maevis breaks my heart, she won't need a bullet to eviscerate me. I should slow us down. I should stop my forearm from moving underneath her ass. I should stop her needy hand from slipping inside my boxers and gripping my throbbing cock, teasing my length in sloppy jerks.

I should definitely not hoist her up the wall, wrapping her legs around my waist. And for the life of me, I shouldn't line up at her dripping entrance, pushing bare inside her in one savage thrust.

"Fuck, fuck, *fuuuck*," I curse under my breath, my mouth still fused to hers, both panting, our combined moans of bliss filling the hallway.

I still inside her, and all that tight wet heat sheaths me like a perfect glove. *Home. Heaven. Maevis.*

"Tate, God, you feel so good. I'm so full. Move, please. Move," she begs me, her short nails cutting into the skin of my shoulders as my hips move back until only the very tip of me remains inside of her. I look down at where we're joined.

Her rose-petal pink lips part around me, belly quivering in anticipation and need. I slam back into her, her greedy pussy swallowing me whole. "Yes, Tate, fuck yes. Give it to me." Her screams of pleasure spur me on.

My hands are everywhere. I desperately grip her ass, claw at her waist, rip the dress over her head. Her white lace bralette falls around her waist as I fuck myself into her with frenzied long strokes, trying to pound my way into the depths of her soul.

"You're mine, Cupcake! This shameless pussy is mine. Your tight, perky tits, all mine," I growl at her, then lower my head and bite hard on her rosy nipple. A crazy flutter grips my cock, my balls, heavy and achy, drawing tight to my body.

"Say it, Maevis. Say you're mine," I order her, desperate for a promise to bind her to me.

"God, yes, Tatum. I'm yours! I'm yours! Holy fuck, I'm so close. Please, I'm yours," she cries out, her fingers clenching my hair in a death-grip, the sting making me roar in absolute ecstasy.

"You gonna come for me, sugar?" I grit around the wet nipple in my mouth, my tongue swirling at the pointed bud. My hand sneaks between the two of us to her needy bundle of nerves. I clasp her clit between my thumb and forefinger, pinching it in quick succession.

"That's it, sweetness." I pant when the familiar tingles erupt in my groin, shooting through me as I fly headfirst into the Sun with her.

A raspy moan rips from her throat as her back arches, pushing her chest into my mouth. Her pussy quivers and trembles around me, drawing me in, milking me for all I am.

I grip her waist to steady her, her thighs growing lax, shaking around me. I slam her on my cock once, twice, three times before spilling inside of her, hot spurts of cum shooting from me as I plant myself to the root, my spent cock twitching with the aftershocks of the best orgasm of my life.

I slump against the wall, holding her still-shaking body close to my chest. My knees are barely holding me upright, but I didn't even scratch the surface of my hunger for her.

My lips are hot and heavy, kissing her sweat-slicked shoulder, trying desperately to gather all of Maevis into me. "That was spiced-up vanilla," I murmur into her skin.

Her molten-sugar eyes, dazed with post-orgasmic euphoria, blink at me in wonder. "You're going to show me plain vanilla now?"

"Oh, Cupcake, there's nothing plain with what I'm about to do to you," I promise her darkly, hugging her closer to me, one hand underneath her ass, the other fisting her hair.

Blindly making my way to her bedroom, my knees hit the frame of her bed, and we both come tumbling down on her mattress. Her peals of laughter bounce off the walls, forcing my lips into a wide smile.

Her soft fingertip trails the corners of my mouth, a shy look in her glazed-over eyes. "You don't smile much, but when you do, it's blinding. Like that one second during an eclipse, when the Moon shifts away from the Sun, and the first rays escaping the shadows glow brighter than day-light."

My stomach tightens at her words, my lips stretching out even more. "Haven't had much to smile about until now," I murmur, crawling on my knees closer to her, until her thighs cradle my hips.

"I hate being *that* woman, but I have to ask, Tatum. What is this?" she whispers, a shy quality to her question, her voice cracking on the last words.

"This, sweetness, is the beginning of us. I'm too old to play any games. I've waited for too long to get to this point," I confess my greatest wish. *My greatest fear, too.*

"Why now? What changed?" she prods. A pang of regret hits me out of nowhere. All this time I was focused on all the ways she could hurt me. The truth is, I could hurt Maevis in the same manner. She's lived the same agony I lived. Hell, I witnessed her ex-husband on the prowl at JC's Pour until I had Jake ban him. For whatever damned good it did.

I drop my head on her shoulder, pressing my lips to the crook of her neck, chasing the fluttering of her pulse, and sigh deeply. Every cell in me protests when I lift off her and climb out of bed.

I grip my T-shirt at the bottom hem and throw it out over my head into the darkness of her bedroom. Not reacting to her moan when my abs contract and flex, bending at the waist, I rip at the laces of my boots, taking them off and dropping them next to her bed.

My jeans and boxers fall to my ankles with one swift shove down. And then I stand in front of her, naked as the day I was born, cock hard enough to break through walls, in all my tatted-up glory. In all my wounded glory, too.

She climbs to her knees, crawling to me, going straight to the red, angry, crisscrossed scar on my right thigh. Smaller scars, shaped like an X surround it, a gruesome painting of the culmination of all my worst decisions.

My whole upper body is inked. So is my left thigh. I've left the horror of my mistakes untouched, so that every time I glance at my leg, I'm reminded of where recklessness took me.

"Nothing changed," I rasp as she tenderly caresses the shattered muscle above my knee. "For nine years, I've questioned every decision I've ever made. This scar on my body? The metals holding my femur together and setting off every airport security alarm? They all mark the first day I acknowledged my choices could not always be trusted."

Maevis peers up at me from under hooded lids, her bottom lip trembling. My thumb flicks at the plump flesh, and her tongue darts out to lick at my fingertip. My cock jolts in her face, straining to reach her, leaking with need to feel her wet tongue on its steel.

"I'm done denying myself what I want. You have the power here, Mae. You have the power to make me soar and the power to rip me to shreds. I may not trust myself a hundred percent still, but I choose to trust you."

A sweet peck on my angry, red head has me tensing before she swallows me whole. My knees buckle and I fist her hair to remain upright while she takes me to the back of her throat. Maevis Barlowe is a goddamn force of nature. And I'm a defenseless tree, bending at the will of the most beautiful tempest.

It's only in the early morning hours that we fall asleep after she showed me all goddamn night that there's nothing vanilla about her. Her naked peach-shaped ass snuggles closer to my still half-hard cock, and the realization hits me in the chest with startling clarity.

I'm not just flying close to the Sun. I'm already submerged under the molten lava bubbling at the surface.

Chapter Three

Maevis

We're like teenagers—horny, hormonal, out-of-control teenagers—sneaking around, stealing touches here and there.

I'm sure we're fooling no one, especially not Lalah. She may be baring her deepest, darkest secrets to us right now, but she's always watching, always observing everything around her. The thick finger sneaking teasing sweeps between my legs has my cheeks flushed and my eyes glaze over with desire for him. *Only him.* And I'm sure she doesn't miss that.

He's testing my resilience on purpose. I know he's disappointed I want to keep whatever this is between us. *For now.* I've known him my whole life, but I've known him as Tatum—the superstar high school quarterback; Tatum—Amanda's boyfriend and then husband; Tatum—the quiet, grumpy, hot-as-fuck mechanic; Tatum—my childhood crush.

But I don't know the infatuated-with-me Tatum. And I don't know what to do with this knowledge.

The chemistry between us is impossibly strong. The things he does to me, the things I want to do to him. I fear lust is all we have. So if I end up being just a long term sex-buddy to him, I don't want to advertise us.

And if he ends up being everything I've ever wanted, then there's nothing wrong with taking our time to get to know one another.

"I'm really sorry, guys. I never meant to deceive you." Lalah's pleading voice brings me back to the table and to her big reveal.

Am I shocked to learn that she has enough money to buy this town ten times over? Sure, although just looking at her home, it's glaringly obvious she's not hurting for cash.

"Would you have told us?" Annalise asks. My eyes dart to my sister-in-law, watching her brush a strand of caramel-colored hair behind her ear. "If Maddison didn't force your hand, would you have told us?"

Maddison Brown is the daughter of our mayor, and she's made it her life's mission to cross Lalah, ever since our friend moved to Lost Hope. There's not much love lost between Maddison and anyone in this town, to be honest. She's always been a bully and an entitled bitch.

Lege et Lacrima, an angel investor company, had most of the business in town assessed during the summer, with several of us receiving a huge amount of money as an investment to better our livelihood. Maddison's was rejected then. She found out yesterday that Lalah was the assessor, and she posted on social media pictures of confidential documents in retaliation, outing our friend.

And this is the reason we're all gathered in Lalah's home. She's not just an employee of *Lege et Lacrima*, she is *Lege et Lacrima* and she's filthy rich.

Lalah purses her pink lips, hazel eyes pinned to the wall behind Annalise, lost in thought. She nods to herself, as if reaching a conclusion. A conclusion she doesn't particularly like based on the furrow of her eyebrows.

"Unlikely I would've said anything," she declares. Cole's massive arm sneaks around her, squeezing her shoulder in a show of support. "My original focus was Hope Haven. I never expected to come here and find my home. And once I met you guys, I didn't think it mattered," she trails off, and I almost snicker at the blush blazing her cheeks.

Lalah McAdams, cool-as-a-cucumber bad-boss-bitch, blushing.

"You're right," I find myself saying. "For our friendship, the size of your bank account doesn't matter. What you do for a living doesn't matter. We all have things we prefer to keep to ourselves. You weren't judging our trustworthiness and finding us lacking."

My eyes dart around the table, trying to gather my thoughts and gauge all the emotions filling the dining room. "I think I can speak for everyone when I say... we're all very grateful to you. Whether you helped us directly or helped someone we love, what you did is extraordinary. By keeping it all a secret, no one felt indebted to you."

"The friendships you made didn't come with a price tag. They're forged out of mutual understanding, shared pain, and supportive hands. Freedom to choose," Jake, one of Tatum's best friends and the owner of *JC's Pour*, muses.

I nod my head in unison with the others. I don't know if I would have felt comfortable enough approaching her if I knew she was the one pulling me out of debt. The debt would've just shifted to her instead of being gone.

"So, what you're saying is my big brother here found himself a sugar mama, huh?" Blake's teasing cuts through the tension building up between the four glass walls. Cole's chest crowds Lalah in her seat when he thanks his brother with a friendly slap over the back of his head.

Was I hurt to know she held such a big secret? Maybe if I wasn't harboring a secret of my own, yes. But I can empathize with Lalah. Sometimes, secrets have everything to do with us personally, and nothing to do with our close ones.

And most of the time, they're born out of fear and pain. Lalah's fear is that she as a person is not good enough. My fear is being left behind, enough for a taste, too bland for forever.

"You're riding with me," Tatum whispers in my ear, a hot shiver trailing down my spine as his breath fans on the delicate skin of my neck.

"W-what?" I jolt, silently chiding myself for being lost in thought again.

"Are you back with me?" Tatum smirks. That freaking smirk that gets me weak in the knees.

I lean back in my chair and scowl at him, pursing my lips in displeasure. His tongue, pink and wet, darts across his bottom lip, and my eyes fixate on the movement. My body leans closer to him as if invisible strings are pulling at me, pressing at the back of my neck, urging me to kiss him.

"Babe," he laughs, his chuckle deep and rumbly, then once again leans close to me and murmurs, "You gotta stop looking at me like that. Unless you want me to spread you on top of the table and maul you for everyone to see."

I playfully slap his rock-hard shoulder with the back of my hand. "Then you gotta dial down all the alpha-sexy-smolder you've got going on. A girl has only so much restraint," I murmur back.

His smirk deepens until the faint outline of a dimple forms on his right cheek. "Stop it," I hiss since I know the sexy bastard is doing it on purpose.

The high-pitched scraping of wooden chairs on slick marble sounds around us, and I turn my back to Tatum, leaning into him now that no one is paying us any attention.

His nose buries in my hair, his mouth tickling the shell of my ear when he whispers, "We're going to JC's, and I get to hold you and dance with you all night. No hiding, no sneaking around."

"Tatum," I whine for his ears only, not missing the bitter undertones of his last words.

"C'mon, Cupcake. You and Annalise are riding with me."

I know I'm being unfair to him. Part of me is screaming to claim him right now in front of all of our friends. But the other part, the one comparing me with his ex-wife and finding me lacking, that part is adamant that I need to be cautious.

Anything too good to be true lasts very little for me.

I've always been the second choice. The one you go to when your first option doesn't pan out. The one you come back to when the greener pastures wilted on the bright side of the fence.

The bland flavor. The safe, boring option.

Seems fitting since I came second from birth. Don't get me wrong, I love my brother to death. Couldn't have asked for a better human to share a womb or to grow up with.

But, where Drake's an overprotective go-getter, the life of the party, the bubbly champagne on New Year's Eve, I'm the hangover cure.

Safe, necessary, nurturing. Bland at best, nauseating at worst.

"You're thinking awfully hard over there," Tatum observes from the driver's seat.

Annalise is right in front of me, in the front passenger seat. He wasn't happy when I went for the back door, but Anna didn't have any Dramamine for her motion sickness. The road to JC's is full of twists, crests, and dips, so I felt it was best to not tempt fate.

"Nah." I give him a small smile. "Today is a lot to process, that's all."

"On that, we all agree," he mumbles.

"That's why I can't wait to get a margarita in me and shake my worries off on the dance floor," Annalise says.

"Amen, sister." I laugh as Tatum throws the truck into park and jumps out, slamming the door shut.

He rounds the tail to help me out, and I greet him with an open door. His long fingers grip my hips, pulling me closer to him before lifting me up and out of the truck. My arms instinctively wrap around his shoulders, holding on for dear life.

It's not the first time he's manhandled me. It's not the first time either that I expect him to drop me or grunt under my weight.

I may be five-foot nothing, but I own a bakery and indulge every day. My ass, hips, and thighs are the unfortunate victims of my gluttony.

His warm palm sneaks under my coat and squeezes my ass. I yelp in surprise, narrowing my eyes at him in admonishment. His low, rumbling chuckle vibrates from his chest into mine, my nipples furrowing in tight points in response.

He lets me slide painfully slow down his body when Annalise's door clicks open. My panties dampen, my inner core clenching tightly when his thick, hard cock pokes my belly as my feet touch the ground.

"Someone's happy to see me," I tease, skipping to where Anna is climbing out of the truck.

In three long strides he's at her side, helping her down, a mumbled "Sorry," under his breath to my sister-in-law.

Anna curls her plum-painted lips, a mischievous twinkle shining in her eyes as she says, "No worries, we all get distracted when we're happy to see Mae-Rae."

A wheezing sound escapes my throat, thankfully drowned out by Tatum's booming laugh. And what a laugh it is. My stomach flips, a rush of heat buzzing through me. The gravelly sounds of his chuckles slice through the silence reigning in the parking lot as we head inside. His neck tenses as he throws his head back, his shaking chest testing the resistance of every single stitch on his black Henley. Even Annalise looks at him in wonder.

A laughing Tatum is as rare as a selenelion.

He's guarding his smiles, too. He doesn't walk around scowling or glaring at people, but his natural expression is fierce seriousness and nothing in-between.

Since Lalah moved to town, he's smiling more often, more freely. I used to be jealous of their connection, thinking there was more to it than she admitted. Otherwise, why would Tatum, the notorious loner of Lost Hope, spend all his free time with a stranger? Until I saw Lalah with Cole for the first time. Even through the screen of my phone I was able to feel their connection. She was completely smitten with Cole less than a day after meeting him.

And Tatum is in seventh heaven happy for them. Turns out, Cole and Tate are best friends and served together in the Marine Corps, with Jackson too, who's currently slinging drinks behind the bar.

Annalise and I both sigh in unison at the sight of him.

She may be happily married to my brother, and I may be plastered to the man I'm half in love with, but not stopping to admire the scorching hotness that is Jackson Camden is a crime against humanity.

Tree trunk-thighs wrapped in low-slung black jeans lead up to a trim waist, washboard abs, and wide shoulders. And NO shirt.

And all *that* is wrapped in tattoos from neck to... I don't really know where, since the mesmerizing art trails off inside his jeans.

Annalise and I grin at each other like lunatics when Jackson pushes his fingers through his luscious jet-black hair, and all the valleys and ridges under his ink ripple with the movement.

"Seriously?" Tatum growls in my ear. I spin on my heel and, on the pretense of dancing with him, I loop my arms around his neck.

He bends ever so slightly, so I don't have to dance on my tippy-toes, but there's a spark of hurt in his blue eyes. His jealousy I can take, but not his hurt. We're too early in the game to play around with each other's feelings.

He's a safe, an impenetrable titanium box of emotions and reactions. But every once in a while, he lets his feelings bubble to the surface, swimming in the topaz blue of his eyes for me to fish out, one by one.

There's a war he's waging inside of him. So similar to the one raging inside of me. My fear holds me back. His fear is what pushes him forward. In this, I can meet him halfway.

"My dad saw how unhappy I was. All day every day, he witnessed my misery. He begged me to divorce Daniel," I confess. Tatum's thick, blond eyebrows rise to the center of his forehead. I don't let his confusion dissuade me.

"Ah, I wouldn't listen. My parents married for life. They would've still been married today if we hadn't lost my mom. I wanted the fairytale. So I continued lying to myself that I had my storybook love, we just had our particular dragons to slay until the happily ever after." I lift a shoulder in a self-deprecating shrug.

"So my dad, the wonderful man that he is, decided to mortgage my bakery for me. Daniel was completely indifferent. He was a carpenter, worked on plenty of sites. There's not a nail in that entire bakery touched by him. I worked day and night for two years with no help from him to get my bakery up and running. The finances were tight, I just didn't know how tight. He didn't work, incessantly grumbling instead about how little construction companies paid around Lost Hope. I now know how big of a lie that was. He just didn't want to work."

"Mae..."

"Once Suga'High was done, I decided we could get the apartment on the second floor cleaned-up and fixed. The house we were renting at the time took a good chunk of my savings. To me, it made sense to move into a home we owned. He laughed in my face, saying that I wanted to box him up," I continue, my eyes unable to hold his bright gaze, lingering on the sexy triangle of bare skin atop of his chest.

I take a deep breath, feeling my lungs inflate with oxygen and the intoxicating smell of Tatum. He doesn't know, but he is the only person to hear the true story out of my mouth. Drake witnessed it and drew his own conclusions. I never told a soul.

People speculated, guessed, gossiped. I let them. I had my bakery and my broken heart. I didn't need the added drama or to make waves.

"I dropped it for a while. But when he started drinking more and more, spending more nights away from home than there, I went back to the idea. So, armed with a notebook and a pen, I went to the apartment. The apartment was supposed to be empty and unlived in. Instead, there was a mattress, a bedside table, used condoms, and condom wrappers all over the floor."

Tatum's calloused palm cups the back of my head, his forefinger underneath my chin tips my head up so that my eyes meet his. There's fire burning in his gaze, enforced with a sheath of vengeance. He's ready to throw down for me, and I fall a little bit more down Tatum's rabbit hole.

"The worst were all the credit cards he opened in my name. He kept all the unpaid bills in a drawer in the bedside table. I took them all and went home to confront him, only to find my dear husband drunk as a skunk on the sofa, getting his dick sucked by the conquest of the night."

"Stop, Mae. Please stop," Tatum pleads, his voice gruff and strained, a grunt in my ear overpowering the thumping bass in the bar. "You're bleeding right in front of me, and I can't do a damn thing about it where we are."

My fingers have a mind of their own as they trail down his jaw, settling on his scruffed cheek. My thumb caresses his cheekbone adoringly, my whole body vibrating with the need to chase away all his emotional wounds. My lips part and tip at the corners into a wide, toothy smile, my attempt to show him I'm okay now. I'm here with him.

"We're not that different, you and I. I've been there. I suffered through wandering eyes. I suffered through wandering hands that turned into full-blown affairs," I tell him, injecting conviction in each of my words. "I'm not going to lie. Objectively, Jackson is a very handsome man."

His lips purse at my words, his tongue darts out to wet them, so I stop his rebuff before it takes flight. "He's also a handsome man who does nothing for me. There's someone else, though. Now, he's got me all twisted up inside. Just dancing with him in a crowded bar, his fingers fisting my hair, just that is enough to have me dripping between my legs."

Chapter Four

Tatum

Maevis Barlowe is the quintessential good girl. Always with a smile on her pink lips. Always the first to sign up for a charity bake sale. Always the first to offer her help. From the way she carries herself to the way she dresses, when you look at her all you see is a safe person. A good girl.

So, who would have thought the good girl with rich chocolate eyes would have my balls aching, my cock a steel rod in the middle of JC's dance floor, and simultaneously flaying my flesh with her pain?

I guess it's true what they say, still waters do run deep, and Maevis is the fucking Mariana Trench.

The fist I grip her luscious dark brown hair in tightens, and my hips grind against her belly so she can feel what she does to me. I'm pushing the boundaries she has set for us. Anyone looking could tell there's more than just friendship going on between us.

We're fooling no one but ourselves.

While I understand her reasoning for wanting us to get to know each other without interference from our *well-meaning* friends, if it were left up to me, I would've shouted from the rooftop of her bakery the morning after Thanksgiving that Maevis Barlowe is mine.

As it is, I have to settle with sneaky visits to her apartment during the night and walks of shame—not even in the slightest—back to my place in the morning.

"You're playing with fire, Cupcake," I threaten, my neck bent to whisper in her ear over Rihanna's admission of loving the way she's being lied to. My lips twist in a self-satisfied smirk at her gasp, so I close the distance between us even more with my palm splayed open on her lower back.

I rock my cock against her belly and, between the choked-out moan escaping her lips and the pressure of her petite body against mine, I'm extremely close to embarrassing myself.

"But in case I haven't made it clear, I don't share. Wherever this thing between us goes, you're mine and only mine," I growl in her ear, my restraint hanging on a thin, fragile thread.

Her pretty eyes roam my face and her gaze bores into mine, serious and demanding. "It goes for you, too. If you're mine, you're only mine."

"All you have to do is say the word, Cupcake. You know where I stand. I don't want to hide, but I'm doing it for you. I want us to move forward and I want us to be together. Say the word," I plead. I'm not above begging. The risks are there, lurking in the shadows, but I'm either all in or not at all.

"Come on, dance bunnies. I need a drink," Annalise shouts over the deafening bass thundering around us. My teeth sink in my bottom lip so the curse on the tip of my tongue doesn't slip free.

Fuuuck. I was so close. My chin dips in acknowledgement and I usher them to the bar.

"There's a table reserved for you," Jake greets us. "Lawson just headed in that direction."

I turn my head to see where Maddox, the chief deputy in Lost Hope, is seated. The bastard is definitely not one of my favorite people. He's an arrogant motherfucker. The only thing he's got going for him is that Lalah forgave the stunt he pulled when they met, and that she's forcing him down our throats now.

My eyes find Jake's again and a shadow of restlessness washes through me. It always comes whenever I'm near him. I owe him my life and I owe him all the years he lost with the Marines after he got hurt saving me.

"Thanks, man." I clap his shoulder. "A round of margaritas for my lovely ladies here and whatever non-alcoholic IPA you have on tap for me." I'm driving precious cargo home, so I'll have my one alcoholic drink when everyone's here to toast Lalah.

"Coming right up," he says and leaves to work his magic. I can't express in words how grateful I am he is here and he is well. Can't express how much I wish he hadn't followed me to Lost Hope. He's my family, my brother. But every time the darkness in his silvery eyes peeks at me from inside of him, I relive the day I almost died. The day I almost took him with me.

So I choke on my guilt every time he is near, grieving the future I robbed him of.

I'm proud as fuck, though. He built JC's from the ground up and made it the place to be to the point where it competes with big-ass names in Billings. Be it winter or summer, be it weekend or a weekday, his bar is never not full.

Having Cole here too, helps but also doesn't. He knows me too well and sees far too fucking much. There's only one other person who can read me as well as he can, and that's Lalah. My eyes latch on the two of them near the bar and a rush of warmth races through me, chasing away the shadows.

There aren't two people more deserving of happiness. I'm beyond ecstatic they found each other. I snort in my IPA. Lalah has literally built a fortress around her to lock everyone out, and now she has more people in her corner than she knows what to do with.

Maevis throws me a questioning look. I can't tell her that I look at Cole and Lalah and see us. She's not ready to hear everything I have to say to her. She's not ready to know that in the moments I was sure were my last on Earth, it was her eyes I saw.

Her eyes blinking up at me, full of hope and with a spark of hero-worship as they were when I found her on the side of the road with bloody knees and braided pigtails. On that summer afternoon, teenager Tatum learned what it meant to have his first crush—a crush that may have laid dormant up until the day I thought was my last.

And when I returned home, a broken man with a mangled leg and mangled instincts, just seeing her about town pushed me to heal and get better.

She was the hope at the bottom of the hellish pit I pushed myself into. The rope I used to climb up into the light.

It's unfair of me to demand that she'd get to the same place I am right now and match my pace. I took my sweet time for nine years. And yes, I'm counting the years she was married, too. Would've taken more time if Lalah hadn't kicked my ass into gear.

But if the most closed off person I know is able to open her heart, then so can I.

"We were this close to asking Jake for a hose to spray you guys off each other," I quip, holding my thumb and forefinger close to stress my words, as Cap and his woman slide on the bench next to me.

"Phew," Lalah replies, pretending to wipe her forehead with the back of her hand. "We need to thank Jake then for saving us the time needed to attend your funeral."

A surprised laugh escapes my chest. "When did you turn so vicious, baby girl? I thought love was supposed to make you all soft and cuddly, not porcupine prickly."

"Love does make me want to bake cupcakes and shit, but exclusively for Cole. The rest of you get to see the bushy tail of my broom." She bats her eyelashes at me as Cap sneaks an arm around her shoulders, pulling her into him.

Choking on a laugh, I only half listen when she turns her attention to the table. "Alright, ladies and gentlemen. Name your poison. Apparently, drinks are on me tonight!" she says to a chorus of *Hell Yeah* before heading out to the bar.

I'm happy and I'm envious. All in the same breath. I want to be able to hold Maevis close to me like that. I yearn to bend my head and kiss her lips without hearing shocked gasps or having to dish out explanations.

Restlessness swirls inside of me, recklessness too. And we all know being reckless never brought me anything good.

Planting my palm on the leather bench between the two of us, my fingers inch toward hers, hooking my pinkie and ring fingers around her hand. Electricity travels through my veins at the small contact, and I'm once again Icarus flying close to the Sun.

"We used to call you Ghost." Cole's voice takes me by surprise. All my muscles lock tight on instinct, so I don't give away I've been caught unawares. That's the power of Maevis. One small touch, one whiff of sweet vanilla, I see and hear nothing else. All my senses are attuned to her, and only her.

"You're losing your touch, *Ghost,*" he taunts. My head swivels toward him, a questioning eyebrow springing on my forehead. "Anyone with eyes can see there's something going on between the two of you. There's no stealth to your secret."

My breath hitches as I watch Mae with the corner of my eye. She's happily chatting with Annalise, showing no sign that she heard him. She would freak out for sure to know we've been outed. But, between Cole's low voice and the blaring music, she remains none the wiser.

My eyes narrow at him, and his freaky pale irises latch onto mine. Those green eyes still haunt my fucking nightmares. I may be retired, but I'm a Marine through and through. And your captain doesn't need words to read you like a book or to make you spill your deepest, darkest secrets.

That's Cole fucking Hayes for you. He doesn't have to raise his voice or instill fear to command respect. He's one incredible man I'm lucky enough to call my best friend. Like I do Jackson, too.

"Cause I'm not tryin' to hide. She needs more time. And I need her," I spill. By the dip of his chin and the twinkle in his eyes, this is not new information to him. And if he knows, Lalah knows, too. I'd bet my red '69 Impala it was his better half who knew first.

My lips twitch in a half smirk. "You're one to talk, *Lone Wolf*. Took you less than a day to hand your nuts over to her."

"I may be a lone wolf, but I'm a smart one. My nuts are safe in her hands. And if I'm lucky, she'll play with them, too." I nearly spray my fucking beer on the tabletop as he wiggles his damn eyebrows at me.

"Fucking hell, Cap. She's got you all twisted up inside," I laugh.

The laughter all but disappears from his eyes, and the stoicism he's known for coats every line on his face.

"I love her. She's my endgame. Every morning I wake up to her, every night I sleep with her in my arms, there's nothing better. And I can't tell her, not unless I want Lalah running for the hills."

"You have to know she loves you, too. It's written all over her face. I think you're underestimating Lalah. Sure, she's skittish and has trust issues the size of the Grand Canyon. But you're Cole goddamned Hayes. The most loyal and dependable man I've ever known, and that's saying something since I'm the son of Tatum Sr."

"Thanks, man. I do know. But is a different kind of torture holding the words in. Hold up," he cuts off, sliding his phone from his jeans' pocket. "Looks like I've been summoned. Your leading lady, too." He leans over me, "Hey Mae, Lalah needs us at the bar. Join me?"

With a hand on my upper arm, Maevis slides out of the booth over the top of my thighs, lingering a second in my lap. The feel of her in my arms, out in the open, rips a groan out of my chest. Fuck, I need to kick my ass into gear and show her I'm here to stay.

So I can fucking claim her as mine in front of everyone.

My eyes follow the sway of her ass all the way to where Lalah is waiting for them. I can't get over how beautiful she is. Her eyes, a deep brown color like molten sugar, her freckled button nose, her small, perky tits and pale pink nipples, the hourglass, tiny waist my big palm can almost completely cover, her round hips and shapely ass, everything about her appeals to everything in me.

The best and worst part? She has no idea how fucking gorgeous she is, inside and out.

I watch how a smile brightens her face and damn butterflies swarm in my gut. My eyes roll on their own accord. Nine years ago, all my emotions were stuffed into a safe and forgotten. Maevis broke through all my barriers, whether or not I wanted her to. And now I'm hit with every feeling on the spectrum all at once.

Her arm hooks around Lalah's, and together, they disappear down the hallway to the bathrooms. I down the last of my tepid IPA and follow them. If I'm lucky, I can crowd her in the darkened hallway and steal a kiss or ten.

A blonde waitress with a tray full of drinks stops my chase. "Hey, I was just on my way to your table. I have a beer for you."

My eyes narrow at her, my head turning toward the bar where Cole and Jake are talking over the counter. She follows the direction of my gaze and smiles, "Yeah, the big guy at the bar got chattin' with the boss and said you guys may be getting thirsty waiting for him."

"Thanks, darlin'. I'll take it now."

She picks up an open bottle of my favorite brew and hands it to me. I gulp a mouthful of ice-cold, golden beer, relishing in the bitter undertones with a hint of spice, my long legs carrying me toward Maevis.

My eyes find her leaning on the wall next to the Ladies'. A quick scan left and right tells me we're all alone. I cover the distance between us in two heartbeats and crowd her against the wall.

My fist clamped on the bottle hits the cold surface above her head, my other hand cups her jaw. One blink to another, my mouth captures hers, and all the cells in my body shift and realign, centering on the feel of her luscious lips against mine. My tongue sweeps at the rim of her lips, the bitter tones of my beer instantly replaced by the sweet and tangy taste of margarita, with a honeyed aftertaste that's all Maevis.

She opens up to me in a surprised gasp, and I set to conquer, to claim, to own. I don't care if anyone sees us. At this moment, it's just me and the woman I'm in love with.

My lips falter with that sobering thought. *Fuck me, I love her.* My stomach tightens and my cock lengthens behind my fly, trying to reach her. *Mine.*

A desperate groan leaves my throat and she drinks it in, plastering her hips to mine, grinding and rubbing against me. I'm seconds away from lifting her up and carrying her to my car when the door to the bathroom pushes open and a flustered Emma walks by us.

We break apart, both panting and turned on. Her pretty eyes are glazed over with desire, her nipples furrowed in stiff peaks poke through the silk of her blouse. I run my free palm over my face, trying to wipe away the primal instinct to jump her that's riding me right now.

Leaning down, I kiss her forehead in a silent apology, even if I'm not feeling at all sorry. "I'll see you back at the table, sweetness," I say and force my legs to move away from her.

I enter the Gents' and, dropping my beer next to the sink, I undo my belt and move in front of the urinals. My cock is still at full throttle, and I curse under my breath, wrestling him down.

The door to the bathroom slams open, and my eyes roll to the back of my head. Just what I needed—witnesses to my hard-on. *Motherfucker.*

My muscles lock up tight when the cloying smell of overly sweet perfume hits my nostrils, seconds before a manicured hand grabs my shoulder. I rip myself away from her touch, my skin burning, trying to incinerate the cotton where her palm rested.

An indignant huff sounds at my back.

Just my fucking luck, being cornered in a bar bathroom by the bane of my fucking existence.

My two-timing whore of an ex-wife.

Chapter Five

Tatum

I shove my dick back inside my jeans and buckle the belt, not a single glance in her direction. One step toward the sink has me swaying. The world blurs and tilts before righting back on its axis. I stop in front of the mirror and blink the dizziness away.

It's the fucking poison this woman exudes just by breathing. I wash my hands and splash cold water on my face, hoping this out-of-kilter feeling goes away.

"Baby, don't be like this. You can't ignore me forever." She pouts, her overly saccharine voice grating on my eardrums.

You bet your plastic ass I can. I made an oath to myself while lying on scorching sand in the middle of the fucking desert, bleeding to death—if by any miracle I got to live another day, Amanda was dead to me; erased from existence. She played me for a fool. Made me question my sanity, my instincts. You'd think she would've been satisfied with cheating on me, but no.

She took a stand in court, in front of my family and her sugar daddy, and declared I was an abusive husband. That my PTSD made her feel unsafe.

While PTSD is no fucking joke, and far too many of my brothers-in-arms were plagued by it, I had it easy. Sure, I felt guilty. I felt like I could have done so much more every time a mission ended with one of us hurt or intel found civilian casualties—but no PTSD. And I sure as fuck showed no aggression toward her.

The rage and my anger management issues came after; after I interrupted her romantic dinner with her new fiancé while she was still married to me; after she threw tantrum after tantrum when she was served with divorce papers. Definitely after she accused me of abandoning her and abusing her.

And in the after, I nearly got myself, Jackson, and Cole killed because I was so distracted by the signed divorce papers in my pocket.

My stomach revolts, tumbling inside of me. I reach for my beer and gulp down half of it in one swallow. I taste nothing but a faint chalky, nearly artificial bitterness. Glaring at the bottle, my vision shifts in and out of focus, and I drop it in the nearby trashcan and move to leave. The wicked woman plasters herself to the door, and I stop in my tracks.

"You're not leaving here until you talk to me. You're my husband, Tatum. That's the least you could do, fucking acknowledge me." She stomps her feet on the sticky tiles on the floor.

A disgusted growl pushes past my lips when she has the audacity to call me her husband. I lean against the wall for support since I can't forcibly remove the witch blocking my way out, and the merry-go-round I boarded without my knowledge speeds, the room spinning around me faster and faster.

"Are you seriously just going to stay there and not say a word?" she screeches. The sound of her voice sends a wave of nausea to my stomach.

What the fuck? I barely drank half a beer. The first one was non-alcoholic. My mind tries to go back through everything I've done today. We had dinner just before we came to the bar. I ate my weight in pizza, so half a fucking beer should not get me as drunk as I feel right now.

Her amber eyes flash in front of mine before her arms hook around my neck, plastering her tits to the arms crossed in front of my chest.

"Tatum, baby, you don't look so well. I'll make you feel better. So much better." My eyes may be unfocused as fuck, but my mind blares alarm bells so loud my ears are ringing. I move my head just a fraction of a second before her lips would've landed on mine.

Cupcake. Mae. Maevis. I love Maevis.

Why is Amanda of all people touching me?

I rip her arms from around me and step toward the door. I feel like I'm moving through water. My body refuses to listen to any commands. My thoughts are heavy and sluggish. All I want to do is find Maevis and get out of this fucking bar.

The heavy music thumps in my head, a headache pressing down on my forehead and eyelids. I'm lost in a sea of writhing bodies. Lights strobe and pulsate around me, robbing me of all my senses. I beeline to the exit, tripping over my own feet, as I stumble through the door.

The cold air gives me a reprieve, and I inhale the freedom deeply into my lungs. I'm in no condition to drive. My legs are barely keeping me upright.

I squint my eyes at the neon sign across the road from JC's. In massive green lights, the motel advertises available rooms.

I drag my sluggish self to the reception, throwing my wallet on the counter. The man behind the counter doesn't even blink at me as he swipes my credit card. He pushes a keycard in my direction. "Room 109, out the door, to the left, three doors down."

"My girlfriend will join soon. Please give her a card, too," I slur. I'll message Maevis to come as soon as I hit the bed. The need to lie down presses heavily on me as I force my body once more to move toward my room.

I fumble with the keycard, the fucking light flashing red a couple of times until I finally get it right, and stumble inside. I kick my shoes off, nearly faceplanting on the threadbare carpet. Some self-preservation instincts still remain in me when I stop my fall with a hand firmly rooted on the mattress.

I let myself crash down on the cool sheets, the bed spinning over and over, and I wash away into nothingness.

"GOD, YOU'RE HEAVY. COME ON, BABY. Lift your hips. Help me out here," a feminine voice orders me. A grunt rips through my dried-out throat. I force my eyes open to no avail. My eyelids are glued shut. I shift around, and cool air hits my thighs and my calves when my jeans slide off me.

"Mae, sweetness," I croak. "I'm real fucking sorry, Cupcake."

"Shut up, Tatum," she screeches. Fuck, I'm drunk as a skunk, no wonder she's fucking pissed at me.

Her warm, naked body plasters to my side, long, sharp nails cut into my shoulders, moving down my chest. Hot, wet lips are kissing the underside of my jaw. My skin crawls and my stomach rolls. A burst of adrenaline forces my eyes open, ripping my lashes from my cheek.

"What the fuck?" I rasp. "What're you doin' 'ere? Don't t-touch me." I swallow with difficulty, trying to get rid of the feeling of cotton stuffed inside my mouth that's slurring my speech.

"God, Tatum, stop being such a drama queen. There was a time you couldn't keep your hands off me," Amanda says, indignation pouring out of her venomous mouth.

I roll away from her to the other side of the bed. My mouth pools with bile. Can't let myself vomit. I know if I give in to my body's urges, I'll never make it to the bathroom. I can't even pull the covers up on me. I will my legs and my arms to move so I can kick the parasite in my bed out, but my eyelids once again glue shut, and darkness consumes my mind.

The ringing of a phone faintly tickles my eardrum, but my mind doesn't register it. Spinning images of Maevis laughing, smiling at me, snuggling against me as she sleeps flow through the all-consuming murky void in my head.

Heat burns through my side once again, but my body is unwilling to respond. Unwilling to move. A bright flash illuminates my eyes, there and gone a second later.

"Your tastes sure have gone downhill, darling husband. You've gone from *me* to Flat Earth. If you were a better man, a smarter man, you could have continued to have me," the voice spewing venom in my ear whispers seconds before I'm dragged under, complete blackout drowning me.

A BLASTING HONK JOLTS ME OUT OF SLEEP. I'm on my feet in an instant, eyes scanning the unfamiliar room, my mind trying to compute where I am and how I got here and coming up blank.

The room is empty, my jeans and Henley haphazardly thrown on the floor.

My body feels like roadkill. Every bone in me protests when I throw my arms behind my back, stretching my legs and my shoulders in a futile attempt to alleviate the tension-ache radiating through my fatigued muscles.

My throat is dry and my mouth seems filled with cotton. Padding to the attached bathroom, I shove my head under the tap and gulp in cold water. It tastes like expired medicine, but I have to get some liquids in me before I dehydrate into dust.

When my throat feels adequately lubricated and my tongue isn't sticking to the roof of my mouth anymore, I turn my head, letting the cold water splash directly onto my face.

I dry my face with the threadbare towel next to the sink and beeline straight to my phone when a faint beeping comes from under the tousled bed sheets.

The sight of a note on the pillow stops me dead in my tracks. Dread climbs up my spine. *What the fuck happened last night?* The last thing I remember is being in the men's bathroom at JC's, the heinous bitch plastered to the door, trying to rile me up.

> *Took care of your Cupcake. Never say I didn't do anything for you.*
>
> *Your loving wife.*

I crumple the useless piece of paper in my fist as my heart hammers in my chest. If Amanda touched a single hair on Mae's head, she'll wish she'd never set her eyes on me in high school.

I dive for my phone, unlocking the screen. The low battery sign beeps at the corner, the clock showing 3:11 pm. I ignore it and go directly for Maevis's message, front and center on the background.

> *Thanks for the heads up. Don't contact me again.*

Cupcake

"What the fuck?" I below. Pain so fierce that my knees buckle stabs through my chest at her words. Mindlessly, I scroll through our last exchange, trying to piece together what went wrong last night.

My finger pauses on a picture I sent to Maevis... at 2:38 am. My eyes are closed, a dopey smile on my face. Red, angry scratch marks mar my shoulders. Tousled, platinum blonde hair drapes on my chest like Medusa's serpents. A bright-eyed Amanda, with her red lipstick smeared, lays in my arms, a freshly-fucked smirk on her face. Under the picture are the words that sealed the deal.

Know your place, 'Cupcake'.

Me

My stomach flips onto itself, and I drop the phone back on the bed, rushing to the bathroom. My knees hit the cold floor, all the water I drank five minutes ago emptying inside the toilet. Dry heaves wreck my body when my stomach is completely emptied.

I fall on my ass, head bent, palm gripping my hair as a sense of complete loss poisons my bloodstream.

"There's no way in hell I fucked Amanda last night. THERE'S NO FUCKING WAY I TOUCHED HER," I shout to no one, bitter tears streaming down my face as the cold reality sets in.

Maevis will never forgive me. We're done before we even started.

I can't remember a fucking thing from last night, and the picture on my phone is more damning than my lackluster memory.

I can't accept this. I can't let the best thing that's ever happened to me slip through my fucking fingers.

Scrambling to stand, I run back to the bedroom, unlocking the phone once again. With trembling fingers, I hit Maevis's contact. The call connects, ringing once, then twice, before my screen turns black, and the useless device dies in my hands.

"Goddammit," I curse under my breath.

Sliding my jeans on with one hand, I throw the Henley over my head with the other. Thankfully, my car keys are still in my pocket. I shove my feet in my boots, not bothering to lace them up, and burst through the door at a run.

I stop by the reception to pay for my prolonged stay and check out, then jog across the street straight to my truck, aiming it directly to Maevis's apartment.

My lungs heave as I take the stairs three at a time. My fist pounds desperately on her wooden door. I now wish I hadn't replaced the fucking thing and I still had the window to peek inside.

Ten minutes go by with me kicking and pounding at the door like a madman, pleading for Maevis to open up, to come out and talk to me, to give me five fucking seconds to explain.

Dead silence. There's not one single sound coming from inside her apartment. No flutter of curtains. Nothing.

I fly down the stairs and back into my truck. If she's not at home, she's either at Drake's or at Lalah's. My best bet is the latter, so I break all the speed limits in Lost Hope, my foot pressing down on the accelerator, willing my truck to move faster.

I nearly plant the hood of my car into Lalah's gate and curse at all her security measures. My fingers impatiently tap the access code. The gates are not fully open when I race my truck through them and stop in front of her garage.

"One more fucking code. Goddammit!" When the light turns green on the entrance panel, I rush through the hallway and into the living room.

Crickets.

Silence.

No one home.

"Maevis? Lalah? Cole? Anyone here?"

Nothing.

There's no one here but me and my misery. Defeated, I drop onto the sofa. *What now?*

The WI-FI charger lights draw my attention, and I heave a relieved breath as I slide the phone from my pocket and get some juice into it. As soon as there's some semblance of battery, I'll call Maevis until either she answers or her phone blows up from overuse.

My throat clogs, my eyes and nose burning with the tears threatening to spill. I was so close to being happy. Scratch that, I was happy. Yesterday I had Maevis and I had hope for a future together.

Today, I might have cheated on the woman I love with the bitch who's done her damnedest to rip me to shreds.

My elbows drop to my knees, my head bent under the weight of my shame.

I feel his presence at my back, relief that he'll find a solution to this mess hits me straight in the chest.

"I fucked up, Cap."

Chapter Six

Maevis

I'm a coward. And a hot, teary mess. And a coward.

Lalah throws me glances from behind the wheel, her mouth opening and closing, as if she's at a loss for words.

Same, girl. Same.

My eyes burn with the blaze of my unshed tears. I really wanted Tatum to prove me wrong. To show me there are good men out there. Men who keep their word and their dicks in their pants. It's not that much to ask, is it?

"Mae," she breathes in the suffocating silence of my car. "Are you sure you don't want to stay and talk to him?"

"There's nothing to talk about," I cut her off before she starts defending him. I get it, I really do. Lalah and I may be best friends, but she's more connected to Tatum than anyone else, with the exception of Cole, that is.

Right now, I want to be selfish. I want my best friend to support *me*, to have *my* back.

"I do have your back. I wouldn't be driving you to the goddamn airport if I didn't," she scoffs, a sea of hurt painting her words, and I realize I spoke those last thoughts out loud.

"It's not the first time he's done it, you know?" escapes me, my palm slamming over my mouth, trying to stop me from giving up more than I need to.

"What do you mean, hun?"

I fold my arms over my chest, my eyes sliding to the window. We're not far from the airport now. I just need to keep quiet for five more minutes. I jump in my seat when she abruptly pulls to the side of the road and the child locks engage on all doors.

"What the fuck, Lalah?" I turn to her, glaring daggers at her forehead.

Her hands are gripping the wheel so tightly, her knuckles are white, her fingers shaking on their strong hold.

"I've no bloody idea what went down between the two of you. And I don't mean just last night. I didn't pry. I figured you'll both tell us what you need to tell us when you're good and ready. But now you're fleeing to Florida, and Tatum is supposedly sleeping with the heartless bitch, and Emma is in the fucking hospital OD-ing on a drink meant for me."

Her head turns to me then, and I draw in a sharp breath when I see the tears in her eyes.

"He'd dance with me, you know? He'd hold me close, and buy me drinks, and dance with me for hours. Night after night, whenever Annalise and Drake dragged me to JC's. And every time I fooled myself *that* was gonna be the night. The night he'd ask me out on a date. The night he would leave with me," I say, my voice cracking when the realization hits that he did leave with me. Thanksgiving Day. He fucked me, and then he moved on.

I clear my throat and push through. "And every time, like a switch flipped in him whenever I was ready to just give in, he'd make an excuse. He needed a drink, or he was headed for the Gents. And twenty minutes later, he had someone else draped all over him and left the bar with whatever-bimbo-of-the-day he managed to snatch. While I was sitting in my booth, pining after him, Daniel's voice in my ear repeating over and over how boring I was, how easy to forget."

"Maevis..." Lalah sucks in a shocked breath.

"Yeah, I had a crush on him for a long fucking time. I didn't act on it because I *knew* he'd never see me. Why would he? Amanda and I are so different we're not even in the same library, never mind page." I swipe furiously at the tears pouring down my face. "I can't talk to him. What would I say? Thanks for the fuck? I've never had better and probably never will? Sorry it was so boring for you that after you mauled me with your mouth on a bathroom door, you had to go and fuck your ex-wife to feel something?"

Her arms come around my shoulders and my face buries in the crook of her neck. She holds me like that, not saying a word, until my tears dry and my sobs quiet.

When I gain a semblance of control over my tear ducts, I move away from her, my brown eyes seeking her hazel ones. There's not a trace of judgment there, just hurt. She's hurting for the both of us.

"I'll just say this, and please, don't think I'm choosing Tatum over you. If the situation was reversed, I'd have the same conversation with him," Lalah trails off, fidgeting in the driver's seat, her fingers plucking and twisting at the hem of her hoodie.

My stomach tightens and a wave of nausea washes over me. It's moments like this when I wish I had someone who was only mine.

I do have a support system; Drake and Annalise—but they belong to each other first; Lalah, too—but I'm sharing her with *him* and Cole.

There's no one in my corner just for me.

This is who I am, Maevis Barlowe, the second choice, the blandest of flavors.

"I swear to Jupiter and his Great Red Spot, if I ever hear you talk about yourself like that, I'll punch you in the tits so hard, you'll have to suction them back with the vacuum cleaner."

A very *dignified* snort sears my nose, my cheeks pinking up in embarrassment. "This thinking out loud situation is grating on my nerves," I grumble. "All jokes—and alien sounds—aside, just say what you need to say."

"You're not a second choice, Mae," Lalah ignores my prompting, fire blazing in her hazel eyes. "In fact, you are my very first friend here. Before Cole, before Tatum, before anyone else, I met you." Her red-tipped finger jabs toward me with every name she lists. "Amazing, wonderful, brilliantly talented, and I thought that before I even stepped foot in your bakery."

My eyes, once again, water with her praise and kind words. I'm hurting and I need someone to see me. To really see me—and choose me despite my plainness.

"You love both of us," I accept on a shuddered breath. Her hand reaches for me, her fingers twisting around mine, and she gives me a light squeeze.

"I do. And because I love you both—more than that, I *know* you both—I refuse to believe he's done something so cruel."

My lungs deflate as I exhale the breath I didn't realize I was holding. "I thought I healed. I thought I put behind me everything Daniel has done. All it took was one picture for me to spiral." I scoff a self-deprecating laugh.

My head twists around the headrest, my eyes falling once more on our intertwined fingers. "You know what hurts the most? Yesterday, on that dance floor, I told him exactly how my marriage ended. So whatever Tate did or didn't do, I need a break away from everything."

"Alright. You got it, hon. Let's take this show on the road." Lalah gives me a small smile, but I don't miss the flash of disappointment in her eyes.

She's not the only one disappointed.

Intentionally or not, Tatum broke my heart.

I'M LIVING MY LIFE IN CHAPTERS. And each chapter spans two weeks.

The happy chapter—I had two weeks of blissful happiness before Tatum moved on to bigger and better things.

The ugly crying chapter—hiding from the world in my Aunt's Grace guest bedroom, I mourned the dreams I couldn't help but dream when I was too drunk in love to see the consequences lurking in the shadows.

Oh, I pretended during each videocall with Drake and Annalise—each videocall with Lalah, too. *Of course* Christmas in Florida is the best since I don't have to trudge outside in snow and below freezing temperature. *Of course* I'm looking forward to the massive New Year's party my aunt is throwing with all her bingo-playing friends.

And now I'm living the *What the fuck?!* chapter.

Let me tell you how it goes. You wake up exactly five days after the New Year. During those five days, you have been completely deserted by your friends, no messages, no phone calls. So you know the line in the sand has been drawn.

Your eyes are constantly red and puffy because you're crying non-stop. Your stomach is tender and flimsy since you chug water like it's an Olympic sport, trying to remain hydrated. A faint twinge of nausea perpetually follows you, every second of every day.

If it's the industrial quantities of water you're drinking, or the savage conviction that you are now completely and utterly alone, who knows?

Except... I didn't take into account option three. I didn't consider a reckless Thanksgiving night with the heartbreaker of Lost Hope.

My palm reverently settles over my lower belly. A hiccup chased by a sob escapes my chest. "Oh my fucking God," I murmur, my vision blurring under the rush of tears. Except, these are happy tears. Incredulous, disbelieving, ecstatic, *happy tears.*

My fingers are shaking so badly I drop the white plastic rectangle into the sink. I watch it roll once, twice, three times before it stops at the bottom of the sink, face up.

The little electronic screen stares right back at me, *Pregnant 3+* proudly displayed in bold, black letters.

"Oh my fucking god!" I screech the words this time, both my palms cupping my face, as a thousand and one questions assault my mind.

How am I going to tell Tatum?

How will I ever be able to co-parent with him when I can't even look at him?

How am I going to raise a baby on my own, as a single mother, and run the bakery at the same time?

What will everyone in Lost Hope think?

But the loudest thought of them all overpowers the negativity spiral threatening to consume me.

"I'm going to be a mom," I whisper, my voice cracking with emotion and longing. My hand is quick to leave my face and cradle my non-existing baby bump once again. "Don't you worry, little one. Mama's got this. You're going to have to bear with me since I only just found out you're cooking inside of me, but I promise you, I love you already, and I'm going to love you forever."

Picking up the test, I slide it back into its protective foil and turn on the cold water in the sink. I wash my hands and splash water on my face. My rich brown eyes sparkle at me from the tiny round mirror above the sink.

Finding out there's a new life inside my belly has breathed life inside of me, too.

I scramble to the guest bedroom and shove the magic test inside the drawer of my nightstand. Until I speak to Tatum, no one can know. He may be a cheating asshole, but he still is the father. He deserves to be the second one to find out.

I ignore the jolt of pain rushing through my chest. It's not the first one, it won't be the last. It happens every time I think of him. My mind tries to send me images of us being together, staring at the screen of the test, waiting for the result, him hugging me to his chest, spinning me around when we find out we are going to be parents.

But that's not my story. And I'm done crying over *what ifs*.

My vanilla bean deserves a strong mother who loves them and protects them. A happy mother who's not going to poison them against life and against living. My baby deserves the best parts of me, and if I'm not at my best right now, that's okay too. I'll be ready by the time I hold my baby in my arms.

I can resent Tatum as much as I want for not being the man of my dreams. But I'm also grateful, oh, so incredibly grateful to him. I'd let him break my heart a thousand times over, if at the end of every heartbreak I end up with a positive pregnancy test.

Chapter Seven

Tatum

My clenched fists hit the stuffed bag over and over. Sweat is pouring down my eyes, but I don't care enough to wipe it off. Five fucking weeks of total silence. She didn't even bother to send a *Fuck off* text. Nothing.

My shoulders strain on my next hit and the sharp sting of skin splitting registers for one second, and then it's gone. A wave of uneasiness washes over me. It's the only warning I get before my skin starts burning, crawling with a million fire ants. My stomach rolls and recoils, bile flooding my throat.

I hug the suspended bag, my ragged breath fogging on the beaten black leather, my heart hammering in my chest. The scorching flame of un-cleanliness starts from my shoulders. Five jagged lines, invisible on my skin, tattooed directly underneath by the most vicious woman.

Pushing away from the bag, I jog to the locker room, shoving my things in my gym bag and scurrying out across the street to Selena's apartment in the whipping Chicago wind. The gusts are cutting. They should be. I feel nothing but the burn spreading down my chest from my shoulders.

Pacing the elevator's floor like a caged animal, I watch the climbing numbers, begging them to move faster so I can reach the shower before the flames torch me alive. A faint ding followed by the swoosh of doors sliding open has me sighing in relief.

I barrel through the hallway and nearly rip Selena's front door out of its hinges in my hurry to reach the guest bathroom. By the time my clothes are lying in a sweaty puddle on the tiled floor, the flames are halfway up my neck, flickering down my hips.

With a quick twist of my wrist, ice-cold water douses me. Goosebumps erupt on my feverish skin, my lungs stop inflating, my heart ceases its pumping, and my mind cools. Still like a statue, I let the water raining from the showerhead lash at me. I let it smother the raging flames until they're turned into embers. Barely popping, hardly igniting.

Scalding tears fall down my face. And I say out loud what Lalah's therapist has me repeating every time the compulsion to wash the uncleanliness and the unworthiness off my skin hits. My lips thin and cramp as I force them open, my voice hoarse. "I am Tatum Carter, a strong and capable man. I'm also a potential rape survivor. The two aren't mutually exclusive."

Potential was not included by the therapist. Using it shows I'm still in denial. But I refuse to accept it. I want the heinous bitch to look me in the eye and admit that she drugged me. I want her to say it to my face that she took advantage of the state I was in.

At the bottom of the darkest pit, I still have a sliver of hope. The rape kit did not find any traces of DNA around my pelvic area. Saliva on my neck, the scratches on my shoulders, but nothing that should not have been there; no traces of lubricants to show the use of a condom, either.

So I hold on tightly to that tiny hope. Sure, there's always the possibility that she cleaned me up after. But why would she? Never bothered before. And with the way Amanda plays mind games, she would have left something behind to make it clear I cheated on Maevis with her.

I shift the water to scalding now. It's all part of the process. The process in which I purify my body from her touch. Even if we didn't have sex... NO. Even if she didn't rape me, she still sexually assaulted me. My hands soap up my shoulders, savagely rubbing at my skin, trying to wipe away any and all traces of Amanda's touch.

When my skin is scrubbed raw, red and nearly blistered, I turn off the water and secure a white towel around my waist. My palm wipes away the steam from the mirror, and I dare lift my head, looking myself in the eyes through the foggy reflection.

"I am Tatum Carter, former Second Lieutenant Marine Officer, a strong and capable man. I am also a potential rape survivor. The two aren't mutually exclusive," I tell the image in the mirror.

The man looking back at me is a shell of himself; gaunt eyes, sunken cheeks, a perpetual scowl marring his face. His long blond hair sticks to the side of his face and his shoulders. He blinks at me, taunting me to fight back, to wake up, to drag myself away from the ledge and back into the land of the living.

I force my eyes closed. Behind my eyelids, soft hands reach for me. Short nails, clean-cut, on delicate fingers trace my shoulders. There's no burn to this touch, no sting. My lungs fill with the healing scent of vanilla, as velvety fingertips trail down the side of my neck and into my hair.

A statue again, I don't dare breathe. I know that once I open my eyes, she'll be gone. Fury boils deep in my gut. She's gone either way, leaving me behind without a word, without the smallest opportunity to explain.

And then there's guilt. Explain what? That I was set up? That I didn't touch the heinous bitch? There's nothing to explain since that night is a supermassive black hole. All my memories from when she came into the bathroom to when I woke up alone in the hotel bed are lost to the methamphetamines dissolved in one small bottle of beer.

I hurt the most important person in my life. I was careless and reckless with her heart. And with mine.

My hands dive for the scissors hidden in the top drawer of the vanity, and with trembling fingers I lift them to the back of my neck. One snap of the sharp knives and a cloud of wet strands fall to the floor. I'm Edward Scissorhands, hacking and cutting, trimming and snipping, chunks of hair raining down on the tiled floor, one after the other.

"What the fuck, Tatum?" My sister's screech stops me from clipping my hair any further, my hand frozen halfway to my neck. "What the hell are you doing?"

"Is it not obvious?" My eyebrow pops of its own accord high on my forehead.

"It really isn't. You butchered your fucking hair," she says in a calmer tone.

I sigh, my hand dropping along my side, my eyes searching for answers on the light blue ceiling of the bathroom.

"I needed a change, Selae," I murmur, defeat coating my words.

Her forehead touches the top of my arm, her warm breath fanning on my torso. "Alright. Put on some clothes and come sit down. I'll try to salvage whatever was left unharmed in this wreckage."

There's no fight left in me, so I just nod and leave her in the bathroom while I quickly put on a pair of boxers and soft athletic shorts.

"Wrap the towel around your shoulders. I lowered the toilet lid for you, so you can sit there," she tells me, so I plop down and close my eyes.

Selena works her magic, humming softly while her fingers glide through my chopped up hair, snipping here and there.

"You know of any good tattoo studios around here?"

"None better than Jake. What do you have in mind?"

"Nothing... Something... No specific design, but it's for my shoulders," I mumble.

"Dear brother, you must've hit your head under the hood of those cars you're always tinkering at one too many times, but you do know there's no actual space left on your shoulders, right?" she retorts, her finger tapping just above my collarbone to stress her point.

"If the artist is worth their salt, they'll find a way."

"So why not Jake? And why do you want a new one?" Selena fires rapidly at me. She knows why, but has always been a steamroller, and she's decided I need to speak the words out loud.

"So that my skin has an actual reason to burn and hurt," I breathe out, a cooling numbness rushing through my veins.

Her hands freeze in my hair, the clunk of the scissors hitting the floor reverberating inside the four small walls. My hands shoot out and catch her forearms as her knees buckle. Selae's whole body shakes under my touch and her cornflower-blue eyes—an exact replica of mine—rain fire.

Her neck turns an unnatural shade of red that's creeping up her jaw, settling on her cheeks. She rips herself away from my grip, blindly grabbing at a bottle of perfume, hurling it across the floor, where it smashes into a thousand pieces on the wall.

"That venomous, selfish, cheating, fucking whore!" she screams, her hands flailing around as if she doesn't know what to do with all the anger coursing through her. Her finger jabs in my direction, face set in stony determination. "You won't feel this way forever. Tatum, you are my older brother and I'd follow your lead everywhere, but I can't support you permanently branding yourself in remembrance of her malignity. Your tattoo would heal in a couple of weeks, but the brand is permanent. She doesn't get to be on your skin. She doesn't get to haunt you for the rest of your life."

My elbows drop to my knees and my head hangs low, counting the patterns in the marble-like flooring. Selae doesn't get it. And I'm fucking ecstatic she doesn't. It makes me sick to my stomach when I think of how many men and women are out there, feeling the way I feel, burning the way I burn, because someone else decided it was their goddamned right to take liberties with their bodies.

I'm reckless. Again.

Selae drops to her knees in front of me, her still trembling palms cupping my jaw.

"I think you need to go home, Tatum," she whispers, and my eyes close of their own accord.

Her words settle like lead in my gut. *Home.* Lost Hope doesn't feel like home anymore. How would I walk the streets there when everywhere I look there's a piece of Maevis? And Maevis wants nothing to do with me anymore.

For years I pined after her, even with all my solemn oaths to never look in a woman's direction ever again. I held myself back, locked my feelings down. We may have only been together for two weeks, but this was years in the making for me. Ever since Thanksgiving, I allowed my feelings free rein. So I'm not at all surprised I fell in love with her in fourteen days. Hell, I might've been in love with her all this time. For all the good that it does me now.

I knew I needed space from Lost Hope when she ended us through a text message. Not just to deal with my new reality. Not to adjust in the skin of a man that's been turned into a motherfucking joke by the vile bitch his teenage self married. But to understand who I am after the storm that Maevis is rolled through my life, and try to build myself back up.

There's absolutely no hope she'll take me back, I know that in my heart. Why would she? I wasn't able to protect myself from a spoiled slip of a woman. What confidence does it give Mae that I'm capable of protecting her, of looking after her? There's absolutely no fucking indication I would be able to prevent Amanda from getting to me again.

"Tatum, Cole called you about a hundred times this past week. You've completely ignored him. Uhm... there was a fire. A massive one at the Pine Ski, and the resort is nearly destroyed. Drake and Cole—the whole LHFD—were out there for over twenty hours trying to put it down."

An icy current of fear works its way through my stomach. Drake may not be my favorite person, but he is Mae's twin. And Cole is my fucking best friend and the partner of the woman I see as another sister. My eyelids spring open. Selae's eyes are wide and honest. There's worry swimming in them—can't determine if for me or for my friends, or a combination of both—and anger still radiates out of her crystal-clear irises, crinkling the soft skin between her eyebrows.

"Are they ok?" I croak, as guilt replaces the fear. I should've been there and had their back. If the fire was so bad, they could've used any and all volunteers. I had the same training as Cole while enrolled, except the EMT qualification.

Her thumb swipes once at my scruff and I brace. "They're fine. There were many injured, but all expected to make a full recovery. Unfortunately, they also had one casualty, but that happened when the petrol tanks crashed, and one of them exploded. Now, everyone in the county has rallied together to help the resort," she explains, but it's the perfunctory smile on face and the worry flickering in her irises that give me pause.

"What are you not telling me?"

She rolls her eyes at me then, the corners of her lips curving in a genuine smile. "I always both hated and loved the way you read us so easily."

"What are you not telling me?" I repeat. My fists tense and relax at my side, dread curling along my insides. Who have I failed now?

"Lalah's brother visited her..." she hesitates, and my body coils tight. "Their reunion was..." Selae clears the throat, sadness coating her eyes. I know all about *Golden-Boy* McAdams. And I'm also painfully aware that if anyone knows where to hit Lalah the hardest, they are all part of her biological *family*.

"Is she okay?" I cut my sister off, a surge of adrenaline buzzing under my skin.

"She's okay now. According to Cole and Annalise, it wasn't great there for a while. Lalah spiraled, but managed to eventually snap out of it. Obviously, it's something she'll have to live with for the rest of her life, but she's doing the work. She's fighting back. And she needs you in her corner. You need her, too, brother. And you need home."

I guess I'm going home.

Chapter Eight

Tatum

I can't take my eyes off Maevis. The way her fiery-red dress wraps around her, and the curled dark-brown hair falls around her shoulders like a cape of silk drives me crazy. She's out of this world beautiful, and every sight of her is like a knife to the heart.

These past three weeks we've both been back in Lost Hope have been pure fucking torture. I've kept my distance, how could I not? Locked myself in my office at Tate's Shop, got caught up on all the paperwork that seemed to grow exponentially in the month I've been staying with Selae.

Between the work at the garage, the long horrific hours of therapy, and pounding the fuck out of the punching bag I hung in my apartment, I pretty much kept to myself. I can't be near her and not want to touch her, to talk to her, to hug her close to my chest and never let go. And she can't even look at me.

I haven't dared to step foot inside Suga'High. I have not dared approach her. What would I say? Maevis Barlowe is the indiscriminate subject of both my love and my resentment. My heart constantly reminds me that she, too, is a victim of the witch's games, but my ego doesn't allow me to forgive her for leaving me behind.

"Are you going to invite me to dance, or what?" Eliza's silver eyes peer at me from under blonde ringlets.

"Of course I am. Miss Eliza, would you do me the extraordinary honor of granting me this dance?" I bend at the waist, leaning toward her, my hand stretched out in a formal invite. She rewards me with an ear-to-ear smile and hops onto my uncomfortable-as-fuck, wedding-fancy shoes. I twirl us around the dance floor, spinning in circles. Eliza's happy laughter harmonizes with the love song playing from hidden speakers.

A flash of red catches my attention, and I spin once again, watching Maevis sprint toward the back porch, Lalah hot on her heels. A twinge of unease hits my stomach, and I prepare to stop the dance and chase after them.

"Don't do it," Cole mutters in passing, pinning me with a serious look. He was all sunshine and smug smiles today. He just married his fucking prize—he has every right to be as smug as he wants. To see this seriousness on his face on what could possibly be one of the best days of his life stops me in my tracks. He's right. Even if I go after them, the chance she'll actually want me there is null and void.

I give him a chin nod and distract myself by continuing to dance around with Eliza. But my eyes are glued to the two women now talking on the safety of the back porch. They're far enough away I can't read on Maevis's lips the words she's confessing to Lalah.

Her smile hits me with the power of a nuclear bomb. She looks so happy, elated even. My blood begins to boil as rage stirs in my gut. I take a step forward, moving in their direction, Eliza still perched atop my dress shoes.

"You're a terrible dance partner," she chastises me, and while I feel awful disappointing one of my favorite people in this world, my number one person drifts her hand down her waist, resting her palm on her lower belly. My breath hitches, my heart sputters like a car engine in the wrong gear.

Is she sick? The thought fleets through my mind, but somewhere deep inside, I know that's not it. My gut-feeling proves right when Lalah launches herself at Maevis, hugging Mae to her. And I know. I *know.* Maevis is not sick. Maevis is *pregnant.*

"Baby girl, looks like Jackson could do with some dancing. Why don't you go and show him the double flip you learned to do last week?" Cole tells his younger sister in a gentle tone, so at odds with the iron grip he has on my shoulder.

He may be taller and bigger, but I'm not sure he'll win against me right now. My vision is tunneled on the woman I love. Hope and despair are battling to death inside of me. If she really is pregnant, is the baby mine? I'm not sure if I want her tied to me by sharing a child and nothing else. I also can't think of the possibility of that baby not being mine. Would not ever recover from that. She owes me no loyalty, but I refuse to believe she found someone else in the time we've been apart since that horrible day.

If the baby she's carrying—and I'm damned convinced she is carrying a baby—is not mine, I'll be fucking destroyed. Unmoored and untethered from everything I hold true.

"You have three fucking seconds to remove your hand from me," I threaten under my breath, making sure each word is infused with steel and the promise of pain if he dares to get between me and my objective.

"Carter," he barks. And it's *the* tone—the same tone I disobeyed nine years ago and nearly got myself killed—that stops me in my tracks. "Don't go in half-assed. Take a goddamn breath. Think about what you're walking into and how you want to approach this."

My hands fly at the collar of my shirt, unknotting the tie cutting my airflow off, and slam the silk material to Cole's chest. "I'm not going on a rampage," I grit, annoyed that he'll think I'll ever be able to intentionally harm Maevis.

"Congratulations, brother," says Cole and lets me go.

I should've known the bastard saw the same thing I did. His words feed into that ember of hope and dread at the bottom of my stomach. I squeeze my eyes shut for a heartbeat, trying to stuff down any rogue happiness until I have the confirmation I need straight from Mae's lips.

My feet move on autopilot, and before I realize it, I'm in front of Maevis, chest heaving, begging her with my eyes not to ruin the last of me.

Both her hands are now protectively splayed over her lower belly, and there's a fire in her eyes I've never seen before, not even when she was writhing under me, screaming out my name. "Is it true?" I murmur, not daring to lift my voice higher than a whisper.

"Not here, Tate. Everyone and their mother are looking at the two of you right now," Lalah interjects, and it's the first time since I've known her that I actually want to throttle her. A grunt escapes me when she pushes me in the direction of the sliding doors, Maevis following behind us.

Lalah doesn't stop pushing me until we end up in her living room, and I fall with a groan on the soft cushions of the loveseat, while Mae perks herself on the coffee table in front of me. Close enough that if I lean forward, I could clasp her hands with mine. Far enough away to accurately point the distance between us.

"I'll leave you to it." My honorary sister gets in my face. "I trust you, Tatum. I trust you to be the man I know you are." And with those ominous words, she flees the room, all white wedding dress and messy curled hair floating behind her.

Maevis sighs deeply, the silk of her red dress straining over her full breasts. *Fuck me, in less than two months they went up at least one size.* My cock stirs in my slacks and I nearly jolt to my feet in surprise. Ever since that dreadful night and Maevis leaving me, I've not been aroused once. My therapist explained that this is normal. My mind needs time to heal, and my body will soon follow.

"I've tried to reach you for weeks," she whispers, and my eyes fly up to hers. She's not looking at me. She's looking down at her hands, her fingers fidgeting with the hem of her dress. "I called and I texted, and then called some more. I came by the garage at least twice a week. 'Tatum's out', 'Tatum's locked in his office'…" she trails off.

I clear my throat, trying to dislodge the lump choking me alive. *What the fuck?* "I didn't get any calls or texts from you, nor has anyone told me you were looking for me."

Her forehead creases and her pretty pink lips purse in displeasure. "You think I'm lying?"

I scrub my palms over my face, blowing a frustrated breath. *This is so not going well.* "No, Mae. I was not actively avoiding you. If I'd have received anything from you, I'd have come running."

Her head rears back, as if I slapped her, and my heart plummets to my feet. *Well, that's just telling, isn't it?* I maintain my face into a neutral mask. There's no reason to make her feel guilty simply because she doesn't want me. Her mouth opens and closes, and I decide to break the ice and put it all on the table. There's no reason to extend the agony, either.

"You're pregnant."

A breath whooshes out of her. Her eyes soften and her fingers flutter closer to her belly once more. A serene smile plays on her lips. There's nervousness in the tremble of the bottom one, but no indecision, no regret. *She's happy.* I'm broken into a thousand different pieces, scattered in the wind, not knowing left from right, but *she's happy.*

"I am. And I want to make it clear that I'm keeping the baby. The decision is unilateral, and I had time to get used to our new reality. You can be as involved as you want to be… I guess we never really discussed this possibility."

"The baby is mine?" The smartest words ever uttered by a man just being told he'll be a father tumble out of my mouth. "I'm fucking this up," I say before the redness creeping up her neck reaches boiling point and she—justifiably—bashes my head in with her tiny, bare hands.

I drop to my knees in front of her, arm outstretched toward her belly. "C-can I?" I ask through the tears coating my throat.

Her sweet scent of vanilla and heaven welcomes me home. At her minute nod, my palm connects to the silk of her dress, soaking in the warmth of her skin through the flimsy material. Her stomach doesn't feel any different than the last time I touched it. Except now it's baking our vanilla bean. Wait, "When? Uhm, do you know when?"

"Thanksgiving. And the due date is August fifteenth," she says with a smile. "First trimester is just about over. I have an ultrasound appointment on Monday, if you'd like to come."

"Of course, I want. I want to be there for every appointment, and everything you and the baby need. Text me the details."

"Tate... you don't get my messages, remember?" she stammers, pointing out the obvious.

I shoot to my feet and slide the phone out from my slacks' pocket. Tapping the screen a couple of times, guided by instinct and a nefarious feeling in the pit of my stomach, I go directly to blocked contacts. And there it is, Maevis's number in black and white. "I... she must've... What the fuck?" My fingers shake as I unblock her contact.

I never wanted to hurt a woman in my life, but I want to hurt that fucking witch with a rage that scares even me.

"About that," Maevis says in a sharp tone, none of the happiness and serenity from earlier to be found. "I don't want Amanda anywhere near our child. I have no right to tell you who to see and who to spend your time with, but I do have a say on who our child will be spending time with, and your wife is a hard pass."

Her words cut me to the bone. I don't even have the chance to process the confirmation of me actually being a father before I'm hit with the power of an iced-out tsunami. The back of my calves hit the loveseat, and I have to plant my feet firmly on the white, fluffy carpet so I don't fall on my back.

Every muscle in my body shakes. One more thing the bitch ruins for me. Not even the acknowledgement that my friends kept their word and their mouth shut about that night mollifies me. My fingers grip my phone so tightly, I'm surprised it doesn't crumble into dust.

"Got it. I'll see you on Monday," I hiss, marching to the entrance. I need to leave before I fuck this up even more.

And I need to get through my thick head that the woman I love, the mother of my future child, will never see me as more than a cheating bastard.

Chapter Nine

Maevis

If there's one thing I don't like about Lost Hope is the lack of a fully equipped hospital. We're trading amenities between us and Forrest Falls; we have the fire station; they have the hospital. And the services of the GP we do have, do not include OB and prenatal care.

I'm pacing the entrance to the bakery, waiting for Tatum to pick me up. This felt like the best pickup spot if I wanted to avoid him seeing my apartment's boarded-up windows. I'm so ready for less snowfall, so kids would finally stop busting up everything I own.

He insisted on us driving together to Forrest Falls Hospital. I'm dreading the drive. I'm also equally excited about it. Oh, it hurts, it fucking hurts being near him and having to restrain myself even from the simple things, like holding his hand, or brushing rogue lint from his sleeve.

I have been back home for a month now, and the first and last time I saw Tatum was at the wedding. You'd think for such a small town and us sharing a group of friends, running into each other would be bound to happen, but no. I really wanted him to be the first to know about the pregnancy, but for nearly a month, he was nowhere to be found.

When I tried bringing him up during wedding planning, it was like a curtain fell between me and my friends. A wall of sadness and heartbreak for him that didn't make any fucking sense. It was clear everyone knew we were involved back in December—or on the brink of starting something. It was also clear they knew there was nothing between us now but a big fucking void. He cheated on *me*, and yet, my friends were actively protecting *him*.

So that left me not only frustrated for having to keep my pregnancy a secret but also feeling left behind, removed from the circle of trust. The hormones wreaking havoc on my body are not particularly helpful, either. They further the alienation I feel, the distance between everyone and myself. It's like I'm still in Florida, separated from everyone, living on the other side of a glass screen.

My mind also plays on repeat his reaction from last week. The way he looked at me like I was put on Earth just for him, the reverence in his cornflower-blue eyes when he touched my belly, the despair snuffing out his light when I told him I didn't want *her* near our child. It wasn't the reminder of that night what hurt him. It wasn't even my stipulation. My intuition is screaming at me that I'm missing something, something extremely important, but for the life of me, I simply can't put this puzzle together.

The sound of a car door slamming shut takes me out of my head, and my pacing falters as my head turns to the black truck parked near me. Tatum, dressed in a sport jacket and low-slung black jeans, rounds the cab and heads toward me. My knees wobble at the sight of him. Hints of pinewood and motor oil reach me and, like I've been conditioned by scent alone, my core clenches painfully with loss.

I plaster a smile on my face. There's no need to make this more painful than it already is. My heart and my head need to get on the same recipe. Tatum and I will share a child and, hopefully, a friendship as we bring a brand new human into the world, and that's the extent of our connection.

"Morning," I chirp. "Thank you for picking me up."

He stops in front of me and kisses my forehead, lingering for two heart-beats.

Co-parenting, co-parenting, co-parenting. Down, butterflies, or else I'll call Pest Control.

"Morning, b-Mae," he stutters. "Did you eat?"

That's his favorite question these days. After his abrupt departure last week and the daggers Lalah's eyes threw my way when I told her how the conversation between us went, I made a point of texting him daily. I keep him updated on how I feel; share any pertinent information regarding the baby, going as far back as the day I found out about our Vanilla Bean, in an attempt to bridge part of that void suffocating me.

"I was planning to have breakfast once we got back."

"Yeah, that's not gonna cut it," he mutters and heads across the street to *Dine&Dash*, and I scramble to follow him.

Damn those long, strong legs of his. He holds the door open for me, and I duck under his arm, walking straight to the counter.

He crowds me from behind, and flashbacks from our first time together, back in November, race behind my eyelids.

My heart is at war with my head, but I steel my spine and lean on the counter to put as much distance between us as possible. His minty breath washes over the sensitive skin of my neck, goosebumps raising in its wake. "What's our Vanilla Bean in the mood for this morning?"

My head turns in his direction, my eyes wide in surprise. "What did you just call the baby?" His scruffed cheek pinkens, his lips parting and closing, as if surprised he said the words out loud.

Clearing his throat, he mumbles, "Vanilla Bean." This time, a genuine smile adorns my mouth. I don't dare tell him that's also my nickname for our child, and how us being on the same wavelength brings both happiness and heartbreak to me. For the sake of our baby, I have to find a way, maybe not to forgive him, but to extend a bit of grace.

He may not be my forever, but he'll forever be the father of my child. And *our* Vanilla Bean deserves to have parents who get along and have their shit together.

"Morning, folks. Whatcha' having?" Renee, the manager of *Dine&Dash*, greets us.

"Hey, Ren. I'll have a strawberry and banana milkshake."

"Like hell you're only having that," Tatum interjects, and all the warm and fuzzy feelings from just seconds ago evaporate. Before I open my mouth to give him a piece of my mind, he continues, "One Americano to go for me, please. We'll also take... hmm..." He looks at me then, eyes assessing, scanning me from head to toe, before he nods to himself and returns that piercing gaze to Renee. "A bagel, no seeds, with fresh, still-hot scrambled eggs, and two crispy strips of bacon, no fat on them. Throw in a slice of apple pie, too, would ya? Thanks, Ren."

Both of us are gaping at him. I'm gaping because he ordered exactly what I'm craving with the exact requirements. She's gaping because this is probably the first time she's heard Tatum speak this much all at once.

"You got it. I'll be back in a minute with your order," she says, but I don't even have the bandwidth to thank her. Out of nowhere, a warm finger touches my chin, pushing it up.

"Close your mouth, babe," he teases, with a twinkle in his eyes, and for a second, I'm transported back in time. Back to when a future together seemed like such a real, tangible possibility, and my eyes get wet. My soul is mourning the wonderful *would-haves* and dreamy *could-bes*. His calloused thumbs wipe at my cheeks, and he sighs so deeply, with such dejection, I feel his disappointment in my chest.

His palms leave my face, his arms falling at his side as he takes a step away from me. A foreign energy in my chest urges me to make it all better for him. But before I can do anything about it, Renee's back with our orders. Wordlessly, Tatum pays for our breakfast and barely throws a "Don't mention it," over his shoulder when I thank him for caring for me.

The drive to Forrest Falls Hospital is silent. Disquiet fills the air in the cab. There's no music playing from the radio; no warm hands caressing mine; no possessive grips on my thigh. Just two hurt souls so familiar with each other I can taste the yearning on my lips, yet so estranged at the same time.

He throws the car in park and, still without a word, exits the truck. I learned my lesson, so I stay put until he opens the door for me and helps me out. In a sense, nothing's changed between us. Our bodies are still attuned to one another. He guides me to the entrance with his palm on the small of my back; I seamlessly fall in step next to him. We're gravitating around each other, constantly repelling and pulling.

As soon as we're shown to the small consultation room, I take my puffy winter coat off and start unbuttoning my shirt to just below my breasts. The teenager in me is gleeful with the way they swelled and grew in the last few months. The rational adult in me curses my newly developed boobs. They're heavy and aching and so fucking sensitive. All my clothes fit too tightly around the chest now, and with my nipples as fussy as they are, I spend half the time aroused and the other half moaning in pain.

The nurse takes my weight, my blood pressure, and goes over the usual checklist with me before she guides me to a bed that's covered in a blue paper towel.

"Dr. Fritz will be with you in a minute. Get comfortable, mama. Are you excited to see your baby?" the kind nurse asks me, a smile on her weathered face.

"Sure am. We're also hoping to hear the heartbeat and maybe get a recording of it."

"We can definitely do that for you. Sit tight," she advises before disappearing out the door. As soon as she is out of sight, Tatum takes a seat on the stool placed next to the bed, near my head.

"I'm nervous," he mumbles.

"What is making you nervous?" I ask, biting into my bottom lip to prevent the laughter bubbling in my chest from escaping—Tatum Carter, big bad ex-Marine, nervous at the prospect of meeting a bundle of cells the size of a lemon.

"Everything. There's excitement, too. I'm sorry I wasn't by your side the first time you've done this. Please, don't keep me away for all the rest," he pleads, his voice a whisper so raw, my heart sputters in my chest.

"I won't, Tatum. Trust me. Keeping you away from your baby was never my intention. I haven't told anyone yet. I wanted you to be the first to know. Lalah figured it out when the cake made me nauseous, and I didn't want to lie to her face. Tried to call you the same day I found out I was pregnant. Been trying to reach you ever since, but short of showing up at your parent's house, I don't know what else I could've done."

His hand reaches for mine, enveloping it completely in his warmth. "What's done is done. I'm here for you and the baby, whatever you need."

"Good morning, Ms. Barlowe. And... who do we have here?" Dr. Fritz, a no-nonsense looking woman in her forties, asks, her gray eyes scanning the man next to me.

"The father. Tatum Carter," he replies, his hand still holding on to mine, his eyes not leaving me.

I give Dr. Fritz a sharp nod, and she wastes no more time, rolling the ultrasound screen over and popping cool gel on my belly.

My heart thrashes in my chest in eager anticipation of seeing my baby once again. The screen flickers to life and settles. "There's my Vanilla Bean," escapes my lips at the black and white image.

"That's right," Dr. Fritz praises. "And these are their feet. Just further up, you can see their arms too," she points out as she clacks away one-handed at the white keyboard. "Everything measures correctly for the middle of the twelfth week."

Tatum's hand trembles in mine, and I don't dare look at him. I've seen our baby once before. Had a month to get used to the notion that I will be a mommy. The least I can do for him is let him revel in the image of his child and process the news without being pestered. I give him a gentle squeeze, just in case. Just so he knows I am here for him.

"I see you're doing the combined test. Once we're done with the ultrasound, a nurse will come to draw some blood, and then you're good to go. If there's anything of concern in the blood test, we'll give you a call. If not, I'll add the results to your chart, and I'll see you back here at your eighteen-week scan," she informs us.

"Thank you, Doctor," Tatum mumbles, his voice scratchy and full of chocked-up emotion. His thump swipes at the back of my hand tenderly, with infinite care. I still refuse to look in his direction. But now because I'm afraid of what I'll find in his eyes. His reaction to the news? Is better than anything I could've hoped for, but it hurts. Oh, it hurts so deeply.

The rest of the appointment passes in a blur. Armed with pictures of our little moon-pie, a recording of that precious heartbeat pumping life into the tiny baby growing inside of me, and all the prenatal vitamins I need, we're back in the car, heading home.

The drive back is as quiet as before, but there's an air of wistfulness and, dare I say, hope between us now. We're in this together, even if we are apart. My mind is busy building up the fantasy of a happy, healthy child, loved within an inch of their life by both of us.

And it's my daydream that stops me from seeing where Tatum has parked. His snarl clues me in quickly, though.

"What in the actual fuck, Maevis?"

Chapter Ten

Tatum

I see red. My fists clench and unclench on the wheel. I'm ready to rip it off the dashboard and throw it at the patched-up windows of her apartment.

"It's not a big deal, Tate. There's someone coming to replace the windows tomorrow," she whispers, as if afraid to further poke the beast.

She should be damn well cautious. I'm fuming. Every cell in my body is drawn tight, my chest constricted by invisible bands. This is now the second time I've seen her apartment broken into.

"I'm moving in," I force through my clenched jaw, eyes fixed on the cardboard covering the holes in the glass.

"Moving in and what, Tatum? Chase children around the neighborhood?"

"How long, Maevis?" I hiss.

"How long, what?" She abruptly turns to me. I don't have to look at her directly to know that her cheeks are red and her honeyed eyes are sparkling with indignation. My mind and my cock know exactly how fucking beautiful she looks right now. They don't need the visual aid, but I remain firm in my seat. I don't budge. I don't give in. Her safety is more important than her pride. Or my comfort.

"For how long have you been living with cardboards instead of windows?" I bite my tongue on the last word to contain the storm of expletives living just on the edge, waiting to be spit out. She doesn't deserve my rage.

My emotions are all over the place. I felt happy and content when I fed her this morning; utter dejection in the moments of clarity when the illusion of a happy family was broken; the magical moment when I fell in love with a grainy black and white picture of our baby; the static covering my skin in the vicinity of the woman I so desperately need; and last, the pure fucking rage consuming me right now.

"A week," she whispers. My blood freezes in my lungs. A full fucking week she's slept with no windows, when the temperature outside dropped each night below freezing point. A full fucking week she slept unprotected, with anyone able to just climb the fucking stairs and get in through the windows. I throw the door to the truck open with such force, I'm surprised it doesn't rip from its hinges, and stalk toward the stairs, my mind set.

"Where are you going, Tate?" she shouts after me and I only stop when I hear the passenger door open.

"Stay in the fucking car. I'm packing you a bag. You're coming with me," I mutter, then curse under my breath when the stubborn woman climbs down from her seat and rounds the cab in the next second. "Am I speaking Klingon?"

The breath whooshes out of my chest when her pointy finger jabs me in the stomach. "You," jab "don't," jab "get," jab "to order," jab "me," jab "around," jab, jab, jab, "Tatum Carter," she screeches, and I've had just about enough.

My hand wraps around her dainty wrist and I pull her to my chest. Her sweet vanilla and honeysuckle scent envelops me, welcomes me home—and I lose my goddamn mind. My free hand cups the back of her head, fingers fisting her silky hair, and my lips fuse to hers.

Time stands still.

Everything stands still.

It's just Maevis and I, the world around us frozen and unmoving. My heart thunders inside my rib cage, threatening to break a bone or ten just to reach her.

I may have acted like a reckless fool, but now... now I'm waiting her out. And she doesn't disappoint. Her warm breath tickles my beard, and that's all the consent I need. My lips part over hers, and my tongue darts out, licking a path of desperation inside her mouth. When her tongue tangles with mine in soft, caring sweeps, all I taste is sugar and home, cupcakes and love.

A grunt rips from my throat and I lose all control over my fucking body. What started as a tentative, shy spark is now a full-blown inferno. I plunder her mouth, willing her to give in to me, begging her to let me in, pleading my most fervent wish—for her to let me stay at her side.

The sound of snow crunching breaks the spell, and the world comes back into focus. Everything rushes in all at once, the freezing end-of-February air, the distant chatter of the townsfolk, the rippling of my blood as it rushes through my veins, Maevis trembling in my embrace, parted lips still seeking mine.

I slow the kiss with a sigh and rip myself away from the sweetness of her mouth with a timid press of lips to the tip of her freckled nose. "I'm not trying to high hand you, nor do I want to dictate what you do. But your safety—and the safety of our child—is more important to me than anything. How can I protect you, care and look after you if I'm not here?"

She blinks those pretty amber eyes open, a feeble sheen of desire still coating them. Her lips, shiny and swollen from my kiss, purse in an adorable pout. A deep sigh escapes her chest as she tries to free her hand from my grip.

Although it pains me, I let her go. I drag my now free palm over my face, trying to shake the last of my rage and the last of my desire.

"I'm sorry, I shouldn't have touched you like that," rushes out of me. I have no right—as much as I wish that I do—to still treat her as if she is mine. Her whole body jerks away from me and her face falls at my words. I'm fucking this up left and right.

My fingers spear through my much shorter strands of hair that I'm still not used to, my mind frantically searching for ways to make this better.

"I don't know what you want me to say, Tate. We are going to be parents, but we're not together. It's not your responsibility to keep me safe. I'm the only one responsible for myself." Her chin jots up, a gleam of defiance and steel in her eyes, but she can't hide the tremble of her bottom lip. My body doesn't listen to reason, and I take a step closer to her. "What are you doing? Don't touch me, please..."

She keeps talking, but I can't make out the words she's saying. All sounds around me are distorted, drowned by rustling sheets and burning touches on my shoulders. My stomach revolts and my mouth floods with bile. Darkness is creeping at the edge of my vision.

"God, Tatum, stop being such a drama queen. There was a time you couldn't keep your hands off me."

The familiar burn radiates along my jaw to my collarbone. *I need to get out of here.* Hastily, I spin on my heel and, in a few quick strides, I'm in my truck, barreling out onto Main Street.

My hands are shaking and my stomach turns into itself. Nausea and dread burn their way up my esophagus. I slam the brake and pull on the side of the road. Shoving my head out the window, I empty my stomach of all the poison that flashback has pumped into me.

I wipe my mouth with the back of my palm, gulping lungs full of cool air, and settle my head on the backrest, trying to calm my racing mind.

There are quite a few things I need to consider, and a list would distract me enough to keep the panic attack and the compulsive urge to shower at bay until I make it to my own apartment.

"I'm going to be a father," I say out loud and let the surprising joy of this news wash over me.

The foggy darkness settled on my skin since that hateful night in December lifts a little. While all hope with Maevis may be lost, I have a new reason to fight—a guiding star in the pitch-black night.

And Maevis is fucking wrong. For as long as my baby grows and lives inside of her, it is my responsibility to keep them both safe.

With trembling fingers, I tap on the screen of my phone and locate my banking app. It doesn't take long for the transfer to come through.

> *Rent Maevis's family home for the next two years.*

Me

I don't wait for confirmation this time. I know it will get done, so I move to the next pressing thing.

> ***Cole, Blake, Jackson,*** *8 a.m., tomorrow, Mae's apartment.*
> *Bring boxes.*

Me

And the dread, I leave that for last. This is the first time I remember something from that night, if I can call that flashback a reliable memory. Dr. Richards and Dr. Laurean—my psychologist—have both told me time and again there's very little chance for me to remember anything of substance.

So, the flashback and, more importantly, my reaction to it need to be addressed as soon as possible. I refused to take anti-anxiety medication so far, willing to do the work and see the results without medication, but with a child on the way, I need to ensure they get the best of me at all times. I simply cannot afford an out of the blue panic attack of these proportions, especially if it happens in a moment when Maevis or the baby need me.

With the therapist appointment booked and my head clearer than when I left Maevis at her apartment, I start the car and make my way home to pack.

"She's going to murder you, you realize that, no? Hell, she's going to murder us both if she finds out I'm involved," Lalah mumbles, clutching a cup of hazelnut latte to her chest as she paces on the front porch of Maevis's family home.

"You'll live." I brush off her words. Do I expect some pushback from Maevis? Yeah, yeah, I do. But she's by no means an unreasonable person. Her apartment is not safe, and no amount of arguments from her will change my mind. My apartment is far too small. So her family home makes sense. We can both have our own bedroom, with plenty of space left over for a nursery.

The guys helped me move everything from my place to here, late last night, after Maevis signed the agreement. Now, all that's left is to pack her up and move her home.

"I will. Cole has my back. You on the other hand? She'll cut your asteroids and wear them for mood rings."

I scoff a laugh and bend down to kiss her forehead. She lays her head on my shoulder and sighs deeply. "You need to tell her," she murmurs. "For your sake and hers, you need to tell her. If she finds out at the trials, it would be worse. Please, Tate, please consider it."

I scrunch my eyes closed. As much as I hate to admit it, she's right. What I didn't want was Mae's understanding or forgiveness two months ago on a technicality. But now that we'll be living together, having a child together, going through the fucking trials together, she needs to know. I'm surprised no one told her by now, but for once Lawson kept his fucking word and stopped the rumors from spreading.

"If we weren't about to go collect your woman, I'd have a couple of threats for you," Cole grumbles from behind us.

"Just keeping yours out of trouble, Cap. Nothing to see here." I smirk at him over my shoulder, and I'm rewarded for my troubles with a smack at the back of my head. "Asshole," I cough in my fist and choke back a laugh when he rips his wife out of my arms and dips her in a kiss.

I can't help but stare at them. As sappy as it sounds, their relationship is my fucking endgame. Lalah radiates happiness, even as she smacks at his chest to be released, yelling "Mind the fucking coffee, you neanderthal." And Cole, I've known him for seventeen years. In all this time, I have not seen him smile as wide as he does since he moved to Lost Hope. When before he was laid back, but serious, he's walking on fucking clouds right now.

Since the first time I saw them together, I *saw* what a true connection meant, and they were practically strangers at that point. I'd never had that, the full-on communication just by a simple look, the tethers of gravity pulling me closer to my better half, the aura of contentment and fulfill-ment. Not until I gave in to my feelings for Maevis.

We all pile up in a convoy of trucks and head to the bakery. I'm riding alone since Lalah all but forced Blake into Jackson's car. And with good reason, too. Any more eyefucking going on and we'd all be getting preg-nant—necessary reproductive organs be damned. Blake has his work cut out for him if he's determined to win Jackson over.

Jake may be one of the most loyal men I have the honor of knowing, but he's the loneliest motherfucker alive. He also won't touch Blake with a ten-foot pole—it really doesn't help that he's Cole's brother and thirteen years younger. While Jake is very much in the open with his sexual prefer-ences—which is anything willing and over twenty-five—Blake never said outright he's playing both teams. Not that he needs to. I've been aware of the crush he's been harboring Jake for at least the past five years. His brother is also an observant asshole, so most likely, Cole's in the know, too.

While everyone parks at the back of the building, I face the first battle of the day. Maevis is glowing behind the counter, her dark, silky hair in a thick braid thrown over her shoulder. The scent of vanilla and happy family envelops me with every step I take toward her. I'm so enthralled by her bright, sunshine smile, I don't even see Sawyer until she shoulder-checks me.

My baby sister's smile is not bright, but downright evil. Such a disconcerting look on her usually kind, meek face.

"Oh, lookie, if it's not a dead man walking," she chirps. "I'd rub my hands, but I went slightly overboard with all the cupcakes and muffins I bought for the Daycare Centre."

My eyebrows scrunch in confusion as I kiss the top of her platinum-blond hair in greeting. I pluck the Suga'High paper bags filled to the brim from her and ask, "What are you talking about, Sawey?"

"A certain master baker has a very secret mini-cupcake baking in her oven. Mom is going to throttle you if she finds out from someone else."

My mouth opens and closes, all words stuck in my throat. I didn't even consider telling other people. Lalah knows. By default, Cole knows, too. Blake and Jackson are the supportive, no-questions-asked type. I groan, dreading already having this conversation with my parents. Oh, they'll be overjoyed for their first grandchild, but heartbroken at the same time.

"H-How did you... d-did she?" I stammer.

"She can't hide that belly anymore. I work at a daycare. I've seen pregnant women before. Also, you weren't trying very hard to hide after Thanksgiving. I'm the youngest, I see everything. Congratulations, brother," she whispers, giving me a side hug. "Now, you gonna help a girl out or what?"

My brain short circuits. *Belly? What belly?* Yesterday when I left her, she didn't even look bloated. "No can do, Sawey. Apparently, I have to see a woman about a baby."

"Morning Carter, Sawyer." Maddox walks past us, and my hand shoots out, halting his progress.

"Make yourself useful and carry these to the daycare," I snap, pushing the bags to his chest. The way I figure, he still owes us for all the shit he and Maddison put Lalah through.

"Sure thing, boss. Want me to kiss your ass while I'm at it, too?" he deadpans, but throws a wink at Sawyer, the motherfucker. He's lucky my mind is fully engaged in seeing Maevis, otherwise he and I would have some words about boundaries and what happens when you cross them.

My sister's sensibilities are obviously offended as she glares at both of us, but her eyes lose the threat when they return to me, softening instead. "I'll see you for dinner on Sunday. Don't worry, I have your back, dear brother." The smirk she gives me would've earned her a pigtail pull in her youth. She gets a sharp nod instead and narrowed eyes when Lawson escorts her out of the bakery with his hand far too fucking low on her back.

A problem for a different day, I muse, returning my focus to the mission at hand: Convincing the pregnant dragon what a great idea it is for us to move in together.

Chapter Eleven

Maevis

I can't keep the smile off my face; or my palm from rubbing the tiniest baby bump in existence. I woke up this morning, and there it was, literally appearing overnight. Could barely stop myself from calling Tatum and squealing like a teenager at a Taylor Swift concert. I've been walking on clouds for hours now.

My skin raises in tiny goosebumps a fraction of a second before he enters the bakery. I rub the center of my chest with the heel of my palm, trying to chase away his absence. That void only grows, knowing he is so close but so out of reach. I peek with the corner of my eye as he stops and talks to Sawyer and Maddox. He carries himself as tall as ever, with his quiet, larger-than-life presence, but there's this foreign storm cloud constantly hanging over him.

Is he regretting his past actions? He never apologized to me. Fair enough, I didn't give him a chance to apologize, but with our circumstances now changed, I think we're overdue a conversation. *And that damn kiss yesterday.* I can't help but replay it in my mind over and over again. He stole my breath and the last of my sanity, and now the already shaking ground I was standing on is crumbling.

My life plan was always simple enough—or so I thought. Suga'High is my professional dream come to life. Yes, it's hard work, with ridiculous early mornings and even more ridiculous early evenings, but it's my passion, my drive, to create delicious recipes and share them with the world. As for my personal life, all I've ever wanted was a family like the one I had growing up.

Before hit-and-runs and cruel strokes devastated us.

I dreamed since childhood of the day I would find the one meant for me, the same way my dad was meant for my mom. I fantasized about the one who would be my husband, who'd care for me, love me, and give me children.

It was those fantasies that made me blind to Daniel's true nature. It's those dreams that urge me now to open up once again to Tatum. But, in my experience, a cheater will always be a cheater. He never reached out, not once, in the past two months. And his reaction yesterday, when he just up and fled, cut me to the bone. He just left me there to stare at the disturbed gravel as he sped away from me. Tatum's hot-and-cold mood doesn't give me much confidence for a simple friendship, nevermind co-parenting a child, or an actual relationship.

Even if we did try, I'd always wonder when he'll step out on me again, or if the only reason we're together is because he has a misplaced sense of obligation for knocking me up.

"Show me!" His demanding voice gets me out of my head, bringing me back into the bustling bakery.

"Good morning to you too," I can't help but smart at him, my eyebrows scrunching in confusion. "Show you what?"

He doesn't answer but rounds the counter until he is in front of me, clasping my hand and dragging me to the kitchen. I try to pull my hand out of his, to no avail. "You're not allowed to be back here, Tatum. Where are we going?"

He grunts in acknowledgement, the fucking caveman, but doesn't stop dragging me behind him until we're outside and in front of the stairs leading to my apartment. The presence of two black trucks parked nearby doesn't even register when he falls to his knees in front of me and unties my apron, shoving it aside with a flick of his hand. His warm palm sneaks underneath my pink linen blouse and settles on my lower abdomen.

His cornflower-blue eyes glimmer with unshed tears, a look of pure awe and wonder on his face. His mouth falls slack, ragged, foggy breaths escaping his chest. His forehead touches the back of his palm through the material of my blouse, his shoulders shaking gently.

"Thank you," he whispers, his words muffled as he presses kisses all over the skin of my stomach. I'd like to say the goosebumps peppering me from head to toe are from the frosty end-of-February air, but that would be a blatant lie. Liquid heat pools between my thighs, my eyes blind to the audience we've gathered. Distant, faraway sounds of car doors closing, wolfy whistles, and happy cheers hit my ears, but they're drowned out by the rushing of my blood in my veins.

I'm a coil sprung tight, one touch away from orgasming on the spot. These pregnancy hormones are no fucking joke. My fingers fist in his silky hair and I sit on the precipice between pulling him away from me or moving his mouth lower where I need him to kiss away the ache he's building up in me. The warmth of his breath on my skin makes my clit throb and my core clench.

"That was easier than I thought," a deep baritone voice says, and the lusty fog surrounding me shatters. I take a step away from Tatum, heat flooding my cheeks, embarrassment eating me alive.

I am fucking easy.

My eyes drop to the frozen ground, pausing for a brief second on Tatum. He's still kneeling, his eyes scrunched shut, all the wonder erased by disappointment and desolation, his hands white-knuckled in a tight fist at his side.

"Goddammit, JC, do I need to get Astrum to teach you another lesson in how to keep your mouth shut?" Lalah threatens in a dark tone, promising pain and a world of hurt.

Oh, goodie, more witnesses to my humiliation.

"None of that," she commands, her hands pulling my blouse down and smoothing my apron back over my tiny baby bump. "Let's go upstairs and talk, hun."

I let her guide me up the stairs, my limbs shaking, the butterflies in my stomach dancing in a frenzied flight. That man is a fucking danger to my sanity, all-consuming and maddening. When he is near, I forget all hurts and heartbreaks, including the ones he single-handedly inflicts on me.

Lalah shoves her hand in the front pocket of my flowery apron, retrieving the keys and unlocking my front door. She gently pushes me toward the living room, and I collapse on the sofa, giving my weakened knees a break.

My head falls on the backrest cushion, and I keep my eyes on the peach-coloured ceiling. A fuzzy blanket lands on my lap before Lalah also drops next to me, her head resting on my shoulder. Her comforting scent of jasmine and roses, with a touch of mint, calms my racing heart.

"Your apartment is fucking freezing," she hisses. "I can't believe you lived like this for the past week."

"My bedroom is warm enough. It doesn't matter, since I'm barely at home," I defend, although she does have a point. I'm just so sick of everyone feeling like they have to come to my rescue. I wanted for just this once to sort my own messes out, instead of running to Drake or my friends.

"Not good enough. Luckily for you, we're here to take you away."

Before I can protest or refute her statement, the cavalry arrives. Cole plucks Lalah from next to me before dropping down in the middle of the sofa and seating her in his lap. He gives me a quick kiss on the cheek, snorting a "Morning Mae," when a thud comes from the entrance to the living room.

My head darts up just in time to see Tatum plastered with his back to the wall, his fist hitting the doorpost absentmindedly. Cole chokes on a laugh, throws me a cheeky wink, and buries his face in Lalah's hair.

"Can all of you pains-in-my-ass give us five minutes?" Tatum grumbles, blue gaze fixed on me, making me shiver from head to toe under the cloudy-soft blanket.

"Hey, I resent that," Lalah protests. "I'm more of a kick-to-the-crotch kinda gal."

I'm not jealous of the slight way his eyes soften when they dart to her for a fraction of a second. I'm definitely not jealous that his sexy-as-fuck lips twitch in a semblance of a smile. Instead, I focus on being outraged. He got his friends to ambush me, to get his way.

He doesn't wait for the room to clear, prowling to me like a goddamned starved wolf on the hunt, pulling at the strings he buried deep inside of me, playing me like his own personal marionette. And, for the second time in a matter of minutes, he's once again kneeling in front of me, his forearms caging me between his rock-hard chest and the backrest of the sofa.

"You're daydreaming right now of wrapping those soft hands of yours around my neck and choking the breath out of me," he murmurs.

I'd wrap my hands alright, just not around your neck.

"I'm sorry for storming out yesterday—promise that's a conversation we will be having soon—and I'm sorry I'm putting you on the spot right now, but, please Maevis, hear me out."

His eyes search my face, cautious, wanting, determined, and my heart lurches in my throat. Two months have dulled the memory of what is like to have his sole attention on me, of what it feels like for every cell in my body to shift toward him as if compelled by an invisible magnet.

"I'm listening," is all I can get out. At least my tendency to say out loud every pesky thought going through my mind seems to have cured on its own in the past month. I'm not dubbing in real time anymore how I want to hold him close and never let go; how at the same time as I want to push him away and run for my life. *Co-parents, co-parents, co-parents.*

"I don't want to miss out on anything happening in my child's life. I need to see your belly grow round with my baby. I need to help with any craving and discomfort. Us moving in together makes the most sense. There's no need for you to struggle alone, Maevis, not when I want to be at your side every step of the way. Can you honestly tell me it won't be easier having me close by?"

My throat dries instantly. *Move in together?* I don't know what I expected, but us sharing a house for the foreseeable future isn't it. It's my very own definition of heaven and hell. My fantasy is right there at my fingertips, so close, yet so impossibly distant.

He rests his forehead atop my thighs, his fingers gripping my knees, and I'm about to fly off my seat and grind against his stupidly handsome face. Tingles radiate in my body as he begs, "Say yes, Maevis. Please, say yes."

And that *please* is my undoing.

The earnest look in his eyes.

He really wants to be there for me. It would be absolute torture to share such a small space with him, to bump into him at every step, to have his scent permeate the walls of my apartment. But how can I deny my child the presence of his father? Science and medicine can track growth and development in the womb, but they can't track or determine if a baby feels love in there. And I want my baby to receive all the parental love and nurturing they deserve, so they grow happy and healthy even before birth.

"Yes," I whisper back, "but..."

He jumps to his feet, interrupting me. "I know. I swear on my life, what happened yesterday won't happen again. Ideally, I'd like you to let me touch your belly since it makes me feel closer and connected to our child. But I won't ever do it without your very explicit permission. And the house has enough bedrooms, so you'll have your space away from me."

Aaaand he might as well pour an ice-cold bucket of water on me.

Of course, he doesn't want to work on a relationship between us. Tatum wants to be there for our child. There is no reason for him to touch *me*. My eyes sting behind my eyelids, but I grit my teeth until the threat of tears subsides. And then the last sentence he uttered registers.

"What house?"

He stills in front of me. If the situation wasn't so goddamned tragic, I'd laugh at seeing this mountain of a man with an absolute deer-in-the-headlights look on his face.

"Uhm..." He clears his throat then tries again. "Your house. Your windows are far too often broken into, and my apartment only has one bedroom. I... I didn't think you'd want to share a room, so your family home made most sense," he cautiously explains, his throat bobbing in a forced swallow.

"Hate to break it to you, but it was rented for two years just yesterday." I hear the words, and then the meaning registers. I'm on my feet and in his face in less than a second. "You sneaky asshole," I screech, my finger poking him in the chest. "You went behind my back and rented it before I even agreed to the move. What the fuck, Tatum? Who else did you rope into this?"

His face blanches, eyes darting toward the entrance to my apartment. *Of course, I should've known. That meddling...*

"You're the worst friend, Lalah," I shout, knowing good and well all of them are able to hear every word we've said so far. It's not like my cardboard windows are soundproof.

"It's for your own good, you stubborn woman," she shouts right back, not a trace of regret in her voice.

My chin drops to my chest in defeat. I guess Tatum and I are moving in together.

I just hope my heart can survive him being near me for the next months until the baby is born.

Chapter Twelve

Tatum

I'm sprawled on a chair at the island, watching Maevis pace the length of the kitchen back and forth. I bite on my fist to stop myself from laughing. Letting it loose is a sure way for me to experience death-by-frying-pan, and that's not something I'm too keen on.

Somehow, we've survived two weeks of sharing a house, if ships in the night can be called living together. Maevis wakes up at unholy hours in the morning, eats a quick breakfast and leaves to get the bakery ready to open. I'm letting her be for now, but soon the baby will demand more energy than she has to spare, so I'm biding my time in bringing up the subject of her reducing her hours.

While she's not at home in the morning, I'm not in the evening. With my month-long absence and the time I take off for therapy, I still have a lot to catch up on. I'm also working on my latest restoration project, and damned if that car isn't giving me all the hell a '69 Dodge Charger could give me.

So, this isn't working out for me. We've barely seen each other on the days one of us has off and only talked enough to put together a dinner for tonight where Drake and Annalise, my parents, and Sawyer are invited. I'm shocked as fuck that the news of Maevis's pregnancy hasn't hit the town yet, but as gossipy as our friends are, they do know how to close ranks when it's needed.

And us breaking the news to our families is the reason Maevis wears out all the splinters on the hardwood floors.

I'm anxious about a million things, but not about sharing this news. If it were up to me, I would've shouted in the middle of the town's square that I'm going to be a father.

A firm knock on the door stops her in her tracks as if she hit a wall. All color leaves her cheeks as she turns round, wide eyes to me. "They're here," she whispers. "Oh my god, they're here."

In less than two heartbeats, I'm next to her. "I'm going to hug you now." At her nod, I wrap my arms around her upper back and pull her to my chest. She's shaking like a leaf and all humor drains out of me. "Everything's going to be fine. Sawyer knows, and she's happy for us. My parents are going to love the hell out of you. I swear to god, Mae, you have no reason to be worried. If anyone so much as narrows their eyes at you, I'm kicking them out. I've got you, babe, I promise. I've got you."

Another sharp knock, and frustration bubbles inside of me that I need to let her go soon. She fits so well in my arms. I know with every fiber and cell in my body that she belongs here. She belongs to me. But even with this absolute truth, I don't know how to fix what's broken between us.

Even if I place all my cards on the table, I'd always wonder if she forgave me because we're having a child together or because of the circumstances of that night. And if that isn't enough, I'm not sure I'll ever be able to trust her to have my back, to give me the benefit of the doubt.

"I'm okay now, thank you," she murmurs. "Let's get this over with."

"Our guests are going to be over the moon with your enthusiasm," I deadpan as I open the front door with a flourish.

"Good Lord, boy, what took you so long?" My mom fusses, slapping my shoulder before turning her attention to the woman half hidden behind me. "Maevis, dear," she coos, and I can't help but roll my eyes, "you look lovely tonight. Thank you for having us over."

"I'm happy you're here, Mrs. Carter. Please, come in." I feel her relaxing and I bite back a smile. Mom may bring me to the brink of exasperation nearly every day, but she has this easygoing way about her that puts everyone around her at ease. It tracks, considering she has been married to my father for nearly forty years, and the surly grump is still alive to brag about it.

"Sir," I say, extending my arm to greet my father. At thirty-five, I still have a healthy dose of hero-worship going on. Looking at him is like looking into a time-travel mirror. I'm his carbon-copy, just thirty years younger.

He carries himself with the pride only a dedicated military man has. And he has much to be proud of. Honorably discharged from the Marine Corps ten years prior, he built Tate's Shop from the ground up and completely passed it on to me just three years ago. Although he was deployed throughout most of my childhood and my teenage years, when he was home, he was present. He made sure I'd grow up to be a man.

He was always harder on me than on my sisters. I don't hold that against him—never did. His girls, Mom included, are his soft spots, the essence of his heart. I'm an extension of him, so he went harder at me because he trusted me to look after his heart.

Dad pulls me into him, giving my back a firm slap. "Your mother is frothing at the mouth, wanting to know why you moved in with Maevis Barlowe." He smirks that crooked smile, full of endearment toward the woman he married, knowing damn straight what a pain Mom can be when she wants to, but loving her dearly anyway.

"Then we'd better get inside before she interrogates Mae to death," I half-joke, but my stomach tightens, and I find I can't move fast enough to go rescue my girl from Drill Sergeant Sarah Carter.

My lungs deflate on a deep exhale when I find both of them in the kitchen, chatting up a storm about Mae's latest attempt—and failure—at baking a banana bread better than Annalise's.

The smile on her face takes my breath away. She's more animated than I've seen her be in months, basking under Mom's attention. I smile right back, especially when, twice in the span of three seconds, her palm drifts toward her belly and stops just before resting on the bump that seems to grow rounder every week.

Mae perks up when she sees me leaning against the doorpost, her shoulders sagging in relief. "Drake and Anna should be here any second, and then we can sit down for dinner."

"Sawyer is on her way, too," my father adds as he beelines straight to my mom. He wraps an arm around her waist, and a pang of jealousy hits me. I want this—their relationship, their companionship, the lover and the best friend. "Thank you for having us, Maevis. How's Ronald doing?"

Oh, fucking hell.

I'm practically jogging to her side, snatching a handful of paper wipes from the counter. I crowd her against the island and subtly press the wipes into her palm. Her pretty eyes roll at me, but she still mouths a *Thank you* in my direction. Her hand seeks mine, and I clasp our fingers together.

"My father is doing well, Mr. Carter, thank you for asking. I cannot praise enough Forrest Falls Care Home. They tend to his every need, and the staff are absolutely amazing."

"I'm happy to hear that, sweetheart. Ronald is a good man, and what happened is a tragedy. Give him my best wishes when you visit."

Maevis doesn't get to respond when the front door opens, and her brother shouts from the hallway. "Mae-Rae, we're here. I hope you cooked enough food, 'cause I'm just off a twenty-four-hour shift and Rowan can't cook for shit."

Drake stops short at the entrance to the kitchen and his face blanches. Red creeps up in his cheeks, and I can't help the chuckle escaping my chest. It is a fucking sight to see the giant asshole blushing in embarrassment.

"I'm so s-sorry," he stammers, just as Annalise and Sawyer push past him. My sister giggles and waves him off.

"You're fine. They hear way worse at the garage all day."

I busy myself helping Maevis set the table and prepare drinks for everyone. The smell of Beef Wellington makes my stomach rumble when she opens the oven. I snatch the oven-mitts out of her hand and take the baking tray out. My mouth waters at the golden crust of the puff pastry.

My chest swells with the stupid male pride I feel for Maevis when I set the tray down in the middle of the table, and appreciation noises fill the small dining room. Before I slice the beef, I make sure to serve Mae the smaller roll set to the side of the tray. She told me earlier today that she cooked the beef for herself beforehand to ensure she's eating it close to very well done. Pink beef does not mix well with pregnancy.

I return to the kitchen a couple more times to bring the mashed potatoes and the remaining sides, then pull the chair for her at the head of the table, taking a seat myself to her right. I don't miss the nod of appreciation I get from both my father and her brother—who is seated right in front of me, to her left.

Dinner passes in a flurry of conversation, laughter, and jokes, and my mind wanders to the future, imagining many evenings just like this one. The whole family around the table, our kids running around creating chaos and wreaking havoc, Maevis smiling at me with a love-drunk look in her eyes—yeah, that's what my ideal life looks like. That is, if I can get over what happened two months ago, and Drake doesn't stab my neck with his fork for getting his twin sister pregnant.

Once we're all settled in with a nightcap in the living room, I walk behind Maevis's armchair and settle my hand on her shoulder, giving her a reassuring squeeze. She tilts her head back, apprehension swimming in her eyes, so I decide to rip out the Band-Aid and let the chips fall where they may.

"Maevis and I are expecting a child," I announce, and all the happy chatter in the room abruptly quiets.

"Tatum!" Mae breathes on a shocked gasp.

Sawyer and Annalise start clapping and hurry from the sofa to give each of us congratulatory hugs. Everyone else remains frozen in their seats.

"Well, I hope you have that third bedroom ready for a guest because my husband's going to murder me for keeping this from him," Annalise chirps.

That gets him up and marching to us, an impassive look on his face. His hand cups the side of his wife's cheek, turning her head to him. "You better believe we'll be having words when we get home," he rasps to her, but by the mischievous twinkle in Annalise's eyes, I don't think she'll mind those words too much.

"Ugh, stop it. Morning sickness doesn't make me as nauseous as you two do." Maevis fakes a retching sound at the same time my mom explodes out of her chair and launches herself at me.

"Oh my God, Tatum baby! You're giving me a grandchild?" She doesn't linger on me though, but hip-checks Drake out of the way and pulls Maevis into a momma-bear hug. "You, my dear girl, are my new favorite person in this world. Thank you, thank you, thank you," she cries.

My father follows suit and gathers the three of us in his arms. "Darling girl, you let us know whatever you need. We're here for you. Congratulations."

I manage to rescue Maevis from all the well-meaning hugs and get everyone to back off. Taking a seat on the arm of the chair she curled herself into, I'm ready to now face the inquisition. I know my mom, and there's no way she doesn't have questions. By the daggers Drake throws my way through his narrowed eyes, he has more than questions. He has threats too.

To my utter shock, he keeps quiet, letting my family lead the conversation, which doesn't bode well for me. He's taking his time before he strikes. I never particularly liked Drake—mostly because of his association with

Lawson, and because his impeccably stupid decision last year nearly got Lalah killed.

Begrudgingly, I also have to admit that I hold a modicum of respect for him. He admits to his wrongs, and he works hard to make up for them. Unlike his asshole of a friend, Drake's not guided by his ego or an overinflated sense of self.

I keep my body still when Maevis's head rests against my forearm. A sense of accomplishment washes through me at her seeking me out for comfort. My sister also sees Mae getting tired, so she jumps to her feet and claps her hands to get everyone's attention.

"I think we've overstayed our welcome. They're not going anywhere, so you can ask any other questions later," she says, hooking her arm around Mom's elbow and ushering her toward the front door.

"That went better than expected," Mae murmurs to me, giving my shoulder a squeeze. I bend my head, planting a kiss on her forehead. There's relief swimming in her eyes, but also exhaustion. She cooked up a storm today, then stress-cleaned the house to within an inch of its foundation. I offered to help but was commanded to stay out of the way or else she'll find very creative—and slightly disturbing—ways to remove me, using a rolling pin and baking powder.

I can't deny that I, too, am relieved to see everyone leaving. The love I have for my family cannot be put into words, but I'm used to having my own space, so I can only take them in small doses.

"Spoke too fucking soon," I curse under my breath when I find myself face to face with Drake, his arms crossed in front of his chest, stubborn determination glinting in his eyes. Even Annalise looks worried, her eyes darting back and forth between us.

She mouths a *sorry* to us, but her apology is drowned out by Drake's demand. "So, when are you getting married?" I suck in a breath. The motherfucker sucker-punched me with a simple question.

"You have to be kidding me, Drake," Mae exhales, rubbing her forehead.

"I didn't ask you, Mae-Rae. Speak, Carter, when are you marrying my sister?"

Oh, fuck no. He doesn't get to dismiss the woman I lo... carrying my child. But my woman isn't deterred by his tone and gets right into his face. I step closer, ready to move her aside if Drake forgets his place.

"Listen here, you obstinate, overprotective sack of potatoes. You don't get to dictate who I marry and when." Here goes the finger-jab to his chest. "You don't get to make any demands on how I live my life." With the way her dainty nail dents the cotton of his LHFD T-shirt, she's sure to leave a bruise. "Tatum and I share a child. That's all there is between us. We are not together, and we have *no* plans of ever being together."

Fuck me! Twist that fucking knife some more, Cupcake, why don't you?

"Now, I'd appreciate if you'd get the fuck out of my house. You're welcome back when you give yourself a hard reset and bring all the apologies you owe me," she throws out, slamming the door shut right in his face before storming up the stairs and slamming shut the door to her bedroom too, for good measure.

I thump the back of my head on the wall.

"Well, that clears any confusion on where we stand."

Chapter Thirteen

Maevis

Pregnancy horny hormones are no joke. Pregnancy angry hormones are even worse.

Now, combine the two; add a sexy-as-fuck, delicious as a black-forest-gateau baby daddy to the mix; sprinkle a side of asshole, overprotective twin brother on top, and decorate with an army of meddlesome friends. Serve with an overly frustrated, petty, horny, second-trimester-is-kicking-my-ass Maevis.

And voilà, I have the perfect recipe for insomnia.

I punch the wrinkled bedsheet at my side as I toss and turn, turn and toss, restlessness eating away at me. There is no part of this bed that's comfortable enough to get me sleeping.

A hot flash creeps up my neck, the throb between my thighs intensifying. I throw the duvet aside, hoping the cool air will bring me a slight bit of relief, but the soft material of my T-shirt rubs against my overly sensitive nipples, and a moan slips past my lips. I creep my palm down my hip and into the thin elastic of my sleeping shorts. As soon as my fingertips touch my swollen clit, electric shocks of pleasure and need run through my body.

My eyes close when I start rubbing circles with my thumb, dipping two fingers in and out of my soaked channel. I know I shouldn't, but I bring the fantasy of the man living just across the hall from me to the front of my mind.

I imagine him hearing me call out in need. He'd burst through the door and rush to me, his thick fingers replacing mine, easing the ache that arches my back in agonizing ecstasy.

Soft moans slip past my lips, his name a chant and a prayer, as I thrust my fingers inside of me, wishing his fingers were stretching me out instead. My thighs fall open as far as they can go, my pelvis tilting, chasing the pleasure building in my core. I'm nearly there, my moment of oblivion just out of reach.

Frustrated mewls of pain and pleasure mix with my moans. My wet pussy, tender from my frenzied ministrations, flutters and throbs, clenching around my ineffective fingers.

"Mae, are you okay?" His low, gravelly voice, muffled by bricks and wood, spurs me on instead of giving me pause. I'm a tight coil of need and desperation. I have no pride in this moment; I have no hurts, just a dire ache for the inferno blazing through me to finally combust.

The door creaks open at the same time I cry out his name, "Tatum!" desperate and fervent in my desire for him.

"Oh, fuck," he grunts, and my unfocused eyes find him in the darkness of the room. He's drinking me in, his jaw slack, teeth sunk deep in the soft flesh of his bottom lip.

"Tate, please, please," I beg and plead, even if I'm not sure what I need from him. Nothing. Everything. Tatum. My fingers are not enough anymore. As soon as he stepped foot inside my bedroom, my body shifted and realigned around him. There's no easing this pain anymore, not without his touch.

"What do you need, sweetness?" he growls, his voice low, crumbly, and dangerous. And all I want is more—more of him, more of his voice, more.

"You. I need you. Please..." My voice breaks on a sob on the last word. I'm burning alive—incinerating from the inside out.

He drags a palm over his scruff, his eyes shifting from my face to the restless fingers still plunging between my folds—bringing no relief—and back to my face. His shoulders snap straight, and it's like he grows right in front of my eyes, taking all the space inside my bedroom, the same way he took all the space inside my heart.

"Fuck it," he snaps. And then he pounces. One minute I'm sprawled on my back in the middle of my bed, obsessively finger-fucking myself, the next my ass is hanging half over the bed, and my legs are thrown over his shoulders. He hooks two fingers in the elastic of my flimsy sleeping shorts and rips them clean off me, throwing them aside like they personally offended him.

"Show me," he orders in a dark voice that makes me shudder in pleasure from head to toe. His hot breath washes over my quivering pussy, and my fingers obey his command, slowly moving out of me, glistening, coated as they are in my arousal. He moves closer, his hand snatching my wrist, pulling my palm closer to his mouth.

Eyes so blue they shine, even in the faint moonlight filtering through the curtains, find mine, locking me in the primal need radiating from them. I need, but he wants. I ache, he agonizes.

His tongue slips over my fingers, softly, almost tentatively. There's nothing soft about the grunt of pleasure ripping out of his throat, or about the way he sucks them clean from tip to knuckle, his tongue swirling, teeth nipping, me losing my everloving mind.

My eyelids shut when he releases my wrist, and I fall back onto the soft mattress. A breath—that's all I'm allowed before his mouth seals over my pussy. He doesn't waste time or movements, sucking my clit between his lips, teasing, testing, torturing it with his tongue.

"Fuck, you're sweet. I missed you with every fiber of my being," he murmurs between bites, licks, and kisses. "Nothing tastes as fucking delicious as you do." His tongue licks the length of my slit—a path of sin and redemption—that has me cry out for mercy. "You're my goddamned undoing."

Calloused fingers dig into the soft flesh of my thighs, parting me open, spearing me, stretching me to high heaven and back. Stars explode under my eyelids. The universe itself breaks apart and mends back together when his tongue moves inside of me, thrusting, and licking, and sucking, caressing and punishing, until all that exists are us together, my cries for more and him, his growls of unleashed hunger, and the orgasm that detonates inside of me.

I'm lost to the tsunami of pleasure that washes over me in a loop as he drinks in everything I have to give him.

My eyes spring open when he presses a soft kiss to my still quivering bundle of nerves. And then Tatum is on his feet, hand shoving down his sweats enough for his thick, hard cock to spring free. He takes himself in his palm, tugging hard and fast. Every muscle in his body is straining, his neck corded and tense, hips jerking in tandem with his hand.

I'm mesmerized by the agony and euphoria dancing on his strained face, my mouth not my own when I beg Tatum to give me one more gift. "Let go for me, my love. Let me have you."

"Fuuuuck, Maevis, baby," he groans, his hand desperately shoving my T-shirt over my breasts, and then he comes, and comes, and comes, painting me in his pleasure and oblivion. He falls over me, supporting himself on an elbow planted next to my hip.

His chest heaves rugged breaths while his palm spreads his essence all over my swollen belly, tenderly, in reverence and awe, every pass of his hand a caress, every touch a declaration of impossible promises.

He buries his face in my chest, mouth peppering feather-soft kisses to my collarbone, up my neck, and finally my mouth. His lips taste like home and me. He smells like all my wildest dreams come to life and wicked desires. His eyes speak of a thousand love promises, of happiness and bliss.

But all it takes is a blink and a sigh for our heaven to dissipate in the quiet of the night.

He pushes away from me without a word, sliding his sweats up his hips, fingers spearing through his tousled hair. If half an hour ago the fire burning inside of me felt never-ending, the cold that settles over my skin speaks of eternity and loneliness.

I choke back a sob as I scramble to my knees. "Tate," I croak, pushing my wrinkled T-shirt over my stomach.

"Don't," he snaps. "Stay there." And then he's gone, disappearing through the bathroom door.

I'm bereft.

Whatever cloud I was floating on just minutes ago comes crashing down to Earth in a churn of thunder and lightning. My eyes sting with tears, and I tilt my head back, blinking rapidly to stop the waterworks. *I will not cry, I will not cry,* I repeat to myself, despite the quiver of my lips or the shame crawling its way up my spine.

Of course he doesn't want me. We were both here and both in need of sexual release. That's all there is to it.

I flinch when his hand lifts my sleeping Tee and a warm cloth is pressed to my stomach. My eyes are downcast, following his every move, but I don't dare look at his face. I can't take a second dose of rejection, so I keep watching as he sweeps and cleans every trace of him from me.

When he is satisfied there's nothing of him left behind on my skin, he straightens to his full height, and with an "I'm sorry, I'm so fucking sorry" thrown over his shoulder, he disappears out of my bedroom.

The door clicks shut behind him, and that's when I let all my tears loose. I crawl inside the rumpled sheets and hug my pillow to my chest, praying that sleep will numb the pain radiating inside my rib cage.

I DON'T WANT TO GET OUT OF BED.

I don't know how to face Tatum after last night.

Three weeks of living together and I am losing my everloving mind.

The urge to knock on his door and crawl into his arms grows exponentially, day by day. I dug my heels in so far and worked to exhaustion each day, spending more time at the bakery than needed. I'd then come home, achy and tired, cooked dinner for the both of us, and fell asleep in an exhausted heap each night.

However, since the dinner we broke the news to our families, he started to avoid me, too. His plate sits untouched on the kitchen counter every morning, exactly as I left it the night before. There are no more "Thank you" notes on the fridge either, for me to find.

And then, last night happened.

Last night when my body betrayed me, singing for him like a siren call meant to lure and trap. He ate me out like he was starved for *me*. His lips kissed hope into the very nucleus of my cells, only to shatter them one by one with the horrified look on his face and his hasty exit.

I bury my face into my pillow to stave off the tears filling my eyes. My pregnancy is not to blame for this. The longing in my heart and my need to be around him is what causes me to choke back wretched sobs.

The grating sound of my phone's vibrations against the wood of my nightstand makes me jolt. My heart hammers in my chest, my limbs slack with the undercurrent of fear weaving through them.

There's *no* good news when your phone rings at five thirty in the morning and it's still dark outside.

My fingers shake as I clutch it and peer at the screen. The brightness makes me wince, but I push through the discomfort just in time to see the call from a restricted number end.

"Oh god, what if it's the care home?" I mumble, waiting with bated breath for them to call again.

Not even thirty seconds later, the screen illuminates with a notification from my voicemail. Steeling my spine, I tap on it and bring the phone to my ear. Relief spreads through my whole body when I'm greeted with rustling noises instead of the frantic voice of one of the night nurses. The rustling turns into heaving breaths and grunts before the call ends abruptly.

Happy nothing happened to my dad, I delete the voicemail—it's not the first time someone butt-dialed me—and swing my feet out of bed and onto the cold floor.

"Summer can't get here soon enough," I mutter as goosebumps sprout on my skin.

My phone vibrates in my hand, and I freeze. A text message from the restricted number blinks at me from the screen.

> *Good girls don't whore themselves out to married men.*

Restricted

I roll my eyes at the words, even though unease creeps up my spine since they hit a little too close to home.

Surely this can't be meant for me, since the only ones in the know about last night are Tatum and me. If I can trust something, I can trust he wouldn't have said anything to anyone.

Out of morbid curiosity, I scroll to the end of the message. My gasp is drowned out by the clattering of the device on the hardwood floor, cruel words staring back at me from the cracked screen.

> *How do you spell Maevis Barlowe?*
> *D.E.A.D. B.I.T.C.H.*

Restricted

My whole body is shaking, and nausea swims in the pit of my stomach. I barely make it to the bathroom in time for my dinner from last night to make a second appearance. When the spasms and dry heaves finally subside, I fall on my ass on the cold tiles.

When the dizziness passes and I feel steady enough on my legs, with a hand firmly planted on the toilet seat, I push to my feet. *Someone is playing a prank. They have to.* My thoughts are in overdrive trying to pinpoint anyone who I could've upset lately. I know this is about Tatum since news of us having a child together has surely spread through Lost Hope.

So, logically, only one person comes to mind. *Amanda.*

But it makes no sense for her to message or call me. She knew back in December that we were involved. Why wait until now to threaten me? Unless... unless they are still seeing each other and she's marking her territory.

A weight sinks in my soul, my stomach revolting once again. I pinch my nose and gulp deep breaths through my mouth.

I'm the second-choice fool once again.

Chapter Fourteen

Maevis

I'm numb and I don't hate it.

My spoon clinks against the dainty china of my yogurt bowl as I play around with half a strawberry. I'm not hungry and my stomach still feels a bit tender, the occasional wave of nausea making me curl in on myself. But at least I stopped crying.

I don't pay attention to the grit under my eyelids or the puffiness of my face. There's no one home to see me, anyway. He left in the early hours of the morning; a lot earlier than he normally does. My thoughts keep drifting from his unusual behavior to the heinous text I received this morning, and I'm hit with startling clarity.

The timing of the message. The horrified look on his face last night. His early exit this morning.

I push away the bowl and watch it clatter on the edge of the island before settling. *Pity.* It would've been satisfying to see it break into a thousand jagged shards. Just like Tatum keeps breaking me.

My breath hitches in my chest. A boulder presses on me when the horror of our future hits me out of nowhere. I'll have to spend my life watching him run back to her over and over. I'll have to spend the rest of my life sharing a child with a man who keeps throwing me away. *I need to get out of here.*

I jump to my feet and round the corner, only to bump into a sweat-soaked, disheveled Tatum. By pure instinct, I recoil from his hands trying to steady me. His face is red with extortion, an angry vein pulsing on his forehead. The fucked-up cherry on this melted sundae of hell? The grimace twisting his mouth and the pity practically leaking from his blue eyes.

He shoves his hands in the pockets of his low-slung basketball shorts. "Sorry," he mutters. "I didn't expect you to be here."

My throat dries instantly, choking back every and any words I want to throw at him, so I just give him a sharp nod and make for the hallway leading to my bedroom. But I'm not lucky enough to escape, when a knock sounds from the front door.

Unease crawls up my spine, settling in my stomach, like a foreboding coil of dread. I don't dare turn completely toward the entrance, just peeking over my shoulder. The chilly March air seeps into me when he opens the door. I flatten to the wall, even though I can't see anything past his massive frame. All my instincts are screaming at me that I will need the support.

"They set the date," Lalah thunders, the sound of her voice echoing through the small hallway.

"I know," he returns, his tone so dark and cutting, a jolt of fear runs through me.

"Four weeks, Tatum. Four fucking weeks and you'll get the justice you deserve," she cries, and I turn toward them just in time to see Lalah launching in his arms.

What is she talking about?

I don't linger on the jealousy swirling in my stomach—right along that foreboding sense of dread—at seeing how freely she hugs him, and he hugs her right back, curling his whole body around our friend.

My curiosity gets the better of me, her words nagging at my mind, pinching and prodding. For months, the feeling that I am missing something has been eating me inside, and my intuition is screaming at me to brace, to tuck into myself and protect.

"What justice?" I croak when I'm a few steps behind them. Lalah looks at me with eyes wide-as-saucers, all color draining from her cheeks. Her eyebrows scrunch together, and the *oh shit* look on her face twists into the mother of all scowls. To my complete and utter shock, her deadly glare is not aimed at me, but at Tate.

Her forefinger goes right into his face, the dark red nail poking into his shoulder. "You haven't told her? What the fuck, Tatum?"

"Tell me what?" I demand, suddenly all courage, despite my trembling knees and shaky voice. But my bravery is short lived when he spins abruptly and buries his fist into the drywall, dust and debris crumbling at our feet.

I can't move. I'm frozen to the spot.

"Goddammit, Carter," Cole mutters, shoving his hulking form in between the broken man in front of me and Lalah.

Tatum's forehead thumps on the wall, his back at me, shoulders shaking, fist still planted in the indented plaster.

Go to him, mouths Lalah half hidden behind her husband.

My mind is fuzzy with confusion, my self-preservation warring with the desire to comfort the man who broke my heart just hours ago.

"Maevis!" she says louder this time, a hint of warning and agony in her voice.

I force my body to shed the stiffness keeping me rooted to the floor, and I take a tentative step, then another, and another, until my front is plastered to his trembling back. My arms go around his waist, hugging him to me, my forehead resting between his shoulder blades.

"It's okay," I whisper. "It's okay, my love. I have you."

I don't react when Tatum's fingers intertwine with mine, and he presses my palm against his chest. A strangled sob escapes him, his pain so raw, so palpable, I can feel it cocooning us, draining all the light in the room.

That sense of dread inside of me intensifies. I feel it down to my last cell that whatever he has to say, it's not something I'll easily recover from. My curiosity dies a quick death when confronted with the broken man in my arms and the absolute desolation pouring out of him.

"We'll leave you guys to talk," says Cole. "Tatum, can I trust you alone with Maevis?"

I bristle at his question. Tatum has been going to anger management therapy religiously ever since Lalah's car crash, and even if I did notice he had a shorter fuse than usual lately, I know with absolute conviction that he would never lay a hand on me. I'm resolved to go toe to toe with Cole but bite my tongue to stop the lash-out brimming in me when Tate whispers, "No. Give us privacy, but stay close."

My heart drops. If I wasn't wrapped around him like a python, I'm not sure my knees would have supported me. His grip on my hands tightens, and then he pushes my arms away from where they're coiled around him, and turns to face me.

He cups my face with both palms, tilting my head back, forcing me to look at him. I don't think I can, and so I squeeze my eyes closed, trying to push back the moment of truth, because I'm sure I've never lived through a moment when the truth hurts more than being left in the dark.

For the first time in my life, I wish to be left out.

"Please," he croaks. One word. One word so full of anguish, my heart quivers in my chest. That's all it takes for my eyes to spring open—and there he is, bleeding right in front of me. He rests his forehead on mine, blue gaze searching, prodding, testing my strength. He's desolation incarnate, and he's my undoing.

He slides down the wall, taking me with him, until we're both sitting on the cold hardwood floor, face to face, hand in hand, locked in a staring contest that leaves no victors in the end, only carnage.

"I had one beer," Tatum whispers, his voice so low I strain to hear him. I suck in a breath when I realize he's not telling me about his liquid breakfast. *No. This is worse. So, so much worse.* He talks about the night at JC's. "She roofied it."

I part my lips, willing words to form, to chant a prayer that would turn back time to that night. When, instead of being butthurt at him staying in the bathroom with her for too long, I'd go looking for him.

He gives a minute shake of his head, as if disagreeing with the jumbled thoughts in my mind. His eyes drop to where my hand is still clutched into his, his thumb rubbing absentminded circles on the back of my palm. I can't tell if he is trying to soothe me, or himself, or the both of us.

Please, don't say what I think you're about to say. Please.

"She came into the bathroom after me..." He chokes but pushes through. "Next thing I remember is waking up alone, in a hotel room wearing only my boxers."

My stomach rolls, and my skin itches and constricts. I feel too big for my body. There's no place for both me and the guilt bubbling to the surface. Tears are stinging my eyes, rolling freely down my cheeks. He shuffles closer to me, caging me between his knees, thumbs furiously wiping at my face.

"Say it," I beg. "Say out loud what I let happen to you."

His fingers rest at the base of my throat, thumb pushing my chin up. His bloodshot eyes, damp and so, so lost, search mine with desperation. I don't know what he is looking for, since I'm devoid of everything. He's about to strip away from me the very foundation of all I thought true about myself. And I deserve it.

"I won't," Tatum denies, his voice stronger now, gritty and determined. "Not until I know for sure."

"Do you believe there's a chance she didn't?" I dare voice with shaky words, a spark of hope igniting in me.

His shoulders lift in the briefest of shrugs, the movement barely there and gone, before they drop in defeat.

My spine straightens.

This is not the time to feel sorry for myself.

I let him down once; I don't plan to do it again.

Tonight, in the darkness of my own bedroom, I can go over every single bad decision I made that night and every day since. But until then, he's here right now, carving his chest open for me, allowing me to see all his scars, all his jagged shards.

So I sneak my arms around his neck, pulling him to me. I'll hold him together from now on. Nothing will erase my past actions. A good decision doesn't erase a terrible one. A shattered plate never looks the same again, regardless of how tenderly it's put back together. But I'm determined to be his glue either way.

And if, from time to time, I graze and cut myself on his serrated pieces, my whole essence spilling over him would just be another layer to cushion his fall. So he can stumble as he heals without losing any more pieces of himself. I'm safeguarding them with my life.

He comes willingly, an arm banded around my waist, and, in a blink, I'm wrapped around him, and he is wrapped around me, sagging into my embrace. He nuzzles his face into the crook of my neck, soft lips feathering across my collarbone, deep inhales pushing his chest into mine.

I breathe him in, his comforting scent of pinewood, with an undertone of salty sweat and pure man. He is protecting me as much as I'm protecting him right now. Caged between the stone of his torso and the steel of his arms, I've never felt safer.

My shoulder gets damper and damper with every bitter tear he sheds, singeing my skin. I let the burn seep into me. I'll take all he has to give. Muffled sobs reverberate through my rib cage, sending sharp arrows of desolation to my heart.

I scramble closer to him, my tiny bump—the life we created together—plastered against his abdomen, my cheek pressed to his soft hair. I stroke the back of his head, humming quietly "The Sound of Silence".

The tip of my tongue stings with the fervent need to apologize, and I have much to apologize for. I called him a cheater and left him alone when he needed me the most. When he needed me to stand strong at his side, I fled and cowered.

My past with Daniel is no excuse. Comparing the man clinging to me like I'm his lifeline with the scoundrel my ex-husband is, I might as well have taken a knife and twisted it into Tatum's back. He put his heart into the palms of my hands, trusting that I'd protect it. Instead, I am just one more person to betray his trust.

There's nowhere left to go since the roads I take are never right.

Chapter Fifteen

Tatum

W hat the hell is an *I know the gender and you don't* party?

And no. It's not a gender-reveal party. This is Lalah's way of bragging about her having information none of us do.

I'm hiding in the kitchen since Lalah's living room has exploded with balloons, but even here it's not entirely safe. Everywhere I look, there's a wall of pinks and blues. I scoff at an inflatable set of wrenches in the most horrible neon pink I've seen in my life. But my eyes glaze over as images of a dark-haired, pigtailed toddler, wearing pink coveralls, standing next to me and peering inside the hood of a car, play on repeat in my head.

I feel my lips lifting in a mushy smile, much like my insides are right now. Shaking my head to dispel the daydream I now desperately want to will into reality, I scan the room for Maevis.

Lalah nudges me with her elbow, chin pointing toward the sliding doors leading to the back porch. I grab my bottle of water from the counter and follow her, cursing under my breath when Astrum wiggles his way between my legs, making me trip.

She snorts a laugh and turns to me, leaning against the wooden railing of her outdoor terrace, hands shoved into the middle pocket of her hoodie. Her black hoodie is an eyesore, in the same color-scheme as her living room, *Gender Fairy—Keeper of Secrets* printed across her chest.

"You seem to be doing better," she muses.

I plant my elbows on the top ledge, bottle dangling between my fingers, as I look out at the forest surrounding us. The weather has started to improve in the past couple of days, much like my mood. The late afternoon sun is shining, although the air still has a chilly bite to it. I'm not much of a spiritual person, but after all the metaphorical thunderstorms, I really hope the weather is a good omen.

"Talking to Maevis helped." I shrug, fiddling with the blue lid. "I didn't realize how much it weighed on me, her not knowing, until I didn't have to carry it around anymore."

"You know I'll always have your back. You asked for our silence, and we gave it to you. But she deserved to know the truth. Not just now, as the mother of your child. But back then, as the woman you love."

Her words are a sucker punch, and the wince on my face is heavy. Things *have* been better between us in the past days—dare I say, friendly—and she hasn't treated me any differently. There's no pity in her eyes or worse, disgust. She doesn't shy away from touching me, which I feared she would.

We don't talk about the night I ate her out like her pussy was the only form of sustenance I had left on Earth, nor do we talk about the fact that the very next day I fell apart in her arms, looking for understanding, comfort, and home.

I didn't thank her for sitting with me in the hallway of her home for so long that she fell asleep in my arms. We also don't bring up me carrying her to my bedroom, nodding at Lalah and Cole as I passed them, and sleeping curled around her for twelve hours.

"I do love her," I admit, my voice hoarse as I force the words out.

"But you don't trust her," Lalah finishes for me.

The truth spilling out of Lalah's mouth plagues me. I don't dare voice it, but I'm sure she sees my agreement in the scowl I'm now sporting.

Maevis Barlowe is my heaven and my hell.

She draws me in like a magnet. All I want is to hug her to my chest and never let go. When she's near, I'm drunk on her sweet scent and the song of her laughter. Around Maevis, I'm free to be myself. I'm home. Her bright smile, innocent blushes, soothing touch, everything of hers has been designed to be my perfect match.

Except her faith in me. Except her faith in us.

Here starts my hell.

I'm a man of very few needs, of very few words. Unless she's drawing me out, I keep to myself. And I'm loyal down to the soles of my boots. But I also have my pride, my ego. While I understood her request to keep our relationship hidden for a while, it hurt that she didn't feel the need to claim me in front of everyone. While I understood her reaction from that night stemmed from past experiences, I was desperate for her support.

I was broken, on my knees, a shell of a man, and the love of my life dealt the last blow before leaving me alone in the dust. If it weren't for Lalah and Cole picking up the pieces right in the aftermath, I'm afraid to think of how that night would've wrecked me.

Fucking ironic, isn't it? I've seen death and despair firsthand, fought my way to safety through the worst of what humanity has to give—coming out relatively unscathed—and yet, my life and mental stability were only truly in danger twice.

And both times at the hand of a woman.

After a lot of soul-searching, and many, many gruesome hours of therapy, I realized that while Amanda cheating on me showed more about her character than mine, it also wasn't the betrayal I felt at the time it was. We were never a good fit. And while I was certainly infatuated, she was never the love of my life.

What I feel for Maevis is the polar opposite. She's in my blood, running through my veins, the very foundation of my being. The two weeks we have actually been together were the happiest I've ever been. Until she took a sledgehammer to all my hopes and dreams at the first sign of a crack and crumbled them to dust.

I want nothing more than to build a life with her, and at the exact same time, I want nothing to do with her particular brand of destruction.

Amanda fucked with my head and made me question every decision I'd ever made. Even now, I struggle to understand how I'd been so blind to the pure evilness rotting inside of her.

But Maevis... Maevis heals and cuts in the same breath. She's comfort and pain, love and despair. We both have similar brands of darkness on our souls. While I wear mine tattooed onto my skin, the scars carved into my body, she hides hers behind her kindness and desire to help others, coats them in self-imposed loneliness, and runs into hiding at the first ruffled feather.

The gentlest breeze will set off her flight instinct when I need her to fight; even when standing against a tornado.

"I love you, Tatum, I do. But you're being unnecessarily harsh," Lalah whispers.

I turn my head in her direction so fast, for a second I fear I'm giving myself whiplash. "'s not like I can help what I feel."

"How's that any different than what she was doing?" she throws back. Faced with my narrowed eyes, she lifts her palms in front of her, waving them like a white flag of peace. "You are both extremely stubborn, and extremely hurt, too. And yet, you refuse to talk to each other."

She groans, throwing her head back, as if looking for answers and miracle fixes in the slowly darkening sky. I'd pay good money for her to share them with me when she finds them.

"You know what my most hated trope is in the romance books I read?"

The fuck?

At my groan, the back of Lalah's hand stings my upper arm.

Fair, I earned it, but I still reserve my right to be annoyed.

Every woman in my life has driven me up the fucking bookshelves ever since Annalise opened the doors to her To Be Read Café, one week before Lalah's wedding. They have a goddamn book club where they read smut like it's a national sport.

My mom particularly likes to discuss the books she is reading during Sunday dinner. Because what other appropriate place would it be to discuss smutty scenes and book tropes—after the tenth wooden spoon over the back of my hand I learned my lesson and what a trope was—than in between "Pass me the salad," and carving the roast?

And if hearing my mom talk about 'Why Choose' books is not torture enough, my sisters chime in with their personal preferences. I can't help the shudder passing through my whole body. There are some things I really do not need, nor want to know about the women in my family.

"Well?" She stomps her foot, and my eyes roll of their own accord, but I indulge her.

"I don't, Lalah, but I'm sure you'll clear that up real fast for me."

"Don't be a smartass, Tatum. You should pick up a romance book every once in a while. You'll be surprised at the... techniques you learn from them. Just ask Cole." She smirks. The motherfucking woman smirks, an evil twinkle in her hazel eyes while acid bile pools into my mouth.

"Goddammit. What did I do to you, huh?" I hiss, rubbing a palm over my heaving stomach. "I don't need the mental images of the two of you in bed, Lalah, for the love of all that's sacred."

"We're getting off topic here." She crosses her arms in front of her chest, her mouth set in a hard line. She's done playing, even if she was the only one having fun, and I brace myself for the ass-reaming she's gearing up to deliver.

"What's your most hated trope, Lalah?" I ask since I figure indulging her will get me out of this conversation faster and with less details about her and Cole's proclivities.

The corners of her lips hitch, but she doesn't lose her fighting stance. "Miscommunication," she hisses, like every book she's ever read with this plot came to life and kicked Cole straight in the sack while Lalah was forced to watch. "And I'll be damned if you fuck up what could be the best thing to ever happen to you just because you're too stubborn to talk."

"Why's my wife so worked up?" Cole asks, amusement coating his tone.

"Apparently, I'm a dumbass living a miscommunication trope," I explain, infusing humor in my voice too, but my gears are grinding. I've had my head shoved up my ass in the past months, and while the deeds of that ex-witch still burn my skin, therapy and anti-anxiety meds are helping. My head is clearer than it's been in a long time, so what am I missing?

Maevis knows my side of the story. But if Lalah insists we need to talk, she knows more than the gender of my baby—she knows Mae's side of the story, too.

"Ah. Supernova, what did I tell you about plotting other people's love lives?" he teases her, arm hooking around her waist, pulling her to him.

"That I'm a genius and I should do it more often, stranger-to-lover?" she quips, her laugh echoing through the open space as he throws her over his shoulder and strides back to the house.

"TALK TO HER!" Lalah shouts, her hair brushing Cole's calves, her words muffled by the sliding door closing.

Throw a brush at me and color me green. I'll never begrudge them their happiness. They fought long and hard to get to where they are and continue to fight for one another every single day. But sometimes watching the connection tying them together fucking stings.

I rub my palm over my face, trying to dispel the bitterness surging in me. Less than one year ago, I was fine in my solitude. And now I'm full of yearning, of wants and needs, and they all point like metal arrows to a magnetic target toward the woman watching me from behind the glass door with a concerned frown.

A deep sigh escapes me as I will my face to relax into a neutral mask. This never-ending ping-pong game between us needs to be cut short. We have murky waters still ahead of us and not nearly enough time to tame the hurricane tearing us apart.

Even if our foundation has too deep of a chasm to build a bridge over, throwing all cards on the table won't hurt in the long run. She's carrying my baby; she'll always be in my life. I need to learn how to trust her again. Whether the extent of that trust includes my heart, I can only hope that's the case.

Chapter Sixteen

Maevis

I can't take my eyes off of him.

His messy blond hair, the menacing scowl on his face, his large palm rubbing furiously over his scruff, the black Henley with the seams of steel covering all that delicious, eternally tanned skin, the black ripped jeans hugging his strong thighs, he's just so goddamn *fine*.

And I'm a hussy.

A nineteen-week-pregnant hussy with weak knees and damp panties, lusting after the father of my child.

I brace because I've been on this rollercoaster for a week now, and it's always the same. I see, I need, I guilt. Always the same recipe for disaster and chaos. Since he dropped the nuclear bomb on my head a week ago, I've been plagued with guilt. This sick, oily feeling settled at the bottom of my stomach, clutching at my insides, refusing to let go.

Anger at myself and at that vile woman poisons my every waking moment. I can't change what she's done. I can't change what I've done either. So many small things could have altered the outcome of that night. I keep lamenting I'm the second choice for everyone around me, but the harshest truth is I'm a second choice for myself, too.

That night, I chose to flee instead of barging into that bathroom, claiming what's mine. I chose to flee again the very next day, despite Lalah's protests, because I was so sure she was siding with Tatum. And she was—for a damned good reason. What I didn't see was her being on my side this whole time. Always fighting *for* me and *not* against me, not for one second.

The biggest slap of guilt, though, comes from the most recent night in my bedroom. The way I begged for Tatum, not that I'm ashamed of my need, but I'm ashamed of the coercion I didn't realize at the time I was inflicting on him. Trying to judge how much he actually wanted what we shared and how much was obligation is tormenting me. And I feel like a disgusting human being, because even knowing what I know, I can't bring myself to regret those magical minutes.

I see the horrified look on his face before he left every time I close my eyes. The narrowing of his blue ones, the grimace twisting his perfect lips—those memories are harrowing, haunting me in my nightmares.

My phone buzzing in the pocket of my maternity dress startles me. Every time this godforsaken phone vibrates, a chill runs down my spine. The cracked screen flashes another message from a restricted number. They've been coming religiously this past week, morning, afternoon, and night.

And knowing what I know now, I'm not so sure this is Amanda anymore.

Which leaves me with exactly zero guesses.

I have no idea who this might be. I stopped reading the texts after the fifth one. Each message coming through is more disgusting, more demeaning, more threatening. There's nothing to block since the number is restricted. With the trials of both Maddison and Amanda looming over us, I decided the best way to go would be to ignore it for now. It helps that they have not tried to call me again or leave any voicemails.

Shoving the phone back into my pocket, I step closer to the sliding doors. My eyebrows knit together at the distress etched on Tatum's face. I want to run to him and kiss away all his hurts. But my selfish wants are like the poisoned apple from Snow White, all shiny and inviting on the outside, life-threatening on the inside.

My eyes lock with his, and all thoughts of poison and apples and scary messages evaporate in an instant, like a switch is flipped and my entire being is laser-focused on him. His scowl drops, but he doesn't smile at me like he used to every time his blue gaze latched on to mine. His handsome face is decidedly indifferent, except for when his eyes drop from my face to my belly.

The dress Lalah made me wear has the print of a baby, stretching right across my stomach, a message bubble floating above with a horizontal bar filled less than half, *Loading 45%* written across it. That brings out his smile, dimple in the right cheek and all. I'll take it, even if it's not technically mine.

He prowls to me, and my palm finds support on the cold glass of the door since my knees are not capable of their most basic function—keeping me upright. When his large, calloused palm overlaps mine from the outside, my knees buckle in earnest, and I swear to God a moan slips past my lips.

I hate to keep blaming the pregnancy hormones, but never in my life has a haze of want and need so acute, so bone deep, controlled me like it does right now. I'm throbbing, and achy, and completely soaked for him, like he just has to breathe in my direction to cover me in his pheromones.

He slides the door open ever so slowly, ever so carefully, disrupting the precarious balance I found on its cold surface. My knees finally give up when there's nothing between us anymore and his scent of all man, with his signature note of motor oil, hits me like an avalanche.

"Easy there, sweetness," Tatum grumbles, hooking an arm around my waist and pulling me to his chest. It's just the two of us in the enclosed porch and the high pitched-moan reverberating between the glass walls when my impossibly sensitive nipples collide with his chest.

"Fuck," he murmurs, burying his nose in my hair and inhaling deeply, his chest pressing even more against my swollen breasts. My hips rock of their own accord, grinding against the harsh zipper of his jeans. "This pregnancy is really messing with you, huh?" He gives me the cockiest, smuggest smirk I've ever seen a man wearing. And that smirk is my undoing.

I'm like a fucking animal in heat, all purring and rubbing against him. I'm burning from the inside out, and he's the only water that can douse the fire consuming me alive. He cups my cheek with one hand, tilting my head back. His eyes are nearly black, the blue of his irises almost completely drowned by the desire reflecting in them.

I don't know if the *want* I see is mine or his, and I'm too far gone to stop and judge the consequences of my actions. "Please," I beg on a mewl when the molten lava coursing through my veins finds its boiling point in my clit. I'm sure to combust with the softest of touches.

"Not here. Not when anyone can walk in and see you. Your pleasure is all mine, you hear me?" I think I nod, but at this point I would agree with anything if only he'd make this ache better, if only he'd take the hurt away.

He walks me backward until we reach the kitchen. The noises of the party rattle against the bubble of lust I built around us, but the rushing of my blood in my ears is faster in its rapid flow toward that spot between my legs that craves him with all my remaining brain cells.

I hide my face in the soft material of his Henley to muffle the cries so eager to leave my chest. The pain between my legs becomes unbearable with every step back he makes me take, with every rub and press of my soaked panties against my swollen clit.

A door opens, then closes, a lock clicks into place, and then I'm spinning, my back hitting his hard, strong chest, his lips pressing hot, open-mouthed kisses on my neck.

"Tell me what you need, sweetness," Tatum whispers, his breath fanning over my collarbone, feathering across my breasts.

"You," I cry out when his finger slides over one nipple, then the other. They're so tight, so ready to cut through the material of my dress to reach out to him.

"Tell me what you need me to do," he demands now, gravel and darkness coating his tone, and I'm ready to incinerate my clothes on the spot, so I'd feel him directly on my naked skin.

"I need you to touch me, please." I choke on a sob since I can't bear it anymore. But he takes pity on me and snakes his arm under my dress, lifting it above my breasts. I look down, but all I see is the material bunching over my chest, my belly protruding from right below it, and his corded, veiny forearm disappearing under it.

"How attached are you to these panties?" he grits. I shake my head in frustration. I'm desperate for him to touch me, not to discuss my attachment to underwear. "Answer me."

"I'm not," I beg, gasping when his fingers hook into the useless lace, and a tearing sound fills the darkened bathroom. He fists the pale pink material and brings it to his nose, inhaling deeply into his chest. A sound of pure hunger rattles his rib cage, and I feel my arousal dripping down my thighs.

"Finders keepers," he murmurs, showing them into the pocket of his jeans, and then I'm all gasps and cries and pleads when his thick, rough fingers find my clit. He's rubbing, pinching, petting, destroying the little sanity I have left, hungry noises escaping his throat. I ignite under his touch like gasoline hit with an open flame, my hips bucking wildly, pushing against him, his hard, thick cock pushing right back into me.

His teeth sink into the soft flesh between my neck and my shoulders, and I'm done. I soak his palm while my pussy flutters and pulses, clamping onto nothing. My whole body is weightless, no anchor to keep me grounded. He whispers sweet nothings into my ear, but I'm too dazed, too overcome with relief and pleasure to make sense of them.

My heart is hammering in my chest, my breath labored, as his tender kisses slowly bring me back to earth. I sag into Tatum's arms, and he coils his bands-of-steel arms around me, patiently waiting for me to come back to him.

I drop my head on his shoulder, kissing the underside of his jaw. With the haze of lust dispelled at the will of his talented fingers, a new feeling roots into my stomach. *Panic.* Once again, I pushed him to pleasure me. My muscles stiffen and my panic quickly turns into nausea. My flight instinct has me pushing at his arms for him to release me, for me to put distance between the two of us. I'm fucking toxic.

But he's having none of it.

If anything, he's squeezing me tighter, palm spread wide over the expanse of my stomach, his other arm caging my shoulders. Even his legs are caging mine, forcing me to arch my back to keep my balance.

"Don't," he hisses in my ear, the sound low—a promise and a threat. "You were doing so well this week, sweets. Your need for me, your desire for me, all that makes me feel like a man. Don't take it away. Don't second guess this."

A whimper escapes my mouth at the despair coating his words. There's absolutely no denying how much I want him, how much my body craves him, his proximity, his touch. The irrational side of me, however, is still fighting against his reassurance. He's between a wall and a hormonal, pregnant woman. He is wired to take care of me in whichever way he can because I am carrying his child.

"But…" I protest, but I'm cut short.

"No buts. If I didn't want to be here, I wouldn't. I'd buy you the most expensive toys ever made and guard the fucking door while you took care of yourself." His words are harsh, admonishing, not placating. His hips buck against my ass, and I feel the entire length of his steel cock behind the rigid material of his jeans. "Does this feel like I'm not enjoying every goddamn second of this?"

"Tate…" I whisper.

"There's nothing I want more than to bend you over and sink inside your tight pussy so deep, I don't know where you end and I begin." He sighs, a sound so pitiful, so tormented, my heart jolts painfully against my ribs. "But we're not there, Mae."

I turn in his arms, facing him. His bottomless blue eyes drink me in, sadness and pride swirling in the bright depths. My insecurities and fears are snuffed by conviction and understanding. I know what I need to do. Lifting my palm to his face, I gently rub his flushed cheeks.

"We're not there," I repeat his words, my voice soft, my face open, allowing him to see the sincerity of my words. "I won't offend you by apologizing for my past behavior and everything I've done that has landed us here," I say, and his jaw twitches under my fingertips, his gaze falling to the nonexistent space between us.

"Look at me," I demand, and the strength in my voice takes me by surprise, but it's strength I need to show him I possess to be right here by his side. "I'll trust you to tell me when it's too much. There's not one instance in this life where I want to be the cause of your hurt." My voice cracks on the last words, but I push through the guilt and the blame. "And I am, I know I am. I'm well aware of how much I have to make up to. But at least, right here, and right now, I can make it hurt a little less."

I drop to my knees in front of him, goosebumps erupting on my skin at the contact with the floor that seems chilled in comparison with the heat blazing through me. His arms fall helplessly at his sides. My fingers are poised at the button of his jeans, itching to trace the outline of his length. His hard cock twitches under my gaze, testing the quality of the stitches, straining to reach me through the thick denim caging him.

"Tell me you want me," I plead, using the same words he did during our first night together.

Tatum groans pitifully, his eyes scrunching shut, a pained grimace twisting his plump, full lips, but his hips jerk closer, his cock throbbing in response.

"You don't have to do this, sweets," he grits, his jaw clenched tight. Despite his words, he cups the back of my head, fisting his hand in my hair. I keep looking at him, my eyes wide open, begging Tate to let me have him. I crave his taste on my tongue, the stretch of my lips as they part around his cock.

"Please..."

"Fuck. Unbuckle me," Tatum orders, and I'm eager to comply, trembling fingers on the cool metal clunking under my clumsiness. Not deterred by my lack of dexterity, I rip the ends of his belt apart, attacking the button of his jeans like the enemy it is, standing between me and my treasure. His zipper is next, but I'm slow now, careful to lower it over his cock despite the absolute frenzy running through my veins.

The flaps of his jeans fall open on either side of his trim hips, and I lick my lips at the impossible beauty of him. I swallow my surprised gasp at his lack of underwear while my eyes roam over his dark tattoos adorning the Vee of his Adonis belt, the trimmed blonde hair at the base of his cock, and finally the pink, veiny velvet covering the steel length of everything I've ever yearned for.

I gingerly trace my finger on his skin, sucking in a breath when his dick jolts at my nearness, and I hurry to wrap my fingers around him when his own fingers cuff my wrist, pulling my hand away.

A single word freezes me on the spot.

"Stop."

Chapter Seventeen

Maevis

I suck in a breath, waiting for Tatum to make a move, to guide me through what comes next. He releases my wrist, and I clasp my hands together in my lap to refrain from touching him. We're playing by his rules and his rules only.

His grip on my hair tightens and he tips my head up. Gone is the pained strain on his face. His eyes are molten pools of desire, pure, raw hunger radiating out of them.

"At any point you have too much, you raise your hand. Do you understand?" he rasps.

I nod my head eagerly, butterflies of anticipation swarming inside of me. Although I blissfully came just minutes ago, need reignites in my core. The simple thought of having him in my mouth gets me dripping and throbbing again.

"I need words, sweetness. Do. You. Understand?" he hisses, his chest heaving with each strained word out of his mouth.

"I understand. Fuck my mouth, Tatum."

The groan ripping away from his throat is not human—it's primal, animalistic, and dangerous. I live for it.

He shoves his hand inside his jeans and frees himself from the denim confines. His cock juts out, proud and hard, the tip of him glistening in his arousal. He wraps his thick fingers around the base and gives a long, slow jerk of his hand until he grips himself just below the dark pink head.

I can't resist but pull against his hold on my hair and place a chaste kiss right on the tip. The sting of my scalp makes me squirm. I fight with everything in me the need to sneak my own fingers in between my legs and get myself off as I suck him to completion. But this is not about me. I got mine. Now it's time for Tatum to get his.

"Open your mouth," he orders. "Stick out your tongue."

My lips part, forming a wide O—and I know this would not be enough. My tongue darts out, greedy and wet.

"That's my good girl," he murmurs. "So eager, so obedient," he praises on a grunt as he taps himself on my tongue, once, twice, before pushing inside my mouth. He fills me in oh so slowly, so gently, so tenderly, before withdrawing with the same excruciating care. His movements tease me more and more, his cock moving in and out of my mouth in short, shallow strokes.

"Relax, sweetness," Tatum pleads, and I hum around him in agreement. His next thrust is harsh. It's deep. It's punishment. My throat spasms and convulses as he bottoms out inside of me, my lips stretched wide around his base. "Fuck, Maevis. Your wicked mouth will be the death of me," he hisses, withdrawing faster. I suck in a breath, tears springing at the corners of my eyes, spilling furiously down my face.

He shoves himself in my mouth again, but I'm ready for him this time. I hollow my cheeks. My tongue massages his underside, swirling and twirling around him, saliva pooling out of my mouth.

"Yeah, baby, that's it. Take me, fucking take all of me," he moans as he fucks himself in my mouth. I want more, I need more, so I pull again against his hold. He stops abruptly, cock lodged down my throat, and I whimper in protest. His blue gaze finds me, the corner of his lips lifting in an arrogant, crooked smirk.

"You gonna choke on my cock, babe? That's what you want?"

I hum, knowing the vibrations of the sound would spur him on and answer his questions all at once.

"Eyes on me at all times," he orders. "Wrap your arms around my thighs. Don't let go."

I waste no time in following his instructions, gripping the back of his strong legs with my fingers so tight, my nails dig into his jeans. He moves his hips away from me until only the very tip of him touches the edge of my tongue. His fingers in my hair relax and splay, cradling the back of my head.

All so tender, all so deceptive. Anticipation floats in the air. I know he'll take my mouth hard and fast now that he made sure to stretch me out for what's to come.

"You're so fucking beautiful like this," Tatum whispers reverently. "On your knees in front of me, begging the power back into me, your lips puffy and swollen around my dick." A deep inhale glides him up my tongue, and the butterflies in my stomach take flight. *This is it.*

"You'll be devastatingly gorgeous and my absolute fucking undoing gagging on my cock, struggling to take me in." He gives me a wry smile, a resolute look on his face, as if he's ready to sign his life away to me right now. "Are you ready to be my undoing, Maevis Barlowe?"

He doesn't wait for my answer as he thrusts back inside my mouth, pushing past the tiny, resistant barrier at the entrance to my throat. I gag, of course I gag, when all that delicious fury is unleashed on me. My mind empties of any and all thoughts. All I know is Tatum is unchaining himself of all restraints, of all the worries that plague him, chasing his pleasure and freedom using my body.

And I give myself freely to him. Breathing through my nose the musky scent of his arousal, I swallow him down to compensate for my throat relaxing around him, receiving his long, desperate thrusts with greed and abandon.

The small bathroom fills with his animalistic grunts of bliss and my garbled moans as they escape my swollen, stretched out lips. My jaw aches, but I revel in it. This pain heals and redeems, connects and fuses together all the broken parts of us.

"Fuck, baby, I'm so close. You're taking all of me, aren't you?" he mumbles, lost to the frenzy. His hips lose all coordination and control, jerking savagely in and out of my mouth. My breath hitches in my chest. He's lodged so deep inside of me he's blocking my airways. Black spots fill my vision, but I don't dare to force an inhale or move my eyes away from him.

The strain of his chase is evident on his face. A dark, angry vein pulses rapidly on his forehead. His cheeks are red and carved in stone, his jaw clenched tight, lips parted in a snarl. My lungs burn with the lack of oxygen, and just when I think I'm about to pass out, his cock brutally throbs on my tongue, coating the back of my throat with his musky release. He growls out my name, a grunt of curses and blessings, as he finds his freedom and end inside of me.

The pressure at the back of my head disappears. His palm cups my jaw instead, thumb lovingly wiping the overspill of his release. His thighs tremble under my firm grip, and I unfurl my fingers from him, allowing blood to flow back into them.

Tatum sags against the wall, his cock still in my mouth, the hard steel melting on my tongue as I swallow all of his hot, salty essence in between shuddered breaths. I lick him clean from root to tip, pressing a final tender kiss on the softening head before gently tucking him back inside his jeans.

He slides down the dark tiles until his denim-cladded ass rests on the floor, legs stretched out on either side of me. His eyes never leave my face, not for a second. His lips tip in a lazy, high-on-dopamine smile as he pulls me on his lap, cradling me to his still heaving chest.

I rest my head on his shoulder, nuzzling my face in the crook of his neck. His pulse is fluttering erratically under my cheek, and I relish in knowing I did this to him. After everything I took, after everything I destroyed, I also gave something back to him.

Tatum palms my still exposed stomach, caressing it with a gentleness that is in such contrast with the soreness of my throat. My breath hitches when I realize that even as I was on the verge of passing out, I never once considered stopping him. I gave myself to Tate completely in this darkened bathroom. I trusted him with my vulnerability, trusted him to take all he needed without ripping me apart in the process.

"Thank you," he whispers, his tone blissed out and reverent. Warmth surges from the center of my chest, spreading out through my entire body like wildfire. I kiss the prickly skin under his jaw in response, my throat still too tender to sound any words. But Tatum being Tatum understands my kiss for what it is. "Give me one more minute to hold you like this, and then I'll go and grab you a drink."

I pat his chest. I'm not in a hurry. This is the first time in months I feel as close to him as back in November, when everything seemed possible, and happiness was hovering just at the tip of my fingertips.

I don't know what's waiting for us outside of this bathroom and out into the real world. Here, in semi-darkness, loving whispers, and the heady scent of sex, we're Tatum and Maevis, floating in post-orgasmic bliss. We're holding each other tight, clinging to possibilities of more, grasping for hope and redemption.

Out there? Out there are threatening messages and trials for attempted murder, aggravated assault, and rape. In the real world, choices are stripped from us, leaving us behind powerless and fearful—an earthquake of resentment shaking the very foundation of our strongest beliefs.

And so I close my eyes, and breathe Tatum deep into my lungs, the subtle spice of his cologne, the freshness of the pinewood always there like part of his skin, the musk clinging to his frame—a mark of him abandoning himself to me—the safety and home this man always provides.

Bubbly flutters around my belly button rise to the surface, and my lips, exhausted as they are, still tip in a smile against the corded muscles of his neck. I clear my throat and rasp quietly to him, "Although you can't feel it now, your baby's tumbling around in my belly."

He stiffens under me, and a minute jolt of doubt flashes through my body. "She does?" he asks, equally as quiet, as if afraid speaking any louder would make the baby stop.

"She?" I question. If Lalah blabbed already, I have a few choice words for her and a lifetime supply of dried out muffins—there's nothing she hates more out of all the baked goodies, except anything almond flavored.

His palm nudges my stomach tenderly, his fingers flexing on my outstretched skin. "It's the goddamned neon-pink wrenches that put the idea into my head. And now I can't let go of this image of a small girl, running around my garage, bringing chaos and giggles in my favorite bay," he chuckles. "I kinda hope our little Vanilla Bean is a girl."

"That'll be a sight to see," I commiserate on a giggle, the sound gravelly and broken. I'll take the burn as many times as he needs me to, even if my voice turns all Bonnie Taylor for the rest of my life.

"You can feel her, though? What is that like?" he prods, the joy in his voice undeniable.

I sigh happily and nod. "As strange as that sounds, it feels like tiny bubbles popping around my belly button, or fluttering just under my skin. Sometimes, they are so close to the surface I swear I can feel them under my palm."

"How often does it happen?"

"Lately? A lot." I can't see his frown, but I sense it. It's in the way his fingers twitch, the slight hitch of his breath, the speeding of his heartbeat. "It only started this past week, Tate. At first, I didn't know what it was. What would you make of a faint tremble in your stomach, just there and gone the next second?"

The stone wall of muscles under me softens again, and I continue, "They grow stronger every day. But right now? This is the strongest I felt them."

His arms band around me, squeezing me to him, and I understand what this is—a *thank you* and *our time is up.*

Tate helps me stand, then pushes to his feet too. We're a mess of crumpled clothes and disheveled hair. His large palms smooth my dress back down my hips, straightening the creases as best as he can. He's not concerned the flaps of his jeans are still hanging open or that his cock is still half-hard. As silly as it is, a surge of pride rushes through me. He may be conflicted about his feelings, but at least his body still desires me.

When he is happy that I am put back to rights, he bends at the knees and presses his mouth to mine. I freeze. His tongue darts out and circles my lips, slipping between them, plunging inside. His fresh mint taste makes my mouth tingle, and I can't help the keening whimper escaping my throat.

He grunts in response, pressing so close to me, not even air can get between us, deepening the kiss, but his pace never falters. My newly recuperated knees weaken once more, and I lean my whole body weight into him.

This is the first time he's kissed me since December—a kiss not meant to punish or silence me—the first loving kiss since he and I were an us.

He rips his mouth off of mine abruptly, my own lips still chasing his, but doesn't put any distance between us. "Holly fuck, Maevis, the taste of me on your mouth is my goddamn demise. If I don't step away now, we'll never leave this bathroom."

And so, I give him his space with a smile on my face.

Tatum stares straight into my eyes as he adjusts his rapidly hardening cock back into his jeans—a challenge and a filthy promise of delicious things to come—zipping his fly and buckling his belt. A quick brush of his fingers through his hair, a run of his palm over his Henley, and it's like the last half an hour never happened.

I don't like the sense of unease and loss crawling up my spine, so I crank up my smile instead to full power and give him my outstretched hand.

A quick flick of my wrist has the lock unlatching and the door opening. I wince at the bright light coming from the kitchen and the party noises ripping through the bubble.

The magic is officially dispelled.

Time to face the real world now.

Chapter Eighteen

Tatum

I drop the goddamn wrench for the thousandth time in twenty minutes. It clangs against the greasy carburetor before it slips down on the intake manifold. I huff a frustrated breath and kick the deflated tire. "Goddammit."

My hands are shaking under the waves of anger coursing through me—hell, my whole body is. That fucking phone call from the lawyer messed up my whole morning. I spear my fingers through my hair, then curse again as I feel the oil and grime from them sticking to it.

I snatch the cotton rag from the back pocket of my coveralls and wipe my forehead with it first, then clean my hands as best as I can. In the state I'm in, I'm no good here. I'll wreck this car more than restore it. Fishing the wrench out, I set off to clean my tools. At least, this part of the process helps me clear my head.

I dread going home to Maevis and telling her the news. I dread Lalah's reaction to the summons we've been given. There's less than two weeks until the trials, and this is when the wretched woman thought it'll be the best time to throw a bomb at us.

The now all-too-familiar burn in my shoulders ignites. I stride to the sink and, with a flick of my wrist, I switch the tap, shoving my hands under the ice-cold water. Once my body got used to the new anti-anxiety meds, they've been life-changing. Oh, the compulsions to shower the filth and the shame off my skin are still there. The burn and the rage are still simmering just under the surface, and there's not much I can do about that but run it off every morning.

I still repeat the mantra my therapist drilled into me at the start and end of every day. Do I believe it? I'm not sure. The lack of clarity and answers is driving me up the wall. At times, out of absolutely fucking nowhere, the urge to pound on the ex-witch's door and demand the truth hits.

But that would serve no one in the long run. It would simply be reckless.

And being reckless nearly got me killed once.

The only silver lining in the hurricane brewing at the horizon is the shift the dynamics between me and Maevis took. It's crass to say she gave me a life-altering blowjob, but she did. She gave herself to me so completely, Earth fucking moved out of orbit.

After months of feeling out of control, powerless against the hits that kept on coming, Maevis took to her knees and gave me back my control and then some. It never felt this way between us, not even when we gave in to our feelings before our entire world imploded.

There was always this wall separating us, always having the nagging feeling of being kept at arm's length.

My beautiful, shy Maevis took a goddamned sledgehammer to it and crumbled it to dust, allowing new hope to shine on me through the debris.

We're still not there, and I refuse to repeat the same mistakes. I refuse to jump headfirst and drag her into murky waters with me. This time, it's all about careful planning, testing the temperature, the depth, and the swimming conditions.

I thought I'd spend my life alone after the divorce, and I will if I have to. The only woman I could ever see myself sharing a life with is Maevis, and this has nothing to do with the fact that she's carrying my baby.

Lalah is right. We have so many overdue conversations. I've never been one to shy away from the difficult things in life. I know how to show up for the people near and dear to me. My lesson is allowing them to do the same for me, giving a bit of slack even when the rope is stretched so tight I can hear the woven fibers snapping one by one.

My phone rings again. A muffled curse slips past my lips, because I know what's coming. I shove my hand into my pocket and retrieve the damn device, and sure enough...

"What can I do for you, baby girl?" I greet her.

"You really need to drop the cutesy names when talking to *my* wife," Cole's gruff voice rumbles from the speakers.

Despite the annoyance still coursing through me, I chuckle at the under-current of jealousy. The back of my head twinges at the memory of Cole's hand wrapped around my neck, pushing me into the wall when I got in his face thinking he hurt Lalah. She may be his wife, but she's like a sister to me, and one of the closest people I have.

"Now's not the time for pissing contests," she interjects, and my spine straightens at the coldness in her voice. I know all that ice is not meant for either of us, but it's a consequence of the phone call I'm sure she also received.

I wasn't here to witness the aftermath of her brother's visit, the culmination of all the shitshow that was December for us, but from her own tell—and Cole's—we're all scared to death she'll have another episode she wouldn't snap out of so easily. With her depression, we don't know exactly what it'll take to push her over the edge and into the cage of darkness her mind designed for her. So we're watching like hawks for any sign, as small as can be, to ensure we're on the other side to catch her when she does fall.

"You're right, Supernova." The distinct sounds of kissing grate on my eardrum, and I freeze for a second. The pang of jealousy that usually follows any PDA from Lalah and Cole never comes, and I blow a relieved breath.

"Come over with Mae?" she asks. She's still matter-of-fact, but the ice in her tone has slightly thawed.

"I don't want her there," I say and open my mouth to elaborate, but I'm cut off by Lalah's shrill.

"Are you out of your fucking mind, Tatum 'Junior' Carter? Don't make me come over there or, I swear to Pluto and his heart-shaped icy plains, Imma kick you so hard I'll launch you faster to the Moon than Artemis's SLS."

"What the fuck is an SLS? Stop talking astronomy-nerd and focus on the matter at hand," I snap.

"Ugh, is the Space Launch System for the Artemis missions. Have you been living under a rock?" she hisses indignantly, and I can't help the brain-saluting eye roll if my life depended on it.

"Lalah," I sigh. "I mean, I don't want Maevis with us if we do decide to go." One of us has to get back on track otherwise we'll be here until the New Year. There's no denying the smile passing through my voice, though. She got worked up enough to drop the ice completely.

"Shouldn't that be her decision?" she whispers now softly, concern practically dripping from her voice.

"I fear she'll dig her heels in as a misguided show of support for me. We obviously don't know what the viper has to say. Maevis has dealt with enough. She's pregnant, and she doesn't need any unnecessary hurt." I jab my finger into thin air, as if Lalah could see me driving the point home.

"Unnecessary hurt would also be keeping this away from her."

"Babe," Cole's warning tone cuts her off, but she's not deterred. She never is. Lalah's worse than Astrum on the hunt when she knows she's right and would never drop anything until she sees it through.

"Don't you *babe* me, Hayes."

Called it.

"We've been through this before. We've been through this just last week. Yes, this is your personal life, and I have no desire to meddle. But this situation right now, it affects us all. It affects Mae, too, and she has the right to know. She has the right to choose for herself." Lalah heaves in a breath, all good and exasperated. I'd pity Cole, but I'm sure he'll find a way to spin it to his advantage and her benefit.

"I understand your need to protect her, Tatum. But in her shoes, I'd have a hard time forgiving you if you stripped my choices away from me."

She's right. I know she's right. I shove my fingers through my hair, grease and oil be damned, and pull until the sting on my scalp cuts through all the curses running through my mind.

All I want is five goddamn minutes when nothing fucking happens. I want to go home to my pregnant woman and kiss the daylights out of her; I want us to have dinner and talk about our day without any fucking thunderstorm clouds threatening our fragile peace; I want to throw myself on the sofa and cuddle her through the cheesiest of chick-flicks and just have five goddamn minutes to breathe.

"I'll talk to her," I say instead. There's a looming deadline—of course, there fucking is. "We'll see you later on today."

"Pizza for dinner?"

"Pizza's fine. Make sure there are no olives on Mae's. She's taken a dislike to them recently. Oh, and extra mozzarella."

"You got it."

ARMED WITH A STRAWBERRY AND BANANA MILKSHAKE and a scrambled eggs and turkey ham bagel, I stop in front of Suga'High and half pray Mae's too busy to take a break and come for a walk with me.

The newly found trust between us is so fragile, anything can draw cracks in it. Despite her knowing my side of the story from that night, the trial and now the potential visit to the detention center in Forrest Falls can reopen wounds only closed off with Band-Aids.

Maddox, in his chief deputy uniform, exits the bakery and freezes in front of me. All color drains from his face—I swear I've seen people bleeding to death losing color slower.

"You doin' okay there, man?" I ask. He may not be my favorite person, but I'm not completely heartless.

He clears his throat, but his eyes never reach mine, instead remain fixed somewhere behind my shoulder. "Morning, Carter. I'll live," he mumbles, and I swear he adds under his breath "unless you know and you're here to kill me," as he passes by me.

Fucking weirdo.

I pay him no mind. I'm about to ruin Maevis's day. If he needs something, he can ask outright. With a rueful shake of my head, I step into the bakery and draw in a lung-full breath of air. Every single time, it's like coming home—sweet vanilla and the subtle spice of cinnamon. Of course it's home since Mae's signature scent seems woven into the very bricks of this building.

By pure instinct, my eyes seek her at the counter, where she has a palm propped on her hip, the other rubbing her belly absentmindedly. She's happily chattering away with Mrs. Jennison from the Post Office, and here I come like a dark cloud. I swallow the lump lodged in my throat, forcing a smile on my face. I'm sure it comes out more like a grimace, but it's the best I've got at the moment.

My heart is pounding, and I feel sweat peppering at my hairline. *For fuck's sake, just get it over with.*

She perks up when she sees me, her arms now outstretched in front of her, making grabby hands at me. "Is that for me? Please, tell me it is."

I round the counter and beeline straight to her, bending my neck to kiss the top of her head. "Sure is, sugar. Figured you could use the sustenance," I mumble.

"My god, aren't you two as sweet as pie?" Mrs. Jennings gushes, and I brace myself. It seems like this cursed town has nothing to talk about except when Maevis and I are going to... "I can't wait for the day I'm going to receive your wedding invitation."

There it is.

Mae's bright smile drops, and I could throttle the old woman. Maevis made it pretty damned clear she doesn't want to marry me—at least, not because she got pregnant. I throw my arm around her shoulders and pull her to me.

"Thank you, ma'am. We'll be sure to invite you when it happens. Now, if you don't mind," I say, throwing her a smile that for sure doesn't reach my eyes, "I'm whisking Maevis away so she can get off her feet and enjoy her breakfast. I'll get..." I draw a blank as I'm not sure who is working the counter today.

"Tessa," Mae whispers.

"I'll get Tessa to ring you up," I recover. "You take care now, Mrs. Jennings. Give my best to your husband."

Not giving a chance to the old lady to respond and drag out the goodbyes for longer than needed, I nudge Mae to follow me. I open the door leading to the kitchen for her, ushering her in with my palm to the small of her back.

"Tessa," I say to the woman frosting a batch of cupcakes, "do you mind manning the counter for a while?"

Her eyes dart to me and then to Mae, her thin eyebrows rising on her forehead.

"Is that how it is?" I chuckle, hoping to put her at ease. "Whatcha say, boss lady, can I whisk you off for a quick break?"

Mae's cheeks pinken, and I bite the inside of mine to stop the groan rising in my throat. *The V8 engine I inspected yesterday was overheating, much like I am right now—for fuck's sake, this is not helping.*

"Tate, are you ok?" Mae asks. I look around and see Tessa has disappeared from the kitchen. I give her a sheepish smile and a small lift of my shoulders.

"Sure am, sugar. Sorry, I zoned out. Coffee hasn't kicked in yet." She gives me a puzzled look, since we both know everything coming out of my mouth right now is a lie, and pulls me to the back entrance. I follow her to her car and lean on the hood.

"Alright, what's going on? You're worrying me."

I cup her jaw with my free hand, stroking her soft skin as I gather my courage to just get it over with when her stomach rumbles loudly. Yeah, that overheating V8 has nothing on these hungry sounds. And the conversation we need to have is best had in privacy. I figured she could eat while I talked, but the parking lot of her bakery is really not the best place for this.

"There's been a potential new development regarding the trials." Her eyes grow large and round, and she blinks at me as if in slow motion, her lips parting on a soft gasp of surprise. "Ms. Townsend called me about an hour ago with the news. I'd like to talk to you about it, but I think it's best if we have this conversation at home."

Chapter Nineteen

Tatum

I watch her as she slurps the last of her milkshake, gently tapping with a paper towel the corners of her full lips. I'm distracting myself with her beauty, I know I am. But it's a fucking indecent show watching Maevis eat and wrap that pouty mouth of hers around a paper straw.

"OK. You're making me anxious," she says, fiddling with the edges of the napkin. I abandon my chair and, in two quick strides, I'm in front of her, crouching next to the sofa. My palm is drawn like a magnet to the belly that seems to grow rounder and rounder by the hour.

"No anxiety. It's not good for our Vanilla Bean."

She snorts a laugh, and my lips curl up in a smile. "That's not how it works, Tatum. You can't just command my feelings into obedience."

That lights a fire in my gut, and my eyes spring to hers, the molten sugar of her irises drawing me in. I'm sure she can see the exact gutter my mind is currently resting in, reflected in mine.

"No, but I can command you into obedience," I drawl, my voice husky with lust. She leans into me until we're nose to nose, and I suck in a breath, anticipation building, my cock throbbing painfully inside my boxers.

A whack on my shoulder from her dainty palm clears the haze away. "You're stalling," she accuses.

"Maddison wants to meet with Lalah and I, preferably by the end of the week." The words spill out of my mouth in a rush, in fear that if I don't rip the Band-Aid off now, I'll have her writhing under me instead of actually talking.

And then instead of attending the trials, we'll be attending a funeral. Specifically mine, when Lalah gets her hands on me.

"Shit," Mae sighs, the sound drawn out and pitiful, her hand flying to the center of her chest.

"You could say that again," I mumble and let myself fall to my ass, my back resting against the coffee table.

"Are you going to meet with her?"

My earlier burst of courage leaves me, and I know I can't do this part looking her in the eye, so instead I look at the hardwood floor.

"Lalah wants all of us to have dinner together and decide. I can't figure out why Maddison wants to see me too."

She's quiet for so long, I almost risk looking back at her. But with Maevis being Maevis, I don't need to. The rustling of her dress against the velvet of the couch alerts me of her movements before her chest presses to mine, her rounded belly bumping against my abdomen, and her arms sneaking around my neck.

"You're gonna have to stretch out one of your legs. Your baby is too big for me not to squish it between us," she laughs, and I'm quick to pull her into my lap. I band my arms around her waist—she may be complaining the baby is big, but my arms still envelop her fully.

Her head goes on my shoulder, and my breath hitches in my chest. "We seem to be creating a new tradition for ourselves," I murmur, my lips feathering atop her head. "All of our heavy conversations lately have happened with you in my arms, all curled up around me."

"I love our new tradition," she whispers. "We're holding each other together. We're holding steady and strong."

I squeeze her closer—how could I not, since those words from her lips are what my deepest desires are made of.

"You don't want me there, do you?" I stiffen under her, my fingers digging into her hip, but she carries on, paying me no mind. "I let myself be blindsided once by them, Tatum. I won't be blindsided again."

"Maddison is not... right, sugar. I have no idea what she'll say and how that could affect you." I soothingly stroke her skin through her dress with my thumb, to make up for my moment of weakness earlier, and drop my voice to a near whisper as I'm admitting to a new fear. "I don't know how it'll affect me."

Her fingers start playing in my hair, the same hair I butchered in an attempt to gain some semblance of control four months ago. She hums softly in her throat, and my eyes fall close of their own accord, my cheek resting on her head, the comforting scent of vanilla all around us.

"Are you going to grow it again?" she asks.

"I don't know," I murmur.

"I miss it."

"I'll grow it again."

"Regardless of how this will affect you, you're not alone, Tatum." Her lips kiss the crook of my neck, and my stomach turns into a live wire, all conduit and no earth bonding whatsoever. "We're not *there,* but we are. And in this space where we are right now, we hold each other together."

"She's cruel, Mae. You know that."

"What I know is that I haven't given you a reason to believe I have your back."

"Then have my back when I get out of there and don't know which way is up. Have my back by allowing me to take the brunt of her words and trusting me to tell you what went on in a way that won't hurt more than it has to."

I'M SHIFTING ANXIOUSLY FROM ONE FOOT TO THE OTHER, my Converse squeaking on the dull, cemented floors. A coil of uneasiness rests inside of me, making me feel like a thousand ants are crawling just under my skin.

"Stop it," Lalah hisses.

I throw her a side glance. She's anxious, too. We spent three days going back and forth about whether or not we should see Maddison. In the end, it was Jackson who pointed out that whether we expose ourselves to her poison now, or during her trial, we're still going through it one way or another. At least during this meeting, we can leave at any time.

So here we are—me squeaking all the way, and Lalah ready to take over the board of a multinational corporation.

I actually did a double take when we all met earlier in front of Forrest Falls County Police Station. In the nine months I've known her, I've almost never seen Lalah wear anything but black leggings and funny sweatshirts, with the occasional dress during holidays or her actual wedding.

She's now wearing a suit, red of all things. You'd expect the splash of color to soften her up, but she looks ready to rip this place apart brick by brick, especially with the scowling menace hovering at her side.

Said menace is glaring at me now, and I halt my pacing, but my knees are still jittery and bouncing on the spot.

The worst is not knowing what the woman just behind the gray door in front of me wants. According to the updates I've received from Ms. Townsend, she had nothing to do with what went down between Amanda and me that night. Apparently, the ex-witch has been known to pop a pill or two on occasion; Maddison simply took advantage of the situation.

Lalah's icy hand slips into mine, giving me a tight squeeze. "Whatever she has to say, we already lived through it. All she has are words, Tatum."

"I know."

"Words sometimes cut deeper than a blade. But nothing *is* happening to us now. The damage is already done. Let yourself fall on Maevis," she whispers now. "If I fall, even the darkest part of me knows Cole is there to catch me. Mae will catch you, too. Believe me, she's stronger than you give her credit for." She snorts now, a self-deprecating, teasing sound, so out of place in this dreary hallway. "It's why she's currently in her car in the parking lot, and not at home where you ordered her to be."

Maevis and I had our *wires crossed* somewhere along the line. I was resting well knowing she'll wait for me at home. And while I was resting, she was planning all along to be here. The cunning minx kissed me *Good luck* this morning when I left home. I, instead, nearly kissed the fucking ground—and by kissed, I mean fell face-first—in my haste to jump from my truck and rush to her car when I saw her standing defiantly against the passenger door, arms crossed over her chest, round belly front and center.

"I'm not leaving," she hissed before I even opened my mouth to say anything, then leveled me with a glare that put even Cole's to shame. "I'm not asking to come inside, and I don't want to cause you more stress than you're already feeling. But *I am here*, and I'm not leaving."

Back before life chewed us up and spat us out, we were together but hiding. She's not hiding anymore. And we're... *I don't know what the fuck we are.* Not together, but not apart; not keeping our hands to ourselves, but not fucking either—and that's all before we add our baby into the mix.

"We're ready for you now, Mrs. Hayes, Mr. Carter." The nasal voice of Maddison's lawyer brings me back to the task at hand and the dreadful person waiting just beyond the wall ahead.

Lalah's fingers squeeze mine once more before she squares her shoulders and marches inside the room. I let Cole go in front of me, then follow him. The space isn't what I expected. I don't know what the hell I expected to see, but it's not crisp-white walls with colorful artwork, nor the black round table and comfortable looking chairs around it. Only the faint smell of stale air is close to what I thought this would be.

"Oh, don't look so disappointed, Tate," Maddison mocks, "Innocent until proven guilty, remember? I may be detained, but I still have rights."

My eyes find her, perched on her chair, legs crossed, hands resting casually in her lap, a smug smirk on her face like she's one-upping us. Her cold blue eyes flicker from me to Lalah, and I take the time to really look at her.

She may have rights, but not too many privileges. I can't remember a time I didn't see her hair in a fancy up-do or her without makeup. The Maddison in front of me is clear faced with tension lines around her mouth and the corners of her eyes.

The blue of her irises twinkles, and she smiles from ear to ear now. "Emo Barbie, I heard congratulations are in order. You sure do move fast."

I feel more than I hear Lalah's sharp intake of breath. Cole instantly steps in front of her, and I get in her lawyer's face, red creeping at the edges of my vision. "Is this the bullshit you called us here for?"

Maddison makes a tsking sound that grates on my eardrums and starts laughing. I've had just about enough. I clench my fingers into a tight fist, so that I'm not tempted to hook them in the cowering suit's tie and sling him out of my way. Any unease I have is blasted away by the wave of rage washing through me.

"We're out of here," Cole barks. "Ms. Townsend, next time you support a harebrained idea like this, after everything Lalah's been through, you're fired." His voice is so menacing and chilly, even the rage flaming inside of me cools a notch.

"No, *meus bellator*," Lalah interjects. At her words, I turn to her, but she's already pushing past Cole and taking a seat in one of the available chairs at the table, mimicking Maddison's posture precisely, down to the harrowing indifference in her eyes.

The temperature in the room drops by at least ten degrees with the icicles the two are throwing at each other in a twisted contest of stares. The hair at my nape stands on end, and my forearms pepper with goosebumps in the eerie air of otherness surrounding Maddison.

Cole's hands fist at his sides, but he says nothing. Instead, he reaches Lalah's side in two strides and stands to her right like a sentinel. So I follow suit, taking the empty place to her left.

"Apologies, Mrs. and Mr. Hayes, Mr. Carter," Townsend nods at us, her sharp features pulled tight, her eyebrows scrunching together in displeasure. She focuses on Maddison next. "Miss Brown, you request-ed this meeting as you wanted to inform my clients personally of your decision. The court has granted this privilege, despite the restraining orders filed against you, as long as my clients agreed to see you. Should you step out of line again, please rest assured, I will file a report as you are deliberately breaking the terms agreed with the judge."

But it's like talking to a wall. Maddison doesn't even spare her a look, her attention completely on us. Whatever games she was playing five minutes ago, she drops them. Her face completely morphs into arrogant indifference.

"Do you know what antisocial personality disorder is?" she asks, leaning forward, closer to the table, her clean-cut nails thrumming on the polished dark wood.

"Miss Brown," her lawyer admonishes, but Lalah cuts him off with a palm in the air, not even bothering to tell him to zip it.

"We're all well aware you're a psychopath, Maddison."

The wicked woman smiles, a goddamned ear-to-ear smile, and flicks her hair behind her shoulder.

"Close, but no. See, the months spent in here have been produc-tive—mandatory therapy and all that—since Mom insisted on getting me any help possible. The way she saw it, being able to claim temporary insanity could only have helped me during the trial. In her head, I surely had a breakdown or lost my mind somehow. Otherwise, what reasons could I possibly have to attack the town's savior?" she mocks.

"You broke her heart," Lalah says.

It's the first crack in Maddison's armor. A flash of anger crosses her face, her eyes narrowing to slits, before the chilling indifference returns.

"Heartbroken or not, I'm sure she hoped the army of therapists would find something to help me in the trial. Congratulations to me, I have been diagnosed…"

"Miss Brown," her lawyer admonishes.

"What is it, Larry? Or was it Steve?" She turns to him. "You don't want me to tell my visitors I'm a sociopath? That I've been a bad, bad girl because I was not made right?" She winks at him, and I can't suppress my eyeroll.

"See, I'm told people need closure, a reason why depraved individuals do heinous things," she continues, the same condescending lilt to her voice. "Humans are wired to root for the underdog, are willing to forgive the unforgivable if there's a mournful, traumatic story behind the villainous mask." Maddison squares her shoulders and tilts her chin up. Her palms prop against the edge of the table—a direct challenge issued to Lalah—and I brace myself for the blow she's about to deal.

"So, tell me, Alana, does it bring you closure to know I'm evil simply because I was born this way? Are you at peace knowing that I tried to hurt you just because you took what was rightfully mine, and I took immense pleasure in watching you suffer?"

"MISS BROWN!" her lawyer shouts this time, his face red and blotchy, eyes wide and horrified.

Welcome to the club, man.

Chapter Twenty

Tatum

Maddison rolls her blue, unfeeling eyes at him, dismissing his words with a wave of her bony hand.

"What are they going to do to me, Lenny?" She sneers. "Lock me up?"

Lalah is unnaturally still next to me, such a stark contrast with the fury radiating from Cole. His rage is palpable—a living, breathing thing, vacuum-suctioning all the air in the room.

"You didn't take pleasure in my struggles because you're a sociopath, Maddison. There are plenty of people out there diagnosed with anti-social personality disorder and they don't harm others for fun."

Maddison huffs, her mouth dropping in disapproval, accentuating the lines bracketing her lips. "Oh, just look at you, the advocate of the damned and hollow."

"Is there a point to all of this?" Lalah cuts her off. "Or did you just want to play one more game before the trial?"

A wistful haze falls over Maddison's face, a caricature of an emotion she probably can't reach. I don't know if I should feel sorry for her, for being born into living a life dulled to all emotions except anger and depraved pleasure, or if I should be relieved she's giving into her narcissistic side and all but confessing in front of our lawyer.

"I changed my 'not-guilty' plea." She drops out of nowhere, and my stomach falls to my feet. That also gets a reaction out of Lalah, whose loud gasp seems to echo against the white walls and stuffy air.

"You have impeccable timing, though. If you lingered on the decision to visit for much longer, you would have had to take the scenic route about two hours away from Billings. They're transferring me tomorrow to my new... accommodations." Maddison pushes to her feet and stretches as if she doesn't have a care in the world.

Lalah is trembling next to me like a leaf, all color rapidly draining from her face, all semblance of the hardened woman charging into the room like she owned it half an hour ago gone. The red of her suit doesn't make her look all powerful, ready to take on the world. She looks like a broken doll, white skin and crimson garments far too big for how small she looks.

"Why?" slips past her lips, the sound hoarse and raw.

"Because it was my choice, Lalah. Sociopathy won't land me in a nice, cushy, kumbaya place where I'm doped on meds and have hand-holding therapy. I would've landed in prison either way, trial or no trial." Maddison slaps her palm on the table, and it takes everything in me not to give in to my instinct to react to the startle she gives me. All my senses are haywire, attuned now to the predator-in-the-making sharing the same air with us.

"You're one-upping me by changing your plea?" Lalah asks incredulously, her chest heaving, and I throw Cole a side glance. This meeting needs to wrap up, and it needs to happen sooner rather than later, before she works herself into a panic attack. But he's already on it, his hand on her shoulder, thumb rubbing her upper arm.

"Not everything's about you, Emo Barbie. Mom doesn't need to be ripped apart during the trial. I wanted to tell you face to face because I don't want you to think you won. I made the choice. I. Am. In. Control." She's practically screaming the last words, each one overenunciated and heavy.

"There was never a competition, Maddison," Lalah says, pushing back from the table and leaning against Cole. I release the breath trapped into my lungs. She's not retreating into herself; she's drawing strength from him. "You played against yourself, and you lost." The ghost of a smile, carrying much more kindness than the deranged woman in front of us deserves, graces Lalah's face. "I wish you the best of luck. Keep well, Maddison. If not for yourself, then for Gretchen."

And with those parting words, she takes Cole's hand and moves toward the door. I can't help the sense of relief that douses me so abruptly, my knees almost buckle.

This could've gone so much fucking worse.

"Tatum," Maddison yells after me, and I freeze. I turn my head and look at her over my shoulder.

Spoken too goddamned soon.

"You sealed your fate as soon as you humped Flat Earth on the dance floor. What Amanda wants, Amanda takes. She wanted you in high school because you were the only one not tripping over your feet when she came near."

I cave. She baited and she caught. And so, I slowly turn to fully face her. If Maddison's going to bury a rusted knife in me, she should at least do it to my face.

The sparkle in her dull eyes is manic. She's almost giddy preparing for the final blow. I feel hands pulling at my shoulders and arms, but I'm rooted to the spot. Cemented in all my worst fears by the answers she's gearing to throw my way—not to enlighten, but to darken and poison.

"To this day, I don't understand why she married you, you little grease monkey." Her overly large smile is fucking terrifying, never quite reaching the ice in her dazed irises. "You were never more than a toy she got to occasionally parade around, then throw aside when she got bored. Amanda doesn't care for her toys, but doesn't want to share them either."

More hands are pushing at me, this time at my chest, forcing me to take a step back, and then another. I don't see past the malice in Maddison's eyes. I don't hear anything but the rushing of my own blood in my ears and the venom in her voice.

"She didn't fuck you. Not for lack of trying, though. Aren't you too young not to get it up when an actual woman puts her mouth on you? They make pills for it, you know?" Her chortles of laughter ring inside my head, banging like a hammer against my skull.

The air is suddenly too thick, the lights are too bright, my body too stiff, not listening to any of my commands. Amanda might not have full on raped me, but she was not far from it either.

My shoulders burn, jagged scratch marks ripping open under my skin, pure acid pouring from them into my bloodstream. My fingers claw at the collar of my Henley, the collar that's getting tighter and tighter around my neck by the second.

"Why the hysterics, grease monkey? Apparently, even when you were drugged out of your fucking mind and passed out, she still got off with your fingers inside of her."

My knees give out and my stomach empties on the white linoleum, again, and again, and again, until all it's left of me are the flames under my skin and the acidic blaze of my esophagus.

All I hear are the heaves in my chest and the maniacal cackles of rotten laughter spewing out of Maddison.

I think I had an out-of-body experience. There's no other way to explain the feeling of looking down on myself as I was being dragged away by Cole and deposited into the passenger seat of Maevis's car.

I don't remember the drive home. I don't remember being helped to my bedroom. Faint memories of Maevis and Lalah checking in on me flash behind my eyelids. My body is tired and heavy, a chill embedded just under my skin. A soft blanket smelling like vanilla and sunshine covers me from neck to toe.

It's still not enough.

My mind is fuzzy, like a fog has settled over me, and I can't find my way out. I can't tell for how long I've been asleep, but going by the exhaustion weighing me down, it could've been anything between five minutes and a week. I blink my eyes open, and it takes a good minute for them to adjust to the darkness of my bedroom—or should I say the guest bedroom in Maevis's family home that I've occupied for the past month and a half.

My throat is dry and my tongue is glued to the roof of my mouth. A pained grunt escapes my lips when I push myself up on my forearm, swinging my feet over the edge of the queen-size mattress.

"Tatum, love? Are you awake?" Maevis's sleepy voice comes from the foot of the bed, and I nearly jump out of my skin since I did not see her there earlier, nor did I sense the presence of another person with me in the room.

The bedding crinkles and shuffles before a warm, soft palm glides up and down my forearm, chasing the chill away, replacing it with heat and electric tingles.

"I'm thirsty," I croak, nearly every second sound out of my mouth broken and rasped out.

"Stay here, I'll be right back," she says, then disappears out the door, leaving it wide open in her wake.

I test the strength of my legs, and when I feel I can support my own weight, I stand and take small steps toward the same door she left through, and to the guest bathroom down the hall. I don't bother with any lights;

my eyes are fairly adjusted to the dark now. A slight shove down of my sweats and boxers, palm pressed on the wall for balance, and the cramps in my abdomen settle as I relieve myself.

Tucking myself back into the soft cotton of my sleeping pants, I wash my hands and then my face, splashing cold water over my tightly closed eyes until the fog mantled over my mind starts to lift. I don't dare look in the mirror. I'm not ready to face the destruction Maddison's words have caused.

My stomach is tender, like I'm trapped into an elevator going up and down at warped speed, and all I can do is grip the handrail with all my might, hoping I won't plummet to my death. The now familiar burn stings my shoulders. My fingers twitch with the need to scratch my skin right off and expose the venom the ex-witch buried inside of me. To bleed it out with the rot and the despair she cursed me with.

I force a deep breath, and then another, and then another, allowing Lalah's words to spring roots into my mind.

"Whatever she has to say, we already lived through it. All she has are words, Tatum. Words sometimes cut deeper than a blade. But nothing is happening to us now. The damage is already done."

My eyes open. Shadows and the faintest strip of moonlight play all around me. I'm half engulfed in darkness, half in the silvery spotlight provided by the moon. Sure, my skin is ashen, my cheeks hollow, and my lips dry. But my eyes... my eyes glow. There's grit and determination shining through.

I open my mouth to say the mantra my therapist has drilled into me. The words I repeat to myself every morning and every night, even though I don't quite believe them, but nevertheless help me push through each day, seeking healing and forgiveness. Instead of a hoarse, cracked sound, the musical, loving lilt of Maevis's voice cuts through. At the same time, the heat of her arm brands itself around my waist.

"You're Tatum Carter. A strong, protective, and dependable man; an amazing father-to-be; the most loyal friend. You're Tatum Carter, a sur-vivor of sexual assault and the plethora of mental health struggles that come in the aftermath. The two are not mutually exclusive."

All the poisoned air trapped into my lungs rushes out as if chased away by the conviction and strength in her voice. My already weakened knees buckle, and I take a step back, resting against the wall, praying it'll support my weight. She slips in front of me, curling her arms around my neck, head craned back, holding my eyes with her warm, healing amber gaze.

Oh, there's pain there with just the smallest hint of anger. Her molten sugar eyes are like motor oil spilled on a cement floor—dark in their self-righteousness but an array of colors radiate out of them as the faint light hits at just the right angle, and she allows me to see everything she's feeling in their depths.

She forgives. She hurts. She protects. She loves. She stays.

"How?" I whisper, awe and confusion warring inside of me.

"These walls are paper thin, Tate. My bed is just on the other side of this wall." Her pillowy lips twitch in the semblance of a smile, and my cheeks blaze red hot. If she heard my mantra every night, she also heard...

"I did," she giggles, the sound soothing my frayed nerves, bouncing inside my rib cage, and settling around my pounding heart. "It definitely didn't help with the crazy hormones," she admits, a pretty blush of her own painting her creamy, white skin, visible even in the near darkness of the bathroom.

She steps closer into me, as close as her rounded belly allows, and settles her forehead in the middle of my chest. And just like that, we're us—us and our protective bubble of trust and truth. I let the heat of her soft body seep into me, my hands automatically gripping her generous hips.

"Let yourself fall on Maevis. She's stronger than you give her credit for." Lalah's words invade my mind again. With startling clarity, I realize she's not wrong.

Maevis is easily underestimated because of her soft demeanor and kind personality; because she chooses to retreat instead of lash out; but there's tenacity in retreating, there's resilience and patience.

Lashing out is easy. Going on a rampage and dragging everyone around you in a hurricane of anger is even easier. Turning your other cheek, now that's difficult. Stepping back without throwing your own malignant darts takes grit and quiet determination. Living your life in the light despite all the attempts to have it snuffed out, that's pure strength.

"What now, Mae?"

"Now we go to bed. I'll hold you together all night and you'll hold me. And tomorrow? We try again."

Chapter Twenty-One

Tatum

This past week has been its own kind of special brand of pure, fucking torture. Maevis, Sawyer, Selena, Lalah, and Annalise, all descended on my head, just shy of breaking out a PowerPoint presentation persuading me to have daily therapy sessions.

I caved.

There's not a man with a licker of smarts in him who would go against that pack of blood-thirsty hyenas when they set their minds to something. Lalah even went as far as flying Selae here, just so my sister can threaten to go to my mom to set me straight. That's when I drew the fucking line in the sand.

If Sarah Carter gets even the slightest whiff of one of her babies being hurt, she'll rain down hell on earth. No one, absolutely no one, wants an unhinged mama bear on a rampage. I'm quite certain there's a voodoo doll with about a million pins stuck into it, looking a hell of a lot like the witch of Lost Hope, hidden somewhere in my mom's kitchen.

My parents are aware of what went down that night in December. I called a family meeting just before I left for Chicago.

I dreaded telling my father. How could I look my hero into his eyes—eyes I inherited from him—and tell him I failed? I broke all the rules he spent years of my life drilling into me. For a second time.

Always be aware of your surroundings. Keep your guard up. Assess before you act. Think before you speak.

My heart was in my throat when I approached him, my palms sweaty as hell. There was never a time my father was disappointed in me; not when I so rashly married the bitch, despite his urgings to be cautious; not when I told him the news of my impending divorce and had to stand in front of him with my head bowed down, admitting that he had been right all along; not even when, for almost a month, they feared every day I would either lose my leg or die from the infection rooted into my flesh and poisoning my blood that just wouldn't quit.

So to go in front of him to tell him I have once again underestimated her wickedness and put myself in such a vulnerable position made me cower in shame and self-disgust.

Tatum 'Senior' Carter stood tall and proud in front of me, clasped a meaty hand onto my shoulder with such strength I thought my clavicle would crack under his grip, and gave me absolutely no disappointment and all the absolution I so desperately craved without even being aware of it.

The corded muscles of his neck worked on a hard swallow, the crinkles at the corner of his eye the only crack in the mask of stoicism he usually wears. His eyes scanned over my entire frame, as if making sure I'm still whole. The silence in the living room felt suffocating and stifling as he processed everything I laid bare at his feet. My stomach churned as he cleared his throat. The small child inside of me—eager for his father's approval—cowered in anticipation of a reprimand that never came.

"Son," he said in his deep, baritone voice that always seems to vibrate through me with its infallible strength, "the evil of humans knows no bounds. Whether in a warzone or just on our front steps, evil exists like an incurable disease. You either bend when facing it or you stand tall and fight. You're fighting. My faith in you is not misplaced by mistakes you make along the way."

Nausea swirled in my stomach at his words. He too believed I had made a mistake. His fingers dug harder into my shoulder, strangling like a tourniquet the burn rising from the memory of those scratch marks, halting its spread.

"My very soul hurts for you, son. It hurts for every single person, be it man or woman, that has to endure unwanted hands on them. I won't sit here and pretend I understand what goes through your head or how you feel. But," his eyes flashed with sorrow, the whites reddening under the sheen of moisture coating them, as he inhaled sharply through his nose, "not everyone has the power to fight back. You, Tatum, do."

He took a step back and let himself fall into the worn-out leather chair in our family's home living room, looking up at me from his seat. My spine steeled and I stood just a little taller. He purposefully put himself lower than me to show me I indeed have the necessary strength.

"Do whatever it takes to heal. And then be stronger, do better. You have the ability to be the voice of so many others who were stripped of it. You have the support system, the courage, and the fortitude. Heal, son, and then fight back for all who couldn't, yourself included."

My mom was absolutely heartbroken for me, and that only served to further my shame. I couldn't shield her from this, couldn't protect her. It couldn't be hidden either once I made up my mind that night at the hospital to press charges against my ex-wife.

Sawyer wept quietly in the corner of the sofa, bent legs drawn tightly to her chest, her face hidden atop her knees. Selena went deadly quiet as soon as I started telling my family what went down the other night, fire and brimstone swirling in her icy blue eyes. Her only words were, "I'll wait for you at the airport," before disconnecting the videocall.

As lost to my trauma as I was in the first weeks immediately after, my family's unwavering support kept me going, my friends' loyalty kept me pushing forward. So if I can do anything to keep their worries at bay, I'll man up and do it, even if I have to sit on a sofa, stare at the ceiling, and expose all the vulnerable parts of me to a therapist once a day.

"Mister Carter, are you still with us?" My lawyer's hardened voice cuts through the memories replaying in my head.

I clear my throat but refuse to let any shame surface. I'm thankful to her, I truly am, but every single fucking night for a week we've had the same conversation over and over again. For six evenings in a row we've been summoned to Lalah's home, debating the trial to death. She's trying to compensate for the fuck-up that was the meeting with Maddison, but she's overdoing it.

"For the love of all those law books you adore so much, Paola, just call him Tatum," Lalah interjects. Her frustration is mounting—same as mine—and I'd bet everyone else's in this room.

Maevis burrows into me, leaning her head on my arm, and I squeeze her fingers in my hand. Every evening during these *trial prep* meetings, she's been right here by my side, holding my hand, supporting me through the rehash of it all. Every night, she has led me to her bedroom and held me through the night, watching over me, guarding my sleep against all foes, seen or unseen. *My Cupcake is fierce as hell.*

I jolt at realizing this is the first time since that dreadful night that I've called Maevis by the nickname I gave her long before she knew of it—the very same nickname the witch tainted, just like everything she comes near.

Maevis cranes her neck and looks at me through lowered lashes. *Are you okay?* she mouths. Her pretty eyes are sleepy, as they usually get after dinner. Our baby grows bigger and bigger each day and eats away at her energy more. I bend and kiss her forehead.

Yeah, babe, I mouth right back. Turning my head toward the lawyer, I say louder, "Ms. Townsend, Paola, I appreciate everything you're doing, but honestly, we've been sitting here, having the same conversation the whole week. Discussing it to death won't change anything in the upcoming days."

She narrows her eyes at me, angling her sharp chin in the air. Oh, she's getting ready to rip into me, but I've had just about enough.

"I just want you to be prepared for what's waiting for you there," she hisses.

"And I am," I say with finality. "Want me to recap it all for you? Maddison fucked herself over when she changed her plea, falsely believing the judge would be more lenient on her. She got slapped with second degree attempted murder"—my eyes dart to Lalah who visibly shudders at my words—"and got herself locked up for thirty-five years with the possibility of parole in twenty."

"Mist... Tatum, that's not going to..." she tries again, but I cut her off. Maevis just hid a yawn in the sleeve of my T-shirt, and we need to get home and have as good of a sleep as we can before the shitshow tomorrow.

"She also confessed the drugs were Amanda's. The witch saw me dancing with Maevis and decided it was her time to play. She claimed I came onto her on the dance floor, but later changed her statement, saying I messaged her to meet me in the men's bathroom, where I came onto her, and we left together for the hotel." My stomach is in knots, and I absentmindedly rub my palm over it as the next words tumble in a fury out of my mouth. "The lawyer her husband hired wants to have the case dismissed on the basis of me being abusive, a fact that was recorded and later disproved during our divorce proceedings, but now the witch is bringing it up again."

"You're right, T-Tatum, but..." Paola says, her cheeks blazing red when Lalah interrupts her next.

"No buts. We have witnesses. We have evidence. Hell, you were there to hear what Maddison had to say in a room full of people." My friend jumps to her feet from where she is perched in Cole's lap and gets in the lawyer's face. "I like you, Paola, but stop pushing him. He's fucking had enough. We all have. This meeting is done." She slashes her outstretched hand through the air, Astrum immediately moving next to her, hackles raised, growling deep in his chest.

That gets a brief smile out of her, all fight leaving her body as if a switch is flipped, her fingers finding their way into his dark fur. "Astrum, laxo. I'm okay," she reassures him before looking back at the lawyer, who smartly puts some distance between herself and Lalah's guardian. "We'll all be there for the opening statements, but make sure Tatum doesn't have to stay in that courtroom for a second more than he has to."

Paola admits defeat with a weak nod, her fingers shakily collecting all the paperwork strewn across Lalah's coffee table. I turn my attention to Maevis, who somehow fell asleep through the commotion. I slide my truck keys out of my jeans' pocket with my free hand and throw them to Cole. He catches them easily, but glares at me anyway. I shrug unconcerned since I knew he would, although I could've used the laugh if they would've hit him in the forehead. Maybe that would stop him from eyefucking Lalah every two seconds.

"Get my truck running, would you, Cap? And turn the heating on, I don't want Mae to be cold."

"Sir, yes, sir," he drawls, saluting me with his middle finger. I return the salute, 'cause we're all about respect, but our childish behavior breaks the tension in the room when Lalah giggles.

I slowly extract my arm from Maevis's tight grip and get up from the sofa, quickly donning my sweatshirt. With a hand supporting her back and my forearm under her knees, I lift her in my arms, Lalah hurrying to my side with Mae's jacket, tucking it all around my sleeping woman. She stirs, sighing softly, but doesn't wake up.

Kissing Lalah's cheek in goodbye, I follow Cole outside to my car. He opens the passenger door for me, and I settle Maevis in the middle of the bench, then carefully arrange the seatbelt over her belly to ensure it's not too tight.

"Thanks, brother," I say to Cole, clapping his shoulder in a half hug. "See you tomorrow."

"Don't mention it." His freakishly pale green eyes bore into mine, quietly assessing my mental state. I let him read me. He's earned that much from me, and if there's anyone I trust with my life, it's him and his wife. "Don't dwell on the next few days. Whatever happens, happens. Think of the woman you're taking home and of your baby. Think of the gender reveal party. Whatever gets you through another day. We have your back, brother."

"I know you do." I give him a sharp nod, then round the hood of my car, ready to get into bed and sleep the night away, all curled up around Maevis.

She doesn't stir the whole drive home, and I can't help the self-satisfied smile tugging at my lips. I never thought I'd be the type to be aroused because I got my woman pregnant, but I am. Her rounded belly is the sexiest fucking thing I've ever seen, and knowing I did this to her makes me feel things I've never felt before.

It's also fucking weird to be aroused at the sight of Maevis or by the simple fact that she's breathing next to me, while I know that in less than fourteen hours I'll have to be in court where my ex-wife is on trial for sexually assaulting me.

This is something my therapist and I have discussed at length. I've spent countless hours reading testimonies from sexual assault and rape survivors, how their lives have changed after, and their reactions in the aftermath. There's no wrong or right reaction. There's no wrong or right feeling. There isn't a rule to follow or a timeline that fits everyone.

And while we all go through all the stages of grief, because we are grieving—it may be true no one died, but we did lose parts of ourselves at the hands of monsters—there's no predefined time for how long we spend in each stage or a predetermined order we're moving through.

I'm firmly in denial, still. While Maddison's words had a gutting effect on me, once my head cleared, I questioned the truth of what she said. The rape kit found no foreign DNA on my pelvis and genitals. Obviously, I washed my hands god knows how many times before we went to the hospital, so they didn't find anything on my fingers or under my nails.

The anger comes and goes, over and over again. My punching bag takes the brunt of my feelings when red floods my vision, my muscles shake under the weight of my misery, and the pit in my stomach threatens to swallow me whole.

Bargaining—now, this stage I haven't touched much. And if I did, it was related to my relationship with Maevis. Especially during the nights I tossed and turned in my bed, wondering if she was thinking of me, and wishing she was next to me, sleeping peacefully in my arms, her signature scent of love and home chasing away my nightmares.

My therapist says I'm not depressed—I'm sad, which is normal. I'm upset, which is also normal. But I've not reached the catastrophic levels of depression yet. I'm anxious instead, and I cope with the anxiety with rituals that are obsessive-compulsive in nature. Like feeling the burn under my skin and showering to wash the shame off me.

One common theme I have encountered in my reading material that I don't experience is aversion to touch. As before that night happened, I don't go around sharing hugs like candy on Halloween night. But I also don't recoil or shy away from touch now. It may be because I remember close to nothing from what went down then, and this may change after the trial since I might learn more than I want to know. But I also think it's because the only ones who come near me are people I trust with my life and my safety.

There's also the simple fact that I share sexual intimacy with only one person, Maevis—and I'm in love with Maevis. Even when I thought we were done and dusted, whenever I closed my eyes and imagined her next to me, her hands on me were always soothing, were always the calm in the middle of the storm.

And, as I carry her to her bedroom and fumble in the darkness of our home, tingles dance on my skin everywhere her sleepy body touches mine, and my cock is rock solid in my jeans.

I place her gently on the bed and take her dress off, averting my eyes. One side effect of that night? I grew exponentially more aware of respecting others' dignity. While before, I wouldn't have hesitated stripping her naked, sliding into bed next to her, and burying my fingers inside her tight pussy, waking her up with an orgasm, now I need her verbal consent for everything.

Which is why, as soon as she's dressed into one of my large, soft-from-wearing T-shirts, I tuck her into her blanket. Despite the desperate longing in my heart to get into bed with her and pull her to my chest, I walk backward out of her bedroom, closing the door softly.

My forehead thumps on the cold wood now separating me from her, and with a whispered "Good night, Cupcake," I spin on my heel and walk into my own bedroom.

Shedding my clothes at the foot of the bed, I let myself fall on my back onto the soft mattress, the cold air of the empty room prickling at my skin. The exhaustion of the past months hits me square in the chest and my body grows heavy under it.

My eyes close and I allow sleep to overtake me.

Alone.

Chapter Twenty-Two

Maevis

The blaring of the alarm rouses me from sleep. Blindly, I pat around Tatum's chest, hoping to reach the nightstand where his phone is screaming bloody murder. He starts stirring under me, a low, gravelly grunt escaping his parted lips when my palm connects with his morning wood.

His large hand tightens on my hip before cupping my ass under the hem of my sleeping T-shirt, giving it a firm squeeze.

"Baby, what are you doing?" he rasps.

"Turn that alarm off, Tate," I whine. I'm exhausted. I fell asleep last night while we were still at Lalah's. The asshole brought me home and then left me to sleep alone. I woke up in the middle of the night, disoriented and cold, his side of the bed empty and undisturbed. Got out of bed and came to investigate where he was, worried he may be pacing the living room floor, stressing about the trial today, only to find him fast asleep in the guest bedroom.

He is lucky I value his rest more than my butthurt feelings, otherwise he would have woken up this morning wearing two assholes.

The alarm cuts off abruptly, just in time for me to hear him moan deep in his chest when his fingers find me wet and ready for him. I'm always ready for him. All he has to do is breathe in my general direction and I'm soaked, never mind him holding me in his arms as I sleep, a willing victim to his wandering hands.

His free palm grips my thigh and moves my leg to the other side of his hip so I'm straddling him, completely draped over him. With only the barrier of our underwear separating us, his steel cock hits me right where I need him the most, so I bear down, soaking his boxers with my need for him. I rock my hips up and down on his length, desperate mewls rising from my throat.

This is not our first morning dance. For the past two weeks, ever since he fucked my mouth like it was his personal heaven, we always wake up like this—tangled in each other's arms, dishing orgasms like they're the last we'll ever have. We haven't exactly had sex, and despite the horniness craze my pregnancy hormones cloak me in, I've been respectful of his boundaries.

We haven't defined what we are or if this is simply a matter of convenience—I'm horny as a cat in heat because of the baby he put in me, while he needs to prove to himself he can touch a woman intimately if he so chooses to—and we just happen to live together, so it makes sense.

His fingers push my panties aside and dip inside of me. My back arches under the electric currents running through my body at the magical way he fills me up. My palm finds purchase on his ridged, stone-like abs, steadying me. My hips thrash erratically, chasing the promise of ecstasy that is just a breath out of reach. The velvety head of him presses against my clit, and I cry out his name, a beg, a plea for Tatum to take me all the way.

He jack-knifes into a sitting position, his plump lips latch onto my sensitive nipple, and a thousand volcanoes erupt in my body, all spreading with the speed of a wildfire to that special spot inside of me. All it takes is a soft graze of his teeth against my pebbled bud. My eyes scrunch shut against the fireworks exploding behind my eyelids and I'm coming, and coming, and coming, my inner walls clamping tight around the fingers still moving inside of me, in slow, loving thrusts.

"That's it, babe. Give it to me, soak my fucking hand. Give me all your sugar, Cupcake."

We both freeze at the same time, his fingers still inside of my fluttering channel. My eyes spring open, amber gaze melding with his topaz one, a million unspoken words shared between us, but the loudest from him is regret. His lips part, and my stomach tightens with anxiety.

Tatum can make or break us now.

"You smelled of sunshine, forest, and vanilla cupcakes," he murmurs.

"What?" I croak, not expecting those words out of his mouth.

"When I found you on the side of the road, bloodied knees and braided pigtails, your big round eyes sparkling with tears, I picked you up, and you smelled of sunshine, forest, and vanilla cupcakes." He presses his mouth gently to mine, a whisper of a peck, before smiling down at me. "I've called you *Cupcake* in my head ever since."

"Tate," I whisper, my eyes filling with tears. My heart hammers in my chest, and a strange, comforting warmth spreads inside of me as images of a distant memory of Tatum being my hero play inside my mind.

"You were my first crush, Cupcake. So tiny, so trusting, so innocent, and too fucking young at the time," he huffs a self-deprecating laugh.

"You were my first crush, too," I confess. The black of his pupils expands at my words, a flash of possessiveness brightening the thin blue of his irises. I could get lost in them so easily. All the Caribbean seas on their best day in the sun pale in comparison to Tatum's eyes. He is my own clear sky on a hot summer day.

His dark blond eyebrows scrunch together, determination bracketing the sharp lines of his prickly jaw. "I won't allow her to taint that beautiful memory for me."

I rest my forehead against his and breathe him deeply into my lungs. People can only take what we give them. They can only siphon the best parts of us if we let go of them. Tatum is the best part of me, and I'm not willing to let go.

"Then I won't either."

His mouth descends on mine, palm cupping my jaw, angling my head to where he wants me. His tongue, hot and greedy, slips between my parted lips, tangling with mine. Hungry noises escape his throat and I drink them all in. His lips heal and punish, chastise and forgive, bruising over my swollen ones over and over, until I'm a trembling, breathless mess in his arms.

"Tell me you're mine, Cupcake," he begs, his voice gravelly with need and a hint of desperation. "Swear to me you're not leaving me again. Swear you're mine, Maevis."

I lose the fight with my tears. I can't keep them at bay anymore when confronted with the rawness of his feelings, with the grit of his kiss, and the bruising hold he has on me as if afraid I'll vanish from his reach at any given second.

"I swear, Tatum," I sob.

"Swear that regardless of what happens a few hours from now, you're standing tall and proud by my side. Promise me, Maevis. Vow to me you'll always have me."

"I vow myself to you, Tatum," I promise solemnly, meaning every word with every cell in me. "I promise to always stand strong and proud by your side. You're mine to support, mine to love, mine to have." His hips thrust upward, hitting my heated center, ripping a mewled plea out of me. "God, do it again. Please, my love, do it again."

Tatum doesn't listen, of course he doesn't. Instead, his mouth leaves mine, my whole body tilting toward him, chasing his lips, but I'm stopped by a firm grip on my shoulder. I don't have time to second guess him or me. He blinks once, slowly, as if in slow motion, and I expect the desire to be snuffed out of his eyes when they open again, but they blaze with determination and want.

"Fuck everything, I'm there," he declares through clenched teeth, a second before my back hits the mattress, my panties are ripped off me, and he fills me to the brim in one smooth, forceful thrust.

A gasp wheezes past my lips at the absolute completion he brings me. Like two puzzle pieces, always meant to be together, we click and form one whole picture. My body sags as elation and relief dance inside of me. My heart beats so fast I fear it's about to jump out of my chest and into the palms of his hands.

"God, sweets, you feel so good. So tight, so right, so fucking perfect for me," he murmurs reverently, his face the most relaxed I've seen in a long time, like he is finally home, finally where he is meant to be.

"Move, my love," I urge him, spreading my thighs as far as they would go, cradling his hips snuggly, opening me up to him to plunder and love.

Tatum doesn't listen, of course he doesn't, because his mission this morning is to drive me out of my fucking mind. Instead, he sits up, his steel cock twitching inside of me, stretching me around him until I'm close to exploding out of my skin and burrowing into him.

His calloused hands caress my hips, pushing the hem of my T-shirt up, higher and higher, until I'm forced to follow him, gripping his shoulders with one hand, and then the other, as he gets rid of the last piece of clothing between us.

And then it's me and him. Him and me. Skin on skin. Connected. Tied together. Whole.

He lays me back down on the bed, palm pressing in the center of my chest, fingers splayed, stroking my pebbled nipples. I thrash and writhe under him, all my nerve centers primed and ready.

"Look at you, my dirty little Cupcake, all spread out like a delicious filthy buffet for me to feast on." My hips buckle under him, taking more of his cock until he bottoms out inside of me. His pink tongue slips out, wetting his lips, a dangerous glint in his eyes. "Ntz, ntz, this is not how we play, sweetness."

Tendrils of excitement and anticipation unfurl in my lower belly, my inner walls fluttering and pulsing around him, coaxing him to come out and play.

Tatum is usually a mountain of a man, steadfast, contained, caged by his own doing. But Tatum unleashed is an avalanche decimating the steadfast mountain. All that endowment, all that strength, the primal force of nature let loose on me and for me only.

Is a heady feeling, so empowering I'm soaring close enough to the Sun to feel the sting of flames on my wings.

His palm lands on the crumpled sheets next to my head, while his other hand cups a heavy breast. His fingers pinch at my nipple, twisting at my oh so sensitive bud until sharp licks of pain are braiding with the molten pleasure traveling through my blood, pooling all between my legs, coating both of us in the evidence of my need for him.

"My, you're a greedy little thing. Are you ready for me to fuck you, sweets? Is that it?"

I open my mouth to beg him to just fucking taking me already, but no words come out when he slides out of me until only the very tip of him remains inside and in the next breath slams into me so hard I feel him everywhere.

The room fills with the music of my screams, his growls and grunts, and skin slapping on skin as he takes me in long and fast thrusts.

My skin tingles, my muscles shake, my breath is trapped inside my lungs—burning me from the inside out. And his cock? His cock is rearranging my whole body to his command and wish. I'm a puppet pulled by her master's strings, bending to his will, willing him to let himself go into me.

My eyes roll to the back of my head when all that restless desire reaches its boiling point inside my body and my lips part on a moan, incoherent words spilling past my lips, begging him to push me over the edge, praying he'll be there to catch me when I land.

His long, strong fingers curl around my neck, and that edge of danger anchors me. The headboard slams into the wall behind us at the same time he impales himself into me with everything he has, fusing everything of him with everything of me, and I'm gone.

The power of my orgasm bulldozes through my every nerve ending, robbing me of all my senses. Muted cries rip from my mouth, my fingers clawing at his shoulders, holding on to that single point of gravity as my very soul leaves my body and attaches to his.

"Fuck me, you're beautiful," Tatum grunts, fusing his mouth to mine. His hips drill relentlessly into my pussy in frenzied, short strokes, his cock angled to rub against my oversensitive clit, ripping another orgasm out of me. His lips part mine, his tongue making love to my mouth as he bucks inside me and stills, spurting months of pent-up love and frustration when he finally gives in and surrenders, the hot evidence of his release spilling out of me.

His forehead touches mine, his heavy breaths washing over my slick skin. The fingers collaring my neck unfurl, sliding down my sweat sheened chest until they reach my belly. Soft, tender caresses feather over the expanse of my rounded stomach.

"I missed you," he whispers. I angle my chin, kissing the underside of his jaw, my palms stroking the width of his tense shoulders.

"I missed you, too."

His lips press against my damp hairline, nuzzling his nose in my tousled strands. "Don't move. I'll go grab something to clean you up."

I'd voice a protest because I don't want to move from this bed. I want us to remain caged in here, wrapped in our protective layer of affection and sex-scented air. But reality doesn't wait. It slams into my chest like an ice-cold gust of wind, and my throat dries instantly.

Beyond our bubble, there's devastation waiting for us.

Chapter Twenty-Three

Tatum

The air in the courtroom is stifling and suffocating. I hook a finger in the collar of my white crisp shirt and pull it away from my neck. My hands are itching to untie the rope Maevis nearly choked me with, but I'm under strict orders to wear it. I see no reason why a shirt and a suit jacket are not perfectly acceptable, but the woman currently sitting next to me kindly—as kindly as an opinionated pregnant woman can—disagreed.

In front of me, just beyond the dark mahogany barrier rail, Paola Townsend and Joshua Craig, the prosecutor, are whispering to each other. The trial is set to start in ten minutes, and I only just met him. Between Lalah and me, we have decided to keep ourselves as far away from the investigation and the proceedings as possible, for the sake of our mental health.

Any communication was done through Townsend and Townsend only.

Now, I don't feel like this was such a good idea. Craig doesn't look much older than me, and the arrogant set of his mouth and the sarcastic twinkle in his black eyes scream fuckboy to me. He didn't even bat an eyelash when we asked Paola to do all the talking for us. His message to us was, "I'll get it done."

Maybe we should have looked more into him, done our homework. Not that it would've changed much. In a county as small as ours where the most that happens are petty crimes, there aren't prosecutors to choose from. You get who you get and hope for the best. All we know is that he moved from New York City about six months ago and that he's vicious. What that says about him, fucked if I'm the best person to judge.

Dressed in a black suit that screams money and entitlement, his dark hair gelled back and away from his forehead, he sits tall and relaxed, like he's the one presiding over this courtroom.

He turns his head and looks straight into my eyes, his mouth quirking at a corner. The arrogance in him wouldn't be more evident if he had *smug bastard* tattooed to his forehead. As if able to read the thoughts running through my head, he fucking winks at me before pushing to his feet.

Both my forearms are gripped in what feels like sharpened steel. Maevis leans into me and whispers, "The witch is here."

Lalah, seated to my right in between me and Cole, is vibrating in her seat. I can practically taste the anger and animosity wafting out of her. Oh, Maevis is angry, too, but she's far more concerned with keeping me grounded and calm than with glaring daggers at Amanda's head.

I'm surprisingly relaxed. I'd be even more so if it weren't for the fucking tie around my neck. Making love to Maevis settled the restlessness in me. I'm feeling like a missing part has been returned and made me whole once again. We still need to put some cards on the table and discuss our relationship. I'm not willing to repeat the same fucking mistakes we made just months before.

Maevis is my endgame.

But I also can't afford to lose my head again, to jump all in without knowing there's a soft place to land. I'm desperately in love with her, but I refuse to allow myself to be blindsided again.

There are far too many people in my life that count on me to be able to function and remain standing. And I know it deep in my gut, if Maevis leaves me again and I have absolutely no contingency for it, she might as well rip my fucking heart out of my chest and feed it to Astrum for all that'll be left of me.

Our baby also plays an equally important part in my self-imposed cautiousness. My child deserves the very best of me. As much as I long to have a family where she—because I'm goddamned convinced a baby girl is cooking in Maevis's oven—will have her parents together and grow up seeing the right way a woman is to be cherished and loved, I need to make sure first that her father remains sane enough to show up for her every day.

"All rise, the Honorable Judge Trenton presiding." The bailiff's voice booms inside the four walls of the courtroom and, as one, we all push to our feet.

Judge Trenton walks quickly to her bench, black robes floating behind her. Her grayed hair has no strands out of place, tightly constrained into a neat bun at the back of her neck. She pauses by her seat, looking around the audience. Her eyes betray nothing, no emotions showing on her weathered face. She lifts her palm in the air, and with a flourish of her wrist, invites us all to sit.

Her fingers flicker through the thick glossier sitting on the dark surface of her bench, her eyes studying intently the paperwork in front of her.

"Counselors, please approach," Judge Trenton says, her gaze settling first on Craig, then flicking to the far-right side of the courtroom where the witch and her posh lawyer are sitting.

Both attorneys make their way to the judge's bench, and when her eyes settle on me, my stomach ties up in knots—the first sign of uneasiness I've felt all morning—and my hands fist in my lap. But I need not worry. Both Maevis and Lalah slip their palms into mine, pry my fists open, and intertwine their fingers with mine.

Their show of support soothes the unease swirling in my gut, and certainty settles inside of me. Regardless of what the judge will rule, I know my friends and family have my back. And they all made it a point to show up here for me today. My parents, my sisters, Lalah, Cole, Blake, Jackson, Annalise, even Drake and Maddox are seated somewhere behind me.

"Ladies and gentlemen of the jury, my name is Joshua Craig, and I am representing the state in the case against Mrs. Stranton. These are the charges being brought forward as defined by the State of Montana's Code, title forty-five, chapter five: criminal possession of dangerous drugs; partner assault against Mrs. Stranton's ex-husband, Mr. Carter; criminal endangerment, and finally, aggravated sexual intercourse without consent."

He strides intently in front of the jury box, not sparing the witch even a single look. I don't plan to either, so I keep my eyes firmly affixed to the empty witness stand, drowning out everything around me, except Maevis's hand in mine and the sickening thought of having to stand in that box, being grilled by Craig and the posh asshole representing Amanda soon.

Mae's pointy elbow hits me square in the ribs, and I have to bite the inside of my cheek to stop the curse at the tip of my tongue from letting loose. But her warning is enough to get my mind back to the courtroom.

"The prosecution invites the defendant, Mrs. Straton, to take the stand as their first witness," Craig booms.

Amanda sashays to the witness box, her white dress swishing around her calves. If you googled *meekness* and *pure fucking bullshit* together, an image of her as she looks right now would show up in your search engine. Her platinum blonde hair is down on her shoulders in soft waves, barely a lick of makeup on her face. There's absolute zero trace of the demon hiding under the saint façade she's showing all of us.

"Please raise your right hand," the judge tells her in the same matter-of-fact tone she spoke in all morning. When Amanda does as she's told, the judge continues, "Do you solemnly swear that the testimony you are about to give is the truth, the whole truth, and nothing but the truth?"

"I swear, Your Honor," she answers in a soft tone I've never once heard come out of that venomous mouth before.

"Please state your full name for the court," Craig addresses her, his tone as soft as hers, like they're having a private conversation, and the witch is a delicate doll that could break at the smallest touch.

My knee is bouncing up and down, restlessness coursing through me. My blood is boiling just at the sight of her. I'm fucking worried I won't be able to just sit through her whole testimony and not lash out.

"Amanda Marie Carter-Straton," she replies, and my eyes fly to her, my stomach heaving with the hit I take at hearing that she kept my fucking last name. She maintains the same innocent expression, but the glint of malice flashing over her face is not lost on me.

How the fuck didn't I know until now that she kept my name?

"Breathe, my love," Maevis whispers in my ear, her palm rubbing the back of mine tenderly.

"What is your relationship with Mr. Carter, Mrs. Carter-Straton?" Craig asks, and I force myself to pay attention to his questions instead of giving in to the nausea burning in my throat.

"Tatum is my ex-husband," she replies, her dainty hand wiping at invisible tears at the corner of her eyes.

Conniving, lying bitch.

"Can you explain to the jury what led to your divorce?" Craig prompts her.

"Objection, Your Honor. The question is irrelevant to the case," the posh asshole she has for a lawyer protests.

"Counselor Craig?" asks the judge.

"Just trying to establish the grounds of their present relationship, Your Honor." He smiles sheepishly, and, for a second, I'm taken aback at the innocence on his face. This man is a fucking wolf in sheep's clothes.

"Overruled. I'd like to hear what the witness has to say. In your opening statement, you claimed Mr. Carter sought your client that night, so I'm interested to know the exact nature of their relationship. Answer the question, Mrs. Carter-Straton."

She closes her eyes, and I swear to god her skin is about to crack under the profound sadness she displays. Give the woman a fucking Oscar for best performance of a dramatic act. A wistful smile plays on her lips as she answers.

"We married young, Counselor. Far too young to understand the intricacies of married life and what a strain him being deployed for so long would be for our lives." She brushes her fingers over the sleeve of her dress before placing her hands on the wooden desk in front of her. Her wedding ring sparkles under the white light of the courtroom, but my eyes aren't drawn to her ring finger. No, instead they hook onto her middle finger, where she wears the wedding ring I gave her.

I heave a breath and nearly double over when my stomach does absolutely all it can to empty its contents on the dark hardwood floor under my feet.

"We decided life on base wasn't for me. I had no education apart from high school. I needed to do something with my life. And so, together, we agreed it would be best if I returned home and went to college," she continues.

If by agreeing together, she means she informed me as soon as I returned from my first mission that she's bored and moving home, sure, we agreed.

"It all went well for the first year. He'd call me whenever he could while he was away, he'd come home between deployments. We were happy," she sighs, once again blotting at her eyes with a fucking handkerchief. "It all changed during the following year. He called less, the visits few and far between. When he did visit and call, it was always fights and jealousy. He didn't like that I was going to study groups where it was a mix of men and women, he didn't like the way I dressed, and threatened to stop paying for my college and the apartment we rented."

She starts crying in earnest now.

And I'm about to explode out of my chair and fucking throttle her. It's the same smoke and mirrors she played during our divorce proceedings. I always fucking encouraged her to go out, to live her life, never once raised my fucking voice at her or been jealous.

"God, the fucking lies out of that woman's mouth," Lalah gasps.

Cole shushes her with a finger on her lips, amusement coating his tone when he tells her, "Keep quiet, Supernova, or you'll get us thrown in jail for disrupting the court."

"In my last year of college, I got an internship at my now husband's company. I found myself working longer and longer hours, especially when Tatum was at home. I was afraid to be alone with him. I was afraid to share the same space with him. Eric, my now husband, found me sleeping in the breakroom one morning after a particularly painful fight I had with Tatum."

My mind is scrambling now, trying to remember any fight or disagreement we had, and coming up empty. *Where the fuck is she coming with this bullshit?*

"I broke down," she cries, "and told him everything that was going on at home. Being the kind man that he is, he helped me by giving me a paid job, so I wouldn't have to rely on Tatum and his moods. Of course, I fell for Eric. Who wouldn't fall for a good and kind man who takes care of you and protects you, when all you had at home was fear and shouting."

"Who filed for divorce, Mrs. Carter-Straton?" Craig cuts through her woe-is-me story.

She blanches, the crocodile tears on her face drying abruptly. Her chin juts in the air defiantly, her meek person act faltering for a breath until she remembers herself.

"Tatum did," she mutters.

"Why didn't you?" he retorts.

"Objection, Your Honor. Relevancy," her lawyer jumps to his feet.

"Overruled, Counselor Garrison. I, too, want to know why the defendant didn't file for divorce herself since, according to her own words, she had the support she needed. Answer the question, Mrs. Carter-Straton."

"I was afraid, Your Honor," Amanda answers, her voice cracking as if expecting me to fly out of my seat and rip her apart. And I'm tempted, oh, so fucking tempted. "I told Tatum during one of the rare times he bothered to call me that I thought we should separate; to take some time apart and consider where we see our lives going. He exploded in anger, spewing threats to me, calling me a whore, swearing he would kill any man that dared touch me."

"Excuse me, Mrs. Carter-Straton. I seem to have trouble following here," Craig says, his shoulders rising and falling on a sheepish shrug. "Please, can you confirm the following for me... You were too afraid to file for divorce because Mr. Carter threatened to kill any man touching you, and yet, you went ahead and not just entered into an extramarital affair with Mr. Straton, but ended up engaged to him while still married to the husband you feared."

Amanda's head rears back as if Joshua slapped her, the corners of her eyes crinkling with annoyance. "Mr. Craig, you must understand..." she pleads, but he's having none of it.

"It's a yes or no question, Mrs. Carter-Straton," he pushes, none of the friendliness he displayed so far to be seen.

"W-well, y-yes, but..." she stammers.

"Thank you, I think I understand now. There's no need to elaborate any further. But, since we're on the subject, please, tell us why did you keep Mr. Carter's last name after your divorce?"

"He was my husband, I loved him..." she wails, but I see the judge rolling her eyes at the periphery of my vision.

"And Mr. Straton must really love you. I know I personally would be offended if the woman I'm saving from a bad marriage and marrying myself would insist on keeping *his* name. But what do I know? I'm a single man." He laughs then, a self-deprecating chuckle, and I'm nearly certain the bitch and the prosecutor should split that fucking Oscar.

"Objection, Your Honor. Prosecution is leading the jury."

"Sustained. Mr. Craig, please keep your opinions to yourself," the judge says, and a smile plays at the corner of my lips. Despite the objection, Craig got what he wanted—exposing her inconsistencies and her fake victim demeanor.

"She's a fucking disgrace to all victims of domestic violence," Lalah swears under her breath, and all of us are nodding our heads in unison. She's not wrong. There are so many people out there suffering at the hands of their spouses, called liars by those around them when they get the courage to speak up because so many others have made a lying spectacle of themselves posing as victims, exactly like Amanda is doing now.

"Apologies, Your Honor, just trying to work things out in my head. Tell me, Mrs. Straton... Oh, you don't mind if I drop the *Carter*, do you?" he asks, the sarcasm heavy in his words, but doesn't wait for her to answer before firing his next question. "In your own words, how are things between you and your ex-husband now? Are you friendly, on speaking terms, avoiding each other?"

"Objection, Your Honor. The prosecution is leading the witness," the posh asshole interrupts again.

"Sustained. Rephrase or skip the question, Counselor," the judge sighs, a hint of annoyance in her voice, which doesn't bode well if she's already losing her patience.

"Once again, apologies, Your Honor. Mrs. Straton, in your own words, how would you describe the current relationship with our ex-husband?"

"We don't have one, Mr. Craig. He'll sometimes call me, especially when he's drunk, or if we happen to be in the same place, he'll seek me out, but I can't say we have a relationship."

What the fuck?

"Why didn't you take a restraining order against him, if he's bothering you?" he presses, and her fingers twitch on the bench, crumpling the white fabric she's clutching at.

"I changed my number several times," she replies in a haughty tone. "He always seems to find it. It's better that I know when he calls or messages so I can ignore it. I didn't consider a restraining order."

"It seems he did think one was necessary," he pauses then, head turned to look at me, a smug smirk on his face. "Against you."

"Objection, Your Honor. Prosecution is twisting the facts. Mr. Carter only took a restraining order after the incident, not before."

"Sustained. Mr. Craig, please keep to the facts," the judge admonishes.

"I was getting there, Your Honor. But dear Mr. Garrison is full of *objections*. Perhaps he shouldn't have skipped the yogurt in his breakfast this morning. I heard it's an excellent diuretic," the arrogant bastard retorts, and I barely keep a snort contained. He'll either win this no questions asked, or he'll have us thrown out of the courtroom if he keeps the bullshit going.

"Counselor…" the judge trails off, shaking her head in disbelief. "Please, refrain from making inappropriate comments moving forward. Do you have any more questions for your witness?"

"Yes, I do, Your Honor." He turns to Amanda once again, placing his palms on the wooden bench, his whole back tensing. "What happened the night of December twelfth, Mrs. Straton?" he booms.

Her hand flutters to her neck, clutching at invisible pearls. I wish she'd choke instead with the tie choking me right now. My stomach knots and my heart pounds against my rib cage. My hairline itches with the sweat peppering my forehead and the back of my neck. I'm not ready to hear her side. I remember close to nothing. I have no way to know if what she's saying is the truth or not.

Amanda's wicked eyes flicker to me, her shoulders slump, her fingers fidget at the collar of her dress. But her eyes, her eyes speak the truth. She's ready to bury me. She's ready to get all her poisoned darts and stab them as deep as she can get them into my heart.

"I met some friends for drinks at JC's Pour. They both live in Lost Hope and didn't feel like driving to Billings. Oh, how I wish they had," she sighs, patting her chest with her palm. "We were at one of the standing-up tables, at the side of the dance floor, when Tatum came in. As soon as he started dancing, his eyes found mine," she says, her gaze darting to me, then back to the wooden desk, "and he scowled at me. I turned away, of course. I was there to have a nice evening with my friends, not to get into a sparring match with a jealous Tatum."

She visibly deflates then, making herself small and subdued. If I didn't know the kind of evil that lives inside of her, I'd buy her act. I draw a deep breath into my lungs, trying to keep myself as still as possible, although there's nothing I can do about my bouncing knee. I have to expel somehow all the nervous energy swirling inside of me.

As if feeling I'm about to be ripped apart, both Maevis and Lalah move closer to me, their fingers tightening around mine. A heavy hand cups my shoulder from behind. I turn my head around and see my father giving me an encouraging smile. Acknowledging his support with a tip of my chin, I turn back around to watch the shitshow happening at the front of the courtroom.

"One of my friends left for the bathroom," she continues, but Craig cuts her off.

"State the name of the friends you were with that night for the court, please."

"Oh, uhm, sure. Maddison Brown and Emma Denvers," she clarifies.

"Which one of them left, Mrs. Straton?" Craig presses, the annoyance in his voice thick.

"Emma did. Maddison and I queued at the bar to get more drinks, and Tatum messaged me to meet him at the Gents' urgently."

"Can you share with the court the phone number from which Mr. Carter messaged you?"

I'm surprised when she starts rattling my phone number. By how Maevis jolts next to me, she's just as surprised.

"Thank you, Mrs. Straton, you're incredibly helpful. Please continue with what happened that night."

"So I went looking for him. As soon as I stepped into the bathroom, he jumped on me, kissed me, and hugged me to him. I tried to push him away, but there was no use. I already had a few drinks by that time, and what can I do against a man, especially in my inebriated state?"

Maevis and Lalah's gasps of outrage explode in the quiet courtroom.

Chapter Twenty-Four

Tatum

I can't stop it now. I double over, slapping a palm over my mouth to try and keep the contents of my stomach inside of me. Sour acid burns my tongue, and I inhale sharply through my nose. A warm palm rubs soothing circles between my shoulder blades, until I feel the nausea recede and I'm once again able to sit up straight.

Maevis uncaps a bottle of water and passes it to me. I gulp at it like I haven't drunk water in months until the acidic burn inside my mouth washes out.

"You doin' okay there, Mr. Carter?" Craig asks, and I want to chuck the empty bottle at his head for drawing attention to my moment of weakness. Instead, I just give him a sharp nod, and take Mae's hand into mine, pressing a kiss to her fingers, breathing in her scent of vanilla and home that always manages to calm me down.

"You were saying, Mrs. Straton?"

I keep my eyes on my lap, watching my fingers play around with Maevis's soft hand. I refuse to look at the vile bitch again. Can't believe she's going as far as saying I sexually assaulted her. But at the same time, why am I surprised, I don't know. I should've learned by now, there's nothing this caricature of a human wouldn't do to ensure she's always emerging the victor.

"He asked me to meet him in the hotel across the street. I refused at first, but he was crazed, manic. He fell to his knees begging me to go," she cries, once more dabbing her eyes with the crumpled material in her hand. "I agreed, thinking I'd go meet him and avoid making a scene in the bar, and explain to him that he can't do this to me anymore, that he needs to learn to let me go."

"And did you?"

"Sorry, what?"

"Jesus Christ, look at her being all confused. Of course, you are you fucking bitch, you're lying through your veneered teeth like the rotten tomato you are," Lalah hisses, and Cole covers her mouth with his palm when the judge's head swivels in our direction.

"For the love of God, Supernova. Keep it together, baby," he pleads.

"Did you tell Mr. Carter to leave you alone, Mrs. Straton?" Craig asks, over-enunciating every word, like he's speaking to a child.

"I didn't get there. As soon as I got to the room, he was on me again, kissing me, touching me. As I said, I already had a few drinks in. He unbuckled his belt, unzipped his jeans, and h-he, he forced me to pleasure him with my mouth," she sobs.

Maevis's short nails cut into the skin of my palm at Amanda's words. My whole body is shaking in disbelief. I'm ready to shoot to my feet and shout as loud as my lungs would let me what a filthy liar she is, but I know it wouldn't win me any points.

"What happened after?" Craig asks, his voice sharp and unforgiving.

"He pulled me into bed with him and went to sleep. I waited until I was sure he wouldn't wake up, and then I left."

"Where did you go after, Mrs. Straton?"

"I-I, uhm, I drove home."

"I see. Even though you were drunk enough to not be able to fight Mr. Carter off, you got behind the wheel and drove all the way to Billings?"

"I was scared he'd come after me. What would you have had me do?" she cries out in outrage.

"Call the police, Mrs. Straton. I would've called 911 as soon as I was safe and secure in my car."

"Objection, Your Ho..."

"Oh, save it for the evidence, Garrison. Don't waste your objections on this," Craig cuts him off, and the derision in his tone has me lifting my eyes from where they are firmly affixed to my lap, and look at him.

He strides decisively in front of the jury, a screen flickering to life behind the box where the twelve jurors are sitting.

"Esteemed jury, you've now heard Mrs. Straton's version of the events of the night of December twelfth. She's made quite a few interesting points in her recount, for which I'd like to present the prosecution's evidence."

He turns back to Amanda, spreading his arms wide, a wolfish smile on his face. I could swear his black eyes are twinkling in anticipation of the pain he's about to rain down on her.

"Mrs. Straton, since your council was far too busy objecting to my questions, I'm doing you a kindness and reminding you that lying under oath is a felony. Is there anything about your testimony you would like to change?"

"I didn't lie, you weasel," she hisses.

"Takes one to know one," shouts someone from behind me, and the whole gallery explodes in curses and yells.

The bang of the judge's gavel travels through the chaos like a lightning strike. "ORDER," she shouts and, like a switch flipping, the chaos mutes in an instant.

"Next time anyone speaks without being given permission, they'll be held in contempt of the court," Judge Trenton decrees in a sharp tone before turning to look at the venomous bitch. "Mrs. Straton, you will refrain from name calling. Counselor Craig is right. If you are found lying under oath, the consequences will be severe."

"I didn't lie, Your Honor."

Craig claps his palms once, walking back to the jurors. "There you have it, ladies and gentlemen. To that respect, I'd like to present to you an extract of Mr. Carter's phone. It contains any calls he has ever made or received, as well as text messages. Mrs. Straton, you'll find the same in the folder inside your desk. Please, study it."

The screen on the far wall shows the same extract he presented to the jurors, with five different phone numbers circled in red.

"Mr. Carter has received over one hundred calls and over two hundred text messages from these five numbers from June of last year to December. There is not a single outgoing instance in the whole document to any of those five numbers." He shrugs now, the glee evident in his tone. "And that's including the twelfth of December."

The prosecutor turns to face me, his eyes determined and serious, not sparing Amanda a single glance as he addresses her, "Mrs. Straton, please tell us which of those five numbers belongs to you."

I can't help but look at her now. Since I know well and good that all five numbers are hers. She's white as a sheet, her eyes open wide, glaring daggers at her lawyer.

"Mrs. Straton, anytime today," the judge urges her.

"A-all of them, Your Honor."

"Please explain to the jurors why the extract shows you contacting him multiple times, and him never at all." Joshua smiles.

"I-I don't know. He must have messed with it somehow, deleted the messages and the calls," she stutters.

"Except I requested the document directly from his carrier, Mrs. Straton. I'm no phone expert, but even I know that even if I delete text messages from my phone, the entry on the extract cannot be modified." He walks to the witness stand, resting his elbow casually on the rounded edge as if they're best of friends having a catch-up.

"I don't know what to say…"

"How about the truth?" Craig cuts her off.

"Objection, Your Honor. Prosecution is harassing the witness," Garrison jumps to his feet, the side of his face that I can see from here red and blotchy.

"Overruled. And I'd like to remind the witness *again* that she is under oath, and lies to this court would not be tolerated."

"Why did you meet Mr. Carter in the bathroom, Mrs. Straton? There was no request from him for you to meet him there."

"Yes, yes, there was. It was the way he looked at me when he was dancing. His eyes practically begged me to go to him," she cries, her fist hitting the wooden bench.

"His *eyes* were begging you? What are my eyes saying now, Mrs. Straton? Can you read mine, too?" He stares at her for a good thirty seconds, none of them saying anything, until his shoulder lifts and drops in a quick movement. "Eh, I guess not. That's a pity."

He turns again to the jurors, his whole back resting casually against the stand, completely dismissing Amanda.

"I'll tell you what happened that night. Some of Mr. Carter's friends went to the bar to order drinks. He saw his girlfriend, Maevis Barlowe, and his friend, Alana McAdams, going to the restrooms, and he followed his girlfriend. On the way there, he was stopped by a waitress, who passed him an open beer bottle, claiming Mr. Hayes bought the drink for him." He pauses then and looks around the courtroom.

"Why am I telling you all this? Why don't we let Mr. Carter tell you what happened that night from the little that he remembers?" Craig walks back to his desk, picking up his laptop, fiddling around with some cables before a massive screen in the corner of the room turns on, and an image of me in Maddox's office flickers to life.

"You get to hear the version of events exactly as it was reported by Mr. Carter the night after the incident. In order to preserve Mr. Carter's dignity and care for his mental health, I am requesting, Your Honor, that he isn't made to sit through the next portion of the trial."

He points at me then before turning back to the jurors. "The woman in the witness stand put Mr. Carter through hell. And I'm here to prove to you beyond any reasonable doubt that she had intent and purpose. Mrs. Straton's actions from that night didn't only harm Mr. Carter, but Miss Emma Denvers, too, who ended up hospitalized after overdosing on the same drugs that were slipped into his drink, but that were meant for another person."

Although he is with his back to us, his reflection glints on one of the dark screens, and I see him placing his palm in the middle of his chest.

"Mrs. Straton sat in that witness box for the past hour and lied to our faces about the events of that night. She posed in front of us as a victim, disrespecting and making a mockery of every single person that had to suffer through domestic violence or sexual assault," he grits, pointing behind him to where Amanda sits like a statue, frozen and pale.

"In her own words, which I'll show after recess, she told Miss Brown and Miss Denvers, just days before the incident, 'I don't see why I should let him be happy without me'. And that, ladies and gentlemen of the jury, should tell you everything you need to know."

"Thank you, Counselor Craig. We'll take a short break for lunch, and we'll reconvene in an hour," the judge says in a loud voice before turning her eyes on me. Where no emotions could be seen before, her eyes are now filled with empathy, downturned at the corners, crowfeet etched deep into her skin. "Mr. Carter, you're excused for the rest of the trial, unless imperative to be called to the witness stand. I shall hope to see you at the ruling."

The loud bang of the gavel against wood reverberates through the courtroom like a shotgun, and the gallery explodes into chaos.

Chapter Twenty-Five

Maevis

The trial drags on for what feels like centuries, when it's only really been three days. One by one, we've all been called to testify. Craig has left absolutely no stone unturned. As long as it brings Tatum the justice he deserves, let him turn the whole damn mountain range upside down. Paola messaged earlier to let us know the jurors have retreated for deliberation and it's all a waiting game now.

I'm desperate to put this entire ordeal behind us. Tatum is, understandably, withdrawn and morose. It was a hard blow for him to sit there during the first day and hear that depraved woman spit lie after lie after lie. I simply can't understand how someone can be so heinous, so rotten to the very marrow of their bones.

We all grew up together. Well, I was always on the outside. Being two years younger than them and a *geek* definitely didn't have me rolling in their circles. But Amanda was evil then, and only grew more malicious in time.

Tatum is blaming himself for not figuring out how vicious she was sooner, for not doing anything about it. I guess, my advantage for being on the outside was seeing what he couldn't. There was no way for Tate to see the true extent of her malice because she kept herself contained around him, and then made a one-hundred-and-eighty turn and rained down all that darkness on him.

He sighs in his sleep, and my eyes dart to my lap, where his face is nuzzled to my belly, lips pressed just below my belly button. I run my fingers through his unruly hair, letting the silk of the longer strands slip through them, then start over again.

I gently trace with my thumb the dark bags under his eyes. He's barely slept in the past few days. By now, he's sure to know every hairline crack of the ceiling, every imperfection in the layers of paint in my bedroom. He's watched over me every night, making sure at least I get some shut-eye, but even when I did, the restlessness bubbling just under the surface of his skin seeped into me, chasing me in my dreams.

I wish I knew the perfect way to make it all better for him. I wish it were as easy as kissing away all his pains and hurts. All I can do instead is hold him, show up every day for him, and let him deal with the turmoil in his own time.

I jolt when something hits the walls of my stomach from the inside, my eyes moving from his face to my belly. Butterflies swarm inside of me when a lump forms near Tatum's cheeks. I'm both elated and horrified, to be honest.

All I've heard about baby kicks is how magical they are. But they don't look magical. My belly looks like it's about to crack open and have an alien crawl out of it. I bite my bottom lip to suppress the laugh bubbling out of my throat, as an image from *Aliens* pops into my head. That'll scar the man sleeping with his head on my lap for life.

Another kick in my lower belly has him grumble, his lips smacking against the cotton of my yellow maternity dress. "Babe, five more minutes, please," he mumbles, his voice gravelly and oh, so hot. The low vibrations travel through me, making me all achy for him.

Sex has, of course, been out of the question for the past days. Tatum's taking more showers than usual, going through the hot water tank at least five times a day. I understand what he's doing. The trial is making him relive those days immediately after everything went down, and so he's trying to scrub away her taint from his skin.

Understanding doesn't make me worry less, though.

A third kick comes and this time it meets his nose. His eyebrows furrow, forming tiny indents between them. "God, sweets, what's gotten into you?" he hisses, just in time for the fourth one to hit him in the chin. I can't stop the laughter now. It spills from my lips until my whole body is shaking, and I'm wheezing for air.

I shriek when my dress is ripped away from me, the chill in the room making my skin pepper in goosebumps. Tatum is kneeling on the hardwood floor in front of me, the sleep in his bloodshot eyes slowly chased away by awe.

His warm, large palms cup my belly on either side, and he bends his neck until he's nose to belly button, blue irises scanning the expanse of my rounded stomach.

"You, little troublemaker," he whispers reverently, caressing my skin with his thumbs and being rewarded with another bump against his fingertips. "You woke Daddy up from sleep, baby girl." His lips press against the place our baby pushes from inside, as if reacting to his words and being drawn to him.

"I can't wait to meet you, Mini-Muffin," he tells my belly like our child inside of me is actually able to understand him. "Can't wait for the day I get to hold you, and read you good night stories, and play with you. I haven't even seen you yet, and I miss you already."

I don't bother wiping away the tears pouring down my cheeks. For once, these are not tears of devastation, but pure, utter happiness.

"Be good to your mommy, babycakes, and don't give her too much grief, alright? She's working hard to grow you healthy and strong," he murmurs, peppering kisses all around my belly button, chasing the little kicks and jolts around the expanse of my stomach with his mouth. His right hand trails on my belly until it stops splayed out in the center. "Give Daddy a belly-five," he says. A smile so wide takes over his face, the elusive dimple pops in his right cheek. "Well done, Mini-Muffin. You're Daddy's girl, aren't you?"

And that's me done for.

My whole body floods with warmth, my heart sputtering in my chest as it inundates with all the love I have for this man. This strong, kind, extraordinary man I'm so fucking lucky to have in my life.

My breath hitches in my lungs, trying to make room for all the feelings that battle inside of me. I don't want to keep quiet; I want to shout from the fucking rooftops how much I love him.

I must have made a sound because his eyes shoot up to mine, and in a second, the bright calm-blue of his irises is swallowed down by the darkness of his expanding pupils. A crackle of danger ripples through the air between us, the room around us charging with desire and unspoken promises.

His hands move from my belly to my hips, gripping tightly onto me. "Come 'ere," he grunts, sliding me over the velvet cover of the sofa and down to his lap. A squeak escapes my lips when my slick pussy touches the steel of his cock caged by the soft fabric of his sweatpants, but it's silenced quickly by his mouth hungrily descending on mine.

His lips coax mine open, low grunts and quiet growls escaping his throat. I drink them in, holding them locked for safekeeping, as his tongue slips inside my mouth, exploring every part of me with abandon and need.

His fingers grip me tighter, rocking me up and down on his hard length, the musky scent of my arousal filling the space between us. My nipples pebble against the soft cotton of his tank, a swirl of annoyance rising in my veins. I need to feel his inked skin against mine. I need to have his strength burrow inside of me and the brunt of direct contact.

But Tatum being Tatum, anticipates my every want and, in a swift move, he rips the frustrating piece of material over his head and bands a stone-like arm around my waist as he rises to his knees. A mewl of protests sounds in the room, clawing out of my throat at the loss of his cock against my soaked pussy when his hips move away from me.

"Patience, you greedy girl, I've got you," he chastises, smacking my ass with his free hand before working it in between us, shoving those pesky sweatpants down his shapely thighs. His cock springs free, thick and proud, slapping against my belly, and my own hips buckle against thin air, seeking him out.

He sits down on his calves, and my arms hook around his neck, holding on to him while he lifts me up with a bruising grip. The smooth head of his cock aligns with my dripping entrance, and in one sharp thrust of his hips, I sheath half his length like I was made for him.

Holding onto his wide, inked shoulders for leverage, I bounce up and down on him, feeling him deeper inside of me, each and every time.

"God, you fill me up so good," I cry out as I work myself onto him, my orgasm just out of reach.

Tatum feels my frustration and a dark chuckle vibrates out of his chest. His palms still my movements, and my tightly shut eyes spring open to glare at him. "Sweets," he murmurs, "trust me to give you what you need?"

His words soften me, the building frustration in my core ebbing, and I whisper a yes in return. He taps my thigh, and that's the sign that he wants me to stand. And so I do, slowly lifting myself off his length, my pussy fluttering around him in protest, unwilling to let go.

When I'm finally up on shaky legs and look down at him, he gives me a lazy, drunk out smile and smacks a kiss against my throbbing clit that sends electric shocks through my limbs.

"Turn around, sugar," Tate orders, his palms already on my waist, spinning me to where he wants me, pulling me back down onto his lap. He rubs his cock between my swollen lips, coating himself in all my desire for him. "Arch your back," he barks, and I'm quick to oblige, my heavy breasts jutting forward, my ass pressing into the hard ridges of his lower abs.

"That's my good girl," he praises, his fingers trailing the side of my waist up to my breasts, cupping them, testing their weight, teasing my tight nipples between his rough fingertips. I know, I know he wants me to keep still and let him explore, but the fire he stokes inside my core has my hips writhing against him and my pussy throbbing for him.

Tatum ignores the increased vexation mounting inside of me, stopping the slow, sweet torture he inflicts on my breasts. He moves his hands to my arms instead, pulling them back and around his neck.

He knows true and well what he's doing.

My back is arched to its very limits, and I can't move, not unless he wants me to. "Hold on to me, Cupcake," he commands, trailing open-mouthed kisses along my neck that have my lower belly clenching and quivering with need.

His palms fasten to my inner thighs, spreading me open, my knees on either side of him. I'm completely at his mercy, his doll to use, his plaything. A scream rips out of me when he plunges his cock as deep as he can go. My tits bounce against his momentum, my ass slapping against his rock-hard hips.

"That's it, sweets. Take it all," he praises, teeth sinking into the sensitive flesh of my neck. I feel him everywhere. He is all hard thrusts, drilling himself into my body, into the very core of my being. I feel his hands everywhere, clawing at my hips, kneading my breasts, plucking at my nipples, thrumming my charged-up clit, and I'm done.

I'm falling and flying and soaring and crashing onto him.

My fingers pull at the damp hair of his nape as I lose myself completely to all that he is, to the pleasure and the pain swirling inside of my body. He has no magnanimity for me, no reprieve, but continues to fuck himself into me in frenzied, wild strokes, building up the orgasm destroying the last of my sanity.

"Tatum," I cry out when his fingers pinch my clit and my nipple at the same time. The nuclear explosion contained in me erupts, blowing me into smithereens as he stills inside my drenched, quivering channel, his arms coiling around my waist, pulling me to his chest.

My vision turns black. My body sags against him. My arms falling limply at my sides. And he pours himself inside of me, hot ropes of lust, love, and pleasure dripping between my thighs where we are still joined.

He nuzzles his face in the crook of my neck, his warm breath washing over me, leaving goosebumps in its wake on my overheated skin. "Fuck, Maevis, you'll be the death of me one of these days," he mumbles, his lips tickling my shoulder.

I open my mouth to answer him, but all my energy is depleted. He literally fucked the life out of me. I'm a rag doll with no control over my limbs or any other part of me. That's the only explanation for the exhale that leaves my heaving lungs carrying words with it—words I have no way to stop or swallow down.

"I love you, Tatum Carter."

Chapter Twenty-Six

Tatum

I'm holding on to her with all my might. I'm completely and utterly depleted. My head drops to the crook of her shoulder, and I nuzzle my face against her neck, basking in the glory of this moment just for us, this moment when we're still joined together, and there's no real life to shove us apart. My nose fills with the sweet, comforting scent of vanilla and the heady musk of sex. My lips taste the candied flavor of her, with the salty undertones of the sweat dampening her soft skin. "Fuck, Maevis, you'll be the death of me one of these days."

She's soft in my arms, thoroughly spent, her ample breasts heaving on my forearm, her inner walls still fluttering like crazy around my cock, still gripping me with all their might. A deep exhale leaves her, and with it a breathless, "I love you, Tatum Carter."

I froze solid where I'm kneeling on the hardwood floor in front of the couch. *Did she just...?* My heart sputters in my chest, like empty bubbles of air pop around its walls, altering the rhythm of its beats, guiding them to follow Maevis's song and dance.

My lips part, ready to demand she say those sweet, sweet words again. I need to know she means them, that this is not just the mind-blowing orgasm that shook us both to the core, when I feel her stiffen in my arms, her knees tightening around my thighs, her fingers pushing weakly at me to let go.

"Oh God," she wails. "Please, please, please, let me go."

Now, I may be a man and by design oblivious, but if there's a time in life when you don't let go of a woman is after she fucked you nearly to the brink of death and then gave you your life back by telling you she loves you. For the first time, might I add.

So I do what every man with two neurons left to rub together does: I hug her closer to me with one arm and thrust my rapidly hardening cock inside of her as deep as I can reach.

I fist my free hand into the silk of her hair, tilt her head just enough so that her golden-flecked brown eyes look directly into my blue ones and demand, "Say it again. Don't you dare take it back. Say"—thrust—"It"—thrust—"Again—" thrust.

Sliding inside her slick pussy in a long stroke has her rolling those pretty eyes to the back of her head. Her luscious lips, reddened by my earlier kisses, part.

"Tatum," she moans, her pussy gripping me so hard I can barely move inside of her. My eyes refuse to leave her, even though I fight to keep them open, I'm so pent up for her. I burn with the need of burying myself in her tight, wet heat and never coming up for air. But what I need more, what I desperately crave, are those three little words on her plush lips.

"Say it, Maevis. Don't make me beg, baby," I grit, my jaw so tense, I swear I can hear my teeth grinding together.

She's close to coming again. I feel it in the quiver of her body. I hear it in the mewls spilling out of her beautiful mouth. I see it in the delicate blush pinking up her cheeks and the light shining on me from her eyes, so I shift my hips, forcing her to lean completely against me. I slow my thrusts, from short, sharp plunges, to long strokes from head to root. Currents of pain and ecstasy roll through me, my balls draw up, heavy and full, ready to empty into her as soon as she tells me what I long to hear.

Every inch of me feels every inch of her, every flutter, every spasm, edging her and myself to the point of no return.

"God, Tate, fuck, I love you. I love the living fuck out of you, please," she screams, her sweet surrender the catalyst I need to detonate inside of her, the tingle at the base of my spine turning into an inferno incinerating me on the spot.

My hand moves to where we're one, her slickness coating my fingertips, and I can't contain the groan ripping from my throat when I feel her pretty pussy all stretched out around me, my cock moving in and out of her, her little bundle of nerves throbbing for my touch. A flick of my finger has her fluttering around my shaft, and all it takes is a featherlike rub of my thumb on her needy clit for her to choke my length like a vise, coming with my name on her lips.

And I let go.

I let myself fall, burn, and empty into her again and again and again, until I have nothing left to give and she has nothing left to take.

With the last spark of energy left in me, I hold a trembling Maevis to my chest, and lay us down on the plush rug next to the couch. She whimpers low in her throat when I slip out of her, my hot release coating her creamy thighs, dripping onto my crumpled sweatpants. But fucked if I care about anything that's not kissing the living daylights out of her and confessing my love in return.

Her dark hair fans out, half on the pastel carpet, half on the floor, wild waves of silk hallowing her blissed out, beautiful face. I brace myself on top of Maevis, her legs curled out around mine, my shaky forearms barely supporting me as I loom above her.

"I love you, too, Cupcake," I confess, my voice clear and strong. "I've loved you for what feels like fucking forever." My forehead touches hers, my nose brushing her freckled one, my lips a breath away from her plump mouth. "I love you with everything in me. The dark, the light, the broken and strong, everything in me loves you, Maevis Barlowe."

I feel more than I see the scalding tears falling from her eyes. A relieved sob breaks out, her chest shaking under me, and I bend down even more, kissing the dampness off her cheeks, the downturned corners of her mouth, her trembling chin. My muscles scream in protest, begging me to lie down next to her, but I refuse to budge even one inch, until Maevis gets on the same page and realizes this is it.

She loves me. I love her. This is us.

I let her have her moment. She can have all the moments she needs from now on. I'll be here for every single fucking one of them. I had plenty of time to get used to my feelings for her, even when I held no hope to ever act on them or have them reciprocated, even when I thought our future was ripped out from our grasp and we'd be damned to pass each other on the street with resentment in our eyes and distance in our hearts.

We both ripped apart the bricks of could have, and now we're both building a new foundation for us.

She quiets under me, her tiny body relaxed, her breathing deep and even. A smile tugs at my lips as I take in my sleeping beauty, and I give into my body's urging and lay on my side next to her, finally catching my breath, allowing my heart to return to its normal rhythm.

My palm splays on her belly, tracing circles with my fingertips from her belly button to the apex of her thighs, where I'm reminded of the mess I left behind. As proud as the primal animal in me is at the simple thought of having her marked in my cum, the rational man knows my pride will cost her, so with a pained huff, I extricate myself from where I'm curled up around her and stand.

I pick up my discarded tank and clean myself up first, tucking my spent cock back inside my boxers and rearranging the waistband of the sweats on my hips. I stride down the hallway to the guest bathroom, throwing my top in the laundry basket. Wetting a clean cloth with warm water, I make my way back to a sleeping Maevis, and, crouching at her side, I clean her up with careful swipes, until no trace of our lovemaking is to be found.

My eyebrows furrow in displeasure, but I shake the thought away. Maevis's comfort comes first, my newly found caveman tendencies second. With my arms under her knees and neck, I hoist her up and gently lay her on the sofa, where she'll be more comfortable sleeping. I swipe the wet cloth and her yellow maternity dress—another vestimentary victim to our frenzy—and throw those into the laundry basket too before returning to her.

Slipping behind Maevis, I pull her to my chest and throw a blanket over us, my palm cradling her belly. I can't help but whisper "I love you" in her ear before I let myself fall asleep, a deep and content smile on my lips.

It's not a tiny kick to my face that wakes me up what feels like only ten minutes later. My eyelids are heavy and gritty, like sand was poured inside my eyes as I slept. A groan rises to the surface, followed quickly by a curse, when my phone doesn't stop vibrating inside the pocket of my sweats.

"For fuck's sake," I mumble. My hand, numb with sleep, fumbles under the blanket, trying to reach the goddamn device and throw it as far away from us as it can get. I squint an eye open, and stare at the name on the screen, *Paola Townsend* flashing at me through the bright light.

I connect the call and put the phone to my ear, croaking a "Hello," at her.

"The jury is ready to deliver the verdict. Court is called back into session in one hour. Get here," she barks. My mind struggles to process her words while adrenaline floods my system, my heart slamming against my rib cage.

My fingers tighten around the phone, anxiety curling inside of me. "This is it?" I ask.

"This is it, Tatum. Get here as soon as possible," she says and hangs up.

I let the phone drop from my hand and hear it clutter on the floor a second later. *It's almost over.* This cursed nightmare I've been living in the past five months is about to end. My lungs deflate on a deep exhale, my mind working furiously to get me fully awake and cognizant.

Maevis stirs near me, turning to her back, and her eyes flutter open. Her lips tip up in a sleepy smile, and the sight of her beautiful face and cute freckled nose calms the hurricane threatening to make landfall inside of me. "Who was that?" she whispers.

"Townsend," I tell her, kissing her forehead. "We gotta get to court."

She jumps up so fast, I barely get out of the way before she gives us both a concussion. "Oh my god," she shrieks. "They're ready?"

"They're ready," I confirm.

"Come on, let's go already." She's on her feet, standing above me in all her naked glory, rounded belly front and center, her dark, silken strands falling around her shoulders and over her pert breasts like a mantle.

I bite my fist to stop my cock from stirring in my sweats. One more time, and I'll be chaffed to hell for the next month. Instead, I clasp her outstretched hand with my free one, and let her pull me off the sofa.

She's a flurry of activity, as if she didn't just wake up from the shortest nap in existence, and before I get my bearings, we're showered, dressed, and driving toward the courthouse in Forrest Falls with time to spare.

I guide my truck to a spot as close to the entrance as possible. Regardless of which verdict the jury reached, I want us to be able to leave as soon as possible. I know our friends will want us to have dinner together and dissect the ruling to death, but I know I don't have it in me. All I want once everything is said and done is to be back home with Maevis and let her hold me while we come to terms with the verdict, and hopefully the end of this nightmare.

Killing the engine and pocketing my keys, I turn to the woman who's made it possible for me to get through this week with my sanity intact, and cup her cheek. She smiles at me, her black lashes fluttering, and I close the distance between us, pressing my lips softly against hers.

"Thank you, Mae," I rasp, the emotions swirling inside of me clogging my throat. "Thank you for carrying me through this trial in more ways than one. I love you so damn much."

Her fingers brush gingerly through my hair before caressing the scruff on my jaw. "Thank you for giving me a second chance, Tate. I love you, too." She nuzzles her cheek in my palm, her amber eyes looking intently into mine. "Now, let's go finish this."

I jump out of the truck, then help Maevis out, too. She takes my hand and leads the way inside. She continues to hold my hand when the judge invites the jurors in. Mae's soft palm squeezes mine and doesn't let go when the head juror clears her throat and stands. She smooths her palms over her black blouse, chin in the air, no emotion on her face, no indication of what the verdict might be.

"Your Honor, the jury has reached a verdict. In the case of the state against Mrs. Amanda Straton, the defendant has been found guilty as charged." My heart seizes in my chest at her words, my stomach flipping when all the tension coiled in my muscles drains into the darkened floor of the courtroom. "It is the opinion of this jury that Mrs. Straton's place is firmly behind bars, that she is a danger to society, and guilty to the very marrow of her bones."

"That's bullshit!" Amanda yells, jumping to her feet at the defendant's table. Maevis intertwines her fingers with mine, her thumb rubbing soothing circles on the back of my hand.

"Order," the judge barks, her voice carrying over the commotion. "Counselor Garrison, please see that your client remains quiet and respectful toward this court."

Craig turns his head to me, a crooked smile on his lips, and once again fucking winks. The arrogant asshole got us full circle.

"Thank you, ladies and gentlemen of the court," Judge Trenton says solemnly, her eyes scanning the jurors briefly before shifting to Amanda. "Mrs. Straton, you have been found guilty on all charges by a jury of your peers and will now proceed to sentencing. Does the prosecution have any recommendation for sentencing?"

Craig stands then, shoulders squared, and struts like a fucking peacock from the bench to the middle of the floor.

"Your Honor, based on the evidence presented during the trial, as well as taking into consideration the severity of the charges, the prosecution recommends that Mrs. Straton receive the maximum penalty for each of her charges."

He points at where Amanda sits, fuming in her seat, glaring daggers at her lawyer's head, throwing some my way for good measure, but I don't give a fuck. I'm floating on the goddamn cloud nine. This day could not have gone any better, maybe only if Maevis married me today, right after this fucking trial.

"Mrs. Straton has not shown one ounce of regret throughout the proceedings. If anything, she stood in front of us, swearing to tell the truth and truth only, and instead lied to everyone's faces. She has shown blatant disrespect to this court, our laws, and everyone involved in this trial, as well as made a mockery out of the tragedy far too many women and men live through every single day. The prosecution is firmly convinced that given the opportunity, Mrs. Straton would, without any shame or second thought, continue to inflict harm on those around her."

Craig continues to argue for his recommendation, but I drown him out. It doesn't matter how many years is Amanda locked away. What matters is that justice prevailed, that all the suffering and pain we've gone through these past months weren't for nothing. Regardless of what happens with the heinous bitch now, Maevis and I can put this behind us and welcome our baby into the world without fearing Amanda's poison.

"Oh my fucking god," exhales Sawyer next to me, and hearing my baby sister swear gets my mind back into the courtroom and to the judge now speaking.

"... a cumulative sentence of seventeen years, with the possibility for parole after half the sentence is carried out."

Judge Trenton strikes her gavel against the wooden block of her bench—a sound I'd die a happy man never to hear again—and sends the entire fucking gallery into cheers.

I'm tackled on all sides by hugs and back claps, while all I can do is take the first full breath of air for the first time in four months. The scent of vanilla settles deep into my lungs, right next to my heart that has *Property of Maevis Barlowe* tattooed on it.

Chapter Twenty-Seven

Tatum

My mom was elated when I visited her earlier today. Thank fuck I didn't bring Maevis with me, because my mother would've given away my surprise plans entirely, she was beaming so hard after our conversation. Mae could've easily read the subtitles plastered to my mom's forehead and figured out what I was up to—Sarah Carter may be a ball-buster, but her poker-face is worth shit.

One hurdle down, one to go.

I'm not a believer in gender roles or archaic traditions. The way I see it, men and women are not equal and would never be. And how could that be the case? It's a fucking impossibility. For as big and brawny as men are, without the women in our lives, we'd be lost. There's absolutely nothing a man can do that a woman couldn't if she put her mind to it.

My mother is a shining example of that. Sure, my father is the big, surly ex-Marine able to command respect just by breathing. But the big, surly ex-Marine answers to a higher power, and that higher power is called Sarah Carter, a five-foot-nothing whirlwind of a woman, capable of bulldozing an entire army out of its trenches if she so feels like.

There's absolutely no fucking difference between my parents and the way I am with Maevis. For as much as I like to hit my fists to my chest and declare I'm keeping her protected and taking care of her, she protects and cares for me just the same.

But as much as I don't believe in archaic traditions, I'm still pretty much set on seeing Ronald Barlowe and telling him of my intentions to marry his daughter. Maevis loves her father with all her heart and makes it a point to visit him nearly every day. And since we moved in together, I have accompanied her, too, as often as I can.

I'm aware there are a number of conversations that still need to happen between us. There is still so much trust lost between us and a whole lot to build, but I'm hopeful for the first time in years—hopeful that together will get through to the other side. The happiness side.

When I divorced the heinous bitch, I was certain I'd never marry again. I was certain I'd never have children, either. And now here I am, with a baby on the way and my grandma's engagement ring burning a hole in my pocket, staring at the entrance to Forrest Falls Care Home.

A knock on my window takes me out of my thoughts and back to the present and the task at hand. My eyebrows rise in surprise when I see none other than Drake beyond the tempered glass. I gesture with my hand for him to step away from the door so I can open it and climb out of the truck. Turning quickly to the passenger bench, I pick up the takeaway bag from Dine&Dash, where Ruth prepared a special goulash just for Maevis's father.

Drake shakes my hand, assessing me from head to toe. He's a big motherfucker, clearly taking after his father. Although his hair and eyes are nearly identical to Maevis's, his build is all Ronald.

"What are you doing here, man?" he asks, his eyes narrowing at me. "Where's Mae-Rae?"

"Mae's at the bakery. Since she's reduced her hours, she prefers to do a full day on Mondays so she can focus on all the admin stuff and be there for the new pâtissier they're training."

He nods at me like it makes sense, but his searching glare doesn't let up.

"Let's get inside before the food I brought gets cold," I tell him. "You've just saved me a trip."

"That for Dad?" he relents, pointing at the Dine&Dash bag. "You're aware he struggles with solids."

"Very much so. Ruth took care of everything."

We walk in silence through the reception and sign the visitor book before climbing the stairs to the second floor where his father's room is. By now, I'm as familiar with the layout of the Care Home as if it were my own home. Although the facility is a medical facility and the residents here need to be cared for around the clock, you couldn't tell from the grounds or from the inside. It looks and feels like a home, and the head administrator has said residents feel much more comfortable in an environment that is not sterile, but warm and inviting. A comfortable resident is much more receptive to receiving help and doing the work to get healthier and overcome whatever tragedy brought them here in the first place.

I knock on the door to Mr. Barlowe's suite and wait to hear the muffled *come in* before entering. His bedroom is large and has a bed pushed into the far corner, framed by windows on one side. The flowery smell of lilac with vanilla undertones greets me as I fully step in. Lilac was his late wife's favorite flower, and vanilla, that's all Maevis.

On the opposite wall there's a two-seater couch and an armchair, which seems to be his preferred place to spend most of his waking hours—reading or watching TV. The rest of his time he spends doing physical therapy or attending one of the various activities the Care Home puts together for residents.

"Ah, my favorite boys, to what do I owe the pleasure?" he says, his speech slurred, barely intelligible, but I've gotten used to the way he now talks, so I don't miss a beat in striding to the armchair and shaking his still functional right hand.

"Came bearing gifts," I tell him. "Ruth threatened to stop feeding me if I didn't come by with her new goulash recipe. We can't have that. I'm a growing boy." I smirk, rubbing my stomach with my palm.

"Hi, Dad." Drake greets him with a kiss on his weathered forehead, and warmth spreads through me. As much as I dislike the asshole, he is all in for his family. The love he has for his father and Maevis cannot be disputed or questioned. I guess I could've done far worse when it comes to future brothers-in-law, even if he has shit taste in friends.

I get a cloth from the cupboard next to the chair and place it under Ronald's chin, then retrieve a spoon from the top drawer. Unwrapping the freshly baked bread, I place it next to me on the little side table and get to opening the tupperware filled to the brim with the deliciously smelling goulash.

Drake catches on to what I'm about to do and strides to where I'm sitting. "I'll feed Dad," he says, arm outstretched for the cutlery.

A garbled laugh comes from Ronald. "He's fine, son. He's an old pro by now. Been doing this every time he visits while your sister fusses about the room."

Drake's eyes laser-focus on mine, but I just brush his questioning stare off. I don't mind helping. His father and I are like a well-oiled machine. I feed him; he cleans himself up and stays alert, so he doesn't choke.

His left side is entirely paralyzed. While he regained some semblance of feeling in his face, his lips are still drooping at the corner, and, as he explained it, his tongue feels like he has a never-ending anesthetic from the dentist. While he can chew some of the softer solid foods, he bit his tongue far too many times in the process, or struggled to swallow some drier cuts. That's why most of his food is blended or made into a thick liquid. It works for him, and it keeps him healthy and as strong as his weakened body allows him to be.

And so, we go about our normal routine, while Drake chatters away about what he and Annalise are up to, the latest shenanigans at the fire station, how much happier his wife is now that To Be Read Café is up and running, how he dreads next week's book club meeting when all the women get together and basically plan world domination. Apparently, it's a book club with a twist. Instead of each reading a book on their own, they meet on book club day, lock themselves in TBR Café, and read the book together.

Fucked if a twinge of fear doesn't crawl up my spine at the reminder.

Last month, Maevis was all fired up. Even if we were still in the *avoid each other* phase at that time, she still ranted for a good hour over dinner the day after their meeting about the book they were reading ending in a cliffhanger and cursing Violet—Eliza's teacher—to high heaven for suggesting an incomplete trilogy.

I even know what a cliffhanger is now. I wish I didn't.

Once Ronald is all done with his early dinner, I clean up the trash and draw a deep breath. He was accepting of our situation when Maevis told him she was pregnant, but, at the end of the day, he is her father. He already got to see her married and that marriage going up in flames. I really hope he will be accepting of me becoming his daughter's husband. Her last husband, if I have anything to say about it.

"I heard congratulations are in order," he slurs. "That was some trial."

"It was," I reply. I respect Ronald too much to brush him off, but if I never speak of last week again, it'll still be too soon. "I'm relieved to know it's over, even if I won't ever know what happened that night. I'll never get back those twenty minutes she was in the hotel room with me. And that's something I have to learn to live with."

His right hand, shaky and dry, pats my knee in understanding. "There are a great deal of things we need to learn to live with in this life. What matters is that we don't allow them to stop us from actually living. You only get one life, son. Give it meaning."

My eyes lift to his and I give him an earnest smile. "'s what I'm trying to do, Sir. I love your daughter. And I want Maevis to be my wife," I say, sliding the vintage box from my pocket and popping it open. There, on a pale white satin bed, sits my grandmother's engagement ring. It didn't seem right to buy Maevis a new one. I wanted the ring I promise myself to her with to have history, significance, and a tie to my family.

"Goddamn," Drake whistles from behind me. "Finally grew a pair, ay?"

I ignore the twat and continue, "I want us to grow old together, for her to always lean on me, and for me to always lean on her. I would be beyond honored if I'd have your blessing before I propose to her."

He says nothing for a good minute, just looking at me, amber eyes assessing the very depths of my soul, the darkest parts and the brightest spots, he sees them all. And I let him. I let him take my measure and decide for himself if he finds me worthy of his daughter.

"You'll respect her," he orders. And even if his words are distorted and garbled, the force behind them is unaffected.

"Yes, sir."

"You'll love her."

"With my last breath," I promise.

"Good. It gives me peace to know Mae has an honorable man at her side. Her kind heart made her an easy target for that unsavory cockroach. I'd rather see her spend her whole life alone than make herself small for someone who refuses to appreciate her worth."

"Maevis won't ever need to dim her light for me. I've loved your daughter for a long time, Sir. I love her for her kind heart and despite it. All I need in return is for her to stand as tall and proud by my side as I stand by hers."

He gives me a wobbly head nod in return, his lips twisting in a half smile, a mischievous twinkle in his eyes. "What would you have done if I said I don't want you by her side?"

"She'd crush both of y'all's nuts and happily sprinkle them on her muffins," snorts Drake.

I bite back the laugh bubbling in my chest and ignore the comedian mammoth behind me. "With all due respect, Sir, I came to inform you of my intention. The choice was always hers. While I'll never stand in between Mae and her family, Maevis is her own woman with her own mind."

"You better believe it. She may be sunshine personified, but my daughter is also a firecracker with a spine of steel."

His right hand grasps my forearm, the strength behind his grip surprising the hell out of me. Ronald pushes to his feet, and I stand with him, holding him upright. Drake's at his side in a flash, and, with an arm around his father's waist, he helps Ronald maintain his balance. "Dad?"

Ronald pays him no mind, but smiles his half grin at me, towering over me, even if I'm propping him up. "Give me a goddamn hug, son. Welcome to the family," he says. A wave of relief washes through me, and I step closer to him, letting him hook his right arm around my shoulder as I clasp his back.

"Maybe wait to welcome him until Maevis actually accepts the fool." Drake smirks, but throws an arm around my other shoulder, a hearty chuckle shaking his chest. "You've no fucking choice but to like me now. But, just so we're clear," he says, and the laughter cuts off abruptly, "hurt my sister, and no one will find your ashes when I'm done with you."

At least both men in Maevis's life accept me into the fold.

Threats and all.

Chapter Twenty-Eight

Maevis

I'm giddy, and excited, and have I mentioned giddy? I love book club meetings. One full day just for us girls, to eat all the baked goodness our stomachs can take, drink all the booze our livers can filter—for those of us who drink—and lose ourselves inside the pages of a good book with no outside world allowed between the walls of To Be Read Café.

"That's what you're wearing?" Tatum says from behind me.

I spin on my fluffy-socked heel and narrow my eyes at him, brushing my braid over my shoulder. "What's wrong with what I'm wearing?"

His cheeks pink up under his dark blond scruff, and I'd find him endearing, if he wasn't such an annoying brute.

"You're leaving in a T-shirt and knee-high socks," he replies, throwing his hands in the air.

"Excuse you, it's called an *oodie*." I point my finger to the gray cotton stretching over my belly where *Blake's first choice* is written in purple cursive.

"What the fuck is an oodie, Cupcake? And why are you wearing Hayes' goddamn name on you? If you're wearing someone's name, it should be mine."

His sheepish-hurt expression must be meant to soften me up, but just because he keeps me well sated in orgasms and love it doesn't mean he gets to comment on my attire. Not on book club day.

"You take it up with Emma. The rule is we all dress in the female main character's favorite item. For the book we're reading today, Blake's oodie it is." My finger finds its way in between his rock-hard pecs, and no, the feeling of all that cotton encased strength doesn't make me back down. Nope. Not this girl. "It's Australian, just so you know. And it's a large, comfy, sleeping T-shirt."

His rough fingers grip my chin, pulling me closer to him. "So, Blake's a woman?" Blue eyes sparkle with amusement as they take me in. I part my lips to confirm, but he slants his mouth over mine, his tongue tracing my bottom lip before slipping past it, searching for mine. His free hand finds its way under the hem of my T-shirt, fingers digging into my hips. "Goddammit, Maevis, you have only panties on underneath?" he growls into my mouth.

I can't bite back the giggle escaping me, but I use this moment of distraction to put distance between us. If I let myself be seduced by that steel pipe in his coveralls, I'll never get to TBRC, and today's meeting is far too important to miss.

"You can peel them off me tonight, and not one second earlier," I tell him. "Come on, caveman, take me to my girls."

"I'll take you, alright, but to the walk-in closet so you can put on some fucking shorts," he grunts and pounces on me, lifting me into his arms, like I'm his bride and he's crossing me the threshold to our home. An unholy squeak rips out of me, my own arms instinctually wrapping around his neck, and I rest my cheek on the crook of his shoulder.

"It's only us girls there, my love," I respond softly. "And I have no shorts that fit around your large baby. I promise I'll have a blanket covering me the entire time."

He turns his head and kisses my forehead. "If Blake sees you wearing that, I'll never hear the end of it."

"I'm yours."

"Forever and always, Cupcake."

I PUSH THROUGH THE DOOR OF TBRC IN A HURRY, a grumbling Tatum at my back, his arms full of bags and blankets.

"Sorry, sorry, am I the last one?" I say, huffing a breath as I plop down in my designated beanbag. "Someone's gonna have to help me out of this later."

Sawyer nudges my shoulder with hers. "I see you have a personalized oodie."

Before I can reply or roll my eyes, Tatum—the proud owner of the sloppy cursive of *Tate's Shop* over my breasts—covers me from chin to ankle in a fuzzy yellow blanket, tucking it around me until I'm resembling a stuffed burrito with a baby bump. He cups my cheek and kisses the tip of my nose, then gives me a quick peck on the lips before tousling Sawyer's hair.

"Oh, stop it. Gosh, why do you have to be such a child?" she screeches, combing her slender fingers through the silvery strands.

"I love you too, little sister." His eyes move back to me, a stern look on his face. "Behave, and for the love of all that's sacred, whatever idea crosses Lalah's mind, don't do it."

I snort a laugh at that. He had to wash body paint out of my belly button for three hours last week after Lalah decided it would be a great idea to fingerpaint a baby with a *loading* bar on my belly. An artist she is not.

"Pick me up later?" I smile innocently at him, all round eyes and pearly whites on display.

"You betcha', I have some peeling off to do," he says, his blue eyes turning dark, his tongue licking seductively at his bottom lip.

"Eww. No. Please, just go," Sawyer cries, pushing at his thigh. I can't help but turn my head and watch him saunter out the door, drooling at the sight of his tight ass and thick, strong thighs. Those coveralls really do wonders for him, and all the squatting around cars all day long doesn't hurt either. "My eyes are bleeding. I love you both, I truly do, and I'm beyond happy you're back together, but this kind of eye-sexing cannot happen around me when we're about to read smut. You're supposed to be my sister, Maevis."

"Sorry," I say, not the least bit apologetic, patting the back of her hand.

"Great, I'm the last one here," Lalah huffs, plopping down in the bean-bag next to mine. "Someone wasted thirty minutes looking for a fucking sharpie," she mumbles, her hazel eyes throwing daggers at a smug-looking Cole.

"Morning, ladies," Cole says, and—because he clearly has no sense of self-preservation—he grabs Lalah's arm and pulls her into his arms, his finger pointing at his name scribbled in black ink on the back of her own oodie.

"Must feel great," Emma sasses, "all that possessiveness floating around." She is a recent addition to our group. She used to be friends with the deranged duo—Maddison and Amanda—but after she bravely stepped up to the plate by showing Lalah a video of Maddison confessing to running our friend off the road and then drank a roofied drink meant for Lalah, we took her into our fold.

Just then, Annalise turns from the coffee machine, and all of us burst into laughter at the ugly handwriting declaring her middle section *Drake's*.

Emma stands from where she is seated and walks behind the counter, picking up a box with an image of pretty flowers in different shades of purple and pink on the lid. She drops it in the middle of the round table holding our snacks and beverages.

"Ladies of the TBRC, I present to you today's read," she says, removing the lid with a flourish. "*Just The Way You Are* by Jayme Louise." She retrieves a paperback, holding it up for all of us to see. "We have a sexy, tatted-up mechanic named Mitch smoldering at us from right here on the cover." She winks at me.

I play along and fan my face, which only earns me a groan from Sawyer. "Denvers, you're so on my naughty list," she says, pointing her finger at Emma.

"You'll live," Lalah interjects. "In fact, I think this book is right up your alley. Guess what? He's a single dad."

Sawyer splutters next to me, choking on her drink, her cheeks turning bright red. "W-what? I-I don't know what you're talking about."

"Sure you don't," snorts the hazel-eyed troublemaker. "Let's go with that while we read about the shenanigans of our redheaded Blake." She laughs then and winks at Emma. "You really chose one that hits close to a lot of homes here, didn't you?"

Annalise groans from where she's sprawled out on a blanket next to the goodie table. "For god's sake, Lalah. You weren't supposed to read the book already."

"Can you blame me?" She shrugs unapologetically. "I mean, look at that cover. He's a *single dad*, Anna. How do you think Hayes got lucky enough to bag me? Apart from the pretty eyes, and his big, massive..."

"NO. Stop right there!" shouts Sawyer. "Let's get to reading already."

"Heart," Lalah whispers. "For the love of Andromeda, Sawey, get your head out of the goddamn gutter. Alright," she claps once, "you'll freaking love this one. I promise you."

And love it, we do. I have not laughed as much in a good while. "God, I can't get over the drunken texting and the sexting," Violet says, twirling one bouncy dark curl around her finger.

Another new addition to our group is the elementary teacher, Violet. She was brought in by Sawyer since they both work together and have formed a friendship. It doesn't hurt either that Eliza is in her class and loves the absolute heck out of her.

We are growing by leaps and bounds, and I couldn't be happier. While I was always treated nicely by almost everyone, I never had a best friend of my own, and now I have four.

"I would've been awkward as fu...dge caramels. Gah, Blake is so endearing," Sawyer gushes.

"You sext your boss a lot, Blondie?" Emma teases my *hopefully* future sister-in-law.

"You're irritating today," she harrumphs, crossing her arms over her chest.

"Actually, I could see it." Lalah wiggles her eyebrows up and down. "Starts innocently enough, a text here and there telling him off when he's late picking up his kid, then full on steam as the night comes."

This is the second time she hinted at Sawyer seeing someone—a *specific* someone. My cogs start turning as I think of all the potential single fathers who have children going to the Daycare Centre, but Lost Hope has only Maddox and a couple other who are recently divorced. It's slim chances she'd be involved with any of them without stirring the rumor mill in town. The glint in Lalah's eyes, though... she knows something and she won't drop it.

May God have mercy if they're on her radar.

My phone vibrates under my thigh and I quickly pull it out, knowing Tatum is checking up on me. He started with messages every hour, but it seems that after he had lunch delivered for us, he's amping the frequency to every half hour.

> *You're sitting all mighty and pretty on that bean bag.*

> *I wonder how pretty or mighty you'll look bleeding on my bedsheets, begging for your slutty life?*

> *Is it worth it, you little whore, selling yourself to others? Or is it a sport for you to destroy marriages left and right?*

Restricted

I feel the color draining from my cheeks and can't help a gasp slipping past my lips. With shaky fingers, I shut the screen off and shove the phone back under the cover. These messages keep on coming daily since they started a month ago. I now have over three hundred unread. I hoped that ignoring them would make them stop, hoped Amanda just had a cruel sense of humor, but she's locked away now, and the messages keep coming.

"You okay there, Mae?" Annalise asks, and I realize with horror that all of their eyes are laser focused on me. I debate for less than a second what to say. We've had such a great day, and since the trial, it feels like a dark storm cloud has been lifted from our skies. All I want is for one freaking week to be normal.

One week when I don't blame myself for my boyfriend being sexually assaulted by his ex-wife, there are no threatening text messages, and me and my friends can just exist and laugh and live.

"Yeah. I had an overdue bill payment." The lie tastes bitter on my tongue, but I want this day to be a happy one more than anything, and so far, the threats have been limited to deranged texts. "I still overreact when I see them. It'll be a while until my anxiety gets with the program and understands I don't have anything to worry about." At least that part is true.

Lalah narrows her eyes at me. There's worry swirling in her mostly green eyes, and goosebumps sprout on my arms at the chill coming from her irises. *Oh goodie, she smells the bullshit.*

"Oh shit," Emma shrieks when Annalise, as plastered as the redhead, bumps into her and a whole glass of red wine drenches her face. They both promptly start laughing and stumble to the staff bathroom at the back.

I make grabby hands at Lalah—the only sober one here apart from me—to help me up, and together we mop up the red puddle on the floor and clean up the empty containers of food. By the looks of this party, we're ready to wrap up. Sawyer is half asleep on her beanbag, while Violet messily braids her silvery hair. Of course, the wild-haired primary teacher is swaying more than sitting upright since the four of them have drunk their body weight in red wine.

Can't blame them either. I'd have devoured a crisp glass of white if I were allowed to drink.

We're all a group of responsible women, but sometimes it's nice to let your hair down and just breathe. When there's so much piled up on your plate it's constantly overflowing, taking a step back to just exist is the best medicine.

Even in a town as small as ours is, I feel like we all live life in the fast lane. Work, responsibilities, obligations, chores, bills—it all just builds and builds, and you run around putting out one fire, only for another to sprout out of nowhere.

So having this one day a month just for the five of us, with the occasional visit from Sarah, Ruth, Renee, Beth, Emmeline, and Lucy, is like a breath of fresh air. We built our own bubble of support and empowerment.

"What the fuck?" Lalah shouts, startling Sawyer from her drunken nap. "Who did this to you?" She points her finger at Emma, who just returned from the bathroom. "Someone bring me a fucking shovel, I have a motherfucker to hunt."

Chapter Twenty-Nine

Maevis

I spin on my heel as fast as the watermelon-sized baby in my belly allows, and I feel the tears springing under my eyelids. Emma's face is black and blue, her makeup smudged, and finger marks collaring her neck. My knees buckle as the sight of her brings back memories from the night Daniel and I parted ways.

MY BLOOD IS BOILING IN MY VEINS. My asshole husband has gone too far. There are tens of thousands of dollars worth of debt clutched in my trembling hands. I push the door open, and I'm immediately assaulted by the putrid smell of stale alcohol and vomit.

The garbled moans and grunts coming from the living room assure me that my absentee husband is finally home, and he's not alone.

My cheeks flame up in anger and humiliation, bile rising up my throat. It's not the first time the good-for-nothing waste of space has cheated on me, but it's the first time he is bringing his affairs home. I flip the switch and yellow light floods the four walls.

And there he is. The prize and glory of Lost Hope, the man who married me and swore to love me until the day he dies, with his jeans around his ankles, sprawled bare-assed on my goddamn couch. A blonde woman—young, too, by the looks of it—is kneeling in between his legs, his stump of a cock lodged inside her throat.

"DANIEL," I shout, my body frozen at the doorstep, startling the cocksucker, a nausea-inducing choking sound coming from the girl's throat.

My husband's eyelids spring open, his mouth twisting at the corners before his eyes blank and a vein in his forehead pulses to life. His palm cups the girl's head when she's trying to pull back, and he pushes her down, face-first into his crotch. "That's it, darling. God, you suck me so good, your mouth is pure fucking honey. Don't stop, baby. Let the old lady watch. Maybe she'll learn a thing or two and stop being such a boring fuck."

That springs me into action. In five long strides, I'm at their side, throwing the papers at his face. "You two-timing, lazy fucker. How dare you?" I scream. My blood thrums in my veins, swishing in my ears. My heart is pounding so hard, my vision darkens at the edges.

That's when he moans long and low, more choking sounds coming from the girl on the floor, and I make the mistake to look at her. With spittle and cum dripping down her chin, she finally lifts her head from his lap, releasing him with a wet pop. My stomach turns, and I bite my tongue so hard, I swear I can taste blood in my mouth.

"Get out, get the fuck out of my house!" I screech, my voice cracking. This is what rock bottom feels like. In debt up to my eyeballs, my husband emptying himself in the mouth of a barely-legal girl right in front of me. My trembling fingers knot in my hair, pulling at the wayward strands, the sick feeling traveling through my spine nearly bringing me to my knees.

I turn around, not able to watch the scene for one more second—the woman getting dressed in a hurry and my husband's sated, limp dick slugging on his hip.

I'm so fucking done with this farce of a marriage. I'm just so done with everything. My chest is heaving, my lungs burning under the pressure of the sobs I won't allow to rise to the surface. When I feel the moisture gathering in my eyes, I scrunch them shut.

Don't you dare cry, Maevis Rae Barlowe. He's not worth it. Don't cry. Don't cry. Don't cry.

"You too, Daniel. Just... leave. We're over," I whisper.

Maybe the blood thumping against my eardrums is the reason why I don't hear him. Maybe my tightly closed eyelids stop me from seeing him move in front of me. The all-encompassing sense of dread flooding my stomach warns me just one fraction of a second too late.

The feeling of his palm connecting with my cheek knocks the breath out of me. A ringing sounds in my ear when his fingers clip the side of my head. Stars burst behind my eyelids. My hands are fisted at my sides, stiff and unmoving, my legs weigh a thousand pounds, so heavy I don't even stumble under the force of the hit turning my head sideways. I'm frozen.

A deer in the headlights.

There's no warning amping up in me when his fist connects with my jaw. My bottom lip bursts on impact. The metallic taste of blood floods my mouth, crimson rivulets spilling down my chin, and I choke on my tongue.

He'll kill me.

He'll kill me and there's nothing I can do about it. My soul has left my body. I have no control over myself; I feel nothing but pain. It's all-consuming, engulfing me whole, like I've been doused in gasoline and set on fire. So I let myself burn.

My legs buckle—left tripping over the right—when his fingers fist into my braid and he pushes me to the floor. At the very last second, my forearm shoots in front of my battered face, and stops me from completely smashing it against the hardwood floor littered with cigarette butts and empty beer bottles.

"You dumb fucking bitch," he growls, his speech slurred. Or maybe the flames burning through me are roaring far too loud for me to hear him correctly.

The tip of his steel-toed boot connects with the center of my stomach, and I feel my ribs cracking at the contact. I suck in a breath as agony travels through my body with the speed of an electric bolt, but there's no air to inflate my lungs, just a void where my chest once was.

"Look at you, the blandest cunt to sheath my dick," he spits. His rotten saliva and stale breath drench my throbbing face. His fingers snake around my throat, constricting the last free trickle of my already clogged airway.

I sputter and choke, my arms flailing helplessly, short nails clawing at his forearm, my body combusting, begging for a sliver of oxygen. "You dare order me around? You, you insipid bitch?" he roars, the rage in his voice cutting through the veil of numbness settling over me.

He picks me up by my throat, and my limbs twitch, but not even the adrenaline flooding my bloodstream is enough to chase away the fear-induced paralysis that overtook my body. His dark eyes are unhinged and glassy, soulless pits of cruelty staring back at me, drinking up my terror, feasting on my suffering. The back of my head hits the hard brick of the wall he pins me to, and more stars burst before my very open eyes.

His lips twist in an evil smirk, his fingers tighten around my throat, thumb pressing down on my larynx, and a flash of startling clarity washes through me. This is the end.

I should've listened when Drake and Dad sat me down and told me to divorce him. They begged and pleaded, but I dug my heels in. I wanted a love like my parents had. I knew the road to happiness was full of compromise and setbacks. A Barlowe doesn't run scared at the first sight of a storm.

I wish I did. I wish I turned tail and scurried like a defenseless rabbit. Even prey knows to take shelter when the hurricane hits.

My body crumbles to the floor, bruised and defeated, when Daniel's hand, keeping me upright, releases my neck and he crumples on his back on the sofa. A wet, rasped out cough wracks my swollen throat, my ribs screaming in pain with every shudder passing through my body.

Strong arms cradle me to a wide chest. The scent of home and safety settles all around me as a warm palm strokes the back of my head. An agonizing whimper spills past my busted lips when his fingers connect to the goosebump hidden by my hair.

"Fuck, Maevis. You're fine, little sister. God. You're fine," he murmurs, and my heart stutters, skipping a beat as the adrenaline is rapidly draining from my body.

My brother came for me. I can let go now.

"Maevis," a sharp voice cuts through the memory of one of the worst days of my life. I blink my eyes open, my vision blurred and hazy. "Are you with us, hun?" Lalah's face comes in and out of focus.

Every single part of my body is shaking, cold sweat dripping down my back. I suck in a breath, my lungs inflating painfully, a ghost jolt of pain from my now healed ribs coiling around my chest. Cold, hard plastic touches my bottom lip, and I take a startled step back. The hand gripping my biceps tightens around me.

"Maevis, hun, it's Lalah. Easy now," she says, her voice low and soothing. "Deep breaths now. Inhale with me." I hear her drawing a deep gulp of air, and I follow suit. "Keep for four—one, two, three, four," she guides me, and I let the calming tones of her voice wash over me. "Now exhale." I scramble to follow her instructions. "That's it."

Her hand leaves my arm and settles between my shoulder blades, moving in slow circles on my tensed back. My knees buckle but continue to support me. I clutch at the bottle of water she was trying to get me to drink and chug half of it in one big gulp. I might as well have drunk rusty razor blades at how much the cool liquid stings as it slides down my throat.

I haven't had a flashback of that night since December, and even then, it wasn't as strong—just the oily feeling of being discarded, the disrespect, or what I thought to be disrespect, shoved in my face. My cheeks flush red and my eyes frantically search for Emma.

"She's okay. Here, sit down," Lalah says, guiding me to a chair. Thank fuck, otherwise I don't think my knees would be able to support me when I have to stand again. "Annalise is force-feeding her coffee. Hopefully, they'll both sober up quick enough."

"What happened to her?" I whisper. I'm honestly not sure if I want to know. But during my darkest days, I had Drake to lean on. Hell, I even had Maddox, who watched over me like a hawk, and sadly kept the habit. She needs to know she's not alone, and I'd bet my life that all the women present here would move heaven and hell to band around her.

"Richard the dick," she hisses. Her eyes glint dangerously, the warm brown full of concern for me completely drowned out by icy green. "Emma testified against Amanda. The scum wasn't impressed. Turns out the psychotic duo and the nutless asshole were going behind Emma's back." She shakes her head, her trembling fingers pushing some wayward strands of hair behind her ear.

Nausea swirls inside of me, my heart breaking for Emma. To be betrayed in the worst way by her childhood best friends and her fiancé is fucking cruel. I swallow down the unease crawling up my spine, leaving a cold trickle of fear in its wake. I know these are not true feelings, but ghosts of everything I felt that night. Emma's story is not my own. But my story gives me the necessary tools to support her if she'll allow me.

"You good? Do you want me to call Tatum?" Lalah nudges me with her shoulder.

"I'm a bit shaken, but if Emma's good to stay, I'm good, too. Took me by surprise to see her like that, and it reminded me of D-Daniel," I whisper. "I'd appreciate it if you kept this to yourself, though."

She recoils away from me, her arms crossing across her chest, and she scowls in my direction with all her might. "For fuck's sake. Here we go again. Honestly, Maevis, did you not learn anything from the past few months? All that fucking pain you guys went through. All the misery could have been avoided if you'd just *talked* to each other. You guys are doing so well now."

"Precisely," I cut off her rant. She could go on for hours if I let her. "I *will* talk to Tate, Lalah. I just want a fucking week to be happy. He went through absolute fucking hell. He's still healing. I just want to let him fucking breathe for a goddamn minute."

"Goddammit," she huffs. "I'm not looking forward to the day I get to tell you 'I told you so', but I will help your stubborn ass when you need to grovel." She rolls her eyes at me, and I release a sigh of relief. The list of secrets is getting bigger and bigger.

Annalise and Emma return, and I notice Emma wears once again a thick layer of foundation, her hair now loose around her shoulders, covering the worst of the bruises around her neck.

"I'm going to take self-defense classes at the Hope Haven," she announces, plopping down in her beanbag.

"They have those for people not living there?" Lalah asks, and I can practically see the cogs in her head moving. Oh uh, she's cooking something.

"They do. Kept separated from the residents since not everyone is comfortable with outside interactions. Jackson's one of the trainers."

Now that little bomb has us all gasping and fanning our faces.

"I knew I liked him for a reason," Annalise laughs.

"I'll join," slurs Sawyer from her beanbag.

"Sure you are, doll, as soon as you survive the hangover." Emma smiles, but the relief swirling in her copper-brown eyes is in direct contrast with her words.

"All of us are," declares Violet. "Well, maybe not the Kinder Surprise here, but the rest of us."

The most unholy of snorts comes out of my nose. While self-defense classes sound appealing to me—I've been defenseless once, I do not care to repeat the experience—there's no way in hell I'll be able to attend them until my bun is nice and baked.

"Speaking of Kinder Surprise," Emma says, shifting the attention from her to me. "Are you guys doing the gender reveal party any time soon, or are we waiting for the baby?"

I rub my hands together, because Lalah may usually be the woman with the plan and the crazy ideas, but this time?

I WIN.

Chapter Thirty

Tatum

"**W**as this one of your wife's ideas? Because if it walks like a Lalah and it quacks like a Lalah, it's most likely a Lalah," I grumble, rearranging the goddamn tie for the thousandth time in the past thirty minutes.

Who turns a gender reveal party into a black tie affair? We do, apparently. Everything lately has been black tie, and everything has been goddamn weird. Ever since that book club meeting they had last week, Maevis has been a little withdrawn, worried every time her phone buzzes, taking calls or even checking her text messages as far away from me as possible.

No, I don't think she's cheating. It's the last damned thing on my mind. But there's that niggling at the back of my head, itching and prodding that I'm missing something, I'm overlooking something important. I can't shake the feeling of impending doom unfurling at the bottom of my stomach.

Oh, she chatted all the way home about the book they read, and how the main character was a mechanic *just like me*, but that his best friend—who is also a mechanic *just like me*—resembles me the most because he's as tatted-up as I am. And I could tell she was genuinely excited about the book. Hell, I'd offer to read any book that gets her happy and fired up, even if I have to learn about tropes and more abbreviations than we used in the Marines.

I actually had to ask—wish I didn't, though—what the fuck was an MFMMM. Piece of advice for future-me: do not ask questions you don't want to know the answer to. Because *the answer* left me scratching my head for a good thirty minutes, thinking about the logistics of such a situation and how people deal with jealousy. The conclusion is simple—I'm a possessive motherfucker. And much like Joey in *Friends,* "Tatum doesn't share..."

Well, Joey's problem is different, but my problem can be eaten, too.

"Sorry to disappoint, brother, but this was all Maevis," Cole laughs, his eyes scanning the expanse of their backyard. Once again, a mountain of neon pink wrenches and blue cupcakes are strewn around. For some godforsaken reason, more than a dozen balloons—of a glittery Saturn of all planets, rings included—are also tied up all around a blue and pink arch, with Lalah's pond behind the ballooned monstrosity.

What feels like half of Lost Hope is meandering around from table to table, munching on appetizers and cakes and fruit-whatevers. Go ask in town, see if they have any food left after the book club devils descended on them with my credit card.

"Has she seemed any different to you lately?" I turn to face my oldest friend. His black eyebrows rise on his forehead, a perplexed look washing over his face.

"Can't say that she's been any different around me, no," he says cautiously. "Why'd you ask? I thought things were smooth sailing with you since before the trial. Speaking of before," he drawls, his lips twisting in a half smirk, so at odds with the eyes narrowed at me, "next time, scrub the fucking bathroom yourself, for fuck's sake."

I bark a laugh at his comment. Can't find it in me to feel a single ounce of shame. Those moments with Maevis, locked together in their downstairs bathroom, were a turning point for me—and our relationship.

"I'll send you a case of bleach and some spare cleaning gloves," I retort and brush my fingers through my hair. The sides have definitely grown. I've considered keeping them short, but Mae made a passing comment that she liked it longer, so I guess I'm growing it again. Gotta add to my online order, along with the shampoo and conditioner, a carton of pink razors to shave my pussy while I'm at it.

"She's been... cagey lately. My protective instincts are flaring up. I can't fix a problem, if I don't know what the problem is."

He clasps my shoulder with one palm and looks straight into my eyes. "It takes a great man to put aside small things and let his woman take the power from his hands. *Especially* a man who had his power taken from him without his agreement. But when you have your person by your side, does it even matter?" He lifts a shoulder in a careless shrug. "She'll never abuse your trust. She may push your boundaries, and you will question your sanity more than once, but at the end of each day, it's your arms she sleeps in. It's you she trusts to hold her hand in the dark."

I take my best friend in—the lone wolf that's *lone* no more. He always had this seriousness about him, a quiet stoicism deployed like a wall of separation. He wielded loneliness as a shield, much like his wife did when I met her. Together though? They're a team. They're not invincible, but goddamn close to it.

Lalah flies high without a net because she trusts Cole to be there, just one step behind, to catch her if she falls. And she's his vault, his safe place, where all his soft spots come to light, and she protects and cherishes them. They orbit each other with the understanding that it's okay to fall. And it's okay to be soft, too.

I want that unity. I desperately crave for Maevis and me to reach that level of trust and devotion. After all the growing pains, after all the darkness and hell, we have more than earned our happily ever after. And the ring in my pocket is a big step in the right direction.

"Thanks, man. I'm already questioning my sanity, so I must be doing something right." I chuckle. "Let's go find out if I'm painting flowers on the walls of Tate's Shop after all."

My eyes search automatically for Maevis as soon as we step onto the outside porch. When the peals of her musical laughter reach me, I jog in her direction, suit trousers be damned.

Fuck, she's beautiful today.

Her lacy white dress hits just above her knees, the fabric hugging and stretching over her rounded belly. Her dark hair, left loose over her shoulders, falls just below her waist. Round eyes are accentuated by discreet makeup, the early afternoon sunlight making them sparkle like igniting embers.

I'm helpless to her draw. My arm hooks around her waist, my other cradling her neck, and I dip her low, my mouth hungry for her peach flavored lips. I hold her like this, pressed to me, kissing her like it's my last day on earth. *I'm ready.*

I'm just about to pop down on one knee and ask her to take a chance on me, to take a leap of faith and be mine officially and legally, in front of our families and friends, when Sawyer cuts through, poking her sharp nail in my shoulder.

"Oh goodie, you're both here. We have a hose on standby too, if needed. Come on, lovebirds. I'm here to find out if I have a niece or a nephew, not to get a first-row seat on how they came to be."

I never wanted to be an only child. Believe me, I want it now.

A mewl of protests slips past Maevis's lips when I pull her upright and take a step back. Her cheeks are flaming red, and I want to kiss every flushed part of her soft skin, to follow that pretty blush under her dress and see how far it travels down her body. Despite her obvious embarrassment at being called out by my brat of a sister, an ear-to-ear smile brightens her face.

"You're good at distracting me," she murmurs, her thumb lovingly sweeping at my bottom lip, wiping away all traces of her lipstick. I catch her wrist in my hand and suck her finger into my mouth, licking it clean.

"That's it," Sawyer says, hooking both her arms into the crook of each of our elbows. "Let's go people, it's reveal time. If I have to sit here for one more second and hear Lalah brag that she's known for close to a month and we don't, I won't be responsible for my actions," she threatens, marching us under the balloon monstrosity of an arch.

Lalah and Annalise come running, arranging us this way and that, until we're positioned with our back to the rainbow from hell. We're facing all of our close ones, all sitting on—you guessed it—alternating pink and blue chairs.

Jackson strides purposefully over to us, carrying a giant balloon that could've been used as an inflatable mattress considering how big it is. He stops just to the right of me, followed closely by Cole. By the looks of his tightly pressed suit jacket, the lovely ladies got to him, too. In fact, they got to everyone, since we all look ready to attend a Bond party rather than a gender reveal.

Emma and Sawyer take the square privacy screen from him and shove it between me and Maevis, forcing me to take a step back.

"What the hell is this?" I demand, moving around to get back to my woman, but I'm stopped when a hard hand clamps down on my shoulder. A long needle is shoved in front of my face, and that's my second step away from her. "Seriously?" I snarl at Jackson, who only grins at me like the dickhead he is.

"Sorry, man. The rules were clear. Now, stop bristling like a poked bear and prick the living hell out of that balloon," he says, raising his voice on the last words. The whole backyard explodes into cheers and my shoulders sag.

I imagined this going differently. Maybe Maevis and I cutting together into a cake, and the color inside told us the gender—not having a freaking security fence between us and a needle in my hand to try to poke my way to her.

"We'll do it together on *three?*" Maevis asks from behind the black monstrosity, the sweet lilt of her voice carrying a trace of amusement.

The things I do for love.

"Alright, Cupcake. You lead, I follow," I tell her. At the end of the day, what my woman wants, my woman gets.

"Three, two," she giggles, "one and a half." My hand twitches at that, fingers ready to stab through the inflatable wall, so I steady myself and let her make the first move since she was excited all week for the reveal.

I mean, I'm beyond thrilled to find out if I'm going to have a baby girl or a boy, but ultimately, all I want is for the baby to be healthy and for Maevis to be okay at the end of it all.

"ONE!" she shouts, and I brace myself for the pop that... never comes. "Taaatuuuum," she whines. "You were supposed to use the needle."

I don't bother arguing that she, too, was supposed to use hers. I just stab the sharp needle through the balloon and sputter when a million and one confetti explode out of it. They glint and sparkle in the sunshine, and I squint, trying to make out the color when one lands on my forearm.

"Gold? What's that supposed to mean?" I ask no one. I turn to Maevis to watch her reaction and freeze. My heartbeat slows to nearly imperceptible pumps. My breath is trapped inside my lungs and my throat closes off.

She beams at me with a smile so bright it overpowers direct sunlight. Her amber eyes shine as golden as the glittery papers still raining down on us, tears building up at their corners.

"Tatum," she says, her voice strong despite the small trembling of her chin. "I was afraid. I was afraid of so many things; standing up beside you, claiming you as mine for all to see, supporting you when you needed me the most." A shadow falls past her face and now her tears fall in earnest.

My knees shake and buckle, and I let myself fall down on the soft grass where she's kneeling in front of me. My palms cup her rosy cheeks, thumbs sweeping away the moisture her eyes can't contain. My stomach is a mess of tingles, warmth spreading through my chest and to my limbs.

"I'm claiming you now, if you'll have me," she whispers. My heart flutters in my chest, my mouth curving in a smile so wide, my fucking jaw hurts.

Sneaky little Cupcake.

"I know I broke your trust, and that it's not something easy to gain back. But I'll fight as hard as I have to, all day every day, to show you that I'm deserving of trust. I'm strong enough to withstand any storm. At your side," she says, louder now, stronger too. She's resolute in her conviction, not a single trace of doubt on her beautiful face.

I'm itching to open my mouth and shout the speech I've practiced a thousand times in the mirror ever since I spoke to Ronald. I'm bursting at the seams to shout my love for all of Lost Hope to hear, but this is her show. This is her moment, so I bite the inside of my cheek until I swear I can taste blood, and let Maevis slay me open.

"I love you and I want to spend the rest of my life with you—with you, and our little Vanilla Bean. Marry me, Tatum. Please, marry me."

I'm done for when her dainty hand sneaks up her chest and withdraws a box from the inside of her bra. She winks at me, her watery smile not wavering in the slightest as she pops it open, presenting me with a dark wedding band. She shifts the box just so, outside of where my own shadow covers it. When the sunlight hits the ring, a million colors explode on the surface, creating an effect just like the thin-film interference phenomenon I see in oil spills on a daily basis.

My eyes jump back to her face, and I drink in the hope glinting in her amber eyes, the love she carries me spilling in gentle rivulets down her cheeks. I bend my head, resting my forehead on hers so we're nose to nose and mouth to mouth.

"Yes," I whisper, "you little thunder-thief."

A breath passes, then two more. And then her arms are around my neck, her belly bumps against my abdomen, and her hungry, ravenous lips are on mine, coaxing them open with her tongue, tasting me, fusing us together.

Catcalls, whispers, and a chorus of claps explode all around us.

I drown them out, attuned only to the little hums of contentment escaping her throat as she kisses me desperately, like any minute I'll disappear from her embrace. My fingers tighten on her jaw, pulling her closer to me until there's not even room for air between the two of us.

"Marry me now," Maevis murmurs. And I choke on my fucking tongue in response.

Chapter Thirty-One

Tatum

"What was that, Cupcake?" I rasp, my blood rushing through my veins, pounding inside my eardrums.

"Marry me now," she says, blinking up at me. A rosy blush spreads from inside her cleavage and up her jaw, burning my fingertips. "I know you had but a second to get used to us being engaged, but why wait? If we're doing this, I want to be married to you when I give birth to our child."

I push to my feet, my injured thigh screaming in protest. I pay it no mind—I had nine years to get used to the sharp pains radiating from it from time to time—and help Maevis stand as well.

"You're serious," I confirm. I have to, since right now I can't tell left from right with how hard my heart is thrumming and how my fucking blood rushes from my eardrums to my cock. Maevis could be my wife as soon as tonight. All my fucking dreams as of late are coming true.

"Very much so."

"But h-h-how?" I stutter. "We need... a marriage license and... someone ordained to perform the ceremony."

A throat clears from behind me before the subtle scent of smoked pinewood hits me. "That'd be me." Jackson grins, and I choke out a laugh. *Out of everyone...* I shake my head in disbelief. She really thought of every-thing.

"Say yes, Tatum," Maevis begs.

A smirk spreads on my lips, crooked arrogance and all that. "Good thing I came prepared, then." I pull on her arms, where my fingers are still hooked above her elbows, and kiss the gasp right from her parted lips. "Yes, Cupcake."

I swear I don't finish the last word before she's whisked from my arms again. I grumble a curse, but the whirlwind named Sarah Carter barrels straight into my chest, slapping at my shoulder.

"You're getting married now?" my mom squeals and pulls me into her arms, squeezing the life out of me. The distress sounds escaping my throat must clue her in that I'm about to keel over, because she releases me abruptly, planting her palms on my shoulders. "I'm so happy for you, baby." She gives me a watery smile that hits me straight in the chest. I've not seen her smile like this—so openly, so freely—since December.

Before I can open my mouth and respond, her navy-blue eyes narrow at me, her eyebrows scrunching together. "God Lord, boy, I didn't help with anything for the wedding. Couldn't you have told me sooner?"

My teeth sink into my knuckles, a jolt of pain traveling through my hand where they cut into my skin, stifling the laughter that bubbles in my throat. *Typical Sarah Carter.*

"Wife," my father says, hooking an arm around her waist and kissing the side of her head, "our son just got proposed to. I'm sure Maevis and the rest of her friends have things well in hand."

"Mr. and Mrs. Carter, nice to see you," Jackson interjects, hand outstretched toward my father. An honest-to-god smile spreads across my dad's face as he clasps Jake's hand and pulls him into a back-slapping hug.

"Son, good to see you, too. You're a sight for sore eyes. Ever since you moved into our town, I see you less than when you two were enlisted," he chastises, his voice taking a commanding tone. He doesn't ask any direct questions, but they're there. *Why are you staying away? Why don't you visit?*

I know the answer to all those questions. *Guilt. Shame.* Very much similar to everything I feel whenever Jake is nearby. I've learned how to live with the consequences of my actions and these lingering feelings clawing at the pit of my stomach. He didn't. Jackson's wounds run far deeper—etched into his very marrow. They keep him tethered to us and push him away at the same time. To Jake, we're both the gravity grounding him and a same pole magnet repelling him.

He is cursing himself to eternally look in while wanting out and forever being out while yearning to be in.

"I'll stop by for Sunday dinner, I promise. Although, by the looks of it, you'll have a full house soon enough," he says. And he fully intends to keep that promise, although everyone here knows he is absolutely not able to.

My mom pinches his cheek, her shrewd eyes scanning him from head to toe and back again. "Next time, maybe you'll actually come in."

He gives her a small smile, a genuine-Jackson, the usual ice in his silvery eyes giving way to warmth and fondness. He clasps her palm and kisses the back of her hand. "I'll do you one better, Mrs. Carter, and sit at the table, too. Now, let me get this son of yours married so he can start his happily ever after already."

"Oh, you charmer," my mom laughs bashfully, her cheeks pinking up. There's no fist-biting in the world that stops my laughter now when my father cocks an unimpressed eyebrow at them and steers his wife away from the ordained Casanova at my side.

"Ready, brother?" Jackson asks me. There's no trace of humor in his voice or on his face. That tightening in my gut whenever he is near lessens. Right now, in front of me, it's not the playboy of Lost Hope—the indifferent shell of a man he became after our discharge from the Marines. It's the brother who always has my back, his loyalty and affection for me nearly palpable in the space between us.

"Ready," I say, with a sharp jot of my chin.

He takes a step back to the center of the arch, and I move to the left, turning completely to face the aisle created between the rows of chairs. A soft violin sound comes from the speakers hidden somewhere around us. The fine hairs on my arm stand to attention despite the warm May afternoon as tingles of anticipation travel through me.

Arm in arm, Lalah and Cole make their way to me. They both hug me tightly, Lalah sandwiched between me and her husband, and there's no need for words. I feel their approval and happiness for both me and my future wife.

Lalah moves to Maevis's side, and I stop Cole with my hand on his shoulder, giving the ring I planned to propose to Maevis with to him. "Hold this for me, would you?"

He looks at the delicate, wooden box in my palm, his eyebrows lifting high on his forehead. *When?* he mouths.

"Tonight." I grin.

"She was faster," Cole laughs.

I don't get to reply, when a bundle of sky-blue silk and long blonde hair launches into my arms. "You're getting married without me?" she demands.

"Selae," I exhale, relief coursing through my veins at the sight of my sister. "You're here."

"You're lucky your future wife thought of everything," she teases me, a wide smile spreading across her face. "I'm so happy for you, Tate. You deserve all the happiness in the world. There's no one more deserving than you. I'm so, so proud you are allowing yourself to move forward and heal." Selena's cornflower-blue eyes twinkle with sincerity and love. I squeeze her to my chest, when another set of arms wrap around the both of us.

"Just because I'm sitting on Maevis's side doesn't mean you get to forget about me," Sawyer teases. She rubs my back affectionately, her head resting on my shoulder. We remain like this for a good minute until Annalise clears her throat from behind Selena.

"Come on ladies, let's get our favorite mechanic hitched." Her tone is light, but I hear the threat for what it is.

"Ball-buster," Lalah coughs from the side.

"Don't get me started on you, *Mrs. Hayes*," Annalise huffs as she takes her place next to Lalah, followed closely by Sawyer. Selena winks at me, stepping next to Cole.

A charge of electricity travels through the air, an unseen pull settling across my skin. And then she's there, just a few feet away. She's breathtaking, the most beautiful woman I've seen in my life. Ronald is standing proud at her side, their hands clasped tightly, with Drake supporting him as they shuffle slowly toward me.

It takes everything in me not to run up to them and let them have this moment instead. My eyes burn, and I feel the moisture gathering at their corners. I don't bother wiping away the tears that spill down my cheeks. I'm finally getting everything I ever wanted. Maevis is all I ever needed and never realized I did.

Her soft palms clasp mine, and I bring her hands to my mouth, kissing each knuckle, breathing in her delicious scent of honeysuckle and vanilla—of home.

"Hi," I mouth to her.

Maevis is all smiles, and warmth, and beauty. And she's all *mine*.

"Hi," she giggles, the sound traveling straight to my heart. Oh, Jackson talks, too. I'll be damned if I hear one word of what he is saying. I'm sure he's spewing poetics with the best of them, but I couldn't care less. All I care about is the woman in front of me, the woman who took a leap of faith and is now claiming me for everyone to see.

A sharp elbow in my back has me shaking my head. My eyes spring to Jackson, who's watching me with an amused smile on his lips, his dark eyebrows disappearing under the hair touching his forehead.

"Now's the part where you stop staring at Maevis and actually marry her," he whispers. Based on the laughter coming from our guests, he might as well have shouted into a microphone.

Cole places her ring in my hand, and I bend down to kiss her bare ring finger. I poise it at her fingertip, the delicate white gold sparkling in the sunlight. Her gasp of surprise has me lifting my eyes to her instead of continuing to admire how good her finger looks wearing *my* ring.

A flush travels up her jaw, pooling over her cheeks, her luscious lips curving in a small O. Delight and shock dance in her amber eyes as Maevis studies intently the band I finally settle at the base of her finger. The two pear-shaped sapphires—one light blue and one amber—curl around each other, much like Maevis and I do when we need to bare our souls and our innermost turmoil.

I pull her hand to my lips again and whisper against the coldness of the stones, only for her to hear, "The blue sapphire stands for loyalty, faith, and devotion. And you have mine from this day to my very last. The amber sapphire stands for happiness and love, and that's what you mean to me." I clear my throat, trying to dislodge the lump of emotions coating it, then speak louder, "I, Tatum Carter, give myself to you, Maevis Rae Barlowe, as your loving, faithful, doting husband. I give you all my bent and broken pieces, not in the hope of you mending them, but knowing you'll treasure and love them for the rest of our lives. From this day forward to all eternity, you'll forever be my one and only choice. Always and forever."

The smile she gifts me is radiant. Her hands leave mine for a quick second, enough for her to get my wedding band from Lalah, and then her trembling hands push the black ring on my finger. "I, Maevis Rae Barlowe, give myself to you, as your loving, loyal, and devoted wife. I give you all my fears and vulnerabilities, not in the hope of you fighting them, but knowing you'll stand by my side as I conquer them myself, for the rest of our lives. From this day forward to all eternity, you'll always be my one and only choice. Forever and always."

My hands cup her jaw, pulling her closer to me, my mouth ravenous over hers, at the same time that Jackson says, "By the power vested in me by the great state of Montana and some obscure site on the internet, I declare you husband and wife. You can now k... Oh fuck it, you're already at it. Ladies and gentlemen, I present to you Tatum and Maevis Carter."

My eyes close when thunderous applause and catcalls rise all around us. All I feel is Maevis in my arms, finally mine. All I hear is my heart pounding in my chest and *my wife*'s hungry whimpers.

"I HAVE SOMETHING FOR YOU, LOVECAKES," Lalah says, plopping into a chair right across from Maevis and me.

"Revealing the gender of our baby, finally?" I snort while my wife giggles next to me. I squeeze her bare shoulder, her skin warm and soft under my fingertips. I can't stop touching her. She's been legally and officially mine for less than five hours, but I feel her deep in my soul. A sense of rightness and completeness settled over me as soon as our lips touched after we exchanged our vows, and with it, the need to have her glued to me intensified.

"Have a little patience, would you?" My friend rolls her eyes. "The night is still young."

"My husband and I are eager to go home," Maevis purrs, the innuendo in her voice going straight to my cock. Not that it needs any extra help. I've been rock hard all fucking afternoon, images of her in our bed, wearing nothing but my ring on her finger, playing over and over in my mind.

"It's not like he can get you any more pregnant than you are." Lalah scoffs.

"Oh, I can certainly try," I retort, grinning like a fool.

"Did you tell them?" Sawyer interjects, her hands gripping the back of Lalah's chair, careful not to touch her.

"I would've, but they have sex on the brain," she whines at the same time Cole covers her mouth with his palm, only to yelp a second later and whip his hand away.

"For god's sake, Supernova, I know now how Clara got into her biting habit."

"She came by it naturally." She flutters her eyelashes at him, and I know we're going to be here a long while if someone doesn't steer the conversation back on topic. And considering the wandering fingers stroking me under the table, it needs to happen fast-like before all our friends get more of a show than they bargained for.

"You had something for us." I grunt when Maevis cups my balls through the material of my trousers and squeezes. The little minx really enjoys playing with fire and I look forward to burning her.

"Pack your bags, newlyweds. Tomorrow evening we're going on your honeymoon."

Maevis jumps to her feet, crushing my fucking sack in the process when the heel of her palm presses down on me. I bite my cheek, trying to swallow down a howl of pain as waves of nausea hit my stomach. "Well, there goes our fucking wedding night," I wheeze as my forehead hits the table in front of us.

"Oh my god," my wife—the nutcracker—yells, finally removing the fucking hammer scrambling my eggs.

"Go get your fallen comrade a bag of ice, *meus bellator*," Lalah orders between snickers.

I turn my head on the cool surface of the table enough to catch Cole's retreating back before Maevis's concerned face appears before my eyes.

"Oh god, Tate, I'm so sorry," she whispers, genuine worry swimming in her eyes.

"He'll live," Sawyer comments. "That's what he gets for playing under the table."

Kill me now. At least most of our guests left, with only our closest friends here to witness my wife neutering me in public.

I scrunch my eyes shut as waves of pain travel through my body, all aiming for my stomach. Nausea is buzzing inside my abdomen, ready to empty me of everything I ate today, right here, on the pristine tablecloth.

Warm fingers brush through my hair, the touch caring and tentative. A breath of relief escapes my chest when the chill of ice seeps through my lap, calming my throbbing groin.

"See, that's exactly why I don't understand where the insult 'pussy' came from. A pussy is tough. I could take a knee to my clit without my brain suffering a short-circuit," Lalah comments matter-of-factly, and a chorus of male groans rise around us, mine included.

"What? It would hurt, sure, but I wouldn't be crumbling like a sack of potatoes dropped from a skyscraper."

"No one will take any knees to your clit, Supernova," Cole laughs, but we all hear the threat behind his words. He'll rip apart whoever even thinks of harming one hair on her head. And that's true for me too, with Maevis. Hell, when it comes to any of my close ones, but my wife in particular.

When the spiral of death originating from my groin lets up enough that there is no risk of the steak I ate earlier making a reappearance, I sit upright, but keep a firm grip on the ice bag resting on my lap.

Everyone and their mother are now gathered around our table, looking at me either in concern—Maevis and Annalise, in amusement—Lalah, Selae, Sawyer, and Emma, or with pity and understanding—Cole, Drake, Blake, Jackson, and Maddox.

"Alright, now that we know for sure our groom survived"—Lalah claps—"let's plan for tomorrow. We"—she points at Cole and Blake—"can pick up Jackson on our way to the airport."

"Airport?" I dare ask.

"It's your honeymoon." She smiles, her eyes twinkling in delight. "About three years ago, Marcus put me in contact with Weston Castling."

Jackson whistles long, interrupting her at the same time that Selena screeches, "Fuck me, *the* Weston Castling?"

My mouth falls open. It's in moments like this one when Lalah's wealth slaps me over the face. She's so down to Earth, so normal, it's difficult to put her and a shit-ton of money in the same picture. But then she goes and throws names like Weston Castling, as if she talks of Mr. Jennings from the Post Office, not about one of the wealthiest men in the country.

"Well, yeah. Weston owns the investment firm handling my money." She shrugs. "We collaborated together on a project around domestic violence, but then he lost his wife, and the project was dropped," Lalah clarifies.

"Oh, shit, that's right." Jackson snaps his fingers. "He's rarely seen nowadays, although all his companies are thriving."

"It goes to show how much it doesn't matter the amount of money or power you have. Death forgives no one. That's why we need to make each day the best day of our lives. You never know when it's our last," Sawyer comments.

"Aaand that went dark real fast. Guys, Weston is fine," Lalah says. "Obviously, he was devastated when he lost Charlotte, but he stepped back from the spotlight for their son, Landon. Anyway, he now lives on an island, on the West Coast. He has a resort there that's absolutely amazing.

Sandy beaches, mountains, forests, everything you want, it's there. And we just so happen to have some cabins for ourselves booked there. I figured we could all use a long weekend away, and Mae and Tatum could do with a two-week honeymoon." She grins.

Her eyes are glinting, a flash of trouble ahead reflecting in her hazel irises, and I brace myself for the pearl that's sure to pop out of her mouth next.

"Plus, what better way to celebrate having a girl? She might be their only child, considering the vasectomy Maevis just gave Tatum."

Chapter Thirty-Two

Maevis

I'm so tired, my coffee needs coffee. And considering I was *persuaded* to switch to decaf, there's not a coffee in the world to help me. The three-hour flight definitely didn't help, nor did the one-hour drive around the island from the airport. I couldn't even enjoy the sights, since I was more focused on not peeing my pants, what with my little Vanilla Bean tap dancing on my bladder.

Tatum opens the car door and helps me out of the rental. Every muscle in my body sighs in relief as I finally manage to stand up straight. But my relief is short-lived when the evil baby in my belly kicks at my bladder again, and my knees nearly buckle with the need to just... let go.

"Oh shit," I squeak and push away from Tatum, rushing through the resort's reception area. I'm panting by the time I reach the desk, where a tanned man in his thirties wearing a black polo T-shirt sits. "Hi," I heave. "We have reservations. Lalah," *heave* "Hayes. BATHROOM. NOW."

His brown eyes widen comically, but he quickly springs into action. "Just through that door." He points to a sign marked as *Staff Only.* "Here, use this key."

Huh, I guess being pregnant with a watermelon hidden under my dress has its perks.

I snatch the keys out of his hand and run—fine, speed-waddle—to the bathroom. In the next breath, my dress is under my neck and my panties drop around my ankles. Aaand... "Fuuuuuuck," slips past my lips when pee-squatting does not happen as easily as it normally does.

For god's sake. I'm a woman. I have the pee-squat down pat. It's basically ingrained into our DNA, instinctual like breathing. But try to do this yoga pose with a bowling ball rolling around inside your body, kicking at your internal organs like it's the Olympic games of Whack-A-Mole, while your bladder screams bloody murder.

There aren't many instances when I wish I were a man, but right now I'm ready to worship at the feet of whatever god is willing to magic my vagina into a penis.

One ruined pair of panties and a lot of curse words sent to high heavens later, my bladder is blissfully empty, my hands are washed, and I'm once again at Tate's side, waiting for Lalah to deal with the check-in.

"Here we go," she says. "Tate and Mae, you have a cabin to yourselves." She gives us a card key first before passing one to my brother and his wife. "Maddox, this is yours. Jackson, you have your own, too. Emma, Selae, and Sawyer are sharing," she continues, but I'm not paying attention anymore as my eyelids flutter closed and my body sags into Tatum's.

I feel him bend at my back and in the next second, I'm airborne, cradled in his arms. My fingers weakly grip his T-shirt as I settle my head on his shoulder. The rhythmic thud of his heartbeat and the gentle sway of his walk lull me into a deep sleep.

An annoying light flashes over my face, rousing me from sleep. I stretch around in bed, grabbing Tatum's pillow and plopping it over my eyes. *Tatum's pillow?*

I jolt upright, scanning the expanse of the room, but my husband is nowhere to be seen. My eyes dart around the large, unfamiliar space. The walls are made from dark wood with huge windows on two of them, a mahogany bookshelf brimming with books pushed on the far wall. A round, cream-colored carpet sits at the end of the four-poster bed I'm currently occupying. I rub my eyes, taking in the delicate flower carvings on each of the four posts and the white, sheer curtains of the bed, falling around the corners like bows.

The sound of a shower running and the low moans coming from the bathroom draw my attention, and I scramble out of bed, pushing the soft blanket covering me aside. I tiptoe to the door and open it gently, trying not to startle Tatum. The steam in the bathroom makes it hard to see, but I don't miss his tall form behind the privacy glass of the shower, nor his slightly hunched shoulders.

I remove my sleeping T-shirt he must have dressed me in last night when we went to bed, and let it fall to the tiled floor, as I move closer to where Tatum is. My teeth sink into my bottom lip as more of him comes into view. His veiny forearm flexing and relaxing, the ruthless grip he has on his hard cock, the punishing pace he is using to jerk off.

A flame of annoyance and insecurity flares inside of me. Why is he rubbing one off in the shower when I was right there next to him in the bed? I look at my round stomach that's growing bigger by the hour and the red, angry stretch marks that appeared around my belly button. My eyes dampen, tears collecting on my bottom lashes.

I shake my head, trying to dispel the negative thoughts. No, my husband is not a shallow man. He spends hours each and every day kissing my belly, talking to our baby, nuzzling his scruffy cheeks against the tender skin.

Drawing a deep breath, I slide the glass screen open and step inside the shower with him. He spins toward me, hard cock still in hand, and his beautiful eyes, although hazy with desire, widen comically. Tatum definitely gives a new meaning to the deer-in-the-headlights look. His plush lips part—my name a breathy whisper on them nearly drowned out by the water pouring down on him.

I take a step closer, my hand finding purchase on his slick hip for balance. My free hand circles the fingers clenched tightly around his steel length. He relaxes his grip at my touch, and I guide his fist up and down his cock in slow strokes, my eyes never leaving his. He looks at me like he wants to devour me whole, like I'm his sole reason for existing.

Any trace of insecurity evaporates out of me when he lets go of the throbbing thickness between us, and my fingers touch the hard velvet pulsing with want in my palm. I cuff him at the base, squeezing tightly, and his chest trembles with the growl rattling his rib cage. My knees bend until my chest is level with his dick. I bring my arms close to my body, pushing my breasts together, caging all his hardness between the softness of my swollen breasts.

His hips rock, pushing his cock between my tits. The hot water pouring down on us makes my skin slippery enough that he slides against my breastbone with ease. I lower my chin, and on his next thrust up, I suck his slick head into my mouth, my tongue twirling around him, teasing him with gentle flutters, licking the saltiness of his precum clean off before releasing him.

"Baby," he grunts. "Goddamn."

I pay him no mind, squeezing my tits together harder, my nipples pebbling with need, a bolt of electricity traveling to my core. I moan around his length, my lips sheathing my teeth as I draw him into my mouth once again and suck hard, hollowing my cheeks. His knees buckle, his whole body taut and stiff under my palms. I hook my hands around his hard glutes and pull him to me until his cock is lodged deep in my throat.

The delicate muscles spasm and flutter as I gag around him, and I will my throat to relax, swallowing around his cock, massaging the underside of his thick length with my tongue. His hips try to shift back, but I press my palms on the back of his thighs, pushing him further into my mouth.

"Maevis," he begs on a pained wheeze, but I refuse to let up, choking myself on everything that he is. "Baby, please…" he moans, "I'm so close. What are you doing to me?"

I can't answer with my mouth stuffed full of him, so instead I hum my response, unsheathing my teeth so they gently scrape at his oversensitive skin. And that's all it takes. His cock throbs and jerks, and I pull back just in time for him to come all over my tongue. I heave in desperate gulps of air as I swallow his very essence.

The very next second I'm hoisted up, and my back meets the cold, wet tiles, his mouth against mine devouring me whole. His tongue doesn't ask for permission, plundering my swollen lips, much like his cock did just seconds before. I'm putty in his hands, a mess of trembling limbs and all-consuming need.

He falls to his knees in front of me, pushing my legs apart with his thighs, and then his insatiable mouth is on my slick flesh, kissing, licking and slurping. It doesn't take much, not when I'm so primed up for him, so ready to fall apart knowing he'll catch me.

His rough scruff scraping the inside of my soft thighs, his hungry mouth devouring my needy nub, two thick fingers spearing inside of my channel, and I'm done for. My pussy grips them inside of me, fluttering and pulsating, as my own orgasm courses through my body. I'm a ship lost at sea, overwhelmed by the waves of pleasure washing me ashore.

His mouth continues to make love to my pussy, peppering soft kisses on my clit, licking me clean of everything I have to offer, just for him.

"You're goddamn perfect," he rasps, pushing to his feet in a slow ascent, as he continues to trail kisses up my belly, to each of my breasts, sucking and nipping at my fevered skin, then at the hollow of my neck, and finally my mouth.

His arm sneaks around my back, and he pulls me close to him, as his lips touch mine, softly, tenderly, with all the reverence he has to give. "I love you so fucking much."

My heart hammers inside my chest at his words. Oh, he tells me daily—hundreds of times a day even—but I'll never tire of hearing him declaring his love to me.

"I love you too," I whisper, my voice scratchy and hoarse.

We help each other shower in silence after. He turns the water off and steps out of the steamed-out glass enclosure, then picks up a large, fluffy towel and wraps it around me. Using a smaller one, he pats my hair slowly with it, draining all the excess water, before using it on his own hair.

We make our way back to the bedroom, me wrapped like a burrito, him naked as the day he was born. In the bright sunlight shining through the windows, my insecurities return. I fidget on my feet, my eyes darting around the room, trying to locate our bags. When I find them next to the bed, I walk quickly to them and pick up the first maternity dress and pair of panties I find, then run back to the bathroom, locking the door behind me.

I drop the towel to the floor and pull the soft cotton up my legs, nearly slipping on the wet tiles when the door rattles.

"Maevis? Are you okay? Open the door, baby," Tatum demands from the other side.

"I'm fine," I squeak.

"Why'd you lock the door?" he asks, a faint thump in the wood resounding inside the ensuite.

I have no answer to that. What do I say to the man resembling a marble statue of a freaking Greek god? That I'm an insecure mess and even though he has shown me nothing but love and devotion, my mind is betraying me and draws parallels between him and my past in a vicious cycle?

My cheeks flame with embarrassment. How do I step out of this bathroom and look him in the eye and tell him I'm afraid he doesn't find me desirable anymore when he came on my tongue less than ten minutes ago?

I quickly pull my dress over my head and, with a deep breath, I unlock the door. My eyes refuse to leave my toes, refuse to look around as I quickly open it and step out, only to walk straight into the warm, rock-hard wall of muscles poised right over the threshold.

"OK. You're freaking me out," he says. "Why are you not looking at me? Did I do something you didn't like? Because I swear to god, Maevis, all you have to do is say 'Stop' and I'll always stop, baby."

I lift my head so fast at the anguished tone of his voice, I nearly give myself whiplash. "What? No. I loved everything we shared in that bathroom," I tell him, my voice resolute, if still a bit scratchy, my finger pointing behind me to the still steaming room.

His palm cups my jaw, tilting my head further back until his cornflower-blue eyes bore into mine; serious, intent, laser-focused. "Then what happened, Cupcake? Why are you acting so strange?"

My cheeks flush so fervently, I'm surprised his fingertips are not incinerated on the spot where he holds my head up. "I-I... uhm... you were... uhm pleasuring yourself... without me," I whisper, my eyes stinging. I swallow the pesky tears, gulping down their bitterness.

His blond eyebrows furrow, confusion all but tattooed on his forehead. "You were sleeping."

"Before the trial, you put me to bed and then went to the guest room," I press. Of course I feel like an asshole throwing in his face past behaviors, but it's like my common sense took a step back, allowing my insecurities to drive this train straight into a wreck.

"Because you were asleep, Maevis," he repeats.

"What does that mean?" I snap.

He pushes back from me, releasing my cheek and spearing his hand through his wet hair instead. "It means that both times you were not awake to give me permission, Maevis, goddammit."

Wait. What?

It takes but a second for the bulb in my sluggish mind to light up. "You never needed permission before."

He looks at me then, his pain and hurt bleeding out of his eyes. "Before? Before I took consent for granted. I've learned differently since."

Understanding courses through me, nausea pooling in my stomach. *This* is another consequence of that night. I grab his hand and pull him toward the bed. "Come with me," I urge over my shoulder.

When we get to the foot of the king-size frame, I point at the fluffy rug on the floor. "Sit," I order. An eyebrow curves up on his tanned forehead, but he does as I ask, and lowers himself down on the floor, his naked back resting against the dark wood of the frame.

I plop down on his lap, and his arms immediately band around me. Warmth spreads through my limbs, radiating from my chest. His reaction is automatic, like he knows there's no better place for him to hold his arms than around me. This is our bubble of trust, the bubble where we confess our darkest fears and deepest desires.

My cheek rests on his shoulder, and I allow the up and down movement of his chest as he breathes to lull me into a state of security. I need all the security I can muster to force the next words out of my mouth.

"Drake saved my life."

He stiffens under me, every hard muscle pulled taut. He's so tense and still, he's not even breathing, so I bring my palm up to his chest and rub soothing, calming circles above his heart.

With a kiss under his jaw, I tell him all about the night Daniel finally lost his goddamn mind and tried to choke the life out of me with his bare hands; how Drake and Maddox dropped in unannounced for a visit and had to physically rip him away from me; how my twin had to carry me, battered and bloodied, to the hospital.

And finally, I confess how being choked, regardless of the manner in which it happens, it's a trigger for me, taking me back to that night, reminding me of the moment I gave up and accepted the death I was sure would come, dealt so cruelly by someone I called *husband*.

The sob ripping out of his throat is inhumane. A wounded animal sounds less anguished than Tatum's howling pain on my behalf. His arms coil around my waist impossibly tight, his heaving breaths washing over me in a breeze of heat and despair.

"God, Maevis, and I did all those things to you..." he rasps, his voice thick with self-blame, jagged shards cutting deep into his very soul.

My fingers abandon his chest, cupping his prickly jaw instead. My thumb presses on his chin, forcing his head down, so he can look at me and see for himself the sincerity of what I'm about to say. "You didn't do anything to me. You didn't take anything from me. I trust you. Never for a second was I afraid you were going to hurt me. I was with you in the moment, giving you my trust in the only way I knew how."

His mouth opens, ready to protest, his doubt palpable between us. I shift on his lap, my knees falling on either side of his thighs, and intertwine my fingers at his nape, lowering his forehead to mine.

"I trust you with my life. I trust you with the life of our baby. I trust you to love and protect me. I trust you so much, I took to my goddamned knee in front of you and married you the very same day."

My lips brush the tip of his nose, a tiny smile playing at the corners of my mouth. "You have my absolute consent to freely touch me whenever you want, however you want. All I ask in return is a sliver of your faith. Husband, have faith in me to voice my refusal if any of my limits are ever crossed. Please, Tatum, please," I beg shamelessly, my heart breaking inside my chest at the scalding tears falling from his blue eyes, disappearing into the blond scruff of his cheeks.

Chapter Thirty-Three

Tatum

I'm hiding in the kitchen of the main cabin. Well, the cabin Lalah, Cole, and Blake are sharing that was designated Honeymoon Central since no one else felt like having their space invaded.

After the heaviness of Maevis's confession, I just couldn't see myself locked between four walls alone with her. Not with this all-consuming rage thrumming through my veins. Not with the irrational sense of betrayal poisoning my mind.

My fists clench and unclench on the black countertop of the island, all my nerves overshot by the anger boiling in my gut. That motherfucking weasel put his dirty, unworthy hands on her. And I never knew. Not until now.

A brief sliver of rationality shouts at me, trying to make me see sense, trying to get me to the understanding that even though we've known each other since childhood, we are in fact still getting to know each other. That our timeline is incredibly accelerated.

It was the still rational part of me that got me to bring Maevis here, knowing everyone will trickle down to this cabin for breakfast, even if they are worse for wear after their night partying at a local club. What I didn't know was the fucking tension they would bring with them.

Jackson and Blake are sitting on opposite sides of the room, not even looking at each other, their fucking animosity more palpable than ever. Emma is torn between the two of them, making herself as small as possible on one of the couches. That's one fuckery well on its way to blowing up in their faces.

Sawyer is hiding behind zombie-lookalike Selae, radiating guilt through every pore of her hungover body. The dumbass, Lawson, sits in the only free corner, hunched over and probably praying for death too by the *what have I done* look on his face.

The only ones looking remotely okay are Annalise and Drake. And of course, my wife, curled on the sofa, is eating the fruits I cut up earlier for her, balancing the plate on her belly.

A loud squeal comes from upstairs, followed by the sound of feet softly slapping against the hardwood floor, and deeper thuds chasing them. And there they are, Lalah in a pair of male boxers and a crop top, Cole in a pair of sleeping shorts, the mother of all hard-ons tenting them, both frozen still at the bottom of the stairs looking at the people milling in their cabin with wide eyes.

"For fuck's sake. Put that thing away," screeches Selae, her palm spread in front of her eyes.

That spurs Cap into action, throwing Lalah over his shoulder, and racing back up the stairs with her in tow.

"Someone make me a coffee," she yells. "Not Blake. Twenty minutes, please."

"Make that an hour," Cole shouts, his voice drowned out by the sound of a door slamming closed.

My eyes roll of their own accord, a deep sigh escaping my chest, as my mind turns back to the problem at hand. Maevis and I may be married now, with a child on the way, but based on this morning's events, I have a long road ahead of me to full trust.

Every little morsel of pain she drops in my lap, I can't help but look at it as a lack of faith in me. She says she trusts me. Hell, she's showing me through her actions, but it doesn't feel like enough. I know deep down that night in December affected me in ways I don't even realize yet. There's this need to know every single thing about her, every one of her experiences, what hurts, what soothes, and I possess very little patience inside of me for her to feed me crumbs.

And that's on me.

Godfuckingdammit, I'm an asshole.

I have every expectation of her to open up to me, and when she does, I dump her on a fucking sofa with our friends to keep her distracted so I can take time for myself. Even I have a shit ton of things I need to tell her and it will probably take the rest of our lives to do so.

Each memory, be it happy, vulnerable, or a downright depiction of hell, needs its own safe space to be shared. No two are the same, and no two require the same exact conditions to come to light.

With that resolve deeply planted in my mind, I stride with decisive steps to my wife, and kiss her stupid.

"WE NEED TO TALK," Jackson says, his voice cutting and serious.

We're all at the local steakhouse for dinner. I wanted a quiet night in with Maevis to actually practice my resolution from earlier today, but I've been outvoted. As *nice* as it is to spend the start of our honeymoon with our friends, I'd rather they just fucking leave already. But no, I still have to put up with them for another day. And then it's just my wife and me for another ten.

"Something wrong?" I question.

"Not sure yet. Grab a beer and meet me on the terrace."

My eyebrows lift to the middle of my forehead, but I give him a chin nod and make my way to the bar, ordering two non-alcoholic beers and asking the bartender to leave them sealed. I look at the table we've commandeered when we came in earlier. Maevis is laughing with my sisters, her hands moving about, her smile a mile wide. I type a quick message to her to let her know I'm having a quick catch-up with Jake before pushing through the door. The salty Pacific breeze greets me as soon as I leave the air-conditioned restaurant.

I find him at the furthest table from the entrance, pacing the width of the deck, an unlit cigarette dangling from his lips. With a lightning-quick move, I snatch it out of his mouth and crush it in my hand, throwing it in the ashtray bolted to the wall.

"I thought you quit," I note.

At the same time he barks at me, "What did you do that for, you cunt?"

He pushes his fingers through his hair, messing it up. He's all coiled tight, like a panther ready to pounce. Except there's no prey around—unless the prey is me. I offer one beer to him, and his unholy silver eyes jump to mine. There's a world of questions in them.

"I know you, dickhead. You walk around like you're a walking, talking goddamned enigma. You ain't."

He blinks once, and when his eyes open again, they're devoid of any emotion. Of course they are. Jackson thinks he's a one-way street. Information, emotion, your deepest darkest secrets—all are free to enter. Nothing's allowed to exit. He's an impenetrable vault. Or so he likes to think.

"You haven't touched alcohol in the past five years," I tell him because like calls to like, and I'm as big of a dickhead as he is, and this dickhead really likes to push his buttons. "You also don't touch anything you haven't made yourself or isn't sealed. Especially since December, but that's not new. So stop trying to decipher what I know and how and tell me why I'm here."

A muscle in his clean-shaven jaw ticks, the only outward sign of displeasure he's showing. Jake doesn't like that I know this about him. He blows out a breath and plants his hands on the wooden railing of the porch, looking out in the distance at the waves hitting the shore.

His refusal to look at me is telling. I won't like what he has to say. So I lean against the same railing myself, twist the lid off the beer and sip at the cold, bitter liquid, mentally bracing myself.

"I thought you were paranoid," he says, his voice so low I barely hear him over the sound of the restless ocean behind me and the faint music trickling from inside. "When you asked me to install security cameras on Maevis's apartment."

A jolt of dread hits my spine, the chill spreading through my body, my fingers clenching so tight against the reinforced glass I swear I can hear it cracking against my hold.

"What did you see?"

"There was nothing for months. I was ready to laugh in your face that you're as whipped as Hayes is and lost your everloving mind to a woman, seeing danger everywhere you look. Until this morning when I looked at the feed. Out of curiosity, more than anything." He shrugs. "And I saw her windows smashed again."

"What the fuck?" I hiss. "Who?"

"Don't know yet. But it was definitely not kids, and it was one hundred percent targeted. There are no fucking snowballs in May and no rocks or footballs thrown by mistake. I played the feed back. Around 3 a.m. a hooded someone took a fucking baseball bat to the windows, everywhere they could reach from the stairs. The door is dented, too. They tried to get in, but the lock held."

My mind is working furiously, trying to fit the puzzle pieces together. Three times that I know of her apartment was broken into—that's not a fucking coincidence. It can't be the bitch rotting in prison, since the first time it happened Maevis and I just started. The very same night.

"Man or woman?"

"Can't tell. Too dark. They held their head down. They also seemed to know about the camera I put in the visor since they avoided looking that way the entire time."

"Fuck," I exhale, the now familiar rage igniting deep in my gut. My hands tremble with the anger coursing through my veins, and I shove one down in my pocket, the other holding on to the now-warm beer bottle like a lifeline. I can actually feel the fucking vein in my forehead swelling and pulsing in the same rhythm as my thumping heart.

"There's more," he says, and my head whips in his direction.

"What fucking now?"

"I asked Rowan to drive by your house to check on things, just in case, after I saw the video. There was a package just thrown on the porch. He noticed the wrapping at the bottom was wet, even though it didn't rain last night in Lost Hope. The package was addressed to Maevis. He might've broken several federal laws, but he opened it. A gutted rat was inside."

I blink, sure I didn't hear him right. When I open my eyes, I see nothing but red, my very blood frozen inside my veins, the rage stalking my insides buzzing in my eardrums.

"Keep it together," he barks, his lethal tone cutting through the haze. "You need to talk to Maevis and find out if she received anything similar, if she's seen or noticed anything at all, or hell, if she suspects anyone."

"No," I snap. "Until we know something for sure, it'll only frighten her."

"And what's your plan, you lump? Glue her to you until we find out who that is?" he snarks back to me.

Now it's my turn to pace. I set down the beer bottle with more force than I intended, but my hands are still shaking. I need to punch something. I need to expel this heinous energy constricting my lungs.

"FUCK!!!" I bellow, and without any conscious thought, my fist hits the closest wooden post. Sharp jolts of pain travel through my knuckles to my elbow and shoulder, my skin smarting against the splinters sticking out from the post. It does nothing to calm the all-encompassing rage flooding my bloodstream.

Jackson restrains me from behind, holding my arms at my back in a steely grip. "Don't lose it on me now, *Ghost,*" he grits, his voice strained as he struggles to keep me contained. But the beast rattling at my rib cage somehow hears him, recognizes the call name I've been given by my brothers in arms, and backs off a notch. Jake's hold on me weakens slightly, but I know he's ready to knock me unconscious if I don't chill.

"All I wanted was a fucking week where nothing happens. One goddamn week when Maevis and I can just exist. She's six-months pregnant, for fuck's sake. The OB-GYN already told her at our last visit that her blood pressure was slightly elevated, and that we need to watch out for signs of preeclampsia. She needs to be relaxed and loved on, not threatened with dead fucking rats."

"I know, brother, I know. We've got your back. I fucking swear to you, we've got your back."

My shoulders slump, all fight leaving my body, the adrenaline evaporating as if it was never there.

"Get Cole involved and install security cameras at the family home, too, when you go back. I'll see what I can find out from Maevis, in a roundabout way. She deserves this fucking holiday, and she deserves to enjoy it before I break the news to her."

"Lawson?"

"Not yet. He'll want Drake to be involved, and as much as I appreciate him being protective of his twin, he may overreact before we get a sense of what we're dealing with."

"Overreact like you did just now?" I'm still with my back to him, but I *hear* the smirk in his tone.

"Fuck off!" I scoff, but there's no bite to my words. "I'll get to throw these words in your face sooner rather than later."

He ignores me, of course he does. Jake is convinced he'll spend his whole life alone and unattached, but the young Hayes is a stubborn asshole and he's had his eyes set on Jake for quite some time now. Blake's infatuation will either be the best thing to ever happen to Camden... or his fucking demise.

Chapter Thirty-Four

Maevis

This whole week has been bliss. Seven days of just my husband and I walking on the beach, trying all the restaurants and little shops the island has to offer, talking to each other, sharing stories, and memories, tears and laughs, ending each night with him buried inside of me, holding me tightly to his chest as we sleep. A whole week of bliss.

Sure, when you've been burned once, you test even the ice cream fresh out of the freezer, after. Not because you remember the pain, no. Tendrils of pain tend to linger inside of you, creating a strand of tension that pulls taut whenever you find yourself in a similar situation. But no memory of the pain itself, since the absolutely delicious taste of your favorite ice cream floods your body with dopamine, overloading all your pleasure centers. And your common sense.

The dopamine overload makes you drop your guard.

It's the reason why women all over the world have more than one child—voluntarily. The birth part? Splitting apart their bodies, feeling as if every single muscle and bone in their bodies shatters and fuses together as they bring new life into the world? As soon as their beautiful baby is placed into their arms, puff, like magic... it's gone. Forgotten. Dopamine overload. So they put themselves through the hell of labor again, and again, and again, because at the end of all the pain, all that *natural* torture, there's love and healing and happiness.

It's easy to get used to the good times. Right now, I'm in a bubble of my own making, so it's effortless to forget real life exists.

I stretch on the lounger like a lazy cat woken up from the best nap of her life. The sun is shining brightly, not a cloud in sight on the blue expanse of the sky. I'm tucked away in a corner of the deck of our cabin, under the biggest beach umbrella Tatum could get his hands on. No heatstroke for this lady here. Now, he's rummaging through the kitchen, putting together a fruit platter for me, whistling softly a love song I'm sure to tease him for what remains of our time here.

And the decade ahead.

Our baby girl kicks happily inside of me, and a giggle spills from my lips when I see the weird shape my distended belly takes. I rub on my tender skin affectionately, willing all the love I have for our growing baby to seep into her through my touch as I chase her movements with my fingertips.

A buzzing sound comes from behind the wide-open French doors leading to our bedroom. I swear to God, Drake calls at least five times a day to check in on me. I'm very much tempted to just turn off my phone, and if it weren't for my father and the possibility of the care home calling, I would have.

"Tate, could you please bring me my phone or answer my brother and tell him to kindly fuck off?" I laugh.

"Wife, you do love me. Look at you giving me the best honeymoon gift," he rumbles from somewhere inside, the sound of his faint chuckle trailing off as he moves away from the door.

I know he doesn't mean it. It's no secret Tatum used to despise Drake and Maddox. Mostly Maddox. It didn't help matters when my brother lost his goddamn mind and followed his best friend blindly into ignoring Lalah, a mistake *she* paid dearly for. But now, Tate and my twin seem to have reached some semblance of a truce.

Confiding the details of when Drake saved my life definitely went a long way toward improving my husband's opinion of my brother.

"What the fuck is this?" Tate asks, and everything in me freezes. My body stiffens against the hard plastic. Even my heartbeats slow for a moment as if afraid that if they pump at normal rhythm the sound would set Tatum off.

No. He's not shouting. In fact, his voice is deep, low, and raspy—and devoid of all emotion.

"Fucking answer me. What is this?" he repeats, pushing the phone with the screen unlocked in front of my face.

> *Did you like my carving? I made that especially for you, so you could see how you'll look soon enough.*

Restricted

> *Has no one taught you it is disrespectful not to thank people for their gifts? I've been patient, bitch. I'm coming for you.*

Restricted

I blink once. Twice. Three times. The burn stinging my eyes is similar to the burn in my lungs. It forces me to suck in a garbled breath, but words and sounds refuse to leave my mouth. My vision blurs under the torrent of tears coating my eyelashes.

"You looked me in the eye and swore that you trusted me. You fucking swore that you trusted me," he yells then, a slight tremor to his chilly words. "But you don't, do you? You don't trust me as far as you can throw me." He drops the phone on top of my thighs and storms off, the entrance door slamming closed behind him with such force, even the wooden deck under my lounger shakes.

See? I told you. I dropped my guard and became too comfortable in my bliss.

I'll have nightmares for months from the hundreds of times I heard the pre-recorded message of his voicemail today. He's been gone for hours with no sign, no message, not even a carrier pigeon or a smoke signal.

I sat for an hour on that sunbed, still like a marble statue, crying my eyes out as soon as he left, contemplating all my life choices and everything that led us here.

He honestly believes I don't trust him.

Do good intentions really matter when they cause the same ripple of destruction as selfish ones?

Maybe his assumption isn't entirely skewed. I trust him with my life, but my actions as of late and my deep-rooted instincts show me that I don't trust him with his.

That night, back in December, when faced with the picture of him and the rotten witch, I was overwhelmed by the flashbacks of a life I'd thought I left behind. I was convinced I was protecting myself while taking the time I needed to heal the wounds his actions inflicted on me. But, deep down, I had an inkling there was more to the story. Clad in my armor with all my shields up, I stuffed that feeling down. Smothered it under one prevailing thought—blame.

I blamed Tatum for putting himself in a vulnerable position, a position where she could take advantage of the softness he hides under his gruff and silent exterior. My mind, in its self-righteousness, decided on two likely scenarios. Either he was already drunk when he kissed me outside the bathroom and thus, susceptible to her vile charms, or she played the damsel in distress card and tricked him—and he let himself be tricked.

I held his mile-wide hero streak against him. The blame was born. Of course, it's always easier to blame the victim.

When the messages started, and we were just finding our footing, wrapping our minds around me being pregnant and our future of co-parenting, I didn't trust him to handle the disturbing but harmless messages.

When I found out the truth—a truth that everyone withheld from me—and witnessed the extent of all the darkness he carried inside, I decided I could help him shoulder the burden and glue all his broken pieces back together, but didn't trust him to handle my burden, too.

Visiting Maddison, listening to Amanda's lies during the trial, him reliving that night over and over again—I didn't trust him to be strong enough to carry me as well, to challenge my demons and conquer my fears.

Because guilt also joined the arena then.

I had to prove myself. Not him.

Fearing harmless texts meant weakness. And there was no space for weakness when I had to show him that *I* was strong enough to stand by his side.

Except, we are stronger when we lean on each other, not when we stand tall with a wall separating us. And I built the damned thing while he fought hard to dismantle it. A brick of misguided protectiveness, a layer of mortar blended out of guilt and blame, and a whole slew of egotistical intentions. And then I threw a triple-layered waterproof tarp over it—denial, denial, denial—to make it truly impenetrable.

For almost three weeks, there were no more messages. I thought whoever was sending those bone-chilling texts finally got bored with my lack of reaction and stopped. And I could carry on living, blissful and unaware, just me and my idiotic wall.

I was wrong.

And my passiveness may have cost me my husband, just one short week after he married me.

After another hour of waiting for Tatum to return, I tried calling. I sent maybe a hundred messages. And all for naught. Voicemail and the useless *Delivered* status.

The pretty blue sky from earlier this afternoon is now dark and gloomy. Even the stars twinkling above by the thousands seem to be dull and mocking.

I crumble in a heap next to the bed, the skin of my cheeks chafed and sore as I dry with the back of my hand another torrent of tears. My heart sputters and starts as it did for the past six hours since Tatum left. Not for the first time, it leaves me dizzy and weakened. Unease pools in my stomach, as my sobs give way to hiccups and heavy breaths.

Breathe, Maevis. For the sake of your daughter, just breathe.

The weight of how alone I truly am settles on my chest like a boulder. I can't reach Tatum; I can't call any of our friends and tell them what happened—how once again I let him down and left him in the dust; me running away even though I was right next to him the whole time. Reaching out to Drake is even more out of the question. My twin will overreact and point his finger at the wrong person.

My body sags against the hardwood footboard, but I have no strength left inside of me, so I let myself slide down until I'm a tight ball of sobs, tears, and regrets on the creamy soft rug.

I STARTLE AWAKE WHEN AN ECHOING THUMP sounds inside the bedroom, my heart hammering in my chest from the fright chasing away the last of my sleep. My eyes are gritty, as if a sandstorm blew every single

Saharan grain behind my eyelids, and I wince when the sunlight streaming through the windows stabs painful jolts into my retina.

With my elbows firmly planted on the soft mattress, I push myself into a sitting position, resting against the headboard. *Wait. Mattress? Headboard?*

A spring of heartbreak coils and unfurls inside of me when the events of yesterday slam into me; the text messages, Tatum leaving, me falling asleep on the floor. He must have come back sometime during the night and moved me to the bed.

I douse the spark of hope trying to ignite in my chest with an imaginary bucket of icy water. Him coming back doesn't mean anything, yet. I'm alone in bed. His side is as pristine and unwrinkled as it was after I made it yesterday morning. He might have taken pity on me and moved me from the floor, but he didn't sleep next to me.

I shove the sheets aside and force my feet to swing over the edge of the mattress and onto the dark hardwood of the floor, even though every single part of me screams not to leave the bedroom. Between these four walls and the closed bedroom door, nothing bad will happen. In here, there's uncertainty. But surely uncertainty is better than the guaranteed soul ripping that is to come as I leave my safe space.

Alone in this bedroom, I'm a Schrödinger experiment; both married and abandoned; both loved and despised; all I have to do is open the door to be faced with the cold hard truth.

But I'm not given that much reprieve. No. The door to the bathroom opens, and Tatum, fully clothed in jeans and a V-neck dark T-shirt, steps into the bedroom, our travel bags firmly held between a veiny forearm and his chest. His legs don't falter when he sees me, his blue eyes don't light up, there's no twitch at the corner of his mouth. Instead, he's donned a mask of indifference so cutting, I feel myself lose all my blood as if he sliced each one of my arteries open.

"Ah, you're awake," he says. There's no depth to his voice, no hitch in his breath, his tone as flat as his face.

"Tatum…" I try, my own voice shaky and trembling, but he doesn't even spare me a second glance, striding instead to the walk-in closet and pulling our suitcases out.

"We have one hour to check out," he informs me conversationally. I also hear what he doesn't say. *I'm checking out in one hour, with or without you.*

My knees buckle, but I keep myself upright, swallowing down the nausea inside the endless pit his words just opened in my stomach. My feet pad tentatively in his direction, each step a hollow echo in my ears.

"Please," I say, my trembling hand outstretched, reaching for him. Tate turns just then and flinches away from me. His impassive mask cracks—his eyes narrow at me and his nostrils flare. A purple angry vein pulsates across his forehead. My shoulders hunch on reflex and I instinctively make myself smaller.

I've never been afraid of Tatum and his anger.

Until right this very second.

The way he looks at me now, like I'm the bird shit stuck to the soles of his shoes that he simply can't get rid of, has my instincts screaming at me to hide. My throat constricts under the steely, cold grip of fear that's coating the inside of my rib cage. The fine hairs on my arm stand on point under the current of dread washing through me. I drop his stare, unable to hold it for a second longer, and look at the black hem scuffing his Converse.

I take a step back, and then another, and another, until the back of my legs hits the edge of the bed, and then, as quickly as I can, I spin on my heel and run to the bathroom, locking the door behind me. I'm frantic, my movements disjointed. My lungs barely inflate with the little oxygen I give them as I push the wide linen cabinet over the door, blocking it. And then I'm on my knees, hugging the white toilet, heaving down the drain acidic bile, bitter tears, and the last of my hopes.

Chapter Thirty-Five

Maevis

A gentle knock on the bathroom door forces me to scramble up on shaky legs from my rock-meet-bottom place on the tiled floor.

"Maevis?" he asks, the same coldness in his voice, but there's the tiniest thread of caution, too. "Are you ready to go?"

"Not yet," I croak. My throat burns as I force the words out, and I rush to the sink to rinse my mouth, gulping at the cold water coming from the tap. "Give me five more minutes, please."

"Maevis... open the door."

My stomach turns again. The pit inside grows larger. I startle when the knob turns, my palm flying to my chest, trying to steady my racing heart, and I involuntarily take a step back. A gasp slips past my lips when the useless slab of wood flies open.

So much for the linen cabinet being a layer of protection since the fucking door opens toward the bedroom.

And there he is.

In all his indifferent glory.

He wears the same unreadable mask on his face—lips set into a thin line, jaw clenched. All that's missing is the angry vein that scared me out of my mind but has since made a swift disappearance. His hands are straining into tight fists on either side of his trim hips, and his strong legs are planted firmly into a shoulder-width stance.

His eyes, though, his eyes are bleeding a world of hurt. They drop to the linen cabinet in front of him before moving back to me. Betrayal screams at me from the dimmed blue of his irises.

"Why?" he breathes, his chest expanding on a deep inhale before shrinking again, the movement making Tatum somehow look smaller.

I look anywhere but at him, my fingers fidgeting with the hem of my T-shirt as I replay in my mind our interaction in the walk-in closet. My heart falls to my feet as a sinking feeling bulldozes through me, and I'm forced another step back.

"I... I d-don't know," I stutter. "I just reacted."

"You thought I'd lay my hands on you?" The pained shock in his words feels worse than a slap. My palm, still resting on my chest, twitches as if it reflexively wants to lift up in the stale air between us like a shield. Who to protect? Right now, I'm not sure the answer is me.

"I don't know what I thought. I feared you," I murmur and chance a peek at him. His fingers are buried in his hair, one palm planted on the door frame, his flexed biceps supporting his weight, his head bent low, chin nearly touching his chest.

"So this is how it feels to hit rock bottom," he murmurs, the sound so low, I don't think I was meant to hear.

Fuck, what am I doing to him?

I physically recoil when startling clarity hits me without mercy—much the same like I've done to Tatum—and my back meets the wall. My weakened legs finally give up on me, and I slide to the floor, goosebumps spreading on my skin as my ass touches the cold tiles.

"They started two months ago," I hear myself saying, my voice monotone and soulless. "In fact, the first ones were sent the morning after you helped me with my... uhm... hormonal situation. At first, I thought it was Amanda. I thought you and her were still seeing each other."

"Holy fuck, Maevis. Your opinion of me is really that low? You honestly thought I'd eat you out like your pussy is my favorite meal and then turn around and run to her?"

Despite the chill on my skin, a flush burns its way up from my chest to my cheeks. I bet if I were to look in a mirror, I would find them beet red, both from his words and from the memory of that night coming to the front of my mind.

"You looked horrified before you left," I defend.

"Because I thought I'd taken advantage of your state. For god's sake, Maevis," he snaps. "I walked in on you playing with yourself and I lost my goddamned mind. All I knew was that I needed a taste of you. Nothing else mattered in that moment but you writhing under me, you coming on my tongue."

I have no arguments for that. It was what I fervently wanted then, too. "I knew what I was asking for, Tate," is all I can say, trying to at least erase the worry of him preying on me.

"What else did you get?"

"Just texts. All day, every day, at random hours. I stopped reading them after the first couple of days," I reply truthfully.

"When did you know they weren't from Amanda?" he asks, and I can't help but feel as if I'm interrogated. The most bizarre interrogation of my life, where the bad cop can't even look at me, and I'm a mess of a woman lying on a bathroom floor.

"At the trial. I received one while she was in the witness stand."

"Fuck!" A loud thump and the screech of wood sliding against marble drown out the curse when he hits with his foot the linen cabinet still poised between us.

"They stopped just after the book club meeting last month, just like that. No word, not even an emoji, until the ones you read yesterday." I draw my knees to my chest—well, to my belly—and rest my arms on top of them. "I thought they were done. Whoever it was got bored playing one-sided threat games and left me alone."

He slips inside then, turning sideways to fit between the cabinet and the wall, then plops down on the floor in front of me, one leg stretched out, nearly touching mine, the other bent at the knee, supporting the forearm dangling from it.

"Why did you hide it from me?"

I know the honest answer. I've thought about it hard and long all day yesterday, but the absolute truth is... "I didn't."

He scoffs at me then, a derisive snort full of indignation and disbelief. "I didn't," I insist. "I never hid my phone from you. You know my passcode, too. I did not actively hide the messages, simply didn't mention them." And I hoped in the deepest most selfish corners of my heart that he'd find the messages on his own, without me having to bring them up.

"Right." He shakes his head in derision. His eyes burn holes into the wall behind me, but never once seek mine out.

"We were hit with one thing after another," I cry then, unable to contain the sob stabbing at my chest for a second longer. "Messages without the smallest hint of follow up felt insignificant in the face of everything else we were dealing with."

My fingers fiddle with my messy braid as I wait for him to say something, anything. He remains quiet, though. Still as a statue, Tatum is the very epitome of a broken man. I sigh, my mind working overtime, trying to choose the right words to fix this wrong.

"All I wanted was to give you a bit of time to breathe. For us to experience happiness without any speed bumps for a little while—a misguided attempt on my part to protect you. Instead, once again, I took the choice from your hands. I decided what was best for you and what you could take on. And for that, I'm sorry," I say, biting on my cheek until I taste blood on my tongue to stop myself from spewing what feels like more empty excuses.

I feel it then, the absolute strength of his undivided attention, burning a path of redemption and punishment on my skin as it travels from my knees to my face. There's longing in his blue gaze, calculation in his blatant perusal of me, but also defiance in the jarring sound of his teeth grinding together.

"It's my job to protect you."

"Is it?" I ask, my voice cutting like a whip, a fire lit in my belly. "Maybe this is where we both went wrong. *Our* job is to be a team. Protection? Love? Caring? We're a couple, we're supposed to share. Share the pain, share the happiness, share a future."

His eyes widen and... *Is that guilt on his face?*

"What are *you* hiding?" I demand, the accusation lingering between us, thick and suffocating.

He draws in a breath with such urgency it feels like all the oxygen in the room is vacuum-suctioned.

"The apartment above the bakery was broken into... again," Tatum whispers, his voice hoarse, as if his vocal cords refuse to sound the words.

Fucking denial. It's too easy to live in denial. And I clearly choose the easy way, each and every time. When my mom died and my father succumbed to his grief, I denied my own chance at grieving to support him. If I didn't think of the unfairness of the hit and run, I wasn't hurting. My mom lived a full and happy life. She was loved. She was cherished. I clung to that.

Daniel wasn't a cheating alcoholic, just misguided and hurt by the lack of jobs. Denial, denial, denial. Until denial wrapped its cold fingers around my throat and tried to choke the life out of me.

Visiting my father in the care home every day, looking at his weathered face, I wasn't dying inside every time half of his smile refused to cooperate and remained in a lopsided curve. His handsome features weren't the very definition of *one eye smiling, one crying.* No, spoon-feeding him blended vegetables and seeing his pride withering under my very own eyes wasn't any cause for pain. Denial.

The chill crawling up my spine every time I went into that apartment and found a window broken or some random item misplaced or just... not quite how I left it before opening the bakery—it wasn't anything serious. Nah, that was just my imagination.

"What else?" I croak. Because that chill I just mentioned? It's still weaving its scaly talons through my vertebrae, puncturing my very marrow.

There's pity now in the blue depths of his irises—pity and heartbreak. Fear, too. He's afraid for me. The veil of denial suppressing my vision lifts. I gulp down the lump in my throat. I'm scared, too. But the truth I was too cowardly to stare in the eye?

It's right here, sprawled out on the cold marble floor, all six feet, inked up skin, and messy hair of him, wedding band heavy on his finger, taking front and center.

All I ever wanted was to have my own person.

And he is right there in front of me.

All I have to do is let him in. Truly let him in. To give him the power to destroy me yet trust he'll never do it.

Except, I got it all wrong. He let me in, and in my misguided attempt to protect my heart *I* was the one destroying him.

I hurt him repeatedly, and all he has done is come back for more.

"Tell me," I insist, my voice lighter than just a minute ago, the weight crushing my chest vanishing under my sobering thoughts. Whatever it is, I can take it. And if I can't? He'll hold me up when my own legs fail me.

"A dead rat."

I blink once.

Twice.

I'm tempted to stick my finger in my ear to release the pressure that's surely blocking my eardrums because I'm not hearing him correctly, right?

"A dead rat in the apartment?" I confirm.

"No, Mae," he sighs, dejection pouring out of him. "A dead rat in a box addressed to you. Left on our porch."

The room sways, the image of my husband less than two feet in front of me blurring. My hands fall to my sides as arctic tingles race through my veins. A heave crawls up my esophagus, bile pooling in my mouth.

"Mae?" I think Tatum is calling my name, but I'm underwater and can't reach him. "Baby? Shit, you're white as a fucking ghost."

A warm hand cups my cheek and, with the last of my energy, I nuzzle my face into it. *Safe. Home. Tatum.* Gentle strokes of a calloused finger smooth down from my temple to my jaw.

"Breathe, baby. Come on, Cupcake, breathe."

I would laugh, but my body refuses to answer any of my commands.

Harmless texts. How stupid am I?

That's the last thought I have before darkness overtakes the blurry image of a freaked-out Tatum, and I succumb to my own fright.

Chapter Thirty-Six

I watch her as she sleeps, her palm protectively nestling the roundness of her belly, wavy hair spread on the white pillow cradling her head, pink lips slightly parted, and marble white cheeks.

I died a thousand deaths on that fucking island waiting for an ambulance. I died a million more pacing the Emergency Room at the hospital, waiting for a doctor, a nurse, or even a janitor to come and bring me news of my wife.

As it turns out, Maevis was severely dehydrated and her blood pressure skyrocketed. The on-call doctor at the ER kept her there overnight to monitor her, recommending upon her discharge that we return home and see her OB-GYN. After the longest flight of my life and a stern soaping from Doctor Fritz, we finally got home about five hours ago with strict instructions for Maevis to rest, hydrate, and avoid anything that could get her blood pressure up.

Guilt and shame war inside of me.

I overreacted like a fucking dickhead, and instead of talking to her like I should've, I shut down. My own actions harmed both my wife and my child. When those texts shone at me from the screen of her phone, I blacked out. Fear clawed at my insides, all the fucking insecurities from *that* night flooded my bloodstream.

I watched myself on that deck, confronting Maevis, and I couldn't fucking stop the trainwreck from happening. When I finally got some semblance of control over myself and saw the tears falling down her cheeks, I had to remove myself from the situation before I made it any worse. I walked around the island for hours, talking to my therapist, all but begging her to reveal some miracle coping mechanism, some magic tool to right all my wrongs so I could go back to the love of my life and be the man she needed me to be.

Trauma, however, doesn't work that way. Even when I have no clear memory of what happened *that* night, my body remembers it. It remembers the tension and sends distress signals to my brain, my therapist explained. Maevis was and remains my beacon of hope. During my darkest moments, my single focus was to get to her. And she ran away from me.

When I questioned who I was as a man, as a partner, as a human being, I rightly or wrongly made her to be my fountain of answers, my tether to balance. But she turned her back on me and left me unmoored.

I thought that throughout the past few months, I've worked through a lot of my issues; that I managed to understand them and move past them. But that was my recklessness talking. The impatience of wanting to be a whole man for the love of my life blinded me to a fundamental truth.

There's no self-imposed timeline to the trauma. Murky waters don't bend to the will of a fish. Swishing my tail as fast as a hummingbird flaps its wings won't clear the water and make it an oasis. I swam headfirst into the muddy bank.

And now I need to proverbially remove my head from my ass.

And fucking do better.

Skip no more steps.

Keep my eyes wide open and my mind clear.

The ironic, cutting truth is... at my very core, I don't trust my wife to trust me. Because I don't trust myself.

Make that make sense, if you will.

I drag my palm over my face to dispel the negativity I'm losing myself in. Blame and guilt are the easiest rabbit hole to fall down through. And let me tell you, I'm no *Alice in Wonderland.* More like the Mad Hatter.

Just a week ago, I made vows to my wife. I pledged myself to her entirely. She deserves the best of me, and she'll get exactly that. I simply need to accept that sometimes, the best of me means sunshine and roses, and sometimes it means standing back, supporting her quietly. It means allowing her to see me at my weakest and learning all over again that with her by my side, even my most vulnerable parts are strong.

Fear is a holdback. Sure, I'm giving her the power to ruin me, but everything Maevis touches is pure magic. I'm so fucking in love with this woman. My knees grow weak every time she gifts me one of her shy smiles. So instead of letting fear control me, I'll let my love for her guide. And hope with every fiber of my being, she'll be there at the end of the road to receive me.

"She's going to wake up if you keep creeping on her," Lalah says softly from behind me.

"You know?" I ask. I don't dare turn around to face her, though. Fear may be a holdback, but I like my balls intact, thank you very much, and when it comes to my best friend, fear is a very, very healthy feeling.

"I do." Her palm lands on my shoulder in a gentle squeeze, a show of support. "It's impossible for Cole to keep secrets from me."

Her words are not reproachful, not even the smallest hint of chastising in them, but they cut, and cut deep. Because I have kept secrets from Maevis. The first secret was a punishment painted as self-preservation, the second I named it protectiveness when it was simply a feeble attempt for me trying to prove myself.

"I fucked up," I admit.

"Did you, though?"

Her question takes me aback. So much so, my head whips in her direction. She's watching me intently, not a trace of judgment on her face. Well, except for that cocked eyebrow arched in a *Let's hear the dumb thought process that led you to that conclusion.*

"You urged me to talk to her. I did everything but talk."

Her arm sneaks around my elbow, and she pulls me away from the door and to the entrance. I plant my feet on the hardwood floor, refusing to move when I realize she wants us to go outside.

"I need to be near," I plead. "In case she needs me."

"Blake's in the kitchen cooking. If she needs you, he'll come get you." Her voice is resolute. There's no arguing with Lalah when her stubborn streak hits. And then she fucking pushes me out on the front porch. "Sit." She points at one of the rocking chairs.

And sit, I do. My eyes squint in the bright sunshine, but I can't deny being outside does me good. Feeling lighter somehow as I inhale the crispness of the mountain air and the sweet fragrance of the linden tree flowers, I slump into the wooden chair. A cool bottle is pressed into my chest next.

"No alcohol for me," I tell her. Jake and Cole might have installed security cameras to rival Lalah's, but I need to remain sharp and in control of myself.

"When have I ever given you an alcoholic drink, Tate?" she scoffs and drops it in my lap before backing away a couple of steps to sit in the other rocking chair. She leans back, her fingers fidgeting with the label on her own bottle.

"How are you not melting in that sweatshirt?" I laugh. I know she's gearing up to chew my ass, and as much as I'm determined to learn and grow, getting my ass reamed after the hell of the past two days is not something I signed up for.

"This thing?" She laughs right back, plucking at the black material on her chest where in large red caps *I like big books and I cannot lie* is written. "I'm part lizard, always running cold." Her fingers fly from her sweatshirt to her lips, her pointer and middle finger drumming against them for a beat before moving back to peel at the label some more.

"Quitting sucks balls," Lalah declares with a huff. "Never get addicted to shit. It's downright painful to give up."

"You quit vaping, too?" I ask, the corners of my lips tugging up with pride. I've been on her case since I met her to drop the fucking things.

"I'm not counting those. They were a stepping stone from cigarettes. I used them as crutches, kidding myself that smoking took the edge of my anxiety. The things we tell ourselves to help us get through the day," she laughs derisively. "I fucking hate vaping. And the only reason I did vape was because I wasn't ready to completely give up my crutch."

"You don't need one anymore," I conclude.

The smile on her face is brighter than the fucking sun. "Nah. I'm strong enough on my own two feet. And when I'm not? Cole's strong enough to hold me upright. All I have to do is... let him."

"Point taken," I concede. "It's not easy."

"Nothing ever is with us, Tatum. Our trauma may be different, but you and I? We were made to feel deep. We were made to hurt even deeper. Fucking hell, *worthless* might as well have been my middle name as far as my own darn family is concerned. Yours is *loyalty.* A lovely quality to have when it doesn't force you to shoulder the weight of the whole world."

"How'd you figure that?" I ask, bemused. Of all the things I was expecting her to say—yelling, a whole lot of swearing, a threat or two to the family jewels—the downside of my loyalty was not among them.

"You live and breathe loyalty, Tatum. It's your privilege and your burden. Loyal to your father and his expectations of you." She pauses, taking a long pull of the non-alcoholic beer, and I follow suit. Her analysis makes my throat dry out as she cuts into me, exposing all my vulnerabilities. "God knows I love Tatum Senior to bits, but one look from him and I want to stand at attention like a good little Marine."

"How's that the root cause of all my demons?"

"It's not. It's the music they dance to. When you use your loyalty to everyone else except to yourself as a measure of success, you're digging your own fucking grave and get buried under misplaced responsibilities." Lalah's hazel eyes pierce mine, searching, intruding. I almost want to look away from her. It's none of her fucking business. "You proved your loyalty to your father by becoming the man of the house when he was away. You earned his respect and love through acts of service."

"My family's deserving of all my loyalty," I snap, my whole body tightening under her accusation.

"Never claimed otherwise. But you are deserving, too." She straightens in her seat, her feet firmly planted on the floor. "You told me it was your own recklessness that got you hurt in that last mission. If you're being honest with yourself, Tatum, it wasn't your recklessness. It was the ghost of the lingering loyalty you had for a marriage never meant to be."

"You're not pulling any punches today," I deadpan, but her words hit bullseye. She's not wrong.

"I'm done pussyfooting around. It's physically painful for me to watch you and Maevis attract and repel. The angst... bitters my coffee. I'm doing myself a fucking favor."

The snort escaping me is what's physically painful right now. I'm just happy I wasn't drinking since no one needs beer bubbles exploding through their nostrils.

"Apologies, Your Highness. I didn't realize my love life was such an inconvenience to you."

"No one messes with my coffee, Tatum," she says and throws a ball of wet paper at me. "My point is that regardless of how many times you prove yourself, it's never going to be enough. Not when you're not on the receiving end." She points her beer bottle at me. "My demons told me Cole was better off without me. I tried to push him away because I love him. Yours demand for you to be an island, to weather any and all storms alone, keeping the high tide to yourself. By doing that, you're also keeping Maevis away because, in your loyal head, that's your act of service."

"That's never been my intention."

"Your intent may be off, but your aim is true. Be a fucking island if you must, Tate. You don't need to change the fundamentals of who you are. You're a goddamn amazing man. But be amazing with a bridge. Let Maevis be that fucking bridge for you."

I let her words run free through my mind. What would that feel like, I wonder? An island with a bridge. And what a goddamn beautiful bridge my wife makes.

Chapter Thirty-Seven

Maevis

My fists hit the dough like it personally offended me. If I stick a picture of Tatum's stupid, handsome face on it, I might be more effective with my kneading. At least, I get a breather at the bakery. No overbearing, overprotective husbands are allowed in my kitchen.

This past week has been... torturous. The man wouldn't even let me grab a glass of water by myself. It got to the point where I had to call Doctor Fritz, and had her write a note with what I was allowed and wasn't allowed to do. Not that it helped much.

He refuses to understand that basic activity won't harm me. And the things actually causing me stress? Him sleeping next to me in bed but refusing to touch me, except for when he pulls me to his chest and lets me use him like my personal full-body pillow. The constant over-vigilance and him being on edge all the time, which in turn makes me look over my shoulder even as I cross the hallway from the bedroom to the living room. And the big, humongous elephant, taking up air and space between us—his constant struggle between sharing potentially upsetting news and his almost obsessive need to turn me into a bubble-wrapped burrito and hide me in an underground vault.

I huff a breath to push away the wayward, curly tendril of hair stuck to my skin and my left eye. No luck. Bending my head, I rub my forehead against my rolled-up sleeves, and finally, the pesky thing clears out of my vision, which is the only reason I see movement with the corner of my eye, startling the living cookie out of me.

Yeah, that scream... I'm not proud of. My palm, flour, dough, and all, flies to my chest, while my other plants firmly onto the stainless-steel counter to support my weight.

"Holy fried pineapple, you tryin' to give me a heart attack? How did you get in here?" I say, my voice still high-pitched and breathy after the fright my brother just gave me.

"I called your name five times, Mae-Rae," he rumbles, a sheepish look on his face. "Really should lock up when you're all alone back here. Especially if your ears are all stuffed up with daydreams."

My eyebrows jump to my hairline, and my heartbeat speeds up again. "The front door was locked. I swear I locked it," I defend, but his whiskey eyes squint at me, disbelief practically painted on his face.

"Pregnancy brain again?" Drake questions. There's no accusation in his tone, maybe a bit of humor, but it rubs me the wrong way. I distinctly remember locking the front door, locking the register after I spent the morning tallying the weekend sales, then coming into the kitchen.

I spin on my heel and barrel through the door and onto the main floor of the bakery. Nothing looks amiss. Everything's exactly the same way as I left it. Except for... "Why's the register open?" I ask no one, rushing to check it over. Of course, there's nothing missing since I emptied the cash and receipts once I was done with it.

Maybe I wanted to lock both the entrance and the register, and I forgot? This pregnancy has really played tricks on me. At the beginning, everything I was thinking, I was also saying out loud. Then came the horniness, making me climb Tatum every five minutes. For the past week or so, the horniness died down to normal levels, and the pregnancy brain kicked in.

"If you breathe a word of this to Tate, I'll tell Annalise all about your senior year trip to Mexico." My finger finds its way to Drake's chest since he's following me like a shadow.

"You wouldn't dare." He sucks in an outraged breath.

I cross my arms over my chest, chin pointed high at him. "Try me."

"Fine, not a word." He concedes, rolling his eyes at me. Sometimes, it's extremely difficult to be mature, even at thirty-four, when old twin rivalries come to the surface. I have the dirt and he knows it.

"Why are you here, though? I have nothing baked. Tessa will come in later this evening to do the prep for tomorrow."

"You really need to hire someone. Closing on Mondays ain't right. Half of LHFD is walking around in a daze, like a horde of zombies, depleted of sugar." He smiles, and I don't miss the pride shining in his eyes. A surge of warmth pushes back the annoyance I feel toward my brother. He means well, and after our mother's death, Daniel's misgivings, and our father's stroke, I can't really fault him for being all up in my business whenever something doesn't sit right with him.

"I'm working on it, I promise," I assure him and tuck myself in under his arm, squeezing his waist one-handed. Can't give anyone proper hugs anymore, not with the beach ball under my dress growing larger and larger every day. He bends down and kisses the top of my head, his palm moving up and down my upper arm.

"You've been summoned," Drake says. "Carter is waiting for you at the waterfall."

My forehead creases as I shoot him an inquisitorial look. "What's he doing there?"

"Guess you'll find out when you get there, Mae-Rae." He shrugs minutely. "Come on. I'll help you clean up, so you'll be on your way soon."

The whole time we spend cleaning the kitchen and then on the short drive to the waterfall, my mind keeps trying to figure out why Tatum needs me to go there. I tried calling him, despite Drake's protests, but got no answer.

The Teardrop Waterfall is one of my favorite places. As a teenager, I used to escape here every time I needed a moment to myself. I'd read, write recipes and work them out in my head, or simply exist in silence, with just the sounds of the rustling forest and the thunder-like roar of the waterfall.

The slope of the mountain it falls down from is curved, carrying the resemblance of a scruffy cheek, hence the veil of water and mist being called Teardrop. At the bottom, it pools into a round pond before the bank closes in tighter and tighter, and the Forrest Falls river forms again to snake between the town bearing its name and Lost Hope.

It doesn't disappoint now either. With the sun high in the sky, the misted pond looks bridged by rainbows. I lower the window of my car as I near and let the scent of damp earth and evergreens fill the tiny cab. As usual, the place is completely empty.

I turn the engine off, picking up my handbag from the passenger seat, and for the second time in one hour, an unholy scream rips out of me as my door opens.

"Cupcake, fuck, I'm sorry," Tatum rushes out, crowding me inside as he curls around me, unbuckling my seatbelt. He helps me out of the car, and when I'm standing next to him, his palms cup my face, and then he gives me the mother of all kisses. His soft lips meld with mine, his tongue, hot and wet, slips inside my mouth, stroking mine in lazy caresses. My hands grip his muscular forearms as butterflies take flight inside of me and my knees buckle.

His warm, minty breath washes over me when he breaks our kiss. A whimper of protest spills past my swollen lips and my eyes spring open. He smiles at me, the dimple I want to trace with my tongue playing peek-a-boo under his blond scruff. Topaz blue shines at me from under hooded eyes, hunger and affection warring on his face. "Hi," he whispers.

"Hi," I giggle like a schoolgirl, because the sight of a playful Tatum knocks the breath out of my chest. "What's this? A secret rendezvous?"

"I realized that we've been living together for a couple of months now. Hell, we're married, but we haven't been on an actual date. We certainly mixed things up well and good." He chuckles ruefully. "So, this is, I hope, the first of many dates."

"Are you asking me to go steady with you, Carter?" I laugh, even though my cheeks are blazing red-hot and my heart takes flight inside my chest.

A deep sigh slips past my lips as I take in the navy-blue T-shirt that looks painted on him. The soft material hugs his wide shoulders snuggly, tight on the hills and valleys of his chest before falling loosely over those mouthwatering, inked abs and his narrow hips. His low-slung, dark-wash jeans encompass his strong thighs, the hem hitting just below his knee, and from there, it's all delicious skin and swirls of ink, down to his Converse. My husband is one damn fine man. And all mine.

Tatum drops his large palm to my belly. His other clasps my left hand, lifting it to his mouth. "You're wearing my ring and carrying my baby. It doesn't go any steadier than this," he growls, and wetness pools between my tights at the possessiveness in his voice.

Was it me punching a ball of dough while picturing his face on it just an hour ago? Surely not. Not with how my nipples harden and my core tightens in need of him.

"So what do you have planned for us?" I ask, my voice all breathy, my cheeks flushing red.

The smirk he gives me doesn't help any. Tate knows exactly what type of thoughts plague my mind right now. But he doesn't act on them. Instead, he takes my hand, intertwines our fingers, and pulls me closer to the rocky beach of the pond. A large wicker basket rests on a boulder. Next to the weathered rock, a checkered, black and red blanket is spread out on a grassy area.

"I thought we could have a picnic and, as outlandish as it may sound, get to know each other." His own cheeks color red as he throws me a panicked look. I squeeze his hand in understanding. Because I *do* understand. We know a lot about one another, it's impossible not to growing in the same town, but it's all superficial.

Oh, we have deep and intimate knowledge of each other's bodies, and even of some more obscure things that not everyone gets to know. But there are so many conversations we should have had, and we didn't. So many places where we need to get on the same page, but we're coming from opposite directions.

Tatum helps me sit on the soft blanket, and I tuck my feet under me as he plops down on his side. He curls his body around mine, propping himself up on an elbow. One-handed, he opens the basket and pulls out a fruit tray, followed by my favorite milkshake, and a coffee for him. Next comes a big, white box, which I recognize to be one of the insulated food carriers from my kitchen.

"Did you cook?" I ask him.

"As a matter of fact, I did. Everything, except for your milkshake." He throws me a boyish grin, and I sigh happily. How can I not? He's so freaking adorable right now, and this is not a word I've ever thought I'd use when thinking of my husband. Devastatingly handsome? Sure. Hot and broody? Damn straight. Adorable and Tatum don't really go together. Except for right now, when he's all proud, crooked smile, shining blue eyes, and wind-swept blond hair.

I run my fingers through the unruly strands, pushing them away from his forehead. "Thank you," I whisper, choking back the emotion coating my throat. *Damn hormones, now is not the time for me to cry.*

He pushes up on his elbow, his eyes searching mine before planting a chaste kiss on my mouth. "You're welcome. You might not be too impressed, though. I kept it simple—steamed vegetables, grilled chicken breasts, roasted potatoes, and gravy."

My hand curls around his nape, and I pull him closer, kissing him again. "I'm impressed, regardless. You're going to have to live with the fact that you're making your wife swoon all over the place."

A boyish grin tugs at the corner of his mouth as he opens up the box one-handed, taking out two wrapped plates from inside. He carefully peels off the paper from each before passing one to me—steam still wafting despite the warm weather outside. The aroma of rosemary, garlic, and thyme hits me, making my stomach growl.

"This smells... heavenly," I praise, my mouth watering.

"Dig in," Tatum says, kissing my bare knee, before he shifts to a seated position in front of me.

For a little while, only the sound of silverware scraping over porcelain plates, happy groans, and hungry moans fill the air. I stuff my face with the best lunch I've had in forever, my taste buds euphoric with the burst of flavor from each morsel. That my husband has gone to all these lengths to cook for me makes it incredibly special. The fresh mountain air and the thundering of the waterfall only add to the magic of this moment.

A strangled groan leaves his mouth when mine wraps around the paper straw of my milkshake. "What?" I mumble around it, feeling self-conscious at the intense way he stares at me. Tingles rush through my body as his gaze moves from my mouth, down my throat, to the swell of my breasts where he pauses for a heartbeat or two before continuing along to my belly.

"You're so goddamn beautiful, it's sometimes painful to look at you," Tate murmurs.

Heat blossoms in my cheeks at his words and my eyes drop to my half-eaten plate. He's not stingy with his praise and always finds ways to compliment me on my looks. At times, my insecurities make it hard for me to believe him. I'm plain Maevis, Flat Earth, vanilla—the blandest of flavors. But not with Tatum.

The way Tatum looks at me like I'm the best thing to grace the surface of Earth makes me feel his words deep in my soul. But he used to look at me like this even before we had anything going on—back when he'd dance the night away with me at JC's and then leave with another woman.

With shaky hands, I put my plate down on the grass and draw a deep breath. It feels shitty to start *this* conversation after he just complimented me, but someone has to start. It might as well be me.

"Babe?" Tatum asks, and the uncertainty in his tone makes my stomach flip.

I force myself to look into his topaz blue eyes and allow their brightness to ground me. Tatum is mine now. He married me.

"Back in December, it wasn't just my past that made me jump to the worst conclusions," I tell him, my fingers fidgeting incessantly with the hem of my pink maternity dress. "To me, seeing that picture... as hurtful as it sounds, it made sense. In my mind, it wasn't the first time you traded me for someone more beautiful, sexier, just... better."

That scary vein on his forehead? Yeah, that's back, pulsing angrily under the skin getting redder and redder by the second. His eyebrows scrunch together, and the mother of all sneers twists the corners of his mouth down. His hands fist on the blanket, his own plate discarded next to his strong thighs.

"What the fuck? There's no one better than you, Maevis," he snaps. "When did I trade you?"

I swallow the lump in my throat and force the words out. "Whenever we happened to be at JC's at the same time. You'd find me on the dance floor. You would dance with me and pull me close, messing with my head. When you had enough, you'd leave the bar with someone else draped all over you. Hell, Tatum, the last time you did it was just after Lalah's birthday, in September."

Tatum stills when my words hit him, and the color drains from his face. A look of understanding softens his features, and he pushes up to his knees, his palms cupping my cheeks.

"I'm an asshole," he grits. "But, baby, listen to me, please. I haven't been with anyone, except for you, for more than a year. Not just sex, I haven't kissed anyone else, either."

I push back from him. Can't help the derisive scoff slipping out of me as I narrow my eyes at him. "You're telling me that you picked up all those women and then what? Just dropped them safely off at home and went on your merry way?"

Tatum's not deterred by my frost, his deft fingers grabbing my chin. "That's exactly what I'm telling you."

He must see there's no way I believe that. My stomach tightens in annoyance. I'm trying to have an honest conversation here, to explain what led to my actions, but I didn't expect him to lie to my face.

"Babe," he breathes with so much hurt, my heart lurches in my chest. "You were always my endgame, but I wasn't ready for you. With every glimpse of you, dancing, laughing, I couldn't stay away regardless of how much I told myself it was a terrible fucking idea to approach you. You were always so happy to see me. I'd see nothing, hear nothing, feel fucking nothing, but you in my arms, swaying your hips, dancing the night away with me." He trails off and presses his forehead to mine.

"Then why?"

Chapter Thirty-Eight

Tatum

Talk about stupidity coming to bite me in the ass. There's absolutely no good explanation for my past behavior. I don't have an excuse. And if I end up hurting Maevis again... *Goddammit.*

I blow up a breath, my heart hammering in my chest. It seems dancing of any sort is our theme. One step forward, ten fucking thousand back. I lift her up from where she's sitting on the blanket and drape her across my lap. My lips twitch at the cute squeal escaping her lips, despite the heavy air around us. I hook an arm around her back, my palm resting on the swell of her belly where our daughter kicks happily. At least, I hope she's happy, considering how much stress I'm causing her mother.

"I've been in love with you for years," I confess. "And if it wasn't love, it was one hell of a crush. I'd see you around, always smiling, always pushing yourself to your very limits to help and support others. I wanted *that* for myself. But I was scared, Maevis. Hell, I still am."

Her soft palm wraps around my forearm, thumb rubbing absentminded circles on my wrist. She settles her head on my shoulder, tucking in under my chin. At least she's not putting distance between us again.

"Every time the urge to kiss you overwhelmed me or my control snapped under the absolute need to steal you away, I forced myself to take a step back. Back then, I had nothing to offer you, Maevis. I'm wondering even now, what the fuck do I have to give? My mind's a fucking mess. Sometimes, I'm drowning in self-doubt and shamelessly using you as my life-line."

"You give me strength," she whispers, her lips tickling the base of my throat. "You give me courage. Most of all, you give me love. These may seem small to you, but to me, they're everything."

My arms tighten around her. *This fucking woman slays me.* I clear my throat and continue, since I don't want her to have any doubts about me.

"I was trying to force myself to put distance between us; trying to show you I wasn't the man for you. I'd make sure you were safe at your table or with your friends and, much to my fucking shame, saw me leaving with those women."

"You hurt me on purpose?" she cuts me off, the tremble in her voice sitting like a rock in my gut.

"No, babe. I never wanted to hurt you. I didn't know what you felt for me, or if you felt anything at all. My hope was you'd do what I proved to be incapable of... put distance between us." My eyes close as I let the warmth of her body seep into mine. *There'll be no more distance between us. Over my dead fucking body.* "Jake would point out women who had someone harassing them all night long, or women who requested an *angel shot*. We'd pretend to flirt for a while, and then I'd take them home. Absolutely nothing ever happened. I swear to you, Maevis, I've not touched another woman intimately since the first time we danced at JC's."

"I don't know if I should kiss you right now or knee you," she murmurs. My balls are ready to hide in my stomach at the threat. Maevis is a fucking sweetheart and wouldn't normally hurt a fly, but there's truth in her words. "I'm disappointed knowing a lot of pain could've been avoided with just a simple conversation, but I'm also thankful we're sitting here right now, despite the pain."

I sigh. I can't help it. *Simple is downright difficult.* "Sometimes, we make what we think it's the best decision with the information we're given. Looking back, it's easy to see and point out what could've been done better. I don't think that conversation would have been simple for either of us. Not a year ago. Not even in the past six months. Were you ready to listen? Were you ready to believe? Not in me, but in yourself."

"Are you ready now?" she whispers.

I shake my head and ponder her question. "I want to be. Just sitting here with you, opening up, I feel it's a step in the right direction. You're my better half, Maevis *Carter.* Hand in hand with you, I know with every fiber of my being that all the steps I'm taking will lead me to where I'm supposed to go. And, instead of hurrying to get to the destination, I'll just enjoy the goddamn journey."

She lifts her head from my shoulder, whiskey-colored eyes searching mine. Fucked if I know what for, but I let her search to her heart's content. She has mine in the palm of her hand. While the fear of her crushing it still lingers in the pit of my stomach, right here, right now, my faith in us is greater than my fear. Her pouty lips curve in a shy smile, and I swear to god, Maevis shines brighter than fucking sunlight.

She touches her mouth to mine. Softly. Gently. Lazily. And my whole body relaxes. All the tension keeping my frame tight vanishes in thin air, and I sag into her, letting her explore my mouth with chaste kisses and tiny nips on my lips.

"Why didn't you tell me?" she asks then, her lips still moving against mine. I wrap her braid around my fist and pull slowly until her head is tipped back and her eyes are once again locked with mine. I can't stand even simple allusions to the witch in Mae's vicinity. The poison that viper spreads, even from behind bars, shouldn't touch the extraordinary woman in my arms.

"Because I didn't want you to forgive me thinking I'm a victim. My head was a mess, Cupcake. Hiding our relationship then didn't sit right with me. Unwillingly, it stirred up old insecurities. And when you left and I didn't even get the chance to talk to you, to explain myself, I felt that you knowing the truth wouldn't have helped any. You didn't trust in me, and that broke my trust in you."

Her eyes glaze over, misting with tears. A jolt of pain rushes through my chest. The last thing I want to do is cause my beautiful wife more pain. But it's best to shed light on all the ugly things we buried within, so we can move forward without the weight of a past that doesn't define us. Not anymore.

"Do you trust me now?" she asks, her voice cracking at the end. I bend my neck and nuzzle my nose against her freckled one, trying to soften the sting of my next words.

"Most of the time," I admit. It hurts to say those words out loud, but I promised myself she'll hear only the truth from me as we move forward and grow old together. She's my person, my partner in crime, my wife. If there's anyone in this world deserving of all my truths, that's Maevis. "Do you trust me?" I dare ask, when she says nothing, just continues to watch me with those amber eyes that sparkle like campfires during summer nights.

"Most of the time," she whispers. "It's your self-doubts I don't trust. But I also know I played a hand at planting the seed of doubt inside of you. I may not have the green thumb my mom did, but I'm determined. I'm scrappy when I need to be." She giggles and gifts me a half-smile. "I'll help you weed them out, husband. Sometimes they'll grow back. Sometimes they'll wither. But every time? We'll persevere. In that, I have one hundred percent faith."

"What ails me…" I sigh. "It's not easy to fix. It's not easy to cure."

"No, no it's not. But you have all the tools you need to succeed. You have an amazing support system. Heck, *we* have an amazing support system. At the end of the day, Tate, all that's really down to us is to determine if we're leaning on them or not. Some burdens are heavier to carry than others. It's not a matter of who gets first to the finish line. We can put the burden down sometimes and just… breathe. Other times, we can share the load and keep going."

"Speaking of burdens, have you received any more messages? Have you noticed anything amiss?" Just bringing up the vile human gets my blood boiling and my teeth grinding. To make matters worse, we still haven't managed to figure out who the fuck they are.

"No texts today," she says, her eyes looking at something over my shoulder as if she's mentally trying to fit pieces of a puzzle together, when she doesn't have a reference, and all the pieces are the same color. "One thing, though… and, before you freak out, let me explain." Her forefinger presses against my lips, silencing me. "The bakery was unlocked today when Drake came to get me. I could've sworn I locked it before I went into the kitchen. Not sure if this is my pregnancy brain or something more. Everything was exactly how I left it, so there's a high chance your daughter is messing with my memory, but I vividly remember locking it."

My stomach turns upside down with the unease churning inside. It could be nothing—pregnancy brain as she calls it—but at this point, I'm not taking any chances. Not when a deranged asshole is sending threats and dead rats to our doorstep.

I kiss her forehead, trying to soothe both Maevis and myself. She's safe right now. She's right here in my arms. Nothing will fucking touch her as long as I live and breathe. "I'll have Jake look into it," I murmur.

"Thank you," she murmurs back. Her lips touch my neck again, her hot breath breezing over my skin sends a full-body shiver through me. I dip my head gently, burying my nose in her silky hair. A deep inhale fills me with her signature scent of vanilla and honeysuckle. She smells like home and like the happiest of lives. She smells like mine.

Her hand grips my side and she shimmies in my lap, trying to get into a more comfortable position. All she achieves is making me fucking uncomfortable as all my blood rushes south to my cock. He perks up under her, pressing painfully against my zipper.

I know the exact moment she feels what she's doing to me. Her breath hitches and a coy smile graces her lips. "Someone's happy to see me."

I can't help but scoff, "Someone is always happy to see you, Cupcake." A subtle thrust of my hips lets her know exactly how *happy* I am since my cock is just about ready to burst through the metal teeth to reach her.

Maevis shifts again until she straddles the top of my thighs, her long skirt riding high on her creamy legs. Her arms coil around my neck, and my hands grasp her hips on reflex. Her cheeks are rosy and her eyes are sparkling. "I thought this move would be sexier, but we have an effective cockblocker between us," she laughs, rubbing her round belly that keeps her at quite a distance from where she needs to be.

"Shh," I hiss, bending my neck and silencing her with an open-mouthed kiss, my tongue tracing her bottom lip until she parts for me, and I taste all her sweetness in one decisive swipe. "Our Vanilla Bean can hear you."

Maevis throws her head back and laughs with all her might. The warmth that takes over me at seeing her so happy, and relaxed, and carefree? Fuck, I couldn't feel taller if I measured ten fucking feet. I've seen glimpses of *this* Maevis in the past months.

I silently vow to see this version of my wife every day. Even in her saddest moments, she'll look at me and know with dead certainty she'll always have a reason to smile.

She lifts high on her knees until we're once again face to face, her mouth level with mine. Her long, dark lashes flutter, a bashful playfulness in her gorgeous eyes. Which is why I nearly choke on my fucking tongue when her question slips past her beautiful lips. "Husband, make love to me?"

Chapter Thirty-Nine

Tatum

"Here?" I croak, my eyebrows high in my hairline, my heart pumping a thousand miles per hour in my chest. I may be shocked as fuck, but my cock's ready to go, twitching and throbbing behind the fly of my jeans. He's all for having Maevis spread out on this blanket and get to actively participate in this picnic.

"No one ever comes here..." she trails off, and the haze coating her eyes slowly gives way to panic. And I know this for a fact. I've been running the trail to this waterfall ever since I found Maevis on the side of the road with her scraped and bleeding knees.

That's all the green light I need though, and before she fills her pretty head with a million doubts, my lips descend on hers with a growled "Fuck yeah!", hungry for everything she's willing to give me. Mae moans into my mouth, and I'm just about ready to explode out of my clothes like the Incredible Hulk.

I trail a hand from her hip to her full breasts, cupping one, then the other, kneading the soft, heavy flesh, brushing my thumb over her hardened nipple until she's a panting, whimpering mess in my arms.

"Are you wet for me, wife?" I grit, my voice low and gravelly even to my own ears. Not surprised with how hard it is to restrain myself and not rip her dress off, rutting into her like a fucking animal until I'm spent of life and she's full of me. "Does it get you all dripping to know you'll be on your hands and knees for me soon, screaming my name for everyone to hear?"

"Yes, please, please," Mae begs, rocking her hips over my thighs. Electricity runs through me as I feel the heat of her pussy, even through the coarse material of my jeans. I flex the scarred muscle underneath, and she mewls in my mouth her pleasure and bliss.

"That's my good girl. But first, let's see if you can come like this for me, baby. Just from my hands on your tits and my thigh between your legs."

Maevis fastens her fingers in my hair, pulling at the unruly strands, as her hips ride me faster and faster. The sting on my scalp and her breathy moans have my balls drawing tight to my body. "That's it, baby," I murmur, "fucking soak me."

"Yes, holy fuck," she moans. Her eyes spring open, and I swear I could get drunk on the lust coating her golden irises. Her hips jerk, frenzied, uncontrolled, and I bend my head, bringing her nipple to my mouth, and suck hard through the soft material of her dress, teasing it with my teeth and swirling my tongue around it. The scream ripping out of her chest as she comes? The most beautiful fucking sound I heard in my life as it echoes in the forest surrounding us.

Maevis sags in my arms, boneless and relaxed, and I release the hardened bud, letting her head rest on the crook of my neck. I pass my thumb over her nipples once, then twice, a grunt spilling past my lips as she twitches under my touch. I cup the back of her neck, my fingers massaging her soft skin, as she slowly comes back to me from the clutches of her orgasm.

She palms me through my jeans, and I just about come in my fucking boxers. "Nuh-uh-uh," I warn her. "Get up!"

She does so, standing on shaky legs, her hands finding purchase on my shoulders. My own hands find their way under the flowery material of her skirt, trailing up her smooth calves, feathering over the back of her knees, and I bite back a smirk when they buckle at my touch.

"Tatum," she gasps, a warn and a plea for me to quit fucking around and please her. And I'm all about pleasing my wife.

I move my hands higher, gripping her thighs from behind, forcing her to take a step closer to me. Her legs part even more on each side of mine as she has to widen her stance to accommodate me. My fingers reach her wet center, softness and heat enveloping them when I drag them through her bare slit. She reads the delighted surprise in my eye and gifts me with a half needy, half sheepish smile.

"Blame your big baby. Nothing's comfortable anymore," Mae mumbles, crying out the last word as I press my thumb to her clit, punishing her with tight, hard circles. I shift around on the blanket, trying to relieve the pressure on my dick. I'm so fucking hard, it's bordering on the edge of pain.

"Lift your skirt," I bark, and in the next moment, her pink, glistening pussy is revealed in front of my eyes, my thumb slick with her arousal moving up and down between her bare lips. "Pull it over my head," I order, but don't give her time to comply before I dive in and draw her clit between my lips, sucking hard. I groan deep in my throat when I taste her on my tongue. "Fuck, you're so goddamn sweet everywhere," I praise, helpless with the words coming out of my mouth.

I tighten my grip on the back of her thighs when I feel her knees giving up on her. Her fingers claw desperately at my scalp, trying to find her balance. But I'm not giving her a second of reprieve. I part her lips with the flat of my tongue, licking a path of sin and redemption on the length of her seam, spearing it inside of her. I'm this fucking close to getting off myself on her delicious taste alone as she floods my fucking mouth.

Her trembling fingers finally find purchase in my hair, over the soft cotton of her dress, and press against the back of my head as she starts riding my face in earnest. My sweet, sweet wife is fucking my face in the middle of the goddamn forest. If it wasn't for the torturous throbbing of my cock, I would think I died and landed in heaven.

"Take what you want, baby. I'm all yours," I order her before my lips clamp down on her clit, my tongue going to town flicking it as I sink my fingers into her tight heat, pumping furiously, curling them and pressing against that special spot that makes Maevis go crazy for me. And she is gone, detonating in my arms, her whole body writhing upright. Her fingers pull at my hair so viciously, I bet I just lost a fistful to her abandon. It's a price I'll gladly pay each and every time just to see her coming apart for me over and over.

"Oh, fuck, Tate," she cries out as her pussy grips my fingers, quivering around them, her sweet release dripping down my palm. I continue to thrust them gently, in and out of her, while she rides out the aftershocks of her orgasm. I press a last, soft kiss to her throbbing bundle of nerves, then brush my lips to the silky skin of her inner thigh before ducking my head out from under the folds of her skirt.

Maevis looks down on me, all wide-eyed and flushed cheeks, her own lips parting, as I lean on one elbow and suck into my mouth the fingers she just drenched, licking them clean of all her sweetness. My tongue sweeps over my lips, collecting every last single drop of her.

"I could eat just you for the rest of my fucking life and never go hungry again," I confess to her. A dangerous glint washes over her face, her plump lips tipping at the corner. If I wasn't so turned on right now that I'm close to seeing double, I would probably have enough brain power left to realize she's about to spellbind me to her for eternity. Alas, I'm drunk on her vanilla essence and all the oxygenated cells in my blood are currently residing in my cock.

Maevis grasps my chin, her thumb brushing over my beard. She lifts her hands to her mouth, swirling her tongue around her finger. And I'm fucking done for. My chest rumbles like I'm a fucking animal in heat with the growl crawling out of the confines of my rib cage.

"Did no one teach you not to play with your prey, husband?" Maevis taunts me. "Did no one tell you the prey learns to like the chase?" My throat bobs as I swallow back a filthy retort. This is her show now. With the sun at her back and her untamed curls framing her beautiful face, she looks like a damn sex goddess. And I'm fucking ready to worship at her altar for the rest of my godforsaken days.

She moves her bare foot over my hip, trailing up my abs, before stopping between my pecs. Her dainty toes, painted in the color of sunflower and summer, press gently in the middle of my chest. "What are you waiting for, *Hunter*? You caught your prey. Now fuck me."

I'm on my feet in a flash, catching her around the waist before she falls. My chest heaves as pure lava runs through my veins. I'm a fucking volcano ready to erupt, and all thanks to the woman in my arms, who knows exactly which buttons to push.

"Turn around," I bark. She flashes me a victorious smile but does as she's told. I release my hold on her and fist my hands at my sides, reciting the inventory of Tate's Shop in my head since I'm a breath away from coming and my belt is not even fucking unbuckled yet.

I step into her, thrusting my hips against the curve of her back so she feels exactly what she does to me. I grip her wrist, circling my fingers around it, and move her hand between the two of us. Bending my neck, I gently blow a puff of air on the delicate skin behind her ear, tingles running through my spine when goosebumps sprout all over her nape.

I rip my belt open and make quick work of unbuttoning my jeans as I force her to take a step forward, then a few more, until she's face to face with a waist-tall boulder around our picnic area. "Take me out," I grunt, guiding her hand to the zipper ready to burst at the seams. Anticipation courses through my veins like liquid ecstasy, my cock jolting painfully behind my fly as the heat of her palm reaches him. She slowly lowers the zipper over me, and I nearly weep when she drags the waistband of my boxers down, and my cock springs free of its confines, hard and stiff like a fucking steel pipe.

I press my hand to her lower back, a strained growl working its way up my throat when the little minx licks her palm, then fists my length. She strokes me up and down before tightening her fingers just under the oversensitive head. "Fuck, baby," I moan. I curl my body around hers, taking her free hand and placing it firmly on the sun-heated rock. "Arch, sweetness," I all but beg, fucking panting as her strokes grow faster and faster.

She curves her spine, her sexy-as-fuck, thick ass pushing up, her arm trapped between the two of us. I take a step back, ripping myself out of her grasp, my hard dick smacking against my stomach. Moving a hand behind my head, I take my T-shirt off and drape it in front of her on the crumbly rock so she doesn't scrape her palms.

I push her legs open, widening her stance, and flip the billowing skirt over her back, exposing her ass and dripping pussy to me. I sigh. How can I not, when my wife is all but presenting her desire and need for me. She's all creamy thighs and hot, pink, glistening perfection. I swear to God, I've never wanted anyone in my life as much as I want Maevis right now.

I palm her cheeks, spreading them open. My fingers dig into her soft flesh until pale indents form under my fingertips. A thrill runs up and down my spine, knowing that when I release her, she'll bear the mark of my hands on her. My teeth fucking ache with the savage urge clawing at me to brand her, so every living creature—human or animal—knows she's fucking *mine*.

My thighs align with the back of hers, and I rub my length between her legs, coating myself in her arousal. She's so fucking wet, my lazy strokes are easily gliding. We moan simultaneously when the pulsing head of my cock rubs against her clit. I'm not even inside her yet, but I feel her core clenching, anticipating my arrival.

My fingers tighten on her flesh, and I thrust upward, my hard cock sandwiched between her ass cheeks. *Goddamn, motherfucker. Get it together.* I'm torturing both of us, denying us of the heaven that's almost within our reach. But as much as I want to drive myself into her until I lose my fucking mind and what's left of my sanity, I want to savor her too, to cherish her like the fucking goddess she is.

"Please, Tatum," she begs. "I'm ready for you, please. Stop denying me."

"You're ready to take my cock, sweets?" I taunt her. "You'll take me hard and fast, like the good little wife you are?"

"Yes, fuck, yes. Just... God, fuck me already," she cries out when I notch the head of my dick at her entrance. We both groan in pleasure as, in one swift thrust of my hips, I bury myself inside of her.

Bliss.

Heaven.

Euphoria.

My eyes scrunch shut when the silk of her wet, tight channel stretches around me, contracting and relaxing as she accommodates to us being one. "Fuck me, babe. You grip me so good, sweetness." I sink my teeth into my bottom lip until I taste blood in my mouth, my abdomen flexing to the point of pain as I keep myself still to stop from coming too fucking soon.

That's the power she has over me. Everything I am is addicted to everything Maevis is. She fits me so perfectly, so completely, from the way her greedy pussy incessantly milks my cock to the way her whole body aligns with mine when she sleeps in my arms.

This incredible fucking woman is all mine. She may not have been my first, but she's my goddamned last. Maevis Rae Carter is the definition of happiness, created just for me.

I slowly move my hips back, watching my length gleaming in her arousal under the bright sunlight, until only the very tip of me remains inside of her. "Yeees," she moans long and hard, clenching those silky inner muscles around me, and I snap. My hips pound into her over and over again, my breath labors, sweat peppering at my hairline, as I hold on to her, pulling her against me.

The grunts slipping past my clenched teeth are fucking inhuman. I've lost all sense of time and space. She's all I feel. She's all I know. Her soft whimpers and cries of pleasure are all I hear. The ground could crumble into dust under our feet right now, and I couldn't care any less. Tingles and fireworks explode in my lower back, igniting my blood.

I bend my knees, adjusting the angle I'm making her mine, and drive myself with all my might into her needy pussy. My thighs slap the back of hers, the sound of our lovemaking drowning out the thunder of the waterfall. I know I'm touching that magic spot inside of her when she contracts so beautifully around me, she's choking my cock in her need.

So tight. So snug. So... home.

We're as close to being one as we'll ever get, and it still doesn't feel like fucking enough. Nothing ever will be enough. She drives me crazy with want and need for her.

"Fuck, fuck, fuck," I curse, straining to keep fucking her in long, controlled strokes, making sure she feels every damned hard inch of me—every ridge, every vein, every single throbbing ache she instills in me.

"I'm so close," she cries. "Don't stop, Tatum. God, don't stop." And I don't. I couldn't stop if my fucking life depended on it. I drop my forehead to the center of her spine, right between her shoulder blades. My right hand releases the deathly grip I have on her hip. I don't give a fuck that my fingers are cramping. I snake my arm around her belly and between her tits, their soft fullness caressing my skin with every cant of my hips, and fasten my fingers around her delicate throat.

Her pulse is frenzied under my thumb, and when she swallows under my grip, I'm as close to seeing God as I'll ever be. "Be a good little wife and come on your husband's cock, sweetness. Let go, baby. I'll catch you. I'll always fucking catch you," I vow to her as my dick swells and the telltale electric current of my impending release has me crazed and wanton.

My movements lose all semblance of control. I'm fucking myself into her like the apocalypse is chasing us, and this is my last chance to love on my wife. And then... flutters. Pulses. Quivers. "Yes, Tate, fuck yes!" And I'm gone. Completely lost in Maevis.

Incoherent words of adoration spill past my lips. My breath stutters in my lungs. My heart takes flight like a goddamn supersonic plane. Throughout my earth-shattering orgasm, I continue to pump myself into her—soft, tender, gentle thrusts, coaxing and prolonging her own orgasm.

She's putty in my hands, boneless and completely spent, just like me. With the last of my strength, I prop my palm next to hers on the hard rock, my thumb hooking around her pinkie. Our wedding rings sparkle in the sunshine; hers—golden amber and topaz blue; mine—a colorful spectrum rivaling the rainbows of the waterfall. I bury my face in the damp hair at her nape, pushing the silky dark tendrils aside with my nose. I press an open-mouthed kiss on her vanilla flavored skin, tasting the salty undertones of our completion.

"I love you," I murmur in her ear, my voice gravelly and sore after the tests and tribulations we've put our stamina levels to. "I'm not a perfect man, but I know with every cell of my being, there's not a goddamn person on this earth better for you than me."

Maevis turns her head, and I loosen my grip around her throat, allowing her to move freely. Her lips meld with mine in a tender, breathless kiss. "I love you, Tatum." She smiles against my mouth. "And I don't need you to be perfect. I need you to be mine."

"Always and forever, Cupcake," I repeat my wedding vows to her.

"Forever and always, husband," she vows right back.

Chapter Forty

Maevis

I shove another slice of banana bread in my mouth and moan. I've no shame. I also don't care. This is absolutely freaking delicious. Just the right level of moistness, the perfect texture, so fluffy and tasty and... I'm crying again. Great.

The sleeve of Tatum's sweatshirt brushes my fingers. I shrug and lift the soft material to my cheeks, wiping the tears away. Sandalwood, pinetree, and everything Tatum, that's the scent calming me down, erasing the sweet notes of banana, with a hint of almond essence, and hmmm. *No, Maevis. Stop it. Don't go down that road again.*

"You doin' okay here, hun?" Annalise asks me, pursing her lips as she takes me in. I can imagine what she sees—a beach ball with swollen limbs and a dark braid sprouting from the vent. I'm sure my face is all blotchy at this point, with all the rivers flowing over my cheekbones.

"You're a traitor to our family," I huff, crossing my arms under my breasts. Or attempting to, because as soon as my forearm presses against them, a bolt of pure, unadulterated pain jolts my sore nipples and spreads through my entire body.

Oh, yes. The newest, *funnest* development. Tits so tender and sore, even the gentlest of breezes makes me scream in agony. The joys of the last week of my second trimester, I guess. I'm experiencing them all. Mood swings? You betcha'. Demon-spawned boobs? Hell yeah. Astronomical level of tears? I single-handedly raised the global-ocean levels by one centimeter this week. Yes, I'm that potent with my tear ducts.

"Is this about my recipe?" Anna asks in a tentative voice, but she's not fooling me. She's damn proud of herself.

"Of course it is about your recipe. I need it, Annalise," I cry. And yes, I can hear the annoying whine in my tone. Can I do anything about it? Nope. Do I want to do anything about it? Not if it gets me what I want.

"I love you, Mae, I really, really do." She smirks—kindly, mind you, but she's still pissing me off. "But that recipe is for my daughter and my daughter only. Or my son, if I'm blessed with one and he'd be interested in baking."

"Ugh, you're... you're," I stutter, trying to find the right words. "You better be prepared to bake one for me every week for the rest of your life."

Because I'm no monster.

I have my own recipes to share with my daughter that are reserved only for her. I'm not denying my future nieces or nephews a sacred bonding moment with their mother. Even if at this moment I want Annalise's banana bread recipe more than I want Tatum's cock. And that's saying something considering my husband has one big, thick, beautiful...

"Don't you dare finish that sentence, Maevis Carter. I'm warning you. I've had it up to my eyeballs with the details around my brother's sex life. No more," Sawyer warns.

Wait! What?

Oh.

It's back.

Oh no.

My eyes well again. I have no thoughts for myself. Everyone will know everything I'm thinking. The baby I'm doing my damnedest to grow in my belly is compelling me to spill all my secrets out into the world. What kind of vampire-hybrid has Tatum spawned in me?

"What's back, Mae?" Anna asks, her warm hand squeezing mine.

"The thinking with subtitles on," I cry out, looking at Sawyer all apologetic. It's okay for me to daydream about my husband's cock. It's my freaking prerogative as his wife. But it is bad manners to narrate my smutty daydreams in public.

Five pairs of eyes blink at me. Lalah shrugs and plants her hands on her hips, her frame nearly completely engulfed by Cole's sweatshirt. We went rogue with this book club session. Most of my clothes either don't fit me or the materials are downright uncomfortable. So, everyone is wearing an oversized hoodie, either stolen from their significant others—Tatum's clothes are the only ones remotely comfortable for me—or bought with today's gathering in mind.

I love my friends. With all my freaking heart. The support I've received from them in the past few months is incredible. Our close-knit group is everything teenager-Maevis dreamed of. Hell, who am I kidding? Is everything adult-Maevis dreamed of, too.

"Narrate away, woman. Who cares? And you." Lalah turns to Sawyer, narrowing her eyes at my sister-in-law. "I'm no happier to look at Tatum and imagine what's in his pants, thanks to the very vivid visuals our Kinder Surprise here shares, but she's carrying your niece, so suck it up."

Sawyer pulls the hood of her own sweatshirt over her head, hiding inside the light blue folds. *Wait a second, where have I seen that hoodie before?*

"Fine," she groans. "But you're only allowed to for the next three months. Then, I'm canceling my subscription." She makes a cutting gesture with her hand, as if she's ready to karate-chop my inappropriate thoughts before they spill out of my mouth.

"I don't mind," Violet adds, twirling a corkscrew strand of chestnut hair around her finger. "Smutty books are my only sustenance right now. Real life visuals don't hurt me any."

"Hey, that's my brother you're drooling about," Sawyer screeches, playfully pushing Violet's shoulder, only for our drooler to wink at me. At least I'm not on the hot stove anymore. I congratulate myself for my unearned achievement by shoving another piece of banana bread into my mouth. And cue the waterworks...

"Someone please take this plate away from me." I sniff, blinking my eyelids rapidly as I try to stop the next great flood of Lost Hope from spilling out of me.

Lalah plops down in the beanbag next to my armchair—yeah, no more beanbags for me, unless I want to pee my pants by the time I get out of the squishy fuckers—and soothingly rubs my thigh. "Yikes, being pregnant is like being on your period, but on steroids. I need to research a proper moisturizer for you before you scrub your skin off drying those salty lakes."

"Speaking of, how did the doctor's appointment go?" Annalise asks, and I forget all about our family-recipe-feud. A smile so big it reaches my ears blooms on my face as I think back to the visit.

"It went great," I gush. "They did the glucose tolerance test, which was great, and a complete blood count. Dr. Fritz actually called me this morning to let me know that my iron levels are where they're supposed to be, so no fear of deficiency anemia. My blood pressure levels were also normal, but she recommended I visit her every two weeks until birth, just to make sure preeclampsia is not a risk anymore." I take a deep breath and let the good news wash over me for a second time.

The truth is... I was worried out of my mind, especially about my blood pressure. The pregnancy itself has been relatively easy on me, but life during this pregnancy? Well, it has been anything but. So it's a relief to know everything is going great and that our little Vanilla Bean is healthy.

They all descend on me, each of them giving me hugs, and, of course, rubbing my belly. I swear, not even Astrum is petted as often as my beach ball is.

"Did you sign up for those Lamaze classes I sent you?" Sawyer asks.

"I did, but we're still six weeks away from that. The instructor was amazing, though. Good grief, she has six kids of her own." I bite into my bottom lip not to laugh at the look of absolute horror on Lalah's face.

"Yikes." She shudders. "Don't get me wrong, some people are absolutely made to be parents. But I can't imagine putting myself through a pregnancy once, never mind six times."

"Well, I want four," Annalise says, shocking the living daylights out of all of us.

"F-four?" I breathe. "Does my brother know that?" I pop an eyebrow at her.

The grin she gives me is pure evil, and, as soon as her own eyebrows wiggle at me, I groan. "He said he'll enjoy practicing for them."

"Great," I deadpan while Sawyer is close to suffocating on her hyena-on-a-sugar-rush cackle. Taking a page from Lalah's book, I flip her off. All it does is make her laugh even harder, her normally peach colored skin reddening to unnatural levels. "Give the girl some water before she faints," I say to no one, rolling my eyes.

"Are you afraid, though?" Lalah asks, nudging me gently with her elbow. There's not a trace of humor on her face, her eyes wide and honest, as she absentmindedly plays with the strings of her hoodie.

My chest expands on a deep breath, then deflates when I expel the air with a huff. "We've put off making a birthing plan until after a couple of Lamaze classes. Ideally, I'd like to go for a vaginal delivery with all the help modern medicine has to give. I try not to think of all the things that could go wrong or of the pain itself, even if everything goes well. But I know Tate won't leave my side, not even for a second."

She gives me a serene smile and a gentle squeeze on my shoulder. "Good. And we're all going to be there, too. You have a village at your beck and call."

"Speaking of births…" Emma trails off. I turn my head in her direction, where she sits all prim and proper on a stool, her back resting against the wooden coffee bar. She leans forward and pats the top of a green cardboard box. "Last month I fell down a rabbit hole of YouTube videos with men trying period and labor pain simulators."

"Those videos are the best." Violet claps. "They're more efficient at managing my cramps than any painkiller." She sighs wistfully.

"Damn straight," we all agree. There's just something about the look of understanding and horror washing over a man's face when he experiences, for the first time, a similar sensation to a cramp. It gives a sense of justice and fulfillment, complete with the honor of throwing a *Who's a tough pussy now* in their direction, with every labored breath and leg wiggle the men go through during those minutes. It's absolutely incredible.

"Hence why, ladies and babies of the TBRC book club, I am now bestowing on you the select, rare power of making an empath and supporter of our womanly woes out of every man in your life," Emma cries excitedly as she flips the box open. As one, we all lean forward to see what surprises she has for us.

"Fuck yeah," Lalah shouts. "Hayes, I'm coming for your balls, darling!" She cackles evilly, rubbing her hands together.

"Now, why waste any time?" Sawyer says, a dark glint in her eyes I've never seen before on my sweet and subdued sister-in-law. "Let's crash the little get-together our men have going on and bring some pain to the party."

Holy red-velvet cakes, this evening just turned a corner.

Chapter Forty-One

B eing back at JC's for the first time since the incident is easier than I thought it would be. It probably helps that my memory of that night is patchy at best. What I do remember are only the good moments, like dancing with Maevis and kissing her breathless in the hallway before it all went to hell. It also doesn't hurt that Jackson closed JC's for tonight, so everyone here is basically family.

A large round table is placed in front of the wooden bar, with a green felt laid on top of it. One deck of cards and stacks upon stacks of chips tower in the center of the table. Disturbed's *The Sickness* is playing at a low volume in the background. There's only one bright Edison bulb hanging above the poker table that illuminates the large space—well, one bulb, and the mood lights around the mirrored wall behind the black shelves heaving with glasses and drinks.

I was more worried than I cared to admit about how I'd feel being back here when Cap called and said that since the TBR Café meeting is in session, we're all meeting here—and by *all*, I mean Jake, Cole, Blake, Maddox, Drake, and Rowan, who is a volunteer firefighter at LHFD and a goddamn bestselling psychological thriller novelist.

I'm fucking proud of myself to realize that all the work I've been doing in the last six months—all those grueling therapy sessions—is paying off. There's no unease churning in my gut, no flashbacks tormenting me.

I know—despite his reassurance that he understood why I avoided coming back here—Jake was disappointed that the place he built from the ground up and poured all his efforts into was no longer a safe space for me. But it is. And he has gone to great lengths to ensure what happened in December never happens again in his bar, including hiring a security team.

The leader of the team, Xavier, actually lives in one of the two apartments upstairs, and he's currently patrolling the area around the bar, ensuring no one drops in and kicks up a fuss for the place being closed on a Friday night. I did try to convince Jake not to close, but he's a stubborn asshole, and once he's set on an idea, it would take divine intervention to change his mind.

"Do you guys have any plans for Mae's apartment above Suga'High?" Blake asks, leaning next to me with his back against the bar top.

"Not that I know of," I respond with a shrug. "Why?"

He shoves his hands in the pockets of his dark suit pants, slumping his shoulders. "Time for me to stop leeching off Cole and Lalah and move out."

That gets my attention. I narrow my eyes at him and really take in his... *defeat? What the fuck?* He's definitely not looking like himself. Blake Hayes is usually the life of the party, fucking sunshine personified in a six-foot-three man, not this aloof, washed-out version of himself.

"Do they know you're planning to leave?"

He sighs pitifully, shaking his head. "They do. Cole understands. Lalah's five minutes away from locking me in her laundry room."

I whistle. "You sure pissed her off. She could've at least chosen the library."

A self-deprecating chuckle escapes him before he sobers up again. Dammit, *this* Blake gives me the fucking shivers. "The apartment?" he presses.

"I'll speak to Maevis tomorrow and let you know."

Blake pats my shoulder and with a low "Thank you," he strides away from the bar and chooses a seat at the poker table between Rowan and Drake.

The sound of glass breaking has me turning around to where Jake is preparing the last of our drinks before the game starts. The motherfucker has the audacity to glare at me. He heard every single word, and he's not happy. I cock an eyebrow in response, but he flips me the bird and starts cleaning off the broken shards.

I grab the tray of drinks he prepared before he went all Hulk on the poor, unsuspecting glassware, and take it to the table. I plop into one of the available chairs between Cole and Maddox. The mighty Chief Deputy flinches when he sees me, his eyes widening slightly before rearranging his face in his usual, neutral mask.

What the heck is his problem?

I started... *tolerating* his presence, ever since he pulled his head out of his ass and let part of that big fucking ego leak out, but he's been acting strange as fuck lately. I narrow my eyes at him, ready to demand he explain what has his balls in a twist, when the door to the bar slams open, and in strides none other than the motherfucking prosecutor.

Joshua Craig, in all his suited glory, flashes an arrogant smirk and a two-fingered salute. "Evening, gentlemen. Good to see you all. Thanks for inviting me."

The fine hairs at the back on my neck bristle. But before I can open my mouth and ask why he's here, Maddox jumps from his seat so quickly his chair topples backward and goes to greet him.

"Thanks for coming, man," Lawson says, shaking Craig's hand and clapping his back.

Great. Just what Lost Hope needed, the two biggest assholes in the county getting close and friendly. Don't get me wrong, I'm grateful as fuck to Craig for being a ravenous shark and ripping the ex-bitch apart during the trial. But being grateful and liking him are two different fucking matters.

His dark eyes find mine, and he gives me a chin nod, his usual arrogant smirk nowhere to be seen. I respond in kind, then lean over the table and grab the deck of cards, shuffling them.

"Are we playing anytime today?"

"Let's get to it," Jackson says, dividing the chips in equal stacks before pushing them in front of each of us. "Buy-in is five dollars."

We're all feeling lucky for the first hand, and a clank of chips finds its way in the middle of the table. I deal two cards to each of us and peek at mine. *Five and seven of clubs. Not ideal, but not the worst hand.*

"Five here," Cole rumbles. "And raise another five."

Goddamn, stoic motherfucker.

Out of everyone here, Cole and Jackson are my biggest competition. I need a couple of hands to see Joshua in action. Drake and Rowan are out, and I decide to stay at least for the flop. An Ace of clubs is first, followed by a double six—hearts and spades. Drake hisses through his teeth and we all burst out laughing. Someone lost a three-of-a-kind.

Cole bets another ten and flushes out Joshua and Blake. The turn gives me an eight of clubs. Not even a cell in me twitches. But the bastard does bet fifty dollars on the next round. Lawson, to my right, taps his boot once on the polished floor. He'll fold.

"Cunt," bites out Jackson, but Cap doesn't even spare him a glance. "I'm out." And then there were three, soon to be two.

Maddox leans back and taps the floor with his boot once more. "Fuck it. I'm out, too."

Internally, I'm dancing—a full on fucking twerk. Externally, "I see your fifty, and raise another twenty-five." He raises too, but his eyebrow before calling my bet.

I flip the river, cool as a motherfucking cucumber. Cole flips his cards face-up, a five and a seven of hearts, and with a smug grin tells me, "Straight." His hand reaches for the pile of chips when I toss my own seven face-up on the table. He stills, fingers hovering just above this hand's winnings.

"My second one's a five," I say. "As far as I know, flush beats straight." I throw my last card over the river's nine of clubs. "You can cry while shuffling."

"Cocksucker," he mumbles, but does as I say. I bite back a laugh, washing it down with a chug of my non-alcoholic IPA. It's bad form to be smug from the first hand. Bad luck, too.

"Yer giving up completely on alcohol?" Rowan asks, as I study the shit hand Cole dealt for me.

I throw my cards face down in the middle of the table. "Nah, but while Mae's pregnant, I'm not touching the stuff. I need to be able to drive in case of anything." He tips his chin at me, his eyes flashing with pain—there one second, gone as he blinks it away. There's a story here, for sure. In truth, no one really knows much about the Irishman. He moved to Lost Hope about seven years ago but generally keeps to himself.

The fire at the Pine Ski Resort at the beginning of this year forged a bond between Cole, Rowan, and Drake, and since then, he's made an effort to socialize more with us. I'll take the likes of him any day—quiet, sarcastic, and minding his own business—over the likes of Lawson and Craig, *arrogant bastards.*

I win three more hands, much to Cole's annoyance. But fucking Blake nearly cleans out the house. Jackson is about to jump over the table and either kiss him to death or choke him to death. I'd say these two need to sort their shit out sooner rather than later, but the hypocrisy tastes bitter on my tongue.

Maevis and I had a fuckton of issues to work through, and on some, we've barely scratched the surface. But, even though she and I went through hell and back and we're still dealing with the aftermath of that dumpster-fire of a journey, Jackson is made of the darkest corners of hell. When he eventually snaps, not even a nuclear fallout bunker will keep us safe from the blast.

"Any more texts?" Drake asks, the rage in his voice barely contained.

After our heart to heart at the waterfall last week, Maevis and I decided to fill everyone in. What is the point of having a village at our back if we keep them at arm's length? Truthfully, sharing the latest shit stain with our friends felt like dropping another one of those suffocating weights crushing my chest.

"None this week," I answer. "But it means nothing. Last time they stopped it was for three weeks, and then they started back up again. Nothing unusual showed up on the cameras, either. The new security systems for the bakery and our home will be installed next weekend."

"You're changing it?" he exclaims, his dark eyebrows shooting up to his hairline. "Because of the unlocked door?"

"I'm not taking any chances, man," I say, shaking my head. "Even if it was a case of pregnancy brain," I clarify, making fake quotation marks with my fingers as the last two words leave my mouth, "I'm not fucking around with Mae's safety."

He throws me a look full of pride and gratitude that takes me aback. Talk about judging a book by the shelf it's been placed on. Sure, he doesn't have the greatest taste in best friends, and he's had his fair share of fuckups, but Drake loves the hell out of my wife. Despite all my grievances against him, he did prove himself to be an honorable, loyal man, who doesn't shy away from admitting when he's wrong.

Maddox clasps my shoulder, and it's the first time today—hell, in weeks—he actually meets my eyes. "I've increased patrols around Main Street and the edge of town. We've got your back. Maevis might as well be a sister to me too, and I'll be damned if I let anything happen to her."

And that's why I don't feel the need to clock the fucker in the face every time I see him lately. I tip my chin in his direction, then let the subject slip. There's not much to do at this point but be vigilant as fuck and wait.

Waiting is the fucking hardest part when you fear that, at any given second, the ground beneath your feet will crumble to nothingness and the heart pumping life into your veins will be ripped off your chest.

I'm about to throw in my last bet of the night when a commotion in front of the bar has all of us trained on the door.

"You better open that goddamn door right now, or I'll test my shiny new toy on you first. MOVE, XAVIER!" a feminine voice shouts, the threat carrying through the thick wooden doors.

"Mother of god, your bouncer is about to have his nuts fried." Cole jumps from his chair and jogs to the entrance.

Before he reaches it, it swings wide open and the big, burly ex-Special Ops Marine stumbles through the door, dragged in by the collar of his T-shirt by a fuming...

Chapter Forty-Two

Tatum

"M aevis?!"

I'm on my feet in an instant, ready to pummel through the mountain of a man for upsetting my pregnant wife. She pays me no mind. Instead, pushes past him and waddle-runs straight to the bathrooms, her posse of wickedly grinning women at her back.

"Damn, man." Jackson whistles, shaking his head. "I don't know whether to applaud your commitment or to question your smarts. Getting between a pregnant woman and the nearest bathroom just screams of you having a death wish." He cackles, leaning back in his chair.

"Fuck off, Camden," Xavier mumbles. "I'll bet my big, fat paycheck, that in about ten minutes, you'll wish I didn't let them in," he throws over his shoulder, spinning on his boots and marching right back outside.

The guys burst into laughter, but Cole and I exchange an *oh shit* look because our women never cut a book club meeting short. And they *never* do it to crash our "toxic masculinity-filled playdates for little boys".

"And that puts an end to poker night," Rowan concludes and pushes back from his chair, every bone in his back popping when he stretches to his full height.

"Sit your ass down," my wife orders him before snuggling into my side.

Can I just be honest here and say I'm damn happy to see her, but my balls have crawled up inside my body and are hiding behind my kidneys? Maevis is *always* sunshine and rainbows, even when she's upset. But there's a glint in her molten sugar eyes I'm not sure I like. That glint only comes when they've concocted a *plan* that'll have the rest of us pulling out our hair and fearing for our lives. And this bossy, stabby version of my sweetheart of a wife... has me *terrified*.

So, I do what any smart man does when put on the spot. I lean down and kiss the tip of her nose. "Hey, sweets."

She beams at me, all dulcet smiles and pearly whites, and yeah, I steel my spine to stop the chill crawling up my vertebrae from turning into a full body shudder. "Husband, we've brought gifts."

The walls of the bar vibrate under the collective groan rising from all of us poor, unsuspecting men. I swallow the lump lodged in my throat and ask, "What gifts?" I don't think I really want to know. None of us do.

"The priceless gift of empathy," Lalah clarifies for us, even though we're still as confused as we were ten seconds ago. "For centuries, millennia even, men have walked around living in the dark. Oblivious." She points at Cole, and his eyes widen, but *wisely,* his mouth remains firmly shut. "Well, not anymore. Thanks to the wonders of modern technology, Emma's beautifully wicked mind, and the miracle of express shipping, gentlemen, tonight you have the honor to test your endurance against four women."

"What the hell?" Joshua exclaims.

Oh man, and here I am, thinking you are smart.

All five women turn to glare at him. "You, newcomer," Lalah continues, her resting bitch face in full force. "You're with me and Cole." She crosses her arms over her chest, tapping her slipper-encased foot on the floor. "Move then, fast-like," she snaps. Joshua realizes she's not joking and begrudgingly moves to her side.

"Oh, perfect." Violet claps once. "I'll take Snarly One and Snarly Two."

"Who's that?" Blake asks.

She rolls her eyes, but makes a *come 'ere* gesture with her finger to Rowan, shouting at the same time, "Xavier, you're needed."

He shoves his shaven head through the door and snarls, "Nuh-ah. I don't think so."

"Get in here," Jackson sighs. "The sooner we stop fighting our fate, the sooner whatever this is"—he circles his forefinger in the air—"ends."

While the burly man stomps his way inside, Emma bounds to Blake and places a kiss on his cheek. "You're with me, sunshine," she tells him, and a wide smile graces his face, the first genuine smile he had all night. I swear, we can all hear Jackson's teeth grinding. She's unphased by the daggers Jake is glaring at their heads though, because she turns to him with a shy smile and extends her hand in his direction. "And so are you, Camden."

He's about to protest, but Maddox jumps in. "That leaves me and Carter with Sawyer. I assume Annalise is schooling her own husband."

"Anyone care to explain what it is that we're doing? Apart from being gifted empathy, of course." Joshua tries his luck again.

"Period pain simulators," all five women squeal, and my insides turn straight to ice.

"What fecking now? Lassies, yer all outta yer bloody minds," Rowan mutters under his breath.

My wife huffs next to me, and I tighten my hand around her shoulders, plastering her back to my chest. Otherwise, I'm sure I'll be scrubbing Irish blood out of Jake's floors for the next four seasons. "Are you going to push a baby out of your vagina anytime soon?" she asks in her sweet, melodic voice. Yeah, that gets everyone cringing. "I didn't think so. Put on the damn simulator and be thankful we're only doing period pain levels."

The top of his cheeks pink up, and I'd laugh if I wasn't terrified myself of what they're about to do to all of us. "Yes, lass."

And before I know what hit me, Maevis spins around in my arms and shoves my T-shirt up. I grip her waist, rubbing my thumbs over the belly hidden by my large hoodie, and grin down at her like a fool. "If you wanted me naked, all you had to do was say so, wife."

Maevis slaps my abs with the back of her hand and starts sticking squares connected to white cords to my abdomen and lower back before placing a kiss on the center of my chest. She looks at me through hooded eyes and mouths, *Later.*

That promise is almost enough to make me forget what I'm about to subject myself to. In order to speed things along so I can get home and have some alone time with the love of my life, I find myself asking, "How's this supposed to work?"

"The squares are connected to this pretty device here," Emma explains, wiggling a blue plastic rectangle with a small display on it. "There are twenty levels, but we'll only go up to twelve today."

"If you can make it to twelve," Lalah interjects.

If those are not fighting words, I don't know what are. She just lit a fire under every male's ass, because we're all competitive as fuck. While we have enough gray matter to know not to compete against the women, not one single one of us wants to lose face in front of the other. *Fuck me, I just signed up for at least twelve levels of pain.*

"If you can make it to twelve," Annalise agrees and takes over the explanation. "Up to level five, you may not feel anything. Anything between a five and a seven is normal period pain. Keep in mind, gentlemen, you're feeling this for a minute at best. We're feeling it for hours on end."

We nod solemnly. How could we not? But the truth is, I don't think any of us know exactly what to expect. We're all men used to pain. All of us have had our balls kicked at least once. Hell, I've had my thigh nearly blown out from under me, and I still think a kick to the crotch hurts more.

"Emma and I are a seven," Violet clarifies. "So everything above that will be new to us, too. The levels from eight to twelve are considered painful, with twelve being extreme pain. Anna's an eight, Sawyer a ten." She points at each woman, and I cringe in sympathy as images of Sawyer curled on the sofa, crying her eyes out, fill my mind. "Lalah is a twelve or just above. So, you're really going against her. Thirteen to twenty are considered labor pain, but we're not testing this today, as per Maevis's wishes."

"We're starting at level four. We're not wasting time for you to get used to the sensation, because that's not how it works. No period cramp eases you into it. They just come and ruin your day," Lalah barks.

Maevis pushes me to the nearest chair, and I sit down, mindful not to tangle the cords sticking out from under my T-shirt. Maddox sits next to me, looking anywhere but in my direction again, and my sister steps between us, leaning casually against the table, her legs stretched out and crossed at the ankles.

"Start," Maevis cheers.

I brace my arms against the chair. A tingling sensation starts in my lower abdomen, but nothing I would call pain, maybe just a slight pressure. I relax against the backrest, spreading my legs.

"Five," my wife counts, brushing her fingers through my hair. This is not bad at all. I don't know what I expected, but it's just a very slight increase in pressure.

"Six." My right leg twitches, a burning-like feeling igniting in my groin. I stiffen in the chair, trying to stop myself from fidgeting on the cushion. Still not painful, but definitely uncomfortable.

"Seven." A wave of pain hits me suddenly, and I bite my cheek to stop the curse ready to spill through my teeth. The wave ebbs and grows, spreading from my abdomen to my lower back. Shit, *this* is a normal period cramp?

I dare to peek at my sister, but there's no trace of discomfort on her face. If anything, she looks bored. Maddox is scowling at the top of Sawyer's slippers, but that's nothing new, since he was born with a scowl on his face. The rest of the men all wear equally serious looks on their faces, while the women are all relaxed and smiling.

"Eight."

And *goddamn*. Both my legs go lax, my knees numb when the wave of pain extends to them. What the fuck? I flex my thighs. I'll be damned if I'm the first one to even twitch.

"Nine!" Maevis beams. She fucking beams as if my insides are not all twisting around, tied in torturous knots of sadistic cramps. *Fuuuuuck*, I curse mentally when my knees start trembling and I feel sweat gathering under my bottom lip.

"How long does this last?" Blake hisses.

"Is not the same for everyone." Anna lifts her shoulder in a nonchalant shrug. "Some women only feel discomfort for a day or two, others for longer, up to a week."

"Seven fucking days? At this intensity?" Drake spits, outrage bleeding all over his face.

"Or higher," Lalah completes, my eyes darting to her just in time to see Cole snatch her arm and pull her onto his lap.

"Ten."

Blake and Joshua jump to their feet, moving their hips around. "Fuck, fuck, fuck," they curse. I don't blame them. The pressure is everywhere. The urge to wiggle my legs, move around, and drive my fist through a wall repeatedly is strong. It feels as if a hot iron rod is continuously stabbing me through my lower half.

Maevis squeezes my shoulder and whispers, "Eleven."

We're all on our feet now. My knees fucking buckle, and it takes everything in me to remain upright. Even the women are walking around at this point. I feel my neutral mask cracking with each wave wrecking my every nerve end. My stomach churns, and more sweat gathers on my brow and hairline. I swear even my goddamn asshole clenches and contracts with each cramp.

Sawyer suddenly turns around and plants her hands on the edge of the table, dropping her chin to her chest, breath heaving. I can't even find the necessary ire in me to rip Lawson a new asshole when he starts rubbing circles on her lower back. Fuck me, *I'm* close to dropping on my knees in front of Maevis and begging her to rub my back, too.

Every one of my friends is cursing and stroking their abdomen or lower backs. The only one seemingly unphased is Lalah, who sits cross-legged on the chair Cole vacated as he leans over her with a clenched jaw and red in the face.

"Twelve," Maevis whispers, and I scrunch my eyes shut. I don't stifle the groan slipping past my lips, but I do swallow down the bile pooling into my mouth.

"Fecken witchy shit on a broken broomstick. What the heck is this?" Rowan roars.

Lalah pretends to fucking *yawn*, shrugging when all of us glare at her. "What? I feel this shit for four full days. No pause button. I get up every single one of those four and *human*. And I'm not the only one. There are millions of women out there doing the same thing, day in, day out." Then those cold hazel eyes pin on me. "And in three short months, your wife is going straight to level twenty. I love you, Tatum, but you better be worshiping the fucking ground she walks on from now on."

There's a freaking chorus of relieved groans when Maevis whispers, "Stop."

"Feel free to keep them," Emma chirps. "And when you need a reminder in empathy, go straight for level twelve."

Chapter Forty-Three

Maevis

I am humming to myself as I flip the pancakes. As of this week, I'm working reduced hours at the bakery. My ankles are the size of watermelons, and after a panicked call to Dr. Fritz, she has advised me to keep my feet up as much as possible and decrease the time I spend on them. While strolls and leisurely walks are strongly encouraged, standing for hours on end kneading, whipping, chopping, and decorating is a no-no.

My bakery has Tessa, my pâtissier-in-training, a couple of high-school kids manning the counter, and the two college students from Billings, who are doing their internship at Suga'High—after one of my old professors recommended me. They'll be here until October, which works well for me, as I'm hoping I'll be able to spend more time at the bakery by that point.

I grumbled when Tatum initially brought up the idea of reducing my working hours, and I wasn't entirely happy with Dr. Fritz's advice, either.

Suga'High is my dream, a dream I've worked for since I was a toddler and baked plastic toy-cakes for my parents. Taking a step back feels wrong, like putting on a pair of jeans the other way around or wearing your shoes on the opposite feet. But ultimately, my daughter and her health come first, always. And I'm not stepping back completely. I am there on Monday mornings, to cash out the weekend, and four hours each day, even if at this point I'm more of a mascot.

Tatum too, helped by my father-in-law, is training someone new he has hired to deal with the administrative tasks. While Sarah still mans the reception more often than not, Tate also wants his days to be freer, so he can spend as much time as possible with us when our daughter is born.

Once Mike, the new hire, is trained and comfortable to run the administrative part by himself, Tate can focus only on restoring classic cars and on resolving any major issues that may arise. The rest of his team holds the fort during the normal day-to-day operation of the garage. That will give him a lot more flexibility and a lot of time for us to spend together as a family.

So, here I am, on a rainy Tuesday morning, cooking breakfast to share with my husband before he goes to work. I plate the last of the pancakes, just in time for the oven timer to ding. Armed with an oven mitt, I carefully remove the tray of steaming, crispy bacon. Last, I finish up the golden, fluffy scrambled eggs and carry everything to the breakfast nook.

The breakfast nook is my favorite part of the house. When I was ten, I visited a friend who had one of those rounded windows in her bedroom with a built-in bench instead of a windowsill, and that was her reading corner. I desperately wanted one too, but for the kitchen. I must have begged my father for weeks until he finally gave in and built me one. The rounded window is massive, taking half the length of the kitchen wall, with a direct view of my mom's flower garden. A dark wood table is pushed nearly flat to the glass. Two tube chairs, one yellow and one green, sit at both ends, and two stools on the same side.

Twenty-four years and they are still holding strong. They're also a lot of work to maintain. But while most of the house has been updated, I kept the pieces of furniture with most memories and looked after them with the love and respect they deserve. They speak of family, of laughter and happy moments, and I'll cherish them forever.

I doctor my decaffeinated coffee with fresh cream and a drop of home-made vanilla syrup, then raise on my tippy toes to grab a mug for Tatum. A warm hand presses on my lower back a second before his fresh, crisp scent envelops me, and he crowds me against the counter.

"I've got it, babe," Tatum says and passes me the mug. He nuzzles his face in my hair before pressing an open-mouthed kiss on my neck. "Smells delicious." Goosebumps sprout on my skin, and my lower belly tightens under the waves of heat traveling from where his lips still press against my skin to my core. My back arches against him and his hand flexes in response.

I turn my head to him and smile. "As much as I want to play right now, you need to eat and get out the door in less than thirty minutes," I chastise him.

"Or I could just eat you instead," he rasps and plants his mouth over mine, tracing my bottom lip with the tip of his tongue. I gasp when his fingers find their way to my sensitive nipples and brush over them, and he slips his tongue inside my mouth. A whimper escapes my throat at the taste of him—mint and Tatum, the most delicious combination. I'm ready to just give in and say to heck with breakfast, when my stomach rumbles the most unholy sound.

My cheeks flame when Tate chuckles and moves his hand on top of my rounded belly, stroking me through my dress. "Or maybe not. Come, wife, let's get you fed before my daughter starts kicking my face again." He picks up both of our mugs and leads me to the breakfast nook.

"She wouldn't kick you if you'd stop napping with your nose in my belly button." I giggle as I take a seat in my yellow tube chair.

"She'll never forgive me if I miss any of her soccer practices," he mock-gasps, placing his massive palm over his chest.

I laugh harder and push at his upper arm. "Sit down, you goof. Although, you do have a point. When she's using your face as her practice ball, she gives my bladder a break."

He smiles, affection dripping out of his topaz eyes, and kisses my forehead. I sigh, a deep, content breath filling my chest. "Three months, Cupcake. And then Vanilla Bean can play with an actual soccer ball."

"Tessa," I holler. "Where's the desiccated coconut?"

"Coming, Mae," she hollers back from where she's bent over, head hidden inside one of the ovens.

My eyes scan over the ingredients spread out on the stainless-steel counter. I already mixed the batter for the sponges—one simple with vanilla, one with a discreet hint of lemon from the grated lemon peel and honey essence I made, and one with crushed hazelnuts marinated in a rich, dark coffee. I cut the creamy butter into perfect little squares and drop them in a glass bowl.

The bakery closed one hour ago, and Tessa is nearly finished with the prep for tomorrow. I, on the other hand, am satisfying a craving. Turns out watching the *Great Australian Bake Off*—yes, I am *that* baker; I watch all variations of the TV show—when pregnant ten thousand months is not such a great idea. Sprawled out on my sofa, I was drooling on my chest at the sight of all the plates of lamingtons in all shapes and sizes.

So, here I am, baking lamingtons. Sure, I could have made them at home, but I was due to come to Suga'High for two hours before closing to go over inventory, and I love my perfect kitchen here.

"We're nearly out of desiccated coconut. Needs to be added on the shopping list," Tessa tells me, as she passes me one box. She wipes her hands on her stained apron and throws her thumb over her shoulder. "I got the oven all ready for you. Are you sure you don't want me to stay and help you clean up after?"

I give her a warm smile. She's an absolute Godsend. "Nah, thank you. You go home and enjoy your evening. Don't forget we're closing on Thursday, since we're replacing the security system and the cameras in the front."

"Alright, Mae. Have a great evening, and save me some lamingtons, would you?" She winks, pushing the apron over her head and tossing it in the laundry basket before slipping out the back door.

The oven pings when it reaches the preset temperature, and I move the pans of batter, staking all three of them inside. I close the door with my hip and set the timer to twenty minutes. Sweat peppers my hairline, and I brush the sleeve of my chef's jacket over my forehead. With all my ingredients prepped, I can get the chocolate sauce done once the sponges are cooling, so I decide to check once more that the entrance is locked and do a final check out front.

I push through the door and smile to myself when I see all the tables are cleared and everything is spotless. Tessa really is doing a brilliant job and stepping up to the plate. She'll be a magnificent chef-pâtissier soon enough. Although, her true talents lay more on anything requiring to manipulate dough, like cronuts, cinnamon rolls or any kind of rolls, Danishes, sweet and savory breads.

I check the register first since last time I forgot to lock it, but it's nice and secure. Firing up the laptop, I place a quick order with one of my suppliers for coconut, hazelnuts, and several other ingredients on the list Tessa left for me. I'm scanning the list carefully to ensure I don't leave anything out. Pregnancy brain is a real thing, and lately I've misplaced a lot of things. I walk around convinced I've done something, like locking a door or closing a window, only to turn around and find them unlocked or wide open. I'm so focused on my task that I startle out of my skin when someone tsks nearby.

My palm flies to my chest, trying to keep my heart contained inside my rib cage, and my head lifts so fast from my bent down position over the laptop, I get a crick in my neck. A squeal of surprise dies in my throat when my eyes make contact with a pair of bloodshot, black, soulless ones, my fingers fisting the material of my white coat. My stomach turns and my knees buckle as darkness slithers through at the edges of my vision.

"Hello, wife! Did you miss me?" he says, the sound of his voice grating on my eardrums, as he throws his arms wide open.

"Daniel," I exhale. Fear seeps into my bones just from his nearness. "W-what are you doing here?" I press one hand flat on the counter, hoping my arm is stronger than my weakened legs. When Daniel left, I withdrew the complaint I made against him because he swore he'd never get anywhere near me. And now… he's back.

"What do you mean what I am doing here? I own half of this shithole," he hisses. "I've got as much right to be here as you do."

His words are enough to light a fire in my belly. I'm not the scaredy cat I was four years ago. I refuse to cower before him or make myself smaller. And under no circumstance does he get to claim ownership of the bakery I have worked so hard to build from scratch and make a success, the dream my father and brother sacrificed their savings to help me buy.

"You're delusional," I tell him. "Please, leave. You are not welcome here, or anywhere near me, for that matter."

The smile he gives me is absolutely terrifying. His lips may curve up, but his eyes are dead, unfeeling. His rumpled state doesn't help either. The years since I've last seen Daniel have not been kind to him. His skin is tanned a deep brown, but underneath the tan, he's ashen. His clothes are stained and creased, as if they were just tossed somewhere in a messy ball, then carelessly picked up and worn.

"Who's gonna make me leave, darlin'? You?" He laughs derisively, his gaunt eyes narrowing at me as if daring me to try. "Do I need to teach you another lesson in manners?" His words chill me to my marrow, but I can't let him see how much he affects me.

"We're divorced, Daniel. The bakery wasn't mine when we were married. There's no part of it that belongs to you," I tell him in as calm a voice as I can muster. Taking a step closer to the counter, I try to hide my pregnant belly under the wooden partition. My hand trembles when I slowly move it inside the side pocket of my white jacket. My palm, damp with nervous sweat, slips over the screen in my desperate search for the volume button.

See, I'm no dummy. Five quick presses on the down-volume dials Maddox, five on the up-volume dials Tatum. Right now, I don't give a fuck who is dialed, as long as one of them picks up their phone.

Chills crawl up my spine when Daniel moves closer to me. A waft of stale alcohol and the stench of cigarettes hit me, making me heave. I swallow down the bile pooling in my mouth and sink my teeth in my bottom lip to stop it from trembling. I refuse to show him how afraid he actually makes me. My eyes sting under the burn of tears threatening to spill, but I blink them away. *Please, pick up, pick up.*

"The bakery wasn't yours? You and your fucking family pulled one over me. The title might have been in Ronald's name, but make no mistake, the bakery *was* yours. That makes half of it mine." He slaps his palms on the counter between the two of us, and despite my false bravado, I jump. He leans closer, licking his chapped lips. "Empty that fucking register, and give me what's mine, you insipid whore."

I involuntarily take a step back. His stench, the hatred in his eyes, the perverted twist of his mouth, everything screams at me to put as much distance between the two of us as possible. I mentally calculate how fast I can run through the kitchen and to my car parked out back. My stomach drops to my feet when I realize my car keys and purse are in the tiny locker close to the back entrance.

"There's no money in the register," I whisper. My voice comes out shaky and mousey, even to my ears.

"You filthy lying whore," he roars. Spittle flies out of his mouth and sprays my face. I breathe through my mouth, trying to quench the need to vomit, and keep my arms stiff at my sides, despite the incessant urge to scrub at my face.

I shake my head, denying his words. "It's really e-empty," I say. "I can show you." At my words, his cheeks redden and his puffy jaw clenches. He rounds the counter, and with a sinking feeling in my chest, the knowledge that no one will reach me in time rushes through me.

We've been here before. I've barely lived through this once already.

My back hits the wall when I hear a faint voice coming from my pocket. And it's enough to give him pause. I slip my hand in my pocket and retrieve my phone, Maddox's name flashing at me from the screen. *He answered.* I shakily tap my thumb on the speaker symbol.

"I called the Chief Deputy. He's on his way here," I say with more confidence than I feel. "Chief Deputy Lawson, I have my ex-husband, Daniel Johnson, here. He's claiming he owns half of Suga'High and threatening me."

"I heard that, Mrs. Carter," Maddox replies through the speaker. "I'm on my way." His voice is immediately replaced by the deafening siren sounds of his cruiser, coming from both my phone and right outside the bakery.

Daniel's eyes widen for a quick second before narrowing to thin slits. "This is far from fucking over." He spits at my feet, then shoulder-checks me into the wall as he runs out through the kitchen door.

A sharp jolt of pain radiates through me from my shoulder to my lower back, and my knees give out on me. I slide down the wall, my arms flailing, trying to grasp onto something to stop my fall, but to no avail. My ass hits the cold, tiled floor with such force, I bite my tongue and my breath wheezes out of my chest.

My belly tightens painfully before relaxing, and ice floods my veins. I lean my head against the wall, trying to force air into my lungs. *Maddox's on his way here. He'll get here soon. My baby is okay.* My trembling palm rubs tentative circles on my distended stomach, but it tightens again, harder this time. *No, no. no.* The tears I cannot keep contained anymore spring past my eyelashes and onto my cheeks.

I force my knees to bend and lift, pulling them as close to my belly as possible, trying to shield my baby. *These are not contractions, they can't be.* I startle, hitting the back of my head against the wall when the entrance door is slammed open.

"Maevis?!" Maddox shouts.

"O-over h-here." I cry out when another wave of pain circles the lower part of my waist. The sound of his boots thumping against the marble tiles echoes ominously as he runs inside. Maddox stops short in front of the counter and, with his palms firmly planted on the hard wood, he propels himself over it, and in the next second he's kneeling next to me, his palms gripping my shoulders.

"Fuck, Maevis! Are you okay?" Maddox asks, his ice-blue eyes scanning every part of me.

"Something's wrong with my baby," I whisper-cry, then turn my head aside and empty my heaving stomach all over his lap.

Chapter Forty-Four

Tatum

I've been on the brink of death two times in my life. Once as I laid bleeding with a blown-up thigh in the sand of a godforsaken desert. The second time, as I slump in a ratty chair with my phone to my ear while a frantic Maddox yells at me to get my ass to the Forrest Falls General Hospital, where Maevis has been admitted ten minutes ago with labor-like symptoms after Daniel Dead-Fucking-Man-Walking attacked her at the bakery.

He might as well saw through my chest with a rusty knife and rip my still-beating heart out. Crimson fiery rage paints my vision, and my fingers grip my phone so tightly, I'm surprised the flimsy device doesn't crumble to dust in my hand.

"Did he hit her?" I choke through my dried-out throat.

"I don't know. Mae couldn't tell me anything. There were no visible bruises on her, nor were her clothes wrinkled or ripped. My first concern was to take her to the hospital as soon as possible. She said there's something wrong with the baby. I didn't stop to ask questions."

As much as I want to curse him to high heaven, I know he did the right thing. Getting Maevis help comes first—before any questions, before calling me. "I'll be there in ten," I tell him.

"Better be here in thirty, you motherfucker. The last thing Maevis needs right now is for me to inform her you're not coming because your truck is at the bottom of a fucking ravine."

"Fuck off," I roar. "She's there all alone."

"Thirty minutes, Carter. Any sooner and I'll arrest your reckless ass the second you step foot through the ER doors," he hisses and ends the call.

Pain radiates through my shin when I kick with all the rage inside of me at the tire propped on the wall. "That slimy filthy rotten cunt," I shout. My blood rushes through my ears, and I swear I feel it pumping behind my eyes. My stomach churns with fear and unease. I fist my hands at my sides, my blunt fingernails digging in my rough, oil-stained palms.

I can't lose it now. Now I need to get my shit together and go to my wife. Later? Later I have a motherfucker to hunt.

I stride to the reception area where my mom is on the phone with most likely a customer. I snatch the cordless phone from her hand and end the call. Her eyes narrow at me, but before she can rip me a new one, I tell her, "Something happened at the bakery. Maevis is in the hospital. Let everyone know I'm not going to be in for the rest of the week." Her eyes widen, tears springing to life in a quick second. I bend over the tire-shaped counter and kiss her cheek. "I'll call you as soon as I know anything." Then I turn on my heel and run to my truck.

I slam the heel of my palm in the center of the wheel when the car doesn't magically start as soon as my ass hits the leather. "Come on, you motherfucker," I curse, but turn the key again and floor it. The tires eat gravel, dust rising in my wake, as I fly out of the parking lot and merge onto the main street.

With one eye on the road and the other on the touchscreen display in the center console, I scroll through my contacts until I find the number I need and hit call. The half ring barely sounds inside the cab before Jackson's voice replaces it.

"Tatum. What's wrong?"

"It's Daniel motherfucking Johnson. I'm pretty damn sure he's the one behind the texts, and the rats, and the trashed apartment," I hiss.

"How do you figure that?"

"Because he just attacked Maevis at Suga' High." Nothing. I peek at the screen to see if the call is still connected. "Jackson?"

"I'm here," he replies, his voice cold and deadly. "I'll find him."

"You do that," I bark and end the call, my finger scrolling again through my contacts and tapping a second name.

"Yellow," Lalah's cheery voice sounds through the speakers.

"I need you to go to the bakery and check that everything's in order. If nothing's amiss, lock the bakery and keep the keys. Take Cole with you."

"Shit," she breathes. "Maevis?"

"I don't know. I'll call you when I do. Just... do this for me, okay? You can ask all your questions later."

"I'll let you know when it's done," she confirms and hangs up.

I know I should call Drake and let him know, but right now I need five goddamned minutes to breathe. How do I inform everyone who loves Maevis that I once again failed her? Nausea churns in my gut. My lungs constrict with the sob pressing down on them and squeezing my heart. *Fuck.*

With everything going on with the ex-witch, not once has the thought of Daniel crossed my mind. He left town before their divorce, and no one has seen him since. What does he want? Why right now?

My blood fucking boils in my veins and my fingers tighten around the wheel until they turn white from the pressure. "Goddamn. If anything happens to Maevis or our baby, I'll bury the sorry excuse for a man alive," I promise to myself.

I cut off the car in front of me as I take a sharp right next to the hospital. I slam the truck into park in the first available spot before jumping out and taking at a dead-sprint through the ER's doors. By the time I reach the reception, I'm out of breath.

"Maevis Barlowe," I heave. "Where is she?"

The nurse behind the desk gives me an unimpressed look, cocking an eyebrow high on her forehead. "Are you a relative?"

"I'm her husband," I tell her, grinding my teeth to stop myself from shouting. *She's just doing her job.*

"Got an ID, husband?" she asks.

I shove my hand in my coverall's pocket and take out my wallet, sliding my ID out and passing it to her. "Please," I beg, hoping she'll move just a bit faster. She plucks it out of my hand, gives it a thorough read and returns it to me. Her fingers type impossibly slow on the goddamn keyboard, and I'm about to jump over the counter and do the typing myself.

"Maevis Barlowe came in through the ER about an hour ago. She's now been admitted to Birth and Deliveries, fourth floor, room 432." My heart stops. There's a flutter in my chest, a strange bubbling when my blood stalls inside my arteries. I sway on my feet, the reception floor no longer flat and straight, but wavy and unstable.

"Mr. Carter, are you okay?" a faint voice reaches my ears, trying to penetrate through the icy shield that just fell down on me.

"She can't give birth just yet," I wheeze. "It's too soon."

Something warm presses against my fisted hand resting on the white desk. My eyes dart down to see the nurse's small hand patting mine.

"Breathe, Mr. Carter. Come on, in through your mouth," she urges, and there's a soothing lilt to her tone that reaches me enough to comply. My lungs expand painfully with all the antiseptic-tasting air rushing in. "Good. Out through your nose."

I follow her instructions again and exhale all the knives slashing at me from the inside.

"Again," she orders, her voice strangely authoritative, and I scramble to do as commanded. With my second breath, the ground under the soles of my safety boots straightens once more, and my heartbeat resumes its normal rhythm. "You back with me?" At my nod, she smiles kindly. "Good. Your wife is not giving birth. She's currently undergoing a series of tests to ensure all is well with her and your baby. She's not marked as active labor in her chart. Now, go see for yourself how she's doing, okay?"

I squeeze the hand still holding mine, forcing my mouth into a semblance of a grateful smile. "Thank you," I say before taking off at a run to the nearest elevator. I pace the silvery cave as it flies to the right floor, and then I'm running again until I finally reach the correct room number. I stop in front of the white closed door, chest heaving, palms planted on my knees as I try to calm the madness swirling inside of me, demanding that I turn back around and paint my skin in the asshole's blood.

Two more garbled gulps of air settle me enough so that I am ready to face my wife without exploding out of my coveralls with rage. I'm sure she's scared enough as it is and doesn't need my foul mood to add to her tension.

Gently, I rap my knuckles against the wooden door, and push it open. My eyes zero in on Maevis lying on the hospital bed. She looks so small and fragile; my arms physically ache with the desperate need to hold her. Her legs and lower body are covered by a dreary, gray blanket, but her beautifully rounded belly is exposed. A wide black band is fastened around the expanse of her stomach and what looks like a thousand wires connect to it.

"Tate?" she sobs. The agony-filled sound is all my legs need to unglue from the floor and carry me to her in three quick strides. I cup her cheek with my palm, paying no mind to the oil and grime coating my skin, and stroke her tear-stricken face with my thumb, leaving a gray streak in its wake.

"I'm here, Cupcake," I rasp, my throat constricted with tears and relief at seeing her in one piece and talking. I touch my forehead to hers and draw in her sweet scent of vanilla mixed with the stingy smell of disinfectant and hospital chemicals. Her warmth and softness burrow in my chest, a quiet calmness settling over my straining shoulders.

She's here. She's breathing.

Her face nuzzles in the crook of my neck, and I adjust my elbow in the pillow next to her arm, so I don't squish her, as I wrap my other arm around her. Her small frame shakes in my embrace under the grief of her quiet sobs. My mind whirs and turns, a slew of questions piling up on the tip of my tongue, but her comfort is more important than my need to get answers right now. I bury my nose in her hair and murmur soothing words to her.

The device measuring her heartbeats beeps incessantly, but I ignore it as best as I can, focusing all my attention on my wife. I don't know how long we stay like this—it could be minutes, it could be hours—but, eventually, her sobs subside. Her head slides down my shoulder, her body limp in my arms. I lower her down on the bed and fluff the pillow under her head so she can rest more comfortably.

I look around the small, private room and eye a flimsy-looking, plastic chair tucked in a corner. I move it close to the bed and slump into it, sending out a quick prayer it doesn't break under my weight, and I end up next to Mae's bed with a plastic leg stuck in my ass. The door creaks open, and I whirl in my seat, feeling my heart take a dive when the plastic screeches ominously. Huffing the breath I was holding when it doesn't give out on me, I look at the intruder walking inside with light steps.

Lawson is a sight for sure. His brown hair is sticking out in all directions and his khaki uniform shirt is untucked and unbuttoned, his badge clipped to his chest pocket. Light blue scrubs cover his legs, so at odds with his sturdy work boots.

"How's she doing?" he asks in a low voice.

"Distraught." I lift a shoulder in a clueless shrug. "She just fell asleep. What happened?" I demand.

He points his chin to the door, silently telling me to go out into the hallway and have this conversation, but indecision keeps me rooted to the chair. I don't want to leave Mae alone in case she wakes up.

"We'll be just in front of the window. I don't want you to... react," he tells me, a cautious tone to his words, "and wake her up."

Considering the rage ebbing and flowing inside of me, he's not fucking wrong, and fucked if I don't hate that he is reading me so easily. I bring

Mae's hand to my mouth and plant a kiss on her delicate knuckles and her wedding ring before tucking her hand in close to her body.

Maddox leads the way out of the room, and we both stop in front of the window.

"Wait, before you say anything, let me get Drake, Cole, and Jackson on the phone," I say.

"You're not planning anything stupid, are you?" The arrogant motherfucker cocks an eyebrow at me and, if it weren't for the fact that he *did* get my wife help, my fist would've met his face and I could have expelled some of the rage weighing me down, clouding my mind.

Instead, I clamp my lips shut and stare him down with a *What do you think* look on my face. He doesn't need to know that mentally I'm making plans on how slowly I will eviscerate the nutless coward who dared put his hands on Maevis, and drag his pain out until he begs for his worthless life.

Maddox shakes his head at me, moving his hands up, palms facing me in a placating gesture. "I just got off the phone with Drake. Maevis begged me to call him after I talked with you. The oven was still working in the kitchen, and she was worried about a fire."

I nod, slipping my phone out of my pocket and dialing Jackson and Cole, leaving Drake out. Moving the call to speakerphone, I turn down the volume so that the whole hospital doesn't hear our conversation. "I had Lalah go to the bakery to check on things, too," I say, but before I manage more words, the call connects and two gruff *hello*-es sound from my phone.

"I'm with Lalah, Drake, and Annalise at Suga'High," Cole states. "Everything's in order. The girls are just finishing up Mae's cakes. Lalah insisted Mae was craving these and refuses to leave without them. Blake will sleep in the apartment tonight and keep an eye on the bakery. I know he wasn't supposed to move until the weekend, but he's adamant."

"Thanks, Cap. I'm here with Maddox." I look at the man in front of me and give him a nod to start talking. He doesn't hesitate to walk us through the call he received, the muffled words he could make out and realizing the dipshit was there, then talking directly to Maevis when she threatened the asshole, the cunt promising it wasn't over, and finally getting to Suga'High to find Maevis slumped on the floor, complaining of pain in her lower belly.

"I've been kicked out of the room, so I have no idea what the doctor told her. She had an ultrasound done, blood tests, uhm... other more private tests, but all I've been told by one of the nurses is that she'll be fine and that's all she could say since I'm not a family member." His words bring me a sense of relief. I'll have to hunt down Dr. Fritz and find out more from her, but even the little he knows is more information than I had ten seconds ago.

"You'll start looking for him?" Drake demands.

"Yeah, man," Maddox confirms. "I was waiting for Tatum to get here, but I'll be on my way to the station soon."

"Goddamn squirrel of a man. He's like a fucking disease that doesn't quit," Drake curses, his voice loud and clear despite the low volume on my phone. An elderly nurse walks past us just then and shushes us primly, her sharp nose up in the air. I'd roll my eyes, but right now I don't have any bandwidth left for anything but my wife and unborn baby.

"Let us know what the doctor says. If Mae needs to stay overnight, we'll come by and bring some clothes and whatever else you need." Annalise's concerned voice comes from the phone's speaker, mixed with strange thumping and slamming sounds.

"Supernova, for fuck's sake," Cole curses faintly in the background.

Annalise laughs, but I hear the strain and unease in her giggle. "Mae will have a new chair and a fresh coat of pain on the kitchen walls tomorrow. Lalah's... taking her feelings out on it."

"Keep us posted. Pigs are flying during the off-hunting season, and I just got a new permit," Jackson says in a cold, lethal voice, disconnecting the call.

Maddox drops his large mitt on my shoulder, his icy eyes boring into mine. His eyebrows furrow—I'm certain he doesn't like what he reads in my eyes—and gives a minute shake of his head. "Don't do anything stupid," he hisses. "Go and watch over her. I'll do this the *legal* way. Got it?"

I don't bother making promises I don't intend to keep, instead I spin on my heel, and with a "Thank you," thrown over my shoulder, I stride to my wife's side, where I'm meant to be.

Chapter Forty-Five

Maevis

I wake up to a sleeping Tatum. His blond hair, disheveled and sweaty, tickles my arm. His warm breath washes over my skin where his lips are pressed to the back of my hand, even in his slumber.

My own lips curve up in a semblance of a smile. That's all I can muster right now, with the aftershocks of Daniel's visit still making my stomach churn and my limbs numb with fear. I thought all that was put behind me when we divorced. After he nearly made away with my life, I had a restraining order drawn up for him. During our divorce proceedings—all done in his absence since he all but vanished after that last night at the house—his younger brother, Derek, begged me to drop the charges.

He pleaded and swore up and down Daniel would not be bothering me ever again. Stupidly, I believed him. At the time, Derek was in his final year at his seminary, preparing to get ordained and become a pastor. While I am not heavily religious, I am a spiritual person. My naïveté made me think a man of God would not blatantly lie to my face. My former in-laws didn't particularly like me, blaming me for Daniel's decline, but Derek always treated me kindly. So, I dropped the charges, and with them, the restraining order also fell through.

I just wanted it all over with. I wanted the divorce done, and I wanted that man out of my life. All so I could start picking up the pieces and digging my way out of the hole I buried myself in because of sheer stubbornness. Clearly, I wasn't the best at making decisions then, starting with marrying the scum.

A throat clears nearby, and I whip my head around to see Dr. Fritz smiling softly at me, her round glasses high up her straight nose. She taps her pen on the back of the clipboard pressed to her chest, then points at the screen monitoring the heartbeat of our Vanilla Bean.

"She's doing great, Momma." A rush of air is expelled from my lungs, the claws squeezing at my heart retracting at her words. Tears spring from my eyes as the adrenaline leaves my body, relief replacing the turbulent flow of my blood. "The tightening you felt in your belly was what we call prodromal, or Braxton-Hicks contractions. These are normal, especially in the third trimester. Just your body's way of preparing you for birth." She steps closer and lays her hand on my forearm, giving me a reassuring pat.

"I thought these were not supposed to be painful. But some hurt so much, they caused me nausea and made me puke." My cheeks flame at my admission, but there's no room for pride or embarrassment when it comes to the health of my baby. Can't do anything about my racing heartbeat, and the good doctor hears it since the device monitoring it beeps like crazy, causing a downright ruckus.

Tatum stirs next to me, and abruptly he springs up from here he was resting his head on my bed. "Sweetness? What happened? Are you okay? Is the baby okay?"

"Both baby and mother are fine, Mr. Carter," Dr. Fritz is quick to assure him. Tate grabs my hand again, and squeezes gently, pressing my fingers to his lips, his unruly scruff prickling at my skin. His eyes are tired and bloodshot, dark bags resting under his lower lashes. "Now, Maevis, to clarify, Braxton-Hicks are normally not painful, you are right. But the sudden stress you were under, coupled with your fall, might have caused the painful sensation. I won't tell you what you felt, but your nausea and subsequent vomiting might have been due to adrenaline rush, too."

I nod my head at her, trying to absorb everything she tells me when Tatum's fingers tighten over mine. "Fall?"

"He... uhm... ah... shoulder-checked me into the wall when he ran out of the bakery. My knees gave out on me, and I fell on my ass," I explain, a nervous giggle slipping past my lips. No, it's not funny. Nothing about this is even remotely funny. Maybe only heaving over Maddox's lap and the horrified look on his face. I giggle harder, the whole bed shaking under me. I slap my palm over my mouth, choking an apology to my audience. "S-sorry," giggle, "Sorry," more giggles, "I d-don't know what's come over me," roaring laughter.

"Doc, is she in shock?" Tatum asks concerned, jumping to his feet and cupping my face, turning my head so that I can look at him. The slight grease smudges in his beard only make me laugh even harder. "Babe, breathe for god's sake. Are you okay? Maevis!" he whisper-yells, but my laughter cannot be contained. I laugh until I'm straining for oxygen and, as soon as I force a breath past my tired throat, that's when the sobs start. "For fuck's sake, Doc. Can't you give her something?" he asks, outraged. He pulls my head to his chest, holding me tight to his strong pecs, his palms running over my back with infinite care.

It only makes me cry harder.

Everything is just... overwhelming—Daniel attacking me; Maddox rushing to help me; sitting in this hospital bed waiting for Tatum to get here, worried about his reaction; terrified out of my mind that I've harmed my baby in the fall. And so, I burrow my face deeper into his T-shirt, letting his familiar scent of home, safety, and a-hard-day's-work sweat comfort me.

I don't know for how long I cry on Tatum's chest, but at some point, he climbs into my bed. His arms are two bands of steel around me. Even his legs tangle with mine. He's lending me his strength and his quiet support with every inch of his body. My bout of hysteria interrupted Doctor Fritz's explanation, and I'm sure Tatum is dying to get some proper answers, but he puts my comfort first.

"Are you feeling better?" he murmurs, his lips pressed atop my head. I nod minutely, my fingers clutching at the soft cotton of his T-shirt. "Okay. You ready for me to get the doctor back?" I shake my head this time, gripping him tighter. If it is up to me, he'll never leave my side ever again. "I'm not going anywhere, Cupcake, I promise. When you're ready, say the word. Not moving a muscle until you give me the green flag."

I close my eyes and focus on the rhythmic drumming of his heartbeat under my ear. My baby is fine. I am fine. Tatum is here with us and he'll keep us safe, always. I know that with every fiber of my being. This man here will lay his life down before he'll ever let anything happen to us. Tilting my head, I touch my mouth over his chest, right where his heart pumps life through him, underneath velvety skin and rock-hard muscle.

A soft knock on the door has me lifting my head and looking in that direction. A sheepish Dr. Fritz returns to the room. "Sorry to interrupt. I just came to let you know I can start preparing your discharge papers if you're ready to go home."

I give her a wane smile and say, "That's fine, Doctor. Thank you."

"We kept you this long because I wanted to make sure there was no placenta rupture after your fall. Your blood pressure was also a concern. But we've monitored both over the last six hours, and I'm happy to say there's no reason to worry. Your pregnancy will progress fast from now on, Maevis, so expect more false contractions. But if at any point you're worried, please come to the ER or call my office during the day." Her eyes flit from me to Tatum, and I swear I see a faint blush staining her cheeks. "Your coccyx will be sore and bruised for at least seven days. My recommendation is that you abstain from any sexual activities for the next two weeks, just to be safe. While we have seen no anomalies around your placenta, this is not the moment to take any unnecessary risks."

"Understood. Thank you, Doctor," Tatum tells her, and I note the lilt of amusement in his voice. For some reason, she directed her recommendation to him instead of to us. I'd snort if I weren't embarrassed myself.

"Alright, folks. I know it's nearing midnight, so if you prefer to stay until morning, I'll leave the discharge papers at the ER reception for you. But I think you'd want to rest in your own bed tonight."

"Yes, ma'am," my husband agrees. "If you are sure that my wife and baby are safe, I'd like to take them home."

She smiles warmly at us before scribbling some notes on her clipboard, then places a set of stapled-together papers on the nightstand at the side of the bed. "Mr. Carter, if you don't mind stepping aside, I'll call a nurse to have Maevis unhooked from all these machines. Maevis, I'll see you in two weeks at your appointment. Increase your bed rest and no strenuous activities until then. Let your body heal in its own time, even though I know how difficult staying put must be. Any issues, don't hesitate to call me. Have a great night," she says and promptly leaves.

Tatum untangles himself from under me, just as a kind, elderly nurse arrives. She scowls at my husband, but he pays her no mind, bending to kiss my forehead. "I'll go settle the bill and be right back, sweets. Love you." And with those parting words and a gentle caress over my belly, he scurries out the door.

The nurse makes quick work of getting rid of all the cables sticking to me, wordlessly helps me shed the hospital gown covering my body and get into my own dress. I drape my chef's coat over my arm, brushing my tangled hair with my fingers.

"Your husband and his friends are foul-mouthed," the nurse hisses over her shoulder before wheeling one of the machines out the door. I look after her, puzzled, and bark out a laugh. Soon after she leaves, Tatum returns and helps me to his truck since the top of my ass does feel sore and bruised, and I waddle slowly next to him.

He unlocks the car, opening the passenger door for me, then lifts me up inside, mindful of my belly and head. I slide over the buttery leather to the middle of the bench and lean my head on his shoulder as soon as he jumps inside. He fastens my seatbelt first, arranging it carefully over my belly, then takes care of his, and in no time, we're on our way back home.

I STIR, AND MY EYELIDS FLUTTER OPEN. I blink slowly a couple of times, trying to get rid of the remnants of sleep still coating my eyes, but it takes me a good ten seconds to process that our bedroom is still enclosed in darkness. It's the absolute silence that gets my heart hammering in my chest. The absence of Tatum's soft breaths as he sleeps, the lack of warmth at my back.

Blindly, I flail my arm around on my nightstand until I reach the switch, and turn the night light on. The sheets on his side of the bed are rumpled and creased, but his pillow doesn't look slept on. The cold fabric under my palm confirms what I already know—Tatum has left our bed at least an hour or so ago.

I swing my feet over the edge of the bed and check the time on my phone. 4:34 a.m. shines at me from the too bright screen. Sighing deeply, I push to stand. My back twinges in protest, but I pay it no mind. I shove my feet into my pink and fluffy, bunny-eared slippers, which the girls decided were the footwear to have for book club meetings. Throwing a robe over my shoulders that I don't bother tying—it's been at least three weeks since it stopped fitting around my belly—I pad softly into the hallway, looking for my missing husband.

The guest bedroom across from the master is empty, so is the attached bathroom. I spin on my heel and move toward the living room, nearly jumping out of my skin when I find Tatum in the darkness with only the faint glow of a night light illuminating him. He's poised like a sentinel in front of the entrance hallway. I can only see his profile where he sits in an armchair he probably dragged over from the family room, baseball bat front and center on his lap.

"Tatum 'Junior' Carter, are you out of your goddamn mind?" I screech, propping my hands on my hips. I bite my cheek to stop the smile of satisfaction forcing my lips up when he startles and jumps to his feet, baseball bat at the ready. "For the love of all pralines, put the damn thing down," I order him, stomping my foot for good measure.

The wooden bat clinks against the floor as it slips out of his hand, and his eyebrows scrunch together. He has the audacity to scowl at me and point a finger to my chest. "You are supposed to be in bed."

I slap his finger away and move to the kitchen, knowing he'll follow. I beeline straight to the breakfast nook, where the boxes of lamingtons are waiting for me, and snatch one from the top, shoving the whole thing in my mouth.

My waterworks broke again for a full-on hour when we got home from the hospital the other night and found the three boxes of lamingtons on my kitchen island. My friends not only made sure my bakery didn't burn to the ground, but they also finished preparing them for me. Sure, the chocolate glaze has far too many lumps in it, but see if I care. These are the best things I've ever eaten in my life, and it's all about the love, thoughtfulness, and care that went into making them.

I slowly chew the fluffy square, my cheeks puffed out like a chipmunk's, hoping the chocolate and sugar are enough to settle the raging hormones in my bloodstream demanding I pick up the baseball bat and spank Tatum to high heaven.

His hands settle on my shoulders. I whirl around, huffing a breath, and a rain of desiccated coconut flies out of my mouth. I can't find it in me to be embarrassed when I'm so angry I'm just about to take a bite out of him. He lifts his arms in a placating gesture, palms facing me. Yeah, that's not placating this pregnant woman.

"Please, sweetness, you're supposed to be on bed rest."

I forcefully swallow the last of the lamington and lick my lips, my eyes shooting deadly laser beams at his head. "I'm supposed to rest," I hiss. "How do you expect me to rest when you're poised in front of the door with a baseball bat, Tatum? What were you thinking?"

He scrubs his palm over his face before running his fingers through his disheveled hair and tugging at the strands. His eyes close, his mouth pulling taut in the most exasperated expression I've ever seen on someone's face. And that is saying a lot, considering exasperation is Lalah's state of being.

"I can't sleep, sweets," he murmurs. "It fucking haunts me in my dreams that the asshole is still out there. We have no security system and too many goddamn windows. I fall asleep and startle awake five minutes later at every sound or critter rummaging around in the backyard."

My heart sinks to my feet and my stomach flips upside-down. I take a step toward him and circle my arms around his waist, my ear resting against his chest. His heart is drumming against his rib cage so furiously, I can feel each and every pump against my cheek. "I'm sorry," I whisper.

His hand cradles the back of my head, his fingers massaging my scalp. "What are you sorry for, Cupcake? You cannot control his actions any more than I could control the witch."

I tilt my head back, my chin propped on his sternum, and seek his eyes through the veil of tears blurring my vision. "I'm sorry for not shouting from the rooftops that I am yours after Thanksgiving." His eyes widen, the sky-blue of his irises expanding until his pupil is barely visible. "I'm sorry for not marching into that bathroom and fighting for you that night." He sucks in a breath and his jaw clenches. "I'm sorry I didn't look harder for you after, and I'm so goddamned fucking sorry for leaving you."

"Maevis," he whispers, his own tears escaping the confines of his long lashes and spilling down his scruffy cheeks.

"I trusted you then with my life, and I trust you now. Your ability to care for me, to protect me—that was never in question, Tatum. It was the lack of trust in myself. I didn't see how I was good enough to be anyone's first choice, regardless of what made me blind to my own worth. And you paid for my insecurities. I'm so fucking sorry."

"You, of all people, don't need to apologize to me, baby," he growls. "In all that bullshit, you were as much of a victim as I was."

"A survivor," I cut him off. "You're not a victim, Tatum. And I do have to apologize. Your loyalty to me may not let you see right now that I was so horribly mistaken, but I was." I sneak my hand around his neck and press his head down until we're both nose to nose. "You may think you don't need to hear this, but you do. I am sorry, Tatum. And most of all, I'm incredibly sorry how *my* actions from then are impacting you now."

His lips crash down on mine, and he groans in my mouth. I swallow all the desperation, the hurt, and the absolution he feeds me with his lips, teeth, and tongue. I take in his thirst for redemption, his craving to be someone's first choice.

And gasp.

The realization hits me with the power of a freight train.

The woes plaguing Tatum are not at all that different from mine. Sure, they stem from a different spring, but our searches are similar. We both want to be someone's first choice.

He sacrifices himself for everyone in his life. If I were to look up Tatum's name in a dictionary, I'd find references to *always showing up* and *pillar of support and strength.* The protectiveness, the loyalty, the care, and all the goodness in this amazing man are always overlooked.

Because they're expected.

And with that, another epiphany shines inside of me. "We were never second choices. We are expected; we are depended on, but never second. I see you, Tatum. And... for what it's worth, I choose you."

"Forever and always, sweets."

"Always and forever, my love."

Once again, I seek his mouth, but I am immediately pushed behind him when the rounded window of the breakfast nook shatters into a million pieces, shards of glass flying everywhere. My limbs grow numb, and all I hear is the dizzying sound of my blood rushing to my ears and Tatum's inhuman roar.

Chapter Forty-Six

Tatum

I'm imploding under the whirlwind of my own emotions. Her apology both slays and heals my soul. She pushes up on her tippy toes, her plush lips seeking mine. I'm just about to close my eyes and give in, when movement just behind her draws my attention. I don't have time to think. I push Maevis behind me, just as the window shatters, chips of glass flying toward us.

My vision turns to red, every muscle in my body coiled and ready to strike. "Lock yourself in the ensuite," I bark. "Go! NOW!" I roar, pushing Maevis as gently as I can toward our bedroom. "Don't come out until I come to get you."

"Tatum," she cries out.

"Go, baby," I say, trying to soften my voice, and give her one last look over my shoulder before rushing out of the house, chasing after the running figure.

He's not a fast runner by any means. In fact, he staggers and slows, but he did have a two-minute headstart on me. My lungs heave and my injured thigh protests. I push harder, running faster, eating up the distance between us. Just when I think I have him, he jumps into a car parked right at the town's border, in the shrubbery, and speeds away. It's still too fucking dark outside to make the color of the car, but it looks like an older, beat-up Corolla, with no fucking plate at the back.

"Fucking coward," I hiss, and run back home. I don't make it more than thirty yards when a black motorcycle whizzes past me. I follow it with my eyes, as the red-light stop disappears in the distance.

I know that fucking motorcycle.

I pat my sweatpants, but of course, I don't have my phone on me. I might have had enough presence of mind to put on shoes when I was standing vigil at the entrance, but my phone is still on the arm of the chair I sat in.

Not wasting any more time, I head home. I burst through the entrance, quickly swiping my phone in my haste to get to Maevis. Despite the madness of this morning and the anger eating at my insides, I'm pleased to find the bathroom door locked. I knock gently so she doesn't startle before calling out her name. The lock disengages with a soft click, and I push the door open. She rushes into my arms, holding on to my waist for dear life.

"He lost his mind," she whimpers. "I don't understand what he wants or why he's back after all this time."

Flexing my knees, I scoop her in my arms and carry her to our bed. I'm not particularly happy with the window being so close to it, but I also know, deep in my gut, he won't return today. He didn't expect me to chase after him. So if he'll try something, he'll try it later on or tonight.

"I know, sweets," I console her, holding her close and smoothing my fingers through the silk of her hair. "Gonna have to call Maddox to report it. I think it's best if you go stay at Lalah's today. Maybe sleep there, too."

"What?" she hisses and sits up on her elbow. "Don't tell me you plan to stay here?!"

"Mae," I sigh, pinching the bridge of my nose. "I need to be here if we ever want to catch this son of a bitch."

"That's Maddox's job, Tatum, not yours," she yells.

If I wasn't a ball of anger and pure fucking hatred—and all aimed toward one person in particular—I would've smiled at the fire burning in her whiskey-colored eyes and how adorably cute she is right now. The blush staining her cheeks and the smattering of freckles on her nose just make me want to trace them with my tongue. Alas—"Maddox doesn't have enough people. He can't be everywhere. I promise, I'll be careful."

"You'll be reckless," she accuses.

That, too.

Because once I get my hands on him, I won't stop until he chews on his own teeth. No one harms my wife and escapes unscathed.

"Do you know where else he could be staying? Lawson already went to his family home, but there was no trace of him, and his parents swore up and down that he was still living in Texas."

"What about his brother?"

"He lives there," I reply, based on what Maddox relayed to us, even though he's not really supposed to share any details of an 'active investigation'.

"Derek?" Mae adds.

"No, I think Madd said his name was Darren."

"That's his middle brother, but he has a younger one, Derek. When I last saw him four years ago, he was finishing up his seminary, so by now he could be ordained and be a pastor anywhere in the county."

"So, Daniel could be living with him," I finish up for her and smack an open-mouthed kiss on her pursed lips. "You brilliant fucking woman." Her eyes light up, and the suffocating heaviness pressing down over the both of us lightens a touch. "I'm going to call Lawson now and clear the glass in the kitchen after I've talked to him. Stay here and don't move a muscle. Once I have the kitchen cleared, I'll get you some breakfast and drive you to Lalah's."

"Tatum... I don't think it's a good idea for you to stay here alone."

"I'll trade you for Cole, for today only." I grin at her, although I'm sure the fake smile doesn't reach my eyes. I don't think I'll be able to sincerely smile until the fucker is rotting behind bars where he belongs.

I DOWN A STEAMING CUP OF COFFEE IN ONE GULP. The kitchen is cleared, Maddox properly awake and shouted at, and breakfast rolls warming up in the oven. The sun is slowly rising from behind the mountains. While I can't actually see the sunrise for the looming slabs of rock, the sky is slowly changing from pitch dark to blue-navy and orange. I huff into my mug. It seems like a personal affront for the day to just... get lighter when there's so much darkness hovering over me.

I'm drumming my fingers on the counter, waiting for Jackson and Cole to get back to me. I texted both, but they're probably still sleeping, considering it's just before six in the morning. Color me shocked that Lawson didn't kick up a fuss when I woke him up and went on a full-on tirade about the bastard breaking the window in the early a.m., but he's been surprisingly... accommodating lately. And now he's focusing on finding Derek.

My phone finally chirps from the counter, and I frown as I read Cole's reply.

> *Blake's been jumped around four this morning. He heard someone banging around the stairs, so he went down to investigate. Whoever it was hid behind the dumpsters and hit him in the back. Kid's fine. A fat lip and a bruised shoulder. Threw some punches of his own, too. The coward ran, Blake gave chase. He disappeared into an old Corolla. Jake's looking into it.*

Cap

> *The wolves are descending.*

Cap

What the fuck?!

I shake my head and ignore his last text. There's no time for cryptic messages and guesswork right now. But his first text just shows the asshole went to the bakery first. Based on what Maevis told me of their *conversation* the other day, he's after money. So, most likely, the asshole was trying to break in and got interrupted by Blake. And then he came here to take his pathetic anger out on Maevis.

I'll breathe easier when the new security system gets installed today. Even if we catch the son of a bitch sooner rather than later, I need to know Maevis is always safe. And all these fucking windows need to be changed. Too many entry points. The glass is far too fragile. I make a mental note to call Matt later today and demand a quote for replacing all of them with the same kind of windows Lalah has in her home.

I may not be a near-billionaire, but I can afford some fucking bulletproof windows.

Sipping slower at my coffee now, I type a one-handed message to Blake to thank him for going after the asshole, but before I get to press 'send', the squeal of tires over gravel as a car brakes hard in the driveway has me throwing my mug in the sink and diving for my baseball bat.

The front door slams open, and I pause. I locked the fucking door, for all the good that it did with a big-ass hole in the wall where the window was. I shuffle silently toward the entrance hallway, lifting the bat over my shoulder, ready to hit first and ask questions later.

I let loose as soon as I see movement with the corner of my eye before a piercing scream rings out, making my ears bleed, and the bat is stopped in midair by a large hand.

"Goddammit, Carter, what the fuck are you doing?" Cole roars, and Lalah jumps into my arms from behind him. Her arms wrap around my neck so tightly that the hold blocks my airflow, and her legs coil around my calves, making me stumble five steps back.

"Are you trying to hug me or to kill me?" I ask jokingly, although my heart hammers in my chest. For fuck's sake, I was about to bash my best friend's head in with a baseball bat.

"Both. Or impersonate Astrum," she mumbles, then squeaks when her husband peels her off me, tucking her in at his side.

"Supernova, you run *away* from the man with the bat, not jump into his arms," Cole grits. "Took ten fucking years of my life, dammit."

"Swear jar," Eliza pushes between the two of them. "That'll be $25.99."

Blake whistles behind them, a sleepy Clara hoisted up on his hip. "I'd laugh, but it's not funny," he mutters.

And I stay frozen in the entrance hallway, watching as the Hayes horde takes over my home. "Uhm, guys, seriously, what are you doing here?"

"We're having breakfast together before I collect Mae. Then we're dropping Eliza off at school, then Clara at the daycare, and then we'll see where the day takes us," Lalah oh so helpfully clarifies, counting on her fingers. "By the way, your oven is smoking."

"Oh, shit," I hiss and stride to the kitchen, where indeed a fine trickle of smoke floats from the door. Armed with a plastic tray, I carefully open the door and fan the tray as the smoke thickens. My perfect breakfast rolls are halfway to being cremated. *Great.* I let out a string of expletives under my breath that would make even a sailor blush as I turn the oven off and bin the charred bread.

"Seriously, you guys are making me *so* rich." Eliza claps behind me, and I drop my head in defeat.

"How much, you little swindler?"

"$37.54," she states with a serious look on her face, presenting me with her empty palm.

"Approximate that for me, would ya'? Otherwise, I'm expecting change."

Her gray eyes widen comically, and her bottom lip pouts. "I don't have change on me, Uncle Tate."

Be still my heart.

"What did you just call me?" I ask, warmth spreading through my limbs and chest.

Eliza looks at me, confusion washing over her small face. "Uncle Tate? Why? Did I make a mistake?" She rapidly fires questions at me. "Coley said that once the adoption goes through, he'll be my adoptive daddy, and Blakey is both my brother and my adoptive uncle. Coley calls you 'brother', too, so that makes you my uncle as well."

I blink at her once, then twice. That's... a lot of information. I pick her up, playfully grunting when she wraps her legs around my waist. "Man, you're getting so big now. What are you, forty-five?"

She bops my nose with her fingertip and giggles, delighted. "No, silly. I'm ten years and nine months old. I'll be eleven years old in October."

I nod with seriousness. "That's a lot of years," I say and kiss her forehead. "I'll be honored to be your adoptive uncle, baby girl." She wraps her arms around my neck and squeezes tight. I can't help but close my eyes and daydream of the day I'll be able to hug my own daughter like this.

I let Eliza run back to her family and set about cleaning the oven, trying to figure out what to feed all of us for breakfast, when the front door opens again. Seriously, no one around these parts knocks anymore? I turn just in time to see Jackson walk in with a tired scowl on his face, his arms loaded with a giant bag. *Dine&Dash* is written in big red letters across the crinkling paper.

"Your delivery has arrived, princess," he hisses and drops the bags on the dining room table.

"Oh, thank you, thank you." Lalah jumps from where she was perched on Cole's lap to hug Jake, smoothing her palms across his leather-clad back.

I smile. How can I not? My best friend hates being touched with a passion, but she has been warming up to all of us and now is going as far as initiating hugs herself. And, truthfully, if anyone needs a hug every once in a while, that would be Jackson.

Quietly, I walk to our bedroom and open the door to see Maevis sleeping peacefully, curled up on her side, hugging my pillow to her chest. I hate to wake her up, but it's best if we're all just eating now, and she leaves with Lalah. This way, I know she'll be safe while we're looking for the asshole.

I take a seat next to her on the bed and tenderly brush her hair away from her forehead. "Babe, wake up, sweetness." She stirs, her arms moving above her head as she stretches and unfurls from her curled up position, lazily blinking her eyes open. I kiss the tip of her nose and smile softly at her. "Good morning, breakfast is ready."

Her own lips are tugging up in a smile. "What are we having?"

"Visitors," I reply with a chuckle.

"Aw, honey, how many times do I have to tell you not to eat our guests, regardless of how much they annoy you?" She giggles, her eyes shining.

And that's one of the million reasons why I love this woman. This morning has been hell, but somehow, she still brings light and joy, even to the darkest storms.

I help her change into one of her maternity dresses, watching as she quickly brushes her hair and arranges it in a loose braid, then guide her to the dining room table. Maybe for the sake of the girls, we're all refraining from discussing any heavy subjects. The mood around the breakfast table is happy and relaxed. Asshole as he is, Jackson even teases me for being a cheapskate and having my window removed instead of just installing an AC unit.

Despite the dreary reasons we're all here, for the first time in weeks, I'm feeling a semblance of content. Like maybe, just maybe, after all the storms, after all the torment we've been through in the past months, life will finally give us a break and let us just... be happy.

A knock sounds at the entrance door. *Of course, I had to go and jinx it.* I mentally roll my eyes to myself. Groaning, I push to my feet and shuffle to the hallway, surprised to see Maddox through the peephole, decked in his chief deputy uniform, badge clipped to his belt, two other officers flanking his sides.

"Morning," I say, as I open the door.

"Morning, Tatum," Maddox clips. "Is this a good time?"

I lift a questioning eyebrow, but their somber looks are impenetrable and give nothing away. "Of course, come in," I invite them, my hand gesturing toward the hallway behind me, opening the door wider and allowing them to pass by me. They stop short at the entrance to the dining room, and I slip past them, standing behind Maevis's chair, my hands planted on her shoulders. Based on Maddox's face, he doesn't have good news for us.

"Sorry to disturb you so early in the morning. I figured, after our talk on the phone earlier, you'd like to know sooner rather than later."

My eyes dart to the living room, and, through the partially cracked open door, I see the girls cuddling on the sofa, their eyes glued to the TV, then look back at Maddox.

"Daniel Johnson was found dead in a double-wide at the trailer park about fifty minutes ago."

Chapter Forty-Seven

Maevis

My breath hitches. Did I hear that right? Is Daniel dead?

"A neighbor called 911 to report smoke coming from inside his trailer, but Daniel did not open the door despite the many times the neighbor knocked. The trailer was also locked from inside, and Mr. Tyler could not gain access," Maddox drones on, but my ears are buzzing.

Daniel is dead. How is that possible? He was just here, smashing our window to bits less than three hours ago.

Tatum's fingers massage my shoulders absentmindedly. My eyes sting. My ears ring. I sniff quietly and press my fingers to my mouth to contain the sob perched on the tip of my tongue. My mind is a blur of thoughts and mixed emotions. Sure, I wanted him to leave me alone and stay as far away as possible, but not for a second I wished him dead. Relief and guilt tangle inside of me as Maddox's words run on a continuous loop in my head.

The pressure on my shoulder lifts, and Tatum crouches in front of me, his large, warm palms settling on my thighs. "Sweets, are you okay? It's over, babe. You're safe. It's all over." I read the words on his lips more than I hear them since the ringing still drowns out every other sound.

I nod, then shake my head. I'm at a complete loss for words. Tatum's eyes bore into mine, his own relief and guilt screaming back at me. Oh, I know that, unlike me, my husband did wish Daniel dead, preferably at his own hands. Which only adds to my own remorse. I'm relieved Daniel is out of our lives for good. I'm grateful for whatever twist of fate that made him perish, and that Tatum is not a vigilante cuffed in the back of Madd's cruiser. And then guilt crashes through me because a man is dead, and all I feel at the thought is relief.

Lifting my eyes from Tatum's, I give myself a mental shake to come back to the present situation. Maddox and the two deputies remain close to the hallway, all three wearing similar, somber looks. I clear my throat, and like a child, I put my hand in the air and wait to be called on. Maddox gives me a chin lift as a go ahead. "What happens now?" I ask in a trembling, scratchy voice.

"Now, we investigate. What we know so far is that he was alone in the trailer, and that, most likely, the fire started from a cigarette he was smoking. His body is being transported as we speak to the coroner's office in Forrest Falls to establish a cause of death, and, ideally, the time of death. From the preliminary report it looks like a heart attack, but we won't know more until after the autopsy."

I nod like a bobble-head, like any of this makes sense to me. But it doesn't. Investigations, procedures, trials, deaths, so many things in so little time.

"Maevis? Tatum?" Maddox tentatively tries to regain our attention, and when my husband takes a seat on the arm of my chair and faces him, he continues, "There's more. His trailer was chock-full of pictures of you, the bakery, the positions of the cameras, everything. My deputies are currently combing through the trailer and will submit all the findings to evidence. We have also found his phones. He had numerous burners, and, so far, we've been able to determine the majority were used to send you messages. Rest assured, together with the sheriff, we're working with Billing's Police Department too, to ensure no one else helped him."

"Thank you, Chief Deputy," my husband rasps next to me.

"You'll need to come into the station later on today—or tomor-row—and give a formal declaration of what happened here this morning, but that's about it. I'll keep you informed," Maddox says. With a two fingers salute, he and his deputies depart as fast as they came in.

I remain seated, staring at the wall and trying to make sense of the last twenty-four hours, hell, the last six months. I think of Amanda's madness, Daniel's selfishness, the ruins of destruction they have left in their wake, and for what? Now, when the dust is settled, she's locked away, spending the best of her years behind bars, and he'll soon be resting six feet under.

Meanwhile, through the incessant hits, the torrent of doubts, all the hurt and despair, Tatum and I are still standing. Sure, we're a little battered, a bit bent, some wear and tear marks here and there, but together. The love we carry for one another only grows and strengthens. So, if I learned any-thing from the wreckage of greed and selfishness, it's this...

We'll weather this storm, too. And all the ones that are to come. Together.

WHAT A DIFFERENCE THREE WEEKS MAKE. I throw a glance at my husband as he focuses on the road ahead. A small grin tugs at his kissable lips, and I can't help but lick mine. I may have the hugest beach ball attached to my waist, but I'll be damned if it'll stop me from climbing him like a tree as soon as we get home. Or... to our temporary home, I should say.

We've been living in Tatum's apartment above the shop for the past twenty days. As soon as we were left alone, after Maddox shared the news of Daniel's death, Tatum started throwing clothes and toiletries into bags and drove us to his apartment. Then he spent the day draining the battery on his phone, barking orders left and right at poor Matt to start changing all the windows to my family home. Tate went as far as threatening him with a lifelong ban from Suga'High if any of my mother's flowers and trees were damaged.

While I'm sure Matt might have protested since his construction company doesn't hurt for business, once Lalah got involved, it was game over. The very next day, my beautiful home became a war zone of glass, bricks, wood, and steel. I tried to convince Tatum a simple window replacement would suffice, but once my mule of a husband gets set on an idea, good luck trying to change his mind. Especially if it's anything related to my safety or the safety of our Vanilla Bean.

We've all been able to breathe a little easier once Maddox and the sheriff concluded their investigation surrounding Daniel's death. His family consented to an autopsy, and the cause of death was confirmed to be a heart attack. The years he spent poisoning himself with alcohol and, later on, drugs, took a toll on his heart. The fire was indeed caused by him dropping the cigarette on a pile of papers he had in a trashcan next to his bed. They also found out his brother, Derek, was dating Tessa.

While he was aware Daniel came back to Montana, he had no knowledge of what his brother was up to, or that he stole and copied Tessa's keys for the bakery. My pregnancy brain? That was all Daniel, locking and unlocking the doors as he pleased with his personal key.

According to Derek, Daniel returned and asked for his younger brother's help, swearing up and down that he was a changed man—a man missing his home and his family. He pretended for about six months, helping Derek around the church. All the while he was driving almost daily from the small village Derek lives in just outside of Billings to Lost Hope and following me for hours.

In reality, he returned to lick his wounds, after he married someone else down in Texas, and tried to pull the same stunt on her as he did on me, opening credit card after credit card in her name. When that wasn't enough to feed his addiction and his gambling issues, he borrowed money from a shark. Suffice to say, he did not pay the money back. His wife received a midnight visit from the shark's goons; Daniel received broken ribs with a side of divorce papers, and, like the coward he was, he ran for his life.

Tessa was devastated to learn of her involvement in his sick schemes, as was Derek. She wanted to quit, but Daniel had tried to ruin far too many lives. I could not allow him to ruin one more. So, she's staying put and 'making it up to me' by becoming the best baker Lost Hope has ever seen. And, hopefully, figuring out Annalise's banana bread recipe.

"Seven weeks to go," Tatum says from next to me, darting a fugitive look in my direction before turning his eyes back on the road. His large, calloused hand cups my knee, and the rough fingertip of his thumb runs circles on my sensitive skin.

"I'm ready now," I giggle, placing my palm over my rounded belly. And I really am. I'm ready to trade the beach ball rearranging my internal organs with a baby. August seems so far away at this point.

He chuckles, the low timbre traveling through the cab of the truck and straight to my core. I'm definitely climbing my man like a tree as soon as we get home.

"I know, sweets. But our little mini-muffin needs to bake a little more. Can't rush greatness."

"Greatness, eh?" I tease, placing my hand over the back of his. He flips his around, intertwining our fingers, and lifts them to his mouth, placing a kiss over my wedding ring. "Speaking of mini-muffins..."

"Oh, no," he groans. "How are you not sick of those cakes?"

I swat at his arm. "I'm not hungry, you bear. But... since your daughter made me eat them for months now, I've been thinking. How do you feel about her having that name?"

"Mini-muffin? Might be a mouthful, Cupcake. Think of the poor kid in school. How are we even going to shorten it? Mini? Muff?"

"God, you're a pain in my ass," I huff, and rip my hand from his, folding my arms over my bulging belly.

"I can be if you want me to. After all, the good doctor finally gave us the green light." He bursts out laughing at my shocked gasp.

"Oh my god, Tatum, I can't believe you just said that," I squeak.

He throws the car into park, and turns in his seat to face me, unclipping his seatbelt at the same time. His eyes soften, fine laughter lines appearing at their corners. "I think it's a gorgeous name, Cupcake. Sweet and special, just like our daughter is."

I swear the wide smile rising on my face lights up the cab of the truck for a second. I throw my arms around his neck, peppering kisses all over his face. "Thank you, thank you, thank you."

He palms the back of my head and guides me to his mouth, and then we collide in a mess of pants and groans as our tongues meet and battle. All thoughts of baby names, the past, and the present flee my head. All I know is the minty taste of Tatum, the neediness of his palms kneading my sensitive breasts, and the acute throb of my clit inside my damp panties.

"Fuck," he whispers in my mouth as he slows the kiss. "Wait for me." And then he's out the door and opening mine in two seconds flat, dragging me across the leather seat. He helps me down, slams the door closed with his hip, and drags me through the reception of Tate's Shop and up the stairs to the apartment.

As soon as we clear the landing, his mouth is once again on mine, his long, thick fingers tangling in my hair. His grunt of need and want tastes like all my filthy fantasies wrapped up in one tattooed grump of a man. I clutch at the soft material of his T-shirt, pulling him closer to me.

"God, I missed you so fucking much," Tate murmurs. His free hand cups my breast, brushing his thumb over my pebbled nipple. A whimper escapes my throat, and he kisses it better. With slow, measured steps. Our lips not breaking apart, not even for a second, he walks me to the bed, stopping only when the back of my thighs hits the cold wooden frame. He leans away from me, his hand gripping the back of his T-shirt, pulling it over his head in one fluid move.

My eyes roam over his strong shoulders, admiring the dark ink that paints every inch of his upper body. My fingers feather over the expanse of his shoulders, then trail down over his granite pecs, flicking over one dark nipple, and then the other. I press my lips to the center of his chest, licking a path of sin and desire down to the hills and valleys of his washboard abs.

I lower myself slowly until I'm perched on the edge of the bed, my hands making quick work of his belt and zipper. I palm his length through the coarse material, stroking him once, twice, three times, then shove his jeans down his strong thighs in one swift move. My fingers make their way inside of his boxers and wrap around him. With infinite tenderness, I take him out of the cotton straining to keep him contained. He's impossibly hard—velvet encasing pure steel—and when I trace the angry-looking vein on the underside of his cock, he twitches on my tongue. My lips fasten around his head, sucking hard, as my tongue laps at the salty sweetness he's coating my mouth in.

The growl he rewards me with has my pussy clenching painfully, and I bob my head over his cock, taking him deeper and deeper into my mouth until he hits the back of my throat and I gag around him.

"Fuck, sweetness, I could die a happy man with those pretty lips of yours wrapped all around me." His hips rock as he fucks my mouth in slow, measured thrusts. "But not today." He grunts when I swirl my tongue over his salty slit, mewling softly when more of his arousal pools inside my mouth. "Goddamn, not today, babe. Today, I'm going to bury myself in you so deep, you'll feel me inside for weeks." I moan deep in my throat as I hollow my cheeks around his shaft before releasing him with a wet pop.

I wipe my mouth with the back of my hand, feeling my lips puffy and swollen, and grin at him like the cat-that-ate-... well, a monster cock. "Promise?"

My dress is ripped over my head, leaving me in a useless pair of cotton panties only. His palm splays on the center of my chest and gently pushes me down on the mattress. His usually sky-blue eyes are nearly black as his pupils overtake the brightness of his irises, and a wolfish smirk tugs at his lips. "Cross my heart," he rasps.

I trail my fingers over my breasts, pinching my nipples, and arching my back when heat travels to my core, his hungry stare following my every move. I continue my journey down, over the swell of my belly and to the waistband of my panties. "Take them off, husband, please."

"Fuck! You know I'll do anything for you when you beg so prettily, wife," Tatum snarls, his hands clawing at my underwear, forcefully dragging it down my legs. He lets it fall to the floor before gripping the back of my knees and spreading me open in front of him.

The cold air of the AC hits my heated folds, slick with arousal and desire for him. "Beg me now, Cupcake. Beg me to fuck you until your limbs are numb and your pussy soaks my mattress to the floor. Beg, wife," he grits, the muscles of his neck straining and red, his sharp jaw clenched.

And who am I to deny him anything, when Tatum Carter is all I ever wanted in life and didn't dare dream about? "Fuck me, husband, please. Let me feel you so deep inside of me, I don't know where you end and I begin. Please, please, I want you so much it hurts. I ache for you, husband. Every hour of every day."

My words seem to do the trick. He scrunches his eyes shut, a look of pure bliss and agony washing over his face. When he opens them again, the fire in his gaze burns so hot, I feel the flames incinerating me from the inside out. His cock notches at my dripping entrance, pushing inside of me, stretching my walls one agonizing inch at the time until I'm so full I feel him everywhere. He rocks his hips against mine, allowing me to accommodate to his delicious intrusion.

"Please," I moan, desperation rolling past my lips when he finds the end of me and keeps still for a breath.

"Tell me you want me, Maevis," Tatum demands, his voice low and gritty.

"I want you," I cry out when he withdraws slowly, then savagely drives back into me, making stars burst behind my eyelids.

"Tell me you love me, Maevis," he orders, his hand leaving my knee, collaring around my neck instead.

"I love you, Tatum."

"Always and forever, I love you," he vows.

"Forever and always."

And then there are no more demands, no more words. He drives into me, mercilessly, savagely, completely lost to the frenzy of his base desires. The bed creaks. His fingers tighten around my throat. My pussy quivers and clenches around him, and fire consumes my every nerve end. It's just me, and him, and the ravaging pleasure coiling in my lower belly, exploding in a million fireworks as my orgasm overtakes my senses.

My eyes roll to the back of head, and I swear, I blackout for a second, as my pussy flutters and contracts, his pace not faltering for one second. My hands grip his veiny forearm, nails digging into hard muscle, when his fingers find my sensitive clit, stroking my greedy bundle of nerves in tandem with his desperate thrusts. Tatum owns me, body and soul. He bends down and sucks my tight nipple into his hot mouth, and I come and come and come, screaming out his name.

He fucks himself harder into me, stroking his cock in and out in uncontrolled jerks, my name a curse and a blessing on his lips when he marks my channel with his own release.

Tatum falls slack on top of me, his weight pressing my exhausted body further into the mattress, before he lets himself roll to one side and gathers me to his chest. He tips my chin up with one finger, lining up my mouth to his, brushing his lips over mine, oh so slowly, so gently, in such stark contrast with the beast that just fucked me to high heaven.

"Made love to you to high heaven," he mumbles.

I nip playfully at his jaw and nuzzle my face into his chest, the inked skin under my cheek damp with a fine sheen of sweat. A happy sigh escapes my lips. I'm living my dream. Sure, my white picket fence home is currently a construction site, but the absolute truth is I'd live under a bridge as long as Tatum is with me.

I might have walked through life for thirty-four years resenting to be everyone's second choice, but life has made sure to reward me with a second chance. See? Seconds are not so bad. They're downright ideal when it comes to chances and desserts.

And happily ever afters.

Epilogue

"**T**his baby better come out, and she better come out right now," I screech, closing my eyes tightly, focusing all my thoughts on convincing my daughter to just... exit my body.

A wet snort comes from somewhere near me. "I don't know what you're trying to do right now, and I'm no expert, but I'll bet my new telescope that the best you'll get is a fart."

My eyes spring open, and I turn my head slowly, throwing a deathly glare at Lalah, who's laughing her ass off at my predicament. "Come on, baby, get out. Your lease expired eight days ago. This is your eviction notice," I grumble.

Lalah leans forward, placing both hands on my belly, smashing her nose against my belly button. I yelp when out of nowhere Astrum runs, stopping snout first on my stomach. "Bumblebee, if you hear me, hold on for one more day, then we can be birthday girlfriends."

I plant the heel of my palm on her forehead and push her face away from the hot-air balloon that is now my stomach. "You're a traitor." She rolls her eyes at me, then shoves her hand into the pocket of her black hoodie and extracts a crumpled piece of paper and a pen.

"Alright, have you tried walking?"

My hand finds the fuzzy pillow supporting my back, and I throw it at her head. She bats it away, letting it fall with a thump on the wooden deck. Astrum growls at the pillow, his front legs poking at the gray tassels.

"Don't get snippy with me. That's what the internet recommends." She shrugs, unconcerned. And why would she be concerned? She's not the one trying to expel a stubborn baby from her womb.

"I've already clocked twenty thousand steps today. My cankles cannot take any more walking."

She taps the pen over her mouth and sighs. "Alright, crossing this off. Spicy food? I think I have some dried chili flakes somewhere. Could make you some spiced-up pancakes." She looks at me all hopeful, but I'd rather scrub my eyes with that chili than eat any more spicy food.

"Believe me, I have every Indian restaurant in Forrest Falls on speed dial. Ain't working."

"Pineapple?"

"Pineapple? Seriously?" I shake my head.

She perks up and jumps to her feet. "Stay there. I'll be right back with the juiciest, sweetest pineapple to put all pineapples to shame. We're flushing that baby right out of you."

It's my turn to roll my eyes at her as she disappears through the sliding doors of her porch. I lean back on the sofa, trying to get comfortable. Nothing is comfortable when you're more than a week overdue. My skin is stretched to maximum capacity. If I had seams, they would've burst by now. I'm hot, and itchy, and achy. And *desperate*.

All I want is to hold my baby girl in my arms... and to be able to see my toes once again. Surely, that's not too much to ask. I grunt when my lovely daughter hits my kidney, or maybe my liver, or maybe my pancreas. God knows she's rearranged my internal organs to her liking as often as I rearranged her nursery. I'm quite certain nothing is in its rightful place anymore.

Another jab, and pain radiates through my lower back. The nauseating sensation of the impeding *Fuck, I'm gonna pee my pants* rushes through me. With my palm flat on the arm of the sofa, I slide, roll, and eventually push to my feet—a maneuver I've sadly been using for the past two months, once my little Vanilla Bean grew twice in size overnight. I waddle-run to the door, crossing my fingers I'll actually make it to the bathroom.

It's a matter of personal pride that I have not once during this pregnancy peed myself. Although, in all truthfulness, I *did* come close a time or two. I strain to slide the door open, doing a little jiggle on the spot when the stubborn baby celebrates my efforts with another kick at whatever poor, unsuspecting internal organ dared get in her way.

My hands fly to my crotch when wetness drips down my thighs. "For fuck's sake," I shout, throwing my head back and shaking my fist at the clear blue sky. *There goes my record.*

"Uhm," a throat clears behind me, seconds before a pair of large palms grip my hips from behind. "Maevis, babe, you're leaking."

My cheeks flame. Great. Not only have I peed my pants, my sexy-as-sin husband is here to witness my humiliation.

"She's downright flooding, that's no leak." Lalah gasps.

"Can y'all stop gawking and help me to the bathroom?" I hiss.

"Darling," Cole says, caution laced in his voice, and I groan. *Amazing.* The whole family is here to see the beached whale wet her fins. "You don't need a bathroom. You need a hospital."

I spin on my heel, gawking at him as he points at the tiny puddle at my feet. Tatum grips my upper arms to steady me, because *of course* I slip on my own bodily fluids. "Easy, Cupcake. Come on, let's get to the car." He grins, his eyes sparkling with happiness and excitement in the sunlight.

"What are you saying?" I ask Cole, paying my husband no mind. This is not the first false alarm I've had in the past three weeks.

"Your water broke, Maevis."

"I told you pineapple will work," Lalah whispers, rocking my daughter softly from side to side. "Could've waited one more day though, Bumblebee." I snort an incredulous laugh, wincing when the stitches holding my poor vagina together pinch.

Yes, stitches. Ten of them.

One for each day my daughter delayed her entry into this world.

Where did they fit them all... beats me. All I know right now is that it feels like my ass has been stapled to my front, I'm wearing a pad fit for a giant, and, after thirty-six hours of contractions from hell, screaming and pushing for five of those, and most likely some dislocated fingers—Tatum's, not mine—Lamington Faith Carter came into the world on August Twenty-Fifth, at the unholy hour of 4:32 a.m.

My incredible, amazing, out-of-this-world husband cut her umbilical cord, breathed down the midwife's neck as she washed and tended to our brand-new baby, then snatched her right up, and presented her to me like she was a heavyweight champion.

"Measuring twenty-one inches," he sing-songed.

I know, I felt every single one of them.

"And weighing in at seven pounds, fourteen ounces," he continued.

Yup, felt those, too.

"With glass-shattering lungs and the chubbiest, cutest cheeks, meet our daughter, my love," he said, love shining in his eyes as he placed Lamington in my exhausted arms. And then, my brave, loving husband kissed my forehead and the tip of our baby's nose, and went to adjust the blue paper towel covering my legs, still hitched up in stirrups.

And straight up passed out.

His beautiful blue eyes went wide, and his gorgeously tanned skin leeched of color. One minute, he was grinning at me like a proud fool. The next, he was sprawled out face-first next to my hospital bed, scaring the living life out of me. I would've been worried the sight of my bruised and battered vagina scarred him for life, but he's safe, considering I'll never let him around that general area. Ever. Again.

I smooth my fingers over his hair, gently pushing it away from his forehead, where a goose egg has already formed, a ring of blue and black circling it. He tightens the arm he has thrown over my waist, but remains asleep.

"Come on, Supernova, give Lami back to her momma. I'm sure they want to spend some time together as a family before the rest of Lost Hope, and probably half the county, descends on them," Cole whispers to Lalah, but his arm coils around her back, his palm cradling my daughter's head.

Lalah pouts but acquiesces. She walks slowly next to my bed, kissing Lami's forehead before she places her into my waiting arms. "I love you," she says, her voice low, barely audible even though she's standing right next to me. "All of you. I'm so freaking happy to be here right now." She bends at the waist and kisses my forehead, surprising the hell out of me.

Tears spring in my eyes—happy, exhausted tears. I swallow down my emotions, but before I compose myself enough to reciprocate, the two of them quietly slip out the door, closing it with a soft click behind them.

I lean my head against Tatum's and arrange Lamington on my chest, supporting her head and back with my forearm. My husband's warm palm settles over mine, and I burrow further into him. My entire life, my whole reason for being, is right here in this bed with me. I'm sore and in pain, exhausted to the very marrow of my bones and emotional beyond words. I'm also the happiest I've ever been.

"Thank you," I whisper. "Forever and always."

"What you did today, I'm in awe of you," Tatum rasps, startling me since I thought he was asleep. "Your strength humbles me. I'm the luckiest son of a bitch to walk the earth, and it's all thanks to you, Cupcake. I love you, always and forever."

I sigh deep in my chest. Bliss. My head rests on his firm shoulder as my palm rubs love over Lami's belly, her pouted lips suckling at thin air in her slumber.

One month. One month of having our baby girl with us. The very best month of our lives.

I jump when Tate's phone shrills from the pocket of his sweats. Chills slither up my spine and goosebumps sprout all over my skin. His strong arm, coiled around my waist, pulls me closer to him, but even Tate doesn't have enough warmth to chase away the cold settling over me.

"Lawson, to what do I owe the honor?" he mocks, and my eyebrows raise on my forehead, questioning him.

They may not actively dislike each other anymore, but they're not friends either. So for Maddox to call in the middle of the night...

My husband's body turns to stone when he grits through clenched teeth, "The fuck you've just said?"

I snatch the phone from his hand and put it on speaker.

"It's Sawyer!" Maddox sobs, and I have to lock my knees together to stop them from buckling under the fear flooding my veins. "I didn't get to her in time," he grits, his voice hoarse and choked out with tears.

I don't dare look at Tatum. Every muscle in his body is frozen still. If I didn't have his heartbeat next to my ear, I would've thought his heart stopped, too.

"Fuuuuuuck! Goooood, no! Get here, Carter!" Maddox orders through the phone. "I'm going to fucking murder him, rip him limb to limb, godfuckingdammit!" he curses, his words followed closely by a muffled thud.

Tatum is still rooted in place, and when I make to end the call, Madd's anguished voice comes through once again.

"Don't leave me, Fairy! Hold on, just a little longer. Help's on the way. Please, baby, hold on. I'm here!"

> **Curious about what happens next in Lost Hope?**
>
> **Find out in book three,** ***Atramentum et Telum Pulvis,***
>
> **Maddox and Sawyer's story.**

Author's Apology

I know, I know. That ending. It's not me, I promise. That's all on Maddox, he made me do it. I take no responsibility for what my characters do. They're too stubborn for me to try and control. Been there, done that, have the headache and the T-shirt to prove it. And a magnet on my fridge.

I apologise on his behalf. And I apologise for myself, for not teaching him proper reading etiquette. He's a right pain.

And as a peace offering, I promise you, Sawyer makes him grovel.

Can't wait!

So run quickly and grab your copy of *Atramentum et Telum Pulvis*.

Happy reading! ♡

Acknowledgements

My second book—deep breaths, allow for a second of freaking out—what is this? My very SECOND book. It feels… surreal. I never ever, ever want to lose this feeling. Even if everything that could've gone wrong writing VeMO, did.

This book has wrecked me in all the best and worst ways. Such a stark difference from *Lege et Lacrima*. I cried as I wrote it; I cried as I typed *the end*.

Tatum and Maevis are so beautifully broken, each in their own way; their path to healing was certainly full of speed bumps, some taller than others, but eventually they did get to their destination. Regardless of the situation, having your choices taken away from you, that oily feeling of powerlessness carries the phantom of a pain unlike any other.

We all know that sometimes healing aches worse than getting hurt. Sometimes, the darkness is much more alluring than going through the excruciating pain of mending open wounds. It made me so happy to see both Tatum and Maevis getting to the point of accepting that while life is full of trials and tribulations, they're not overlooked, they're not second choices. They are the very foundation keeping everyone else upright.

Speaking of foundation, here is mine—all the gorgeous. amazing, incredible people in my life who support me and this crazy journey I've embarked on.

Siiri, thank you for the absolutely incredible cover you've created for the first edition of VeMO. You so beautifully incorporated both Tatum and Maevis into it, my heart flutters like crazy every time I look at the book. And most of all, thank you for taking a chance on me and editing *Vanilla et Motricium Oleum*. Thank you for taking the time to talk me down from my freak-outs and for all the insightful advice that simply made Tatum and

Mae come to life. You are the best triple threat; a brilliant editor; amazing cover designer; and one of my dearest friends.

Jamanda, from the bottom of my battered heart, thank you. I'm so, so incredibly lucky to have met you. Who knew a Facebook group and an exchange of manuscripts would lead to such an amazing friendship? You are indeed the keeper of my sanity and my biggest cheerleader. For all the times you talked me off the ledge and for all the excruciating hours you spent convincing me my writing is worth it. You are one of the best people I've ever had the honour of meeting and one of the most talented, too.

Bella, talk about a curveball I never saw coming. Thank you for all the late-at-night friendraphy sessions. For all the handholding you've done for me, for being a social butterfly in disguise, and one of the bravest people I have ever made. Yes, I did say brave and I WILL fight you on this if I must. Too bad you like dark chocolate, but hey, we can't all be perfect. Last, thank you for our book club, **S**exy **L**it **U**nder **T**he **Sh**eets. May our books thrive and our *incomings* not getting us fired.

Annie and Lottie, thank you for being the best Beta readers this writing-cave-woman could have. Your support and advices mean the world to me. You are incredible women and I am in awe of you.

Ana Maria and Claudia, thank you for being the bestest best friends this girl could have. There's no geographical distance that matters when you find your people. Always and forever.

As always, a special thank you goes to Mr. Right. You, sir, are everything I never knew I wanted but so desperately needed. Thank you, my love, for putting up with my constant refusal to wash dishes and continuing to love me anyway. Thank you for all the hugs you gave me when this book ripped my heart out of my chest, and I needed to cry my eyes out. I love you more than I love a million M&Ms dipped in hazelnut lattes. **PS: You're still doing the dishes. I'm starting book three.**

The biggest thank you goes to my readers. Thank you for continuing to take a chance on my dream with every page you read. I am overwhelmed in all the best ways for all the love and support I've received so far. It goes beyond my wildest dreams. And it's all thanks to you. You fuel me, give me hope, and keep alive this dream of mine that just one year ago seemed so far-fetched. I hope you found little pieces of yourselves in *Vanilla et Motricium Oleum*, and I hope I've done all of them justice. All my love ♡

For the smallest contribution in the grand scheme of things, I need to mention coffee again. Thanks for keeping me awake. I literally couldn't have done it without you.

Also by Alina

**Lost Hope Series
(small town, contemporary romance)**
Lege et Lacrima— Lalah & Cole
Vanilla et Motricium Oleum— Tatum & Maevis
Atramentum et Telum Pulvis— Maddox & Sawyer

To Have and To Hold— a dark romance standalone

For the most up to date list of released books, please visit
my website www.alinacomsaauthor.com

About the author

Alina Comsa is Transylvanian, and her little vampire soul now lives in the UK with her partner, dodging like a pro her turn to do the dishes—and that pesky little star called the Sun. She dabbles in quality assurance by day, writing and reading by night, and lives with little to no sleep.

In high school Alina was voted most likely to... become a lawyer. What a letdown, right? She aced those creative writing tests, though, worry not. Because she's an overachiever, she was also voted most likely to become a journalist. So far, high school votes have been zero out of two.

Eternally exhausted, she believes that "life was meant for reading" and coffees. Loads, and loads of coffee.

She loves everything romance, but has a slight obsession with shifters. They'll win her heart every single time.

If you'd like to poke the vampire and find out more about other novels she's currently writing, please join her private book cave here:

AC's Book Cave

Since procrastination is an effective punishment tool when her characters misbehave, if she's not waiting for a latte to be delivered, she can (sometimes) be found here:

Facebook—Alina Comsa Author

Instagram—@alinacomsaauthor

TikTok – Alina Comsa Author

Sign up to her newsletter for bonus scenes, character art, and other surprises.

She promises to be on her best behaviour, whatever that means.

For news of upcoming books, trigger warnings, and events, please visit www.alinacomsaauthor.com